ADIRONDACK TRAIL OF
GOLD

A NOVEL BY

Larry Weill

NORTH COUNTRY BOOKS, INC.

UTICA, NEW YORK

ISBN-10 1-59531-042-8
ISBN-13 978-1-59531-042-2

Design by Zach Steffen & Rob Igoe, Jr.

Cover photo of Louis Seymour courtesy of the Adirondack Museum.

Library of Congress Cataloging-in-Publication Data In Progress

North Country Books, Inc.
220 Lafayette Street
Utica, New York 13502
www.northcountrybooks.com

Contents

ACKNOWLEDGEMENTS

There are a great number of people who helped collaborate in the research and writing of this book. Joan Dunseath of the Brookside Museum provided the initial list of resources and references that was instrumental in initiating the research. Barbara Anderson of the Heritage Research Library (Washington County Historical Society) conducted the initial database searches for the life and times of Robert Gordon and passed along numerous articles and references on this topic.

Carol Greenough, Curator at the Skenesborough Museum in Whitehall, assisted with the names and locations of early territorial municipalities and villages, and she also researched the names of several Canadian locations for their earlier appellations. Carol Senecal, the Town and Village Historian of Whitehall, provided estimates of the movement of Gordon and other Loyalists as they fled from the American territories to Canada in the 1770s.

John and Kay Chessers, of Coburg, Ontario, assisted by providing multiple resources regarding the life of Robert Gordon, as well as the details about his store and his land holdings in the U.S. and Canada. Their book, *In Consequence of Loyalty*, was an invaluable reference while developing this manuscript.

Dennis Lowery, Washington County Archivist, spent several hours with me reviewing court dockets and municipal records of Skenesborough. Dona Crandall, Washington County Historian, assisted by providing locations and population estimates of many towns and other landmarks in the county region. Tom Lynch and his assistant, Allison, in the Warren County Records Center, provided numerous maps of the region from Whitehall (colonial Skenesborough) to the areas in the Adirondacks that are featured in the story. They also assisted in the effort to trace the locations of the early roadways around Warren Country and the land surrounding Lake George. John Austin, Warren County Historian, provided additional insights into life in the early years of Warren County and information about the means of travel on and around Lake George.

Christopher J. McKelvey, a Mined Land Reclamation Specialist with the New York State Department of Environmental Conservation, Department of Mineral Resources, answered numerous questions on gold and gold mining within the state and provided resources listing the applicable New York laws on mining precious metals on public and private lands.

Jerry Pepper, the Curator and Librarian of the Adirondack Museum in Blue Mountain Lake, provided numerous details about the museum. He also confirmed several details about the display materials and holdings of Adirondack French Louie that contributed to the accuracy of the text.

Bruce Lomnitzer, the Forest Ranger of Indian Lake, detailed the locations of the trail systems in and around Lost Pond, located between the Moose River Plains and the West Canada Lakes Wilderness Area. He also described the trails and herd paths that existed many years ago and can still be viewed on older, dated versions of the USGS topographic maps.

Countless other organizations were the source of reference material used throughout this text, including the National Geophysical Data Center (NGDC) of NOAA Satellite and Information Service, which provided historical computations of magnetic declination. The websites of the National Register of Historic Places and the New York State Historic Preservation Office were also invaluable resources.

I owe a debt of gratitude to my good friend, Bruno Petrauskas, and my daughter, Kelly Weill, for their endless hours of proofreading this manuscript for content and "fatfinger" errors. Pat Phalen's work inspired the cover design of this book.

Because undoubtedly I have missed or failed to mention each person who assisted me in the development of this manuscript, I'd like to offer a blanket "thank you" to everyone who offered information, suggestions, criticism, or mere words of encouragement. Your involvement in this book, whether active or otherwise, has made it a most enjoyable and gratifying experience.

FOREWORD

I developed the idea for this book by taking some of my favorite subjects and merging them into a single plot. As a lifelong fan of the Adirondacks, many of my favorite memories are concentrated on the lands either inside or adjacent to the Park. Because of my love of the area, the setting is almost entirely concentrated on that part of New York State.

This story is loosely based on the saga of Robert Gordon, an early sympathizer of the British and King George III in the days leading up to the American Revolution. Gordon was a successful and wealthy merchant who lived in the eastern New York town of Skenesborough, which changed its name to Whitehall in 1786. As the early skirmishes of 1775 turned into full-scale battles, Robert Gordon felt the same pressure as other Loyalists, and he feared reprisal for his alignment with the Crown. Therefore, sometime during the middle of 1775, he decided to flee the ever-increasing violence of the burgeoning revolution for the relative safety of Canada. Most of the details of Gordon's exodus from colonial America have been lost, along with a majority of the municipal records of the day. However, legend tells us that somewhere en route, he hid a massive cache of gold in the muddy swamp waters of southern Lake Champlain. That treasure was rumored to be approximately $70,000 in 1775 dollars, which would place the value at about $6.3 million today.

Unfortunately, Robert Gordon was never afforded the opportunity to return for his gold. Following the Revolution, he died in a hunting accident in his newly adopted country, leaving behind a tale of treasure that has fascinated people for centuries. Many have sought out this vast accumulation of sunken gold. However, only one search party came close, and that was by accident. If the legend is to be believed, the locked chest still sits unmolested on the shallow bottom of Lake Champlain, waiting for the right person using modern technology and know-how to retrieve it.

Another New York State historical figure comes to us from the central Adirondacks. In this remote and heavily wooded territory lived a famous French Canadian woodsman and guide, who went by the name of Louis Seymour, more commonly known by those familiar with him as Adirondack French Louie. Louie lived in a log cabin on the shore of West Canada Lake, in the heart of the West Canada Lakes Wilderness Area. He established himself in that setting about 1868, and he lived there until the day before his death in February, 1915. So unique and popular was this larger than life character of the north woods that his story is still read today, by new generations of Adirondack enthusiasts.

My personal introduction to the life of French Louie came in the late 1970s, when I was stationed as a Wilderness Park Ranger in the same area where Louie built his main camp. My weekly route took me past Louie's homestead, which still stands in the clearing that used to be his home. My fascination with his life and the events that shaped that period in time motivated me to bring Louie into this story and throw him into the middle of a search for the gold that had been lost over a century earlier.

The fact that I chose to include French Louie in a search for lost treasure is not entirely without basis in fact. It is known that he was hired as a guide on at least two occasions to help lead parties through the woods with the sole intent of finding Revolutionary-era caches of gold. However, the details of the search in this book, as well as the characters who employ Louie to help them locate the treasure, are entirely fictional. It is my deepest desire to assure readers that Louie never buried a cache of gold anywhere in or around West Canada Lake, so please don't go looking for one.

These are the elements that I selected to use as I developed the storyline for this novel. In a world that values the gleam of gold and the excitement of treasure, what better way to spark the imagination than to start with a massive horde of gold that has been missing in action since the year before our country's birth? The addition of French Louie to the hunt moved the plot into the very heart of the Adirondacks. It also allowed me the enjoyment of spending some time with one of my favorite characters. If I could go back in time to the late 1800s and be afforded the opportunity to meet any one individual, Louis Seymour would be high on my list.

Finally, I have created a contemporary cast of characters who are thrown unwittingly into the search, and then adopt the cause as their own. It all starts with a pair of college buddies from central New York who, with a couple of clues that were passed from French Louie to a deceased great-grandfather, set out to unravel the two hundred thirty-year-old mystery. In the process, they find themselves mixed up in a cryptic maze of ancient maps, skeletons, phantom e-mail clues, and cunning adversaries.

Perhaps I have enjoyed writing this story so much because it allowed me to take a pair of colorful historical figures with real stories, and carry them into the realm of fiction. Through my own invention, with an added dose of creative license, I was able to provide a setting that included two of my favorite locations: the Adirondacks and the Land of Imagination. I hope that you enjoy this journey through these wonderful places, and that you find your own pot of gold at the end of your rainbow.

PART I

BIRTH OF A LEGEND

CHAPTER 1

May 7, 1775

It was a cold and damp night, the sky partially illuminated by a half moon that peeked out from behind the scattered clouds. A light rain had fallen earlier across the south end of Lake Champlain, making the damp spring air feel even colder than it was. It was the kind of chill that could penetrate a person's clothing and go straight to the bones.

In a small ravine next to Halfway Creek, two men hunched down against the elements, keeping a keen eye peeled to the south. Less than a hundred yards ahead of them lay the crumbling walls of Fort Ann. The fort, built in 1690, had been demolished and reconstructed no less than five times. During its lifetime, it had been occupied only sporadically, by the French, the British, and the American colonists. But now it was a beehive of activity, even at this late hour.

The two men watched carefully, noting the activity of the Patriot soldiers as they worked to fortify the aging structure. The term "soldiers" may have been a gratuitous appellation, as many of them were no more than local farmers and merchants who had taken up the cause of national independence from the Crown. Ill-clad and under-armed, they relied on pure willpower and tenacity to overcome their shortfalls in weapons and supplies.

Robert Gordon, the taller of the two men scouting the Patriot soldiers, observed the numbers and locations of the amassed troops, recording what he saw in quickly-scrawled handwritten lines. Relying on the available moonlight, Gordon noted all their movements, along with his assessment that the fort's position on Mud Creek gave it direct access to Lake Champlain and the "northern route" to Canada. He noted that the numbers of men and rifles appeared to have increased every month throughout the year, and that the garrison could be used as a jumping-off point for an attack on Fort Ticonderoga to the north.

As Gordon wrote, his companion, Thomas Swain, kept a close watch for any movement signifying the approach of enemy soldiers. They could ill-afford to be captured spying on the Colonists' activities, as the information they were gathering would be important to their British friends inside Fort Ticonderoga. The countryside was becoming more hostile to the Loyalists, as the opponents of King George III grew stronger and bolder. The battles at Lexington and Concord a month earlier had reinforced the Patriots' notion that they could fight the British troops and win. Perhaps Gordon's notes on the growing Colonist forces would influence the British army leaders to call for more redcoat reinforcements before the rebels could attack.

The protocol was the same as they'd used for the past six months: roll the parchment with the scouting notes into a tight scroll and insert it into the lid of the tin flask tucked inside Swain's belt. Sealed with a cork cap, it resembled any of the canteens of the day, and would never have attracted suspicion if the two men were stopped for inspection. Then, they slowly backed down the ravine and up the other side, being careful to remain in the shadows of the woods until they had cleared the first several bends of the trail leading north. Their job was done for the night.

The return route to Robert Gordon's homestead was over four miles long, and not absent of peril. The "road," like many of the other local routes in the days leading up to the Revolutionary War, was a glorified horse path, not more than ten feet wide and barely cleared of obstacles. In fact, many of the early roads had started out as deer paths, which had been adopted by the early settlers and improved as needed.

It took Gordon and Swain almost two hours to pick their way along the first mile of trail, sometimes feeling their way as much as seeing the correct route. When they reached a small clearing on the west side of Wood Creek, they located the large upright boulder they'd used as a marker and turned into the woods. After about two hundred yards of stepping through wet, mucky soil, they reached their steeds, which they'd tied to a tree several hours earlier. They knew that they could not trust the animals to remain quiet, and so they had left them out of earshot while they conducted their clandestine activities.

The men quickly untied and mounted their horses, both of which appeared to be black in the inky, dark woods, and guided them across the clearing, heading back to the farm. Fortunately, the horses' keen night vision allowed them to trot along at a pace that dwarfed their own progress up to that point. But even with the quick stepping of the steeds, it was well after 2:00 a.m. when the two men arrived back at Gordon's farm. They were extremely tired, but thankful that they had completed another mission without being seen. They knew that they would be paid well for their information, and they were grateful for that. However, they also knew that if they were caught in the act of conducting espionage, the justice imposed would be rapid and harsh. This played heavily on their minds, though neither of the two said a word as they dismounted inside the old corral and parted for the night.

The morning after the scouting mission marked the start of a glorious day in the area now known as Washington County. The clouds of the previous evening had been pushed aside by a brisk wind, and the sun arose over a crystal-clear blue sky. Robert Gordon was the first one to awaken at his settlement, despite the fact that he had been asleep for less than four hours. Rose, his wife of four years, followed shortly thereafter, and prepared a hearty breakfast in the kitchen of the small two-story farmhouse. Once he had eaten, Gordon was out the door and headed toward his shop, which would be open for business as soon as the clock struck eight.

Gordon appeared relaxed and well-rested for someone who had been leading a stress-filled double life. A big man for his time, Gordon stood close to six feet tall, with a clear complexion and a muscular build. At thirty-five years of age, he was in the prime of his life, and his reputation as an energetic entrepreneur and civic leader had spread across the region.

Born in London in 1739, he had come to the colonial territories in 1770 to escape the wrath of the King. While serving as a member of His Majesty's gardening staff, he had performed several personal favors for the Queen, including providing her personal information about the King's private activities. Although he was a talented gardener and a favored member of the crew, he began to fear for his life, and decided to flee the country.

Arriving in Boston in the spring of 1770, he quickly sought out and located an acquaintance from London, Philip Skene. Skene was a Colonel in the British army and a settler along the shores of Wood Creek, in the region of New York State just south of Lake Champlain. He was heavily involved in the effort to organize the area as a municipality, and he had traveled back to England to petition the King to formally recognize Skenesborough as its own entity. Skene quickly arranged for Gordon to acquire and settle a tract of land at the southern edge of the town that is now known as Whitehall.

In the years that followed, Robert Gordon converted his barn into a large, unfinished store, where he stocked many items needed by the local population for farming, harvesting, and furnishing their own homes. A born salesman, he exuded the self-confidence and bonhomie that made him popular with everyone he encountered. His business flourished, and he found a ready clientele among both the local Patriots and those who preferred to remain loyal to the Crown. Gordon tried to walk the delicate line between the two, remaining friendly to both sides while not angering either. But this was difficult to do, and by the beginning of 1775, the rumors were already flying that his allegiance lay with the British.

That morning, as Gordon opened his gates and declared his store open for business, a single individual stood outside the fence, waiting patiently to enter the large red barn. Dressed in a white cotton shirt and rough leather vest, he was unknown to the workers who were already busy in the establishment. He walked past a pair of men who were moving a stock of brooms to a wooden box in front of the store. Stepping up to the rough planking that served as a countertop, he asked Gordon for a bag of iron nails and a metal file.

Gordon nodded in a friendly manner and turned around to retrieve the items from the shelves, which were neatly organized to display the wares. As he turned back to his customer, he displayed no signs of recognition, nothing to give away the fact that the man was not a total stranger. The customer accepted the woven container of nails, and in return slid a leather sheath across the counter to Gordon. There was a silent, imperceptible nod between the two men, who exchanged a quick "thank you" before parting ways. The customer then turned and strode from the building, heading north toward the road that bordered the creek.

Each of the two men was pleased with the business they had transacted. The customer, Richard Gilthorpe, was heading north to return to his unit. A Lieutenant in the British Army, he had ditched his uniform in favor of the colonial garb of the day in order to pass as a frontier farmer. Nestled inside his pouch of nails were two scrolls of observations from Gordon on the Patriot soldiers in and around Fort Ann, including their apparent preparations to deploy somewhere to the north, perhaps towards Fort Ticonderoga and Canada. Gilthorpe would carry that information to his Colonel, receiving accolades for his daring venture into the heart of the rebel territory.

In the meantime, Gordon took his payment, still wrapped in the leather purse, and proceeded into a small building attached to the side of his house. He used a key to unlock a heavy padlock, then opened a trap door and descended a short flight of stairs into a small cellar. A single lantern, the only light in the room, cast heavy shadows against the wooden crates and chests that filled the space. There, in the privacy of the dark, dank enclosure, he opened the pouch and took stock of its contents. The payment for the nails and the file should have been a few shillings, paid for in small denomination coins. However, the pouch contained an array of five gold coins, large and gleaming in the glow of the lantern. The Spanish coins, which the Colonists called doubloons, were valued at well over five British pounds each, a large sum in that day.

Gordon moved to the opposite wall of the cellar and opened a locked wooden chest. He stacked the new currency with a massive number of other gold pieces, arranged in rows across the velvet-lined interior of the container. The center of the chest was filled with gold ingots, stamped with symbols declaring their weight and place of origin. The combined pile of gold filled the chest almost to the top, making for a sight that few men had ever encountered. The monetary value of the stash must have been staggering, as the sheer weight of the chest had grown too large for a single man to lift.

A few of Robert Gordon's long-serving foremen had been present when he had conducted his larger transactions, noting his insistence at being paid in gold. This was most unusual, as silver was far more common in that day and used for almost all commercial transactions. But not for Gordon, who dealt in gold, and gold alone.

What these men did not realize was that Gordon was also receiving money from the British Crown for his services as a spy against the Patriots. Gordon had taken only two of his most trusted foremen into his confidence regarding his allegiance to England and the Loyalist cause: Thomas Swain, who had come to the New World with Gordon, and Alvin Smith, who was his chief storekeeper. Although Swain was officially Gordon's top supervisor, he and Smith regarded each other as equals. Both of these men had been with Gordon since he had moved to Skenesborough, and both were also fiercely committed to remaining part of England. The three of them often took their midday meal together inside the farmhouse, where they could discuss their allegiances and events of the day in private.

As Gordon prepared to leave the storeroom, he returned the lock to the oak chest and latched it shut. He then opened a second chest, slightly larger than the first, and surveyed the contents. It was similarly filled to capacity, but contained silver instead of gold. This chest held the proceeds of his smaller transactions, as well as the profits from his farming operation. Although it weighed more than the first chest, its value was much less due to the lower price commanded by the silver coin. Gordon looked at this stash as an inconvenience, and he wondered how he could convert it to gold in order to make it more transportable.

After a final visual inventory of the treasure, he restored the lock to the second chest and proceeded up the stairs, locking the storeroom door behind him. To most men, it was more money than they would ever see in a lifetime. To Gordon, it presented a dilemma, for he knew that the time might come when he would be forced to flee for his life if the Patriots prevailed in the war that was sure to come. That flight might be difficult or impossible if he was shackled to a half ton of gold and silver. Grimly, he concluded that he might soon be forced into making that decision: to leave his gold behind and make a new start in Canada, or to remain in the colony of New York and risk dying a very rich man.

As it so happened, the choice was forced upon Gordon sooner than he had expected. Two days later, on May 10, a band of over eighty members of the Green Mountain Boys crossed over Lake Champlain in the pre-dawn hours and conducted a surprise attack on Fort Ticonderoga. (Even more of the rebel soldiers were left behind on the east shore of the lake, as they had insufficient transportation to move them across the two miles of water.) The fort, which was defended by about half as many British troops, surrendered without a fight. And so, even though the attack came from the east rather than from the Patriot troops stationed at Fort Ann, the result was the same. The key fort guarding the route to Canada now lay in the hands of the enemy.

News of the successful attack by the Patriots spread like wildfire among the colonies, reaching southward to Albany, New York City, and Virginia. Likewise, the news traveled north and was received grimly by British General Guy Carleton. For the British, the news was troubling for a pair of reasons. First, it meant that the primary route into the revolting colonies from the north was now blocked by a Patriot-held fortification with the means to disrupt traffic along Lake Champlain. Second, and perhaps even more important, was the fact that the fort contained a great number of cannons and plentiful ammunition, both desperately needed by the formative army of the fledgling country. This artillery could be put to immediate use, either to hold the fort or to move closer to the fighting around Boston.

Robert Gordon learned of the attack within a day of the event. It was news of the worst order, as his primary water route of escape was now much more dangerous. It meant that he might be forced to transit that portion of the lake under cover of darkness. Worse yet, he had lent two of the British officers in Fort Ticonderoga his personal riding saddles to use if they needed to make a hasty retreat. Since one of the conditions of the surrender to Ethan Allen and Benedict Arnold was that all of the contents of the fort must be turned over to the rebel troops, he worried that they would find his tack and trace it back to him. If they did, his life would be in immediate danger, along with that of his wife and possibly those associated with his enterprise.

Robert Gordon had always been a man of action with a strong sense of self-preservation. He was not one to sit in place and allow circumstances to dictate his fate. And so, following the fall of Fort Ticonderoga, he began to formulate the escape plan that would take him and his wife out of harm's way. But timing would be everything, and so many questions loomed in his mind. Would the Patriots occupying Fort Ticonderoga be guarding the passageway north on Lake Champlain? Would his saddles be found and identified, marking him as a sympathizer of the Loyalists? What would happen if they attempted to move north with the chest of gold inside the boat? Would they have their life's savings confiscated by the rebels? Would their lives be spared?

Gordon quickly decided that his only option was to pack up a few precious belongings and make a run for the Canadian border. Whether he could get there with both his life and his gold would remain in question.

CHAPTER 2

May 21, 1775

Gordon was well served by a network of influential friends and associates in the settlement of Skenesborough. He was very selective when it came to letting others into his trust, confiding only in those who had affirmed their ties to the Loyalist cause. He relied on this network to keep him informed of the gossip that was passed among the townspeople, as his own activities depended on remaining anonymous as a scout for the British.

So far, Gordon knew that he had not been linked directly to the enemy forces at Fort Ticonderoga. But he also knew that the members of the Green Mountain Boys were in the process of removing and cataloging the storerooms of the fort. They would naturally start with the cannons, ammunitions, and rifles that could be put to immediate use in battle. But next would come the remainder of the stores, and among them would be his personally marked saddles and carrying bags. He cursed himself for making the mistake of loaning these items to his British friends during such a period of strife. One month is what he estimated, one month before the link was established and charges would be brought against him. After that, he would be fined heavily and possibly face the confiscation of all his land and belongings. Or worse. He tried his hardest not to think about the possibilities.

And so, on the night of May 21, Robert and Rose Gordon decided to plan their getaway. It should have been easy: load their possessions into a bateau and sail north on Wood Creek, through Lake Champlain, and eventually on to Canada. They could count on getting aid from the wide-spread network of Loyalists throughout the area, who would help them with food and shelter, if needed. But they would also be susceptible to inspection and arrest by Patriot forces, especially in the narrower waters at the south end of Lake Champlain near Fort Ticonderoga. Once they made it past those troubled miles, Gordon was confident that they could make the rest of the trip in relative safety.

But the gold! In the day when the average man's wage was but a few shillings, Gordon's personal cache could have kept an army of men in pay for months. He was simply not willing to take the risk of losing that to the rebels, who would be looking to loot and steal to support their primitive war efforts. An idea slowly hatched in Gordon's mind that germinated almost overnight. He would make his escape via the expected route, up Wood Creek and into Lake Champlain, accompanied by his wife and a couple of his most faithful employees. However, he would not be carry-ing the gold. He would, in essence, serve as a decoy. Meanwhile, his two most trusted comrades, Thomas Swain and Alvin Smith, would travel overland, west across the forests of the Adirondacks, before turning north and eventually crossing into Canada, where they would meet at a prede-termined location. It would be they who would carry the gold.

The meeting was called in the kitchen of the Gordon homestead on that very night. Since it was a Sunday, the gathering of close friends would not arouse suspicion, as the Gordon family often invited guests to gather for a communal meal in the comfort of their snug home. On this particular evening, though, the topic of conversation would be the escape plan, including the routes and the evacuation of the gold stored inside the cellar.

The Gordons counted on Swain and Smith to transport the gold into Canada simultaneously with their own escape. They had agreed on this arrangement over a month earlier, so the two foremen were already well-versed on the plan. However, three other soon-to-be refugees sat around the large square table that evening, hearing about the mission for the first time. Philip and Elinour Rowe had arrived in Skenesborough two winters past, building a small home just north of the Gordons. Both of them worked on the farm in various capacities. Philip was a carpenter and mason who had built two of the smaller outbuildings with his own hands. Elinour was an accomplished weaver and seamstress who produced high-quality finished garments from raw materials. She was equally as handy with the loom as with a pair of knitting needles. Her products were always in demand by the townspeople, who found her wares for sale at the Gordons' store.

Benjamin Warren was an astute businessman who, unlike Robert, chose not to establish his own enterprise. Instead, he managed the purchasing and inventory of the Gordons' store, maintained records, and sought out new products and suppliers, operating in the background and avoiding any acclaim or public recognition. Although he was both young and attractive, he had never courted any woman that anyone could remember, and he lived alone with his books and papers.

Although the members of this gathering varied in age and disposition, they shared a crucial belief: that the King of England should remain in control of the territories and the rebellious Patriots from Boston to Virginia should be put in their place. They also believed that the well-trained and well-supplied soldiers of King George would be able to put down any rebellion within a few short years, after which their lives would return to normal. Of that one fact, Robert Gordon was certain; he would return to his homestead as soon as the political landscape had stabilized and their safety could be guaranteed.

Within an hour, Gordon laid out his plans for the coordinated escape. It involved timing, daring, and a little luck. First, he would obtain a large, double-ended bateau from his friend, Philip Skene. Flat-bottomed and measuring twenty-eight feet in length and six feet abeam, it was a very stable, seaworthy platform, powered by two sets of oars that could be augmented by a small sail in the forward part of the vessel. It could easily carry the full weight of the gold, along with the family necessities such as clothing and personal goods.

However, Gordon believed that they might be followed as they sailed up Wood Creek, or face boarding in the lower part of Lake Champlain, and for that reason, he planned to carry the lesser-valued silver instead of the gold. Anyone focusing their attention on the bateau would miss the more precious treasure, which would be routed around the southern end of Lake Champlain and then westward. Smith and Swain would take along a contingent of four Indians, also loyal to the British, who would serve as scouts and guides. The Indians had been paid handsomely for their services in the past, and they had been treated well by the Gordon family. Gordon had earned the respect of many members of the local Iroquois tribe, which would serve him well in the weeks to come.

Swain and Smith would bring along two horses, which would carry the gold and the bulk of the supplies and foodstuffs. This would allow the men to walk unencumbered, thus increasing their daily range by several miles. The Indians could also carry supplies, as well as counter any threat en route to the Canadian border, but they were there primarily to provide direction across the many miles of trails and deer paths between Lake Champlain and the great wilderness of northern New York.

Gordon was intentionally vague when it came to discussing the details of the hoard being distributed for transport. Had he chosen to share the specifics, those who were assisting him would have known that the accumulated sum was slightly over $80,000, with about $74,000 being comprised of gold coin and bullion and the remainder in the form of silver coins. The sheer weight of the silver amounted to about 300 pounds, while the gold tipped the scales at about 210 pounds.

To everyone present, it was apparent that Swain and Smith drew the short straws in the bargain. Their journey to Canada would be much longer and infinitely harder. They would have several weeks, if not months, of difficult traveling, facing mountains and unknown terrain before reaching the northern border of the territory. The roads that existed were certainly not improved to any measure of modern terms. West of Lake George was a long stretch of empty woods, after which the maps depicted a long, narrow body of water that today bears the name of Indian

Lake. Beyond that, nothing was known. Not even the Indians knew whether the land was inhabited by a single soul. However, Swain and Smith were not only faithful and trustworthy, they were smart as well. Gordon had promised them both a cut in the treasure once they rendezvoused in Canada, along with a significant plot of land on which to build their new homes. It was a deal that neither man wanted to turn down.

While the foremen and their Indian guides headed west through the woodlands, the double-ended boat would carry the Gordons, Philip and Elinour Rowe, and Benjamin Warren straight up the Champlain waterway. They would load the boat on the night of May 25, and then depart in the pre-dawn hours of May 26. The silver would be carried from the house to the nearby dock on the creek in small loads to avoid raising a commotion. Once in the bateau, the precious metal would then be placed back in the chest, which would be locked and covered with other crates and cargo. With five people in the boat, the oars would be manned by two of the men at a time, while the others tended the sail or kept watch.

The date was carefully selected to permit the craft to move past the occupied Fort Ticonderoga at night under a new moon, which would fall on May 28. Timing was critical. Gordon figured they would need two days to travel up Wood Creek, avoiding traffic whenever possible, to the point where Ticonderoga guarded the junction between Lake Champlain and the outlet of Lake George. Once past the fort, the lake widened considerably until it reached Crown Point in another fourteen miles. After that it should be clear sailing to Canada.

Gordon also had a backup plan that was ready to be executed if necessary. He had scouted a stretch of waterway at the narrow south end of Lake Champlain, about ten miles north of his homestead, where the bottom was only three feet down and covered in mud. It was a reed-filled patch of water that was adjacent to a large fractured rock formation on the west shore. If pursued, Gordon knew that he could dump the locked chest in this pre-designated location and return at a later date to retrieve his stash. In order to find the exact spot, he had asked Swain to drive a long sharpened stake through the weeds the week prior. Once the chest was sunk, he could remove the stake and easily find the spot by referring to the shore topography.

The five men and two women gathered around the table reviewed the plans and posed questions as they arose. Gordon and the others in the bateau would have the easier and more direct route. It was a distance of a bit over one hundred miles to the Canadian border, after which they would sail up the Richelieu River to a location about twenty miles further north. Even at a mere fifteen miles a day, they would cross the border within a week to ten days. The only factors that could slow them down were severe weather or hostile forces.

Gordon had expected that Swain and Smith would take perhaps two months to complete their journey via the planned detour westward. The first part of their route was easy to calculate: pass southwest around the bottom of Lake Champlain, below Lake George, and then west into the wild forests. He figured that if they headed west perhaps twenty or thirty miles, they should be able to make the turn north and proceed unimpeded for the border.

What Gordon hadn't counted upon was the rugged terrain that they would have to cross once they passed into the "dismal wilderness" of the Adirondacks. From the waters of Lake Champlain, they had seen the mountains to the west and guessed that their progress might be slow. But nowhere could they find a map that portrayed the vast expanses of thick woods and swamps, the mazes of lakes, and the endless peaks that characterize the Adirondacks. It would be a challenge for them to traverse this distance across such terrain even without the added complications of a meeting date. However, none of this was known to any of those gathered on this day, and so the planning moved on.

Gordon introduced a map that showed a small town, called Saint Jean-sur-Richelieu. His friend, Colonel Skene, had promised him the rights to some land near the Richelieu River, along with the option to acquire additional properties for his employees. On the primitive map, it appeared as though the village sat about twenty to twenty-five miles north of the border. This distance, thought Gordon, should provide an ample buffer between his new homestead and the rebellion brewing in the colonies.

Gordon planned on making final landfall at this destination by the twelfth of June, give or take a couple of days. He and Swain applied a pair of navigational dividers to the map and arrived at a figure of two hundred miles for the land route. In other words, it appeared that there would be at least a month's wait before Swain and Smith would arrive with the gold, and perhaps even longer if the terrain was as tough as they imagined.

Gordon and Swain decided that they would make their rendezvous at a small pub nearby the old fortification built by the French, Fort Saint-Jean. The pub had been recommended by Skene as a safe location. It was owned by a retired British infantry officer who had offered refuge to any Loyalist passing through from the colonies. The proprietor's name was William, although Gordon did not know his last name. Gordon and his group would check in with William when they arrived and leave directions for Swain and Smith with the tavern keeper. It wasn't a perfect plan, but it was the best they could formulate without arousing suspicion. Although the gold would take longer to reach Canada, at least they should be able to avoid having it captured by the Patriots.

As the sun set over the Gordons' homestead, the lamps were turned on in the dining room, sending flickering shadows dancing across the table. Robert and Rose Gordon looked from one solemn face to the next, assessing their dispositions. Each member of the party knew that it would be a difficult transit, with perils around each bend in the river or rise of the next mountain. But they also knew that they had no alternatives. They had to leave, and time was running out.

Before ending the meeting that night, they all joined hands in prayer, asking for safety and deliverance on the voyage north. They also took an oath to support one another, regardless of consequence, to fight to the death if need be, in order to reach their objective. Captivity in the hands of the colonial army was not an option.

May 26 was now only four days away.

CHAPTER 3

May 25, 1775

They arrived without making sound, shadowy silhouettes that appeared on the edge of the clearing. The Iroquois braves were as comfortable in the woods as most colonists were in their houses. Silently, they crossed the grassy verge of the settlement and slid through the open door of the barn.

It was well past twilight in the village, and the employees of the Gordon establishment had been sent home early. All except Swain and Smith, who were busy moving supplies from a back storeroom to the middle of the main room. Philip and Elinour Rowe were inside the farmhouse, preparing their personal belongings for stowage inside the bateau. Benjamin Warren was also inside the house, checking the final route on the large map of the lake. Very little was said as they went about their pre-assigned duties. The hazards of the upcoming voyage weighed heavily on their minds.

The four Indians moved in single file through the maze of tables and wares. Gordon and Swain raised their hands in silent greeting and were solemnly answered by the leader of the group. The dark-skinned warriors were clad in native clothing, including leather leggings, tall moccasins, and loincloths. To Swain, it appeared as though the fabric of their shirts was European linen, although each was partially covered by a cape that made identification difficult. Three of the four wore feathers in their hair, secured by a headband over the forehead. They all wore nose rings though their nostrils, as well as other silver jewelry and colored beads on their hands and wrists.

Gordon was the only one there who knew the four Indians. Their names were hard for him to pronounce, and he repeated them over and over again as he introduced them to Swain and Smith, looking for approval from each of the braves and taking time to establish a rapport among the six men. The leader's name was Achak, which Gordon said meant "spirit." Achak was a quiet man with a special affinity for the woods. He could "hear" the right path through the wilderness and read the sun and the sky and the winds. He was respected by the other Indians as a wise man who could guide them through danger to safer ground.

The second Iroquois he introduced was Anakausuen, which literally meant "worker." Anakausuen was the tallest of the four braves, with long sinewy limbs and graceful movements. He looked more like a long-distance runner than a fighter, and he could cover great expanses in the woods without ever tiring.

If Anakausuen was the runner, then Machk was the wrestler. A thick, heavily-muscled warrior with several piercings, he was the fiercest-looking member of the lot. Machk's name translated to "bear," and one look at his physique attested to the appropriateness of the name. An Olympic weightlifter would have been envious of his biceps, and the bulging muscles on the tops of his shoulders belied enormous strength. He never smiled, and was always restless to move into action.

Finally, the last of the Iroquois group, Matunaaga, stepped up and grasped hands with the two white men. Matunaaga was not overly impressive in size or build, but his reputation as a fighter was legendary. He was quick as lightning, able to attack without warning before most men could raise a hand in defense. He was also an expert with the spear and war tomahawk, although Achak was a better shot with a bow and arrow. His name was the Iroquois word for "fights," and those who had opposed him in battle had often paid the ultimate price for underestimating his speed and power.

Gordon had selected these four members of the local tribe for good reason. They were symbiotic in their ability to move and fight as a group.

Their individual skills, strengths, and weaknesses meshed closely into a cohesive unit, led by Achak, the quiet thinker and leader. Each of these warriors had also worked for Gordon in some capacity, and while they still relied on their native tongue while addressing one another, they could comprehend the white men's language and reply in broken English when needed. Only Achak, however, spoke English fluently.

The Indians were led into the barn and shown a place where they could bed down for the night in the straw. They had carried their belongings on their backs, packed into leather rucksacks from Gordon's store. Because the distances would be great and the terrain rugged, each had packed a second set of moccasins, along with more sturdy footwear that resembled early European boots, except for the leather tassels and beadwork. Each would also be carrying a supply of dried meat, clothing, and other supplies that would be needed over the extended duration of the voyage. Removing their rucksacks, the braves lay down in the straw and pulled a dyed woolen blanket over their bodies, using their packs as pillows.

As the Indians bedded down for the evening rest, Swain and Smith busied themselves preparing the saddles that would be placed on the two packhorses. The saddles were early versions of "la estradiota," or Spanish war saddles. However, they were constructed nothing like the ordinary riding tack of the era. Elinour Rowe had used her extraordinary seamstress skills to sew a great deal of the gold bullion into hidden compartments in the leather and cloth saddles. It had been tough work, performed over the course of two weeks, with a heavy needle and thick catgut thread. After hiding close to eighty pounds of gold inside and under each of the saddles, she attached an extra layer of material that camouflaged the entire surface, rendering the treasure invisible.

Gordon had already discussed the issue of the gold with Swain and Smith, agreeing that the Indians should never know about the vast treasure riding on the backs of the steeds. The two of them would be the only ones allowed to handle the saddles, since anyone who attempted to hoist either of them would instantly realize that their massive weights were due to something other than cowhide. Additionally, both of the foremen would carry slightly over twenty pounds of the bullion themselves. Once again, it was Elinour who had sewn this stash into the sides of their packs, leaving the main compartment open for their own clothing and personal effects.

By ten o'clock, all members of the ensemble gathered at the Gordons' homestead moved inside the farmhouse for the evening. Only the Indians were left inside the barn, and they were already asleep. The bateau was completely loaded, except for the massive hoard of silver that would be brought onboard just prior to pushing off at dawn. Gordon had this lot divided between ten thick cloth bags, each weighing about thirty pounds, tied closed around the top with a length of twine. The distance between the house and the creek was short, not more than 150 feet. It would take little time for the three men to relay the laden bags from the house to the pier. There, the bags would be brought onboard and packed inside an oak chest, which would then be locked with a secure hasp. That would be the last chore they performed before pushing out into the creek in the early morning haze.

The Gordons' home had three bedrooms, and each was pressed into service that night. Robert and Rose slept in their own room, while the Rowes occupied the other bedroom facing the front of the home. Benjamin Warren was alone in the smaller room that was originally built to be a child's nursery, although the Gordons had not yet produced a child. Swain and Smith occupied the living room, Swain lying across a comfortable couch, while Smith settled for a well-padded armchair. Although the arrangements were not perfect, they served the purpose. In fact, it mattered little, as each of the seven Loyalists occupying the house that night experienced some degree of insomnia. Sleep was hard to find, as the day of reckoning was just hours away.

Although the sky was barely kissed by the pre-dawn light, Rose Gordon was already awake. She had come out of her sleep before 5:00 a.m., preoccupied with thoughts of their new life in the Canadian frontier. She was a healthy young woman of twenty-six who had looked forward to raising a family in their Skenesborough home. And now, this. She made certain to wipe away any signs of her tears before shaking her husband out of his sleep.

Robert arose quickly, pulling on his outer garments as he was stepping out the bedroom door. As he passed from room to room, waking the others from their sleep, Rose hurried into the kitchen and quickly set to work preparing a small breakfast of eggs and biscuits. She looked longingly at her stove, wondering if she would ever see it again. Putting aside her painful thoughts, she quickly produced enough food to feed each of the seven tenants of the house, plus a sufficient surplus to bring out to the barn for the four Indians. Swain and Smith decided to eat in the barn as well, with their soon-to-be guides. It would be their last meal at the homestead.

It took less than twenty minutes to load the silver into the bateau and another ten minutes to bring aboard the rest of the cargo. Benjamin stayed in the craft, distributing the load so that it rode evenly in the water without a list to either side. Meanwhile, the Gordons and the Rowes backtracked to the barn and helped Swain and Smith saddle the horses. Finally, when all hands were ready to depart, they exchanged a series of long handshakes and embraces. Robert Gordon reminded Swain of the rendezvous: the first of July at the Black Horse Tavern. If they couldn't make it by that date, the tavern keeper would tell them where to find the Gordons. It sounded simple at the time.

Swain and Smith backtracked to the creek to see the bateau off. They released the line holding the craft to the small dock, watching as Benjamin Warren and Rowe pulled on the two sets of oars. They quickly pointed the bow north and headed into the waters of Wood Creek. Within two minutes, the boat was lost in the fog.

The two men walked back to the farmyard, where the Indians were already leading the packhorses out of the stable. They were just as anxious to be departing as were the other travelers. They too had been promised land north of the border, and were eager to reach their destination.

Though none of them had been in the territory west of Lake George, they had an uncanny sense of direction and the ability to orient themselves in the natural world. Even without the benefit of the faintest trail, they could keep their heading in the woods and blaze their own route across swamps and mountains. Swain and Smith were grateful that their employer had retained the services of these four men.

The first day of the voyage was routine and uneventful. The territories around Skenesborough and Fort Ann were well traveled, as was the hilly land south of Lake George. Following horse trails that had been hacked out of the woods (some by the direction of Philip Skene himself), the six men were able to cover over ten miles. None of them were under the illusion that would last for long, especially once they cleared the settled region west of Lake George.

After the first day of the trek, the land bound group was overlooking the waters of Lake George. Achak pointed out places where they could camp for the night, and also catch some fresh fish from the cold waters near shore. The two white men were tired from the first day of walking, but it felt good to finally be on their way.

Smith had been astounded by the stealth of the Iroquois over the initial leg of the trip. Although Achak remained close by, he rarely noticed the presence of the other three braves. Matunaaga, the skilled fighter and warrior, was alternately ahead of the men with the horses, then following after them. He seemed preoccupied with the trail behind their group, as though he was looking for someone who might be following in their footsteps. Meanwhile, Anakausuen was some distance ahead, silently surveying the woods surrounding the path. Smith caught a glimpse of him only twice the entire day, and yet Achak was able to effortlessly discern whether his fellow guide had stayed on "the road" or had veered off. Their ability to follow one another despite the lack of visual contact was uncanny.

Smith had also noticed that the Indians were wearing some of the payment that Gordon had given them in advance of their sortie—thick, silver bands with engraved patterns that wrapped around the wrists of each of the four. Payment in the form of silver jewelry and coin was highly valued, and it was considered a status symbol within the tribe. While the land they would receive in Canada was far more valuable, the ornate wristbands and other adornments were a very large perk of the deal.

As they settled down to a small meal around a communal fire that night, Swain wondered just what the Indians would do if they knew the value of the gold that was concealed inside the saddles. He also couldn't help but worry about possible adversaries they might meet in the days to come. Had anyone else known about the vast fortune accumulated by the Gordons over the past five years? How long would it be before the people in town knew that Gordon himself had departed and fled north? Would any of them pursue either the bateau or the group on horseback? Too tired to think, Swain quickly decided to push the worries from his mind and allow himself to drift to sleep. Tomorrow would be another day, hopefully as uneventful as today. He closed his eyes and turned over, feeling the last warmth of the waning flames against the skin on his face.

Considering the primitive conditions of the day, Smith had spent very little time in the woods. Unlike Swain, he had been raised in the city, first in London, then in Boston. Sleeping out in the open that first night, he lost considerable sleep to the constant animal cries and other woodland sounds within earshot of their campsite. On at least two occasions, he bolted to an upright position, startled by the call of a cougar and the scream of an entrapped hare. Yet the calm slumber of Swain and their guides reassured him that this was nothing but ordinary, and he soon returned to sleep. It would remain like this as long as the woods were their home and the stars their ceiling; he just needed some time to get acclimated.

Day two followed in a similar manner, with the Iroquois leading the white men over a series of progressively taller hills as they made their turn around the bottom of Lake George and onto the long leg west. Sometimes they followed trails, while at other times they cut alongside streambeds and over fields. When luck was on their side, they were able to pick up improved military roads that were increasingly evident in the years surrounding the

War for Independence.

During one particularly lengthy transit across an old clearing, Anakau-suen appeared from a clump of brush to their right and spoke rapidly to Achak, who smiled in response. He beckoned to Swain and Smith, who followed them along a detour and into a clearing with an unobstructed view to the east. In the distance, rain clouds were spreading a series of showers over the mountains, and a gorgeous full-spectrum rainbow was painted across the sky from horizon to horizon, filling the heavens with color. Achak explained to Swain and Smith that this was a sign from the gods; they were smiling down on them and embracing them. All would be well for the duration of the voyage.

Swain remembered hearing Achak's prophecy again later that day as he stood at the edge of the river, wondering what to do next. They had completed eight miles and were nearing the end of their travel for the day when they reached the Hudson River. It appeared to be far too wide and too deep to cross, although none of the men had tested its bottom. Swain came to a stop, considering whether the horses could swim with the weight of the gold in the saddles, while Smith stood by his side, devoid of ideas. He amused himself by wondering whether the muscular Machk was able to carry the horses safely to the other side.

As they stood there pondering, Achak calmly surveyed the scene along the banks and pointed upriver. He indicated that they should go north, following the waters towards their source, where the volume might be less. Swain agreed, although he had seen this river on the map and knew that it was far too long to trace back to its origins as a creek that could be stepped over. But since they had to go north eventually anyway, he agreed to the idea of the detour, thinking they might locate a more favorable spot to ford the currents.

Thankfully, they didn't have to travel far. By halfway through the third day, the topography flattened out somewhat, and the riverbed was much wider. Instead of boulders and whitewater, the stream wound its way through a relatively shallow stretch where the round-pebbled bottom sat no more than three feet below the surface. Achak held up one hand and gestured across to the other side. With that one simple movement, the other three Indians turned and started crossing in single file. It was obvious to Swain that he, Achak, was the "guide of guides" among the natives, and that his word was respected as final.

The crossing was made with little difficulty. Even the horses didn't hesitate about following along on their leads, as the water reached less than a foot above their knees. The men briefly considered removing the saddles, lest the horses stumble and toss part of their load into the current. However, since Swain and Smith knew the true weight of those saddles, they had to trust their steeds' balance and allowed the gold to ride across the Hudson on their backs.

Later that afternoon, the men stopped for a short break. Anakausuen and Machk both napped, while Swain retrieved a sheet of paper, a short quill pen, and a small bottle of ink, and prepared to write. Written in diary format, he meticulously charted their progress several times each day, noting directions, distances, and landmarks, drawing diagrams and miniature maps as best he could given his limited navigational aids. Gordon had presented him with a compass that he had received from one of his friends in Fort Ticonderoga, and Swain had become relatively proficient with the device. However, he did not trust it implicitly, and he continuously tried to match the readings with his own observations of the sun.

Once across the Hudson, they ran out of maps. Within another day, they also ran out of roads and trails. They faced a seemingly endless traverse of thick woodland that seemed to get more mountainous by the day. Each time they scaled a new height, they hoped to gain a glimpse of flatter land on the horizon, but only managed to see the crest of an even grander peak further west. None were large enough to show bare exposed rock, but they still required major exertion to climb, and their pace slowed considerably. As he toiled, Swain's mind wandered to the bateau and his five companions who were sailing north on Lake Champlain. They had the easy route over water—as long as they didn't get caught. He wondered where they were, and how much different their plight was from his own.

If Swain had known the full story, he would have been content to remain in the woods, safely concealed amongst the trees. For within two hours after leaving the dock, the boat's occupants knew they had problems.

Benedict Arnold, the infamous "turncoat" Colonel who had led some of the troops in the fort's capture, had already raced down the lake and absconded with several private vessels, including a small British schooner that he desired for his own raids. Later he captured a seventy-ton British sloop, the Enterprise, and headed north, looking for additional targets of military value to attack, leaving several of the smaller craft to lurk in the waters south of Lake Champlain.

It was late in the afternoon when Benjamin Warren made an unsettling discovery. Looking off the back end of their bateau, he observed two of these craft coming into view from the south, both appearing to be larger and wider than their own. While they were still too far away to observe closely, they appeared to be sailing together, with numerous men onboard. With more sets of oars and bigger sails, these vessels were bound to move through the water faster then their own. Gordon guessed that these were two of the British boats captured in Skenesborough by the Green Mountain Boys. This presented them with a problem: they didn't want to be overtaken for fear of being boarded and their valuables confiscated, yet, if they increased their speed by means of aggressive rowing, it would give the appearance that they were running from the Colonists.

Gordon decided to adjust their sail to maximize their forward speed as much as possible without appearing to be evasive. Meanwhile, he took over the oars from Benjamin, being much bigger and stronger and thus able to put more force into each stroke. Philip manned the other set of oars, while Rose directed the movement of the craft from the stern, indicating whether they should move closer to either bank or remain in the middle of the waterway.

To everyone onboard the bateau, it appeared as though the two craft were following them, although it was impossible to be certain, because anyone who was northbound along the creek would naturally have to follow in their wake. But over the next two hours, as the two other vessels slowly closed the gap, they could detect the boats following their movements from port to starboard as they maneuvered through the water. The soldiers on the craft were still too distant to hear or see their faces. However, they were clearly not wearing the characteristic red uniforms of the British military. Worse still, they continued to mimic the movements of the Gordons' bateau as they slowly but steadily grew closer.

Gordon assumed the worst, and his mind went into overdrive as he came up with a plan. They had already decided that they'd have to hide the silver by dropping it into the shallow water of Wood Creek. That part of the plan was pre-determined. It was the rest of the deception that would require the lion's share of good fortune. Gordon calmly briefed the other four members of the crew on what to do and what to say when they were overtaken. It was a mad and somewhat desperate plan, but just crazy enough to work. It had to.

It was getting darker now as the sun was setting to the west. But there was enough light remaining in the sky to see the detailed shoreline on the Vermont side of the river. Gordon quickly identified some geographical points that he could recall at a later date, reference points to use when they returned for their treasure someday—hopefully soon. And then, he turned the boat into the shoreline and sprang into action.

The point selected by Gordon was a low-lying rocky stretch of shoreline that jutted out from eastern side of the water. The bottom was only about four feet deep at that point, with a muddy floor and lots of aquatic plants growing up from the sediment. Gordon directed Rose and Elinour to drop the anchor over the side and then do the best they could to keep the bow of the bateau pointed toward the approaching craft. His reason for doing this was simple: he wanted to use the sail to hide their actions. Timing was everything, so they had to act quickly.

The three men moved to the back of the craft and slid the chest containing the silver to the very edge of the pointed stern. Gordon was concerned, because the trunk felt every bit the three hundred pounds it weighed, and then some. He could not lift even a corner of the chest off the deck; all the while, the two pursuing craft moved closer. Elinour could now see individual men and their weapons as they directed their vessels to the same part of the tributary. The distance between them was now less than a quarter of a mile.

Robert Gordon, Philip, and Benjamin all bent over and heaved simultaneously, each trying to grasp either a handle or part of the chest's frame in order to lift it up over the side of the bateau. But the weight was too great, and the load very cumbersome. Added to that, Gordon had another worry: what if the weight of the three men, combined with that of the chest, placed too much of a load in the stern of the craft and swamped the vessel?

Benjamin Warren was not a very powerful man. But he was a thinker with a mechanical mindset, widely known for finding ways to solve problems with the least amount of exertion. He quickly grasped two thick planks that they had used to stack the cargo on the bateau. As the other two men slowly lifted one side of the chest off the deck, and then the other, he was able to slide the planks underneath. Using the planks as levers, they were able to raise the chest to the rear edge of the boat. Each of the men strained, heaved, and pulled, all the while wondering if they could clear the top surface of the gunnels. Finally, with a muffled splash, the chest rolled over the side and disappeared into a thick cloud of bottom silt.

There was no time to spare. The two hostile boats were now within two hundred yards and closing quickly. Still hidden by the slackened sail, Robert Gordon ducked beneath some empty crates and pulled a linen cloth over his long body. Philip and Benjamin both stacked additional light cargo and sacks over his concealed form. Then, Benjamin grabbed for the bible, and the performance began.

As the first of the two boats pulled alongside, a Lieutenant of the Green Mountain Boys, armed with a long rifle, cupped his hands to demand a boarding. In back of him stood a half dozen armed soldiers, guns at the ready to counter any military threat they encountered on the craft. However, the officer stopped short as he gained his first full view of the smaller vessel's occupants. Benjamin, dressed in black, head bowed, was reading from the bible as the other three visible sailors listened in distress. At intervals throughout the reading, Philip Rowe nodded solemnly and murmured "Amen." Elinour and Rose were both weeping, their heads partially concealed in black scarves, while Philip put on an Oscar-winning performance, filling the role of comforter and consoler.

The Lieutenant watched in silence for a full minute while Benjamin read the Lord's Prayer, milking the act for all it was worth. Finally, unable to remain quiet any longer, the officer made his demand: who were they and what was their purpose for traveling on the creek?

For about fifteen full seconds, the challenge went unanswered as the four continued to stare disconsolately at the murky waters below the river. Then, Benjamin turned slowly towards the Lieutenant and asked him for silence.

"May it please you, Sir, a moment of silence so that we may finish committing this man's soul to the Lord, from whence he came?"

The officer was stunned, momentarily, not knowing how to respond. He had been expecting to engage in a possible skirmish. Instead, he was witnessing a funeral.

"Was that a man's body you dropped into the water?" He was at a loss, not able to dispel his shock. "How did this man die?"

"Smallpox, Sir. We have one more like him with us, only barely alive. I fear that we, too, are infected. Please save yourselves and do not linger in our presence, I beseech you!"

The Colonist officer appeared stunned as he involuntarily backed away from the side of the boat. The other members of the platoon, who had since removed their covers in respect, appeared aghast. Several of them reached for materials to pull over their mouths and faces. Smallpox was among the most feared of diseases known to man, a nearly certain death sentence for anyone in that era. There was not a man among the crew of soldiers who wished to search the infected bateau for even a minute.

As several members of the rebel craft began to pull on their oars, Elinour fell to her knees, reaching for the water while wailing in despair. "Oh, John, John, no, no. I love you, John. Come back to me!" She crumpled over in the stern of the boat, apparently lost in her grief.

From beneath the camouflage of crates and tarps, Gordon listened to the proceedings with hope and encouragement. His comrades were carrying out the plan better than he could have ever dreamed. Not only had their ruse stopped the soldiers in their tracks, it had caused them to retreat without even visually searching their vessel. He silently regretted depositing the silver in the river, although he knew that he could easily return to that very spot and reclaim the chest as soon as the British Army had put down this insurrection, perhaps within the next year. It shouldn't take long, he figured, before he would be back to take ownership once again of his land and material possessions.

Gordon remained under cover of the cargo material until the two raider craft had completed a small circle in the waterway and commenced their course south. Only then, when he was certain that they were beyond visual range, did he chance emerging from hiding. It was getting darker now anyway, and his chances of being sighted were very slim.

As dusk turned to night, the sky grew darker by the minute, with little illumination from the slim new moon above. Rather than linger in the area where they had encountered the soldiers, the group quickly decided to move northward, putting some additional distance between themselves and Skenesborough. By rigging the sail and simultaneously taking turns on the oars, they could power through the water at a reasonable speed. Their eyes became accustomed to the dark, and they moved comfortably ahead.

Benjamin had figured that they were, at most, ten miles south of Fort Ticonderoga. Traveling at three knots, they would pass by the fortification somewhere around midnight. It would make for a long and grueling day. However, each member of the party agreed that it represented the safest way to evade any observers looking down from the fort's walls. And if the Colonists had indeed positioned boats in the water east of the fort, they would have been sitting ducks for yet another attempted boarding by soldiers.

So onward they sailed, feeling their way through the widening waters that poured from Wood Creek into Lake Champlain. The sky offered just enough light to suggest the hint of a tree line to the east of the lake. Gordon directed Benjamin to navigate a course within three hundred yards of the eastern shoreline, as far away from Ticonderoga as possible without endangering the craft in the shallows near the Vermont border.

Fortunately, the crew experienced no further scares for the remainder of the night. Gordon suggested to Rose and Elinour that they try to rest, although sleep would be difficult in the confines of the small vessel. They swept stealthily past the fort at 11:00 that night and continued to sail north until well past midnight. When they could finally stay awake no longer, they pulled their craft to shore near a tight cove of trees and threw out their anchor. By arranging the many crates lengthwise in the bateau, they were able to fashion enough horizontal surfaces to serve as cots, using wool blankets as padding. It wasn't comfortable, but they were all too weary to notice. Best of all, they had completed the most dangerous part of the journey, and they appeared to be safe.

CHAPTER 4

June 2, 1775

True to Gordon's planning, the rest of the voyage was relatively simple. The travelers' cares seemed to evaporate with each passing day as the lake grew wider. Choosing to remain near the Vermont side of the water, they saw an occasional boat sail by from north to south, although none appeared to carry military personnel. These would be merchant vessels, transporting goods and raw materials to various points around the lake. Even if they were surprised by one of these vessels crossing their path, it was doubtful that anyone would recognize the Skenesborough residents and suspect them as Loyalists.

However, things were just starting to get difficult for the two white men traversing the deep forests west of Lake George. They had left the rolling hills west of the lake behind and were now climbing up and over the taller mountains they had seen from the Hudson. Their Indian guides seemed to take it all in stride, threading their way through the brush and thick coniferous growth of the Adirondacks. But both Swain and Smith were burdened by the extra load of the gold bullion in addition to their necessary supplies. It was more than they were used to carrying, and their breath was labored as they heaved their way up and over the successive peaks.

After five days of walking, they arrived at the east side of an extremely long and narrow lake. It was oriented north-south, much the same as Lake Champlain, although Swain guessed that it was probably much smaller. He did his best to map out the cardinal points of the compass on his daily record of the trip, noting the relation of the lake to the orientation of their route. This was important to him, because he wanted to know approximately how far they had traveled in each direction as they navigated their way west, then north towards their eventual destination.

The men had settled into a daily routine whereby they moved from early morning until about noon, when they rested and ate a brief repast. Swain used this time to record additional information in his journal, while Smith and the Iroquois either rested or searched for edible nuts and berries. At night, they gathered around a small fire before settling in for the night. The two foremen removed the laden saddles from the pack horses just before turning in, placing them between their two bedrolls next to the fire. Meanwhile, at least one of the Indians was usually posted in the woods nearby, listening and watching for anything that might be a threat. However, no enemy soldiers, no other people at all, were seen by the men once they entered the deeper forests of the Adirondacks. Instead, Matunaaga and Anakausuen decided to use this time to stalk the rabbit and partridge that were so abundant in the territory, adding these to the nightly meal.

The following day, the men rounded the bottom of the long, narrow lake, and headed west once again. Swain estimated that they had traveled about thirty miles since crossing the Hudson River. According to the plans he had made with Robert Gordon, he would take the group about ten miles further west, and then make the big turn to the north.

The Indians had little difficulty keeping their progress pointed in a single direction as they silently led the way from their nightly camp. Their route took them up and over another seemingly endless ascent, forcing the white men to stop for breath on numerous occasions. The woods were beautiful and not overly thick with underbrush, although they were strewn with large boulders that required frequent scrambling. The next several hours led them over the crest of the ridge, then down a long and sometimes steep descent. They then progressed through a large swampy area, taking time to circumnavigate the wetter acreage, before arriving late that afternoon at the edge of a beautiful lake.

As the Indians set about making camp, Swain once again penned his notations, including mileage and descriptions. The lake, he noted, was probably a couple miles long, but appeared to continue to another body of water at the southwest end. There were other large fingers of water protruding from the main body of the lake, and a river spilling from the northeast end which appeared to flow north. It was, he wrote, among the most beautiful places he had ever visited. The fine cedar and spruce forest mixed with maple and birch hardwoods around the shoreline, and the lake itself fairly teemed with fish jumping at the hatching caddisflies. Above all, the call of the loon was heard echoing about the various inlets surrounding the lake, adding to the mystique of the place.

That night, each of the men tried his hand at fishing along the edge of the lake, and each was rewarded with an almost unlimited catch of fine trout. They ate until their bellies were full, for which the Indians gave thanks by song around the fire. The sun set across the western sky in a brilliant display of crimsons and reds, putting the end on a nearly perfect day. This, thought Swain, was a fitting finish to the first part of their voyage. All had gone well, and now it was time to turn north on the next part of their voyage.

The following morning came late for the travelers, and they spent a bit more time than usual before breaking camp. They fished again for their breakfasts, and then pushed ahead at a leisurely pace through the brush bordering the northwest shore of the lake. Within a mile, they came to yet another part of the lake, a smaller pond that appeared round in shape and barely connected to the rest of the main body. The narrow spillover between the two was so shallow that they could have waded across. It was here that Swain directed Achak to take them north, away from the water, and on toward their eventual destination. Achak quickly spoke in native tongue to the other three and then turned to the right, following the shoreline of the smaller pond.

The day went more slowly than the previous several, and they walked with less purpose. Swain noticed the difference, and he thought perhaps

they should have spent a day resting back at the edge of the l[
many days on the trail without a break could wear on the body, and even
the Indians seemed ready for a day of rest. It took them a couple of hours
to move through the thick woods around the northern extension to the
lake, then continue north over hills and through more dense vegetation.
Late afternoon found them descending a modestly steep hill leading to
another body of water, a mere puddle compared to the last lake. Perhaps
a few hundred yards in diameter, it resembled little more than a large
depression in the earth that had been filled in with water.

Despite the lack of scenery surrounding the pond, Swain and Smith
decided to make an early camp, gaining some extra time to rest for themselves and their guides. They unsaddled the horses and rolled out their
blankets while the Indians scouted the area for fish and game. While
Smith retrieved some dried meat to start supper, Swain led the horses over
to the edge of a clearing where they could graze on some tall wild grass.

It was then, when Swain was least expecting it, that all hell broke
loose. A mother black bear had been resting on her side in the shade, concealed from view in the trees. Meanwhile, her two young cubs played on
the soft, peaty soil nearby, soundlessly trading swipes with their padded
forelegs. The mother bear sensed the man and horses as they approached,
her protective instincts becoming more aroused with every step they took.
Swain walked in front of the horses, now only one hundred fifty feet from
the cubs. Then it was one hundred feet, then seventy-five. He unwittingly
moved closer with every step.

The horses actually detected the bears' presence before they saw them.
Their acute sense of smell picked up their scent almost at the same time
that the mother bear charged from her hiding spot. As the cubs sat up, startled, looking out at the intruders, their mother rushed forward, her mouth
open and teeth bared, a primal snarl emitting from her mouth as she
lunged towards the intruders. It was a sight that would have put the fear
of God into any sane man.

Had Swain been carrying his rifle at the moment of attack, it would have been raised and fired within a half second. He was a superb shot, and his reflexes were second to none. However, he had left his firearm with his pack when they stopped, and he was completely unarmed. The bear flashed out of the brush and directly at him with a speed that astounded him. He was momentarily paralyzed, forgetting that he had a firm grasp on the horses' lead ropes. It would be a recipe for disaster.

The horse on Swain's right side, a large roan mare, immediately reared up on her hind legs and kicked out at the oncoming threat. As she raised her front legs off the ground, the other horse, a black and white gelding, bolted to Swain's left. He was holding both ropes, and the adrenalin only tightened his grip on the lines.

The movement of the two horses in opposite directions had the effect of spinning the large man off his feet. His legs slid out from beneath him, and he landed directly underneath the body of the mare. The bear veered off to her right and collided with the gelding, which broke into full gallop through the clearing. The collision startled the bear, which sprinted across the patch of grass up a nearby ridge, followed by her two cubs. Meanwhile, the mare lost her footing in the mud, her body twisting to the ground on top of Swain in a sickening thud. As she landed, two distinct popping noises punctuated the air, resonating like a large branches breaking off a felled tree.

Smith and Achak sprinted toward the sound of the screams, followed by Matunaaga, Machk, and Anakausuen, who arrived within a matter of seconds. The scene was chaotic. Swain lay pinned on the ground, his legs trapped beneath the fallen horse, his face a mask of pain and fear. The horse was similarly anguished, its rear left leg bent outward and up at a grotesque angle. A bad break of the femur, which would leave Smith little choice but to shoot the animal and put it out of its pain.

With the men lined up against the horse's back, they were able to exert enough force to roll the animal off of Swain's legs and extract him from his position. But every movement, every tug and pull on his body, was accompanied by screams of pain and agony. Only when they had fully moved him away from the mud pit did they see the reason for his intense anguish. His right trouser leg was colored with a rapidly spreading stain of blood, and a jagged, broken bone protruded through the torn fabric. Smith turned deathly pale as he looked at the ghastly injury, then looked away. He knew it would be impossible to doctor his wounds so far from civilization, without proper medical supplies. He felt his pulse race and his logical thought process start to desert him.

Within the span of three minutes, their lives had taken a drastic turn for the worse. Swain was in dire need of medical attention in order to save his leg—and possibly even his life. One of their two horses had bolted into the woods at full speed, while the other would need to be executed. It appeared as though their mission was falling apart before their very eyes.

Smith was pondering his next move as the Indians sprang into action, urged on by the words of Achak. The Iroquois leader always seemed to know how to act in a crisis and address the most pressing problems. With only a few spoken words, he had the men lift Swain over to the dry patch of clearing they had selected as their camp. Anakausuen quickly pared a limb off a nearby sapling and fashioned a splint. Meanwhile, Matunaaga helped Smith cut the pant leg off of Swain's injured leg so they could examine his wounds.

It was an ugly, ugly fracture, with the broken edge of the fibula bone protruding through the flesh. Achak told Smith that he had set this kind of break before, but he would require help from the others. He explained what he wanted to do and directed each man to the desired position. Smith and Anakausuen were stationed by Swain's shoulders and armpits to stabilize his position, while Machk and Matunaaga applied traction to the lower leg. It was a relatively short process, although it cost Swain dearly in pain. His screams were accompanied by seemingly gallons of sweat, which poured off his face and neck and dripped to the ground in small rivulets.

Once the bones were realigned, Achak used a headband to fashion a bandage, which helped to stop the bleeding. Smith retrieved a small flask he had kept hidden inside his pack. It contained a small amount of whiskey, which he had planned to share to celebrate their arrival at their destination. He gave some to Swain to help relieve the pain, and poured the rest on his wound to help disinfect it.

With Swain's injury dressed, Smith considered his options. What should he do now that Swain was disabled and their horses gone? Anakausuen and Machk left to try to track down the black and white gelding, whose tracks they picked up heading south. From the prints left in the soil, they could tell that he had bolted at a rapid pace for about a half mile before settling into a slower trot. But after following the tracks for about two miles in the direction of their previous night's encampment, they still saw no signs of the frightened animal. How far would he travel before turning around? That is, if he turned around at all. The two natives returned to the party and made their report.

Meanwhile, Matunaaga scouted the terrain just south of the pond, along the side of a tree-lined outcropping. His keen eye was scanning the vegetation for squirrel, rabbit, or other meat for the evening meal. Suddenly, he gasped and stood still, his eyes wide in amazement as he took in the natural phenomenon that lay in front of him. Between two boulders in the formation, he had detected an opening in the rock. He approached the black hole slowly, and found himself staring down into the entrance of a moderate-sized cave. As he listened intently, he could hear and feel a current of cool air flowing from the dark interior. He was stunned into immobility, but only for a moment. Then he ran quickly back to inform Achak and Smith of his find.

The discovery of the cave was a lightning bolt of good news injected into an otherwise horrible day. The catastrophic turn of events dictated that they remain in that spot for the time being. To move Swain, they would need to find and retrieve their only uninjured horse, which might be impossible. But at the very least, Smith thought, they could move Swain into the shelter of the cave until they were ready to move on. The fact that Swain would have to ride horseback, which would not leave room for all of the gold, was not lost to him. He felt helpless, as though he was running out of options.

With one man on either side for support, Swain was lifted to his feet and half carried into the cave. The space was fairly large, about thirty feet long by twenty feet wide. It had a smooth floor and a relatively high roof that allowed the men to stand fully erect. The room narrowed considerably towards the back, where two openings led into a series of descending pathways. There was no way of knowing how far the caves stretched under the earth, but Smith guessed that they went quite a bit farther than their current location. He was encouraged to hear the sound of dripping nearby, which meant that they wouldn't have to travel too far to find drinkable water.

They spent the next three days camped in the cave, trying to regroup and plan their next moves. Swain was bandaged again and his leg re-splinted, which did little to quell the extreme pain of the fracture. His spirits plummeted as he thought of their predicament. Meanwhile, the Indians hunted and searched for the second horse, which had disappeared south, then east. Swain had hoped that it would eventually return to their camp, looking for food and water. Instead, it appeared that the horse was retracing its steps in a beeline for home. Regardless, the animal was nowhere to be seen.

The Indians also collected firewood, stacking it in piles along the interior walls of the room. They lit a fire just inside the front wall of the cave, and they kept a small blaze going the entire day. Even as they slept, the embers were covered to keep them ready for cooking their breakfasts the following morning. In fact, the entire arrangement could have been quite comfortable if not for the bats, which passed over their heads in great numbers at both sunup and sundown. The Indians considered them an omen from the demons, and they always left the cave at the earliest sign of the winged mammals' activity.

Meanwhile, Swain and Smith conversed on a great many topics, returning frequently to the irony of the situation in which they found themselves. Here they were, sitting on a vast fortune, and yet it was useless to them in their current predicament. It couldn't help to heal Swain's injury, nor could it purchase another pack horse to carry the gold out of the woods. About all that they could do was to move the treasure into the safety of the cave, and then hope for a miracle.

By the end of the third day of encampment, Swain had relinquished all hope of moving north with his companions. The pain from the broken bone was still excruciating, and the skin near the wound was red and swollen. He knew he needed to rest for at least a month, maybe more, in order for it to heal.

That night, over the fire, Swain voiced his thoughts to Smith.

"Alvin, tomorrow morning I want you to head north towards the rendezvous point. Whether we wait a day or wait a week, I still won't be ready. It would be better if you leave now."

Smith ignored the remark for almost a full minute before replying, "No, Thomas, my friend, we're not going to do that. We're not going to leave here without you. We came in this together, and we're finishing it together. Besides, you know Robert needs at least some of that money to purchase the land up north. If we don't get it to him, what happens then?"

"What purpose will be served if we stay here until I'm completely healed?" Swain replied. "No matter what happens, we couldn't carry those two saddles by ourselves. I can stay here with most of the gold, and you can meet the Gordons like you're supposed to."

"You wouldn't last a week here in your condition," Smith argued. "You can't walk and you can't hunt, so how are you going to take care of yourself? It took us six days to get this far, and there's nothing that guarantees we'll ever be able to find this spot again to get you out of here. Or maybe you think that General Burgoyne is going to ride through here and give you a lift?"

"I was thinking that if Anakausuen stays with me, he could provide all the food I need until I can walk again. It shouldn't be much more than a month. Then we can leave, taking enough gold to buy a couple more horses. We'd probably arrive at the Gordons' about two months after you. It's the only way I see us making this work."

Smith did not relish the idea of leaving his friend and companion in such a desolate location with only a single person to rely on. But given the circumstances, it seemed like the most logical course of action. Swain and the gold could make it to Canada as soon as he was ready to walk again. And in the meantime, the gold was most certainly safe in its current location, concealed in a cave some forty miles into the woods.

To keep the treasure even more hidden from view, Smith decided to move the saddles into one of the passages leading out of the front room of the cave. He half-carried and half-dragged them along the floor, placing them behind a cleft between two larger boulders. He then turned one of the saddles upside down and extracted a knife from its sheath, quickly cutting across the bottom of one compartment. Several pounds of lustrous gold coins spilled from within, making metallic clinking noises as they cascaded onto the floor of the cave. Smith opened a leather satchel and stuffed in as many as he could gather, filling the bag to the top before tying it tightly. This money would have to serve many purposes, including paying the Indians as well as serving as a down payment for the land. He hoped it would be enough. He pushed the open saddle back into place with the first and pulled a few smaller rocks over both, forming a small wall. He quickly inspected his work, satisfied that it would remain hidden from Anakausuen.

After Smith finished, he and Swain described their plan to Achak, who relayed the information to Anakausuen. He would remain with Swain until he could walk again, and then guide him out of the woods. The tall Iroquois brave calmly accepted the news, and let Achak know that he would carry out his task until he had helped Swain to safety.

Before turning in that night, Swain insisted that Smith take the journal he'd been making to record their daily course through the woods. It was relatively crude, with mileage estimates and rough sketches of the mountains and lakes they'd encountered along the way. He only hoped that it was accurate enough to allow them to recreate the same path at a later date, so that they might recover the rest of the gold. Otherwise, Robert Gordon's fortune would be lost to the ages.

The following morning, sensing a growing reluctance on the part of Smith to leave, Swain playfully picked up his rifle and, with a mock frown set on his face, threatened to shoot him if he didn't depart before noon. They traded one last embrace, said one final farewell, and then Smith and the three Indians departed. Anakausuen watched with Swain as Smith as they walked around the other side of the pond and disappeared into the woods beyond.

At that moment, Alvin Smith could not have foreseen how final their farewell would prove to be. Thomas Swain, his friend and mentor, would be dead within the week.

CHAPTER 5

Middle of August, 1775

The much-anticipated reunion between Robert Gordon and Alvin Smith did finally take place. The Gordons, along with the Rowes and Benjamin Warren, arrived at their final destination within eleven days of departing their homestead. They were forced to wait another two months before Smith arrived, accompanied by three of the Iroquois Indians. Without the guidance of an accurate map, the group spent unnecessary days and weeks pushing north into geographically impassable territory, including the area now known as the High Peaks of the Adirondacks. The obstacles delayed their schedule and forced them to detour even further west, resulting in a circuitous route to the Canadian river village.

Although happy to see his faithful employee, Gordon was saddened to hear about Swain's injury and upset that the cache of gold did not make it to Canada with the newly arrived group. It seemed ironic that he had been so wealthy such a short time ago, and yet now he possessed so little. His load of silver was sitting in the waters of Wood Creek, and the horde of gold was imprisoned in a remote Adirondack cave. The net result of five years of hard work and espionage activity was lost to the waters and earth of colonial New York.

All that Alvin Smith could provide to Gordon besides the precious bit of surviving gold was the map that Swain had so carefully prepared. The notations from the first week of the voyage were clear, neat, and detailed. However, once Smith assumed the duties as cartographer, the quality of the account rapidly degraded. On some days he forgot to make any notes at all, which forced him to later attempt to reconstruct two or three days at a time. Once the party moved north, into the higher elevations, their frequent detours rendered the map useless. He finally ceased making any notations about a month into the trip. This meant that if an attempt could be made to find the cave, it would have to be done by retracing their steps from the start of the trek rather than from the end.

Smith also committed some major mistakes when he took over as mapmaker, and those errors were made before he ever left Swain's side. While he quickly mentioned that they could "see the water from the cave," he never took the time to explain the importance of that statement. He also wrote a cryptic line that would further serve to confuse future searchers, which read: "Deposited bags with precious metals behind fake wall in back passageway." But nowhere did he record the fact that the passageway, or even Swain, was tucked away in the underground shelter. It was a critical omission that would cost the family dearly.

Gordon never had the opportunity to ask Swain about his notations on the map, because no meeting ever happened. Within two weeks of Smith's arrival, Anakausuen emerged from the woods along the banks of the Richelieu River. He was thinner than he had appeared during the previously, his face creased and distraught. As he approached the tavern by the fort, he seemed to have aged a number of years.

Because Anakausuen was not fluent in English, Gordon summoned Achak, who translated the somber story. Anakausuen had nursed Swain's injury for close to a week when the leg became badly infected. The only materials he had to fight the condition were herbal remedies, which did not stem the tide of the condition. Swain developed a high fever and lost consciousness two days later. He finally succumbed to the infection, passing away in his sleep as the Indian prayed nearby.

Gordon paid Anakausuen for his dedication with a few of the gold coins that Smith had carried from the cave stash. Anakausuen then joined his three tribal mates, settling a small land claim about five miles west of the town. Meanwhile, Gordon used the remainder of the small parcel of gold to purchase a farm near the village and buy an ownership share in the pub, where he had befriended the British owners. He became both respected and profitable in his new life, surrounded by other refugees from the Colonies who had fled the blossoming revolution. Alvin Smith, Philip and Elinour Rowe, and Benjamin Warren all settled in within a mile of the new Gordon homestead, and they remained lifelong friends.

Unfortunately, the political situation never favored Gordon's plans to return to his New York home and retrieve his fortune. Within the year, rebellious forces from America swept through the area and conquered the British forces. They also defeated the British garrison in Montreal, but they were pushed back from Quebec the following summer. Robert Gordon's plan to reclaim his bullion died before it was born.

Robert Gordon died prematurely. A hunting accident claimed his life while he was stalking game on his newly acquired land. His wife Rose didn't learn how he passed away until several years later, when a few of his personal belongings were returned to his home by some local Indians, who recognized that he was their owner.

Rose maintained possession of the map after her husband passed away, keeping it preserved in an ancient leather holder, its existence a closely guarded secret. Curiously, she considered the treasure to be something of a family curse, believing that the gold would bring ill fortune to anyone seeking to find it. It was a secret she almost brought to her grave. As a matter of fact, she only shared the story with one daughter, Alicia, to whom she transferred ownership of the map shortly before her death in 1810.

Alicia treated the aging document with similar deference, keeping it locked inside a chest with her other valuables. She eventually married a Canadian settler named Robert James Harrison, with whom she had three children. The family moved to Quebec, where Robert James was a partner in a law firm. She passed it down to her son when she died in 1853. The son, Robert James Harrison, was interested in the myth of the gold treasure, but he never attempted to find it. He was a busy merchant who was constantly traveling between his many businesses along the water-front of the Saint Lawrence Seaway; taking the time to depart on an extended treasure hunt was an idealistic luxury that he could not pursue.

Instead, Robert James Harrison passed the map down to his first son, William James Harrison, in the year 1900. William James, born in 1856, shared his father's enthusiasm for the tale. However, unlike his father, he was much less pragmatic and more inclined to dream. He had repeatedly turned down offers to take over the operations of several smaller business interests from his father, instead preferring to travel and see parts of the world. Yearning to see the faraway places he'd visited through his readings, he served as a seaman on a cargo freighter soon after leaving school. He was also a bit of a gambler and was thus naturally attracted to the fable of a mountain of gold that had been left for the ages in the middle of nowhere.

William's eyes practically gleamed as he extracted the yellowed sheet from the cracked leather casing one afternoon in 1900. His father knew very little about it, or about his great-grandfather who had accumulated the gold that became part of the family legend. It was a quiet, forgotten tale—that could make someone very, very rich. It instantly captivated William's imagination, and he knew that he was going to begin his search as soon as possible.

Within a year, Robert James passed away, leaving William with con-siderable wealth to pursue his life's desires. William spent some time organizing his family's affairs and selling the businesses, none of which interested him as a lifelong pursuit. Then he packed up his belongings and moved south, away from Quebec and back towards the region east of Lake Champlain, across the Vermont border.

The story of the silver in Wood Creek had eventually leaked out, and many treasure hunters over the years tried to locate its whereabouts. None were successful, although several parties reported finding the area where the chest should have been. But no one knew about the gold outside of the Gordon family. Alvin Smith swore to Rose that he would never divulge the location of the cache, and he remained true to his word. The only other person who knew of its final resting place had died within twenty feet of the fortune in that cold, isolated cave.

William James Harrison was more than an idle dreamer. He was smart and well educated, and had the benefit of modern mapmakers to aid his search. One of his very first moves was to compare the original notes made by Thomas Swain over one hundred years earlier to a modern U.S. Geographic Survey map that had been produced in 1898. By following the descriptions within Swain's notes, and transferring them from the old map to the new, he was able to recreate most of the route taken by the group back in 1775. There were no markers indicating the presence of a cave, but the map did depict the hills, directions, and estimated mileage. William worked it like a puzzle, meticulously plotting each day's routes, labeling them, and correlating them to the daily journal.

After two days of examination, he had narrowed his search down to a region of desolate woods in the southern portion of the open wilderness. It was inside an area that the State of New York had recently set aside as the Adirondack State Park. The specific location that drew his attention was a group of lakes northwest of the town of Newton's Corners (now known as Speculator.) He couldn't be certain, because so much depended on the descriptions and estimations recorded in Swain's journal. But based on what he'd seen so far, it looked like a good match, and he circled that area on the map in red.

It was a lot of territory. Perhaps two hundred square miles lay inside Harrison's plotted target. But somewhere in that circle lay a lot of gold, and the answer to a mystery that had persisted since the War of Independence. He only hoped that his detective work would put him in the ballpark.

It turned out he was pretty close.

PART II

ADIRONDACK
FRENCH LOUIE

CHAPTER 6

June 25, 1903

His real name was Louis Seymour, although everyone called him "French Louie." Born into a family in the Canadian north woods, he left home at an early age and drifted aimlessly through his adolescent years. He tried his hand at a variety of jobs, including farming, canal work, and even carnival vending. However, he had an affinity for the wilderness that would never die, and it was there that he made his final home.

As a young adult, Louie seemed to enjoy being by himself. He learned to depend on his own abilities to take care of himself rather than seek help from others. He was also a man who was full of built-in contradictions. Even though he was forced into manhood at a very early age, he could enjoy the childhood pleasures of a circus "merry gone-round" (as he called it) as easily as an eight year-old. He avoided people, and loved the quiet and solitude of the deepest woods, even as he was sought by throngs of sportsmen every year as an authoritative guide.

By the winter of 1868, Louie had become established as the sole resident of West Lake, otherwise called "West Canada Lake." This crystal clear body of water is located in the middle of Hamilton County, about fifteen miles north of Piseco. It was prime hunting and trapping territory, filled with virgin forests that had seen little or no intrusion from the white man. Louie built a cabin on the east end of the lake and then set about the task of clearing some land for a garden and outbuildings. He was strong, industrious, and as good a woodsman as ever set foot inside the Adirondacks.

Within a few short years, Louie had constructed camps on many of the nearby lakes and ponds, as well as smaller makeshift dwellings in which he could stay while tending to his extensive winter trap lines.

He had also acquired a number of boats and canoes, which he kept on the various lakes, using them as part of his own personal transportation and guide system. Always looking for ways to economize his movement, he could travel long distances with very little effort. He merely rowed across one lake and then hiked the short distance to the next body of water, where he had another boat hidden away in the brush.

If there was one thing that Louie was not, it was lazy. A tireless worker, he was renowned for the massive loads of furs he'd pull out of the woods on his wooden sled. It wasn't only the deer and bear skins that drew people's attention; the hundreds of otter, mink, fisher, and pine marten pelts were also in great demand. He was a one-man trapping empire, and his fame spread farther and wider, until he had reached legendary status. Articles appeared in New York City newspapers and in hunting magazines and gazetteers about the grizzled mountain man who lived off the land of the West Canada Lakes region.

Louie was also known for a less desirable tendency, which was his consumption of whiskey and other spirits. For as hard a worker as he was in the woods, he was every bit as hard a drinker when out in town. Louie only came out to Newton's Corners about once or twice a year, but when he did make an appearance, the entire town knew it. His famous animal calls and chants of "Louie da boy!" could be heard from the pubs and barrooms of the town for several weeks, until he consumed the profits of his trapping and returned to his woodland home. It was an odd way of life for the popular member of the community, but the people of the town loved him and adopted him as one of their own.

Louie was a man who did as he pleased, who would not conform to others' schedules. He could also not be bought. If he wanted to serve as your guide, he would do so based upon his feelings on that given day. He cared little for the silver that many would pay him for his services. Instead, he selected his clients based on how much he liked them, and how they treated him in the woods. Even though he had little or no formal schooling, he was a keen student of human behavior, and he could quickly summarize a man's character within a few minutes of silent observation.

On one particular afternoon, late in June, Louie was standing in back of the chicken coop he'd erected next to his log home on West Canada Lake. He was filling pails with feed to bring into the enclosure when he saw a stranger emerge from the woods. He was moderately tall, with wide shoulders and a thick head of wiry blond hair. He marched through the clearing with purpose in his stride; he was not there for the fishing or hunting, Louie guessed.

The man approached Louie with a smile and an extended handshake. "Excuse me, Sir, are you Louie, the guide?"

Louie slowly nodded his head, "Yes, ah be da guide. Dees be ma house," he said, nodding to his cabin. (Even though Louie lived in New York for most of his adult life, he maintained his heavy French Canadian accent right up until he died. Most of his sentences were a mixture of French and English, and it took some of his guests a while to understand his speech. This day was no exception.)

"Nice to meet you, Louie. My name is William...or better yet, Bill. Bill Harrison. It's very nice to meet you. I've come a long way to talk to you."

Louie simply nodded his acknowledgement, looking at the newcomer through squinted eyes.

"You see, Louie, I need a guide to help me find something in these woods. I have a friend back home, Dr. Ebenezer Gibbons, who said that you're the best there is. He said that if anyone can help me find what I'm looking for, it would be you."

Louie showed a trace of a smile and shook his head once. "Ol' Ben, he's ma fren. He catch most feesh as I do me."

Harrison looked at the old man with a mixture of respect and amusement. He had never seen anyone who looked so much the role of hermit. Louie was the very soul of the woods.

"So how would you like to guide for a group of us who will be coming back in a couple of weeks? We sure could use your knowledge of the terrain back here."

"Mebbe. Louie don't know if hees be here den. What you looking for? You wan feesh? You wan for bear?"

Harrison smiled. He wanted to answer Louie's question, but he didn't want to give too much away.

"No, Louie, we're not hunting or fishing for anything. Actually, we're looking for something that was left back here a long, long time ago. Some things belonging to my great-grandfather were left in a cave when he was a young man, and I'm interested in trying to find that cave. You think you could help us? We'll pay you double your normal rate to come along, and we'll give you even more if we find what we're looking for."

Louie didn't mind getting paid extra for his work. But he hated schedules, preferring to do as he pleased from day to day. And he had to like a person before he agreed to guide for him, and couldn't be bought if he didn't.

"W'en you come back you to start?" Louie asked, turning the matter over in his mind.

"Right after the Fourth of July, Louie. We'll be here about three days after then. There will be four or five of us."

Louie scratched his beard and looked down, contemplating the proposition.

"You double ma pay? How you know how much I make me?" Louie asked.

"I tell you what, Louie. We'll pay you fifteen dollars a day. And if we find what we're looking for, we'll double that."

Louie's eyes lit up, his teeth showing through a rare grin. His normal rate of pay for guiding was five dollars a day, which was considered top dollar for a professional guide in that era. Many of his contemporaries were not even able to command that fee, depending on the season of the year and the availability of game.

"Yo pay me fifteen dollar each day, ol' Louie guide you, I do me."

"Fine, Louie, fine! Where do you want to meet me and the boys? They're as excited as I am to get started."

"Yo come to da Corners, I come meet you dere," said Louie. "I meet you at da Perkin's store in da Corners on three days after Fourth of July."

"Louie, I don't know if we'll be able to find what we're looking for, but we'll have fun looking. I've got a map that I made and a bunch of old pages of writing and drawing. You want to take a look at it and see if anything looks familiar?"

Louie nodded his head and turned towards his cabin. "Ol' Louie look at da map. He see if he know where you go to find yo things."

Harrison followed Louie into the camp, where he sat down at a large plank table. He took the pack basket off his back and set it down on the floor. He then removed a smaller parcel and unfolded a large map. From a separate pocket of the same bag he removed a cardboard tube, which held a very old and yellowed sheath of papers. They were so aged that small bits of the fibrous material broke off the scroll as he rolled it out on the table.

"A friend of my great-grandfather's wrote down these directions over a hundred years ago," Harrison explained. " I've taken everything that I could read, and I've moved it onto this map. Now the first few pages of writing are easy, because that's where they traveled along early roads and walked west from Lake Champlain. I followed the directions to the south of Indian Lake, because there's nothing else in this area that looks anything like that. But that's when the directions get confusing, because they don't really match up to the water back here, and some of these lakes are awful hard to find."

Louie was amused by that last remark, because he not only knew about all the lakes, but he had fished and trapped in each of them, gaining a familiarity none could match.

"What all dem lines drawn on dat map?" Louie asked.

"Those are called topographic lines," Harrison explained. "They show where the hills are and whether you're walking uphill or downhill. You see, places where there are a lot of lines close together, that means there's a steep hill there. But if there are no lines at all, that means it's kinda flat."

"I got maps, I mek, but I have no de fancy stuff on dem."

Harrison spent the next hour or two poring over the maps with Louie. He explained that he thought they should look somewhere around the shore of either Whitney Lake, or perhaps around the small extension northwest of Cedar Lakes, which some people called Beaver Pond. In either case, he told Louie, he was looking for an area where a very small body of water lay about four miles away from another lake that had lots of finger-like bays.

"Oh, Louie, there is one other thing that I didn't tell you," Harrison said. "We're looking for a place where there might have been a house or a camp. Because the story says that they hid some stuff behind a fake wall in a passageway. So wherever it is, there used to be a building there.

This part puzzled Louie, because he was one of the very earliest settlers back in those parts. He had never found any remains of a camp or building that he couldn't connect to a logging operation or possibly an early mine. He also had never seen a cave in any of those locations, although he did have a "camp" in one location around Cedar Lakes in a small cave-like shelter in the rock formation. Rather than being a genuine cave, though, Louie's cave was more of an enlarged overhang, where the jumbled rock had formed an enclosure that provided walls and a roof. But it made no difference to him, because he was confident in his ability to find just about anything in the woods around the West Canada Lakes and Indian River. It was his home.

"Ol' Louie help yo find yo place, I do me. Yo just get yo frens to da Corners, an Ol' Louie be dere."

Harrison shook hands with Louie and threw his pack back up on his shoulders. "OK, Louie, we'll be there by noon on July 7, at Perkin's place at the Corners. So long!"

The truth of the matter was that even Bill Harrison himself didn't know what to expect from this trip. The water mentioned in Thomas Swain's original notes could have been anywhere within this dense region of woods. And while he had narrowed it down to a choice between three or four bodies of water, he couldn't be sure whether they could still find the place some hundred plus years after the fact. It was certainly going to be a challenge, assuming that the gold was still there in the first place.

True to his word, Louie was in Newton's Corners at the agreed-upon time. Actually, he had arrived the day before the Fourth of July and had been staying in the hotel above the tavern on the main road. For four days, he subsisted on a diet of whiskey and lake trout while enjoying the company of the locals. Even among the town's residents, he was a bit of a celebrity, and he could usually be found conversing with a small knot of fellow sportsmen. The festivities surrounding the Fourth of July had only heightened the level of celebration, adding to Louie's drinking binge.

When Harrison and his four buddies arrived on the seventh, they found Louie in his favorite position: standing at the corner of the bar in his moccasins, head tilted sideways in conversation, two shot glasses of whiskey on the bar. It was five o'clock in the afternoon, and Louie had been there since before noon.

Harrison stepped up to Louie, who barely recognized him from their previous meeting. He introduced his friends, who had traveled a day and a half to make the meeting. They were Jeremiah, Ezekiel, Sheldon, and Gerard. Sheldon and Gerard were brothers. They were both loud and boisterous, appearing to be on the edge of laughter at any given moment. Jeremiah, or "Jerry," as he preferred to be called, was the tallest member of the group, and he wore a serious expression on his face as he shook Louie's hand. Ezekiel, or "Zeke," was also quiet, although he had a nervous demeanor that Louie would have noticed had he been more sober at the moment.

For the most part, Louie ignored the group of newcomers, preferring to talk about the local trapping with his group of friends. Meanwhile, Harrison and his friends lost no time in catching up with the drinks. They bought several rounds of whiskey for themselves and refreshed Louie's glass from time to time for good measure.

By the end of the day, Louie retired to his room in the hotel while the five men of Harrison's group rented another two rooms of their own. They all slept well into the morning of the following day, then repeated the entire drinking escapade for another afternoon. Louie didn't mind, although he had been thinking about getting back into the woods before another day went by. But Bill Harrison and his sidekicks were already too drunk to go anywhere within an hour of hitting the bar that afternoon, so Louie went along with the party.

For those first two days, Louie got along well with Harrison, Jerry, and Zeke, although they didn't spend much time conversing. But Louie quickly decided that Sheldon and Gerard, the brothers, were not men that he would choose to guide under normal circumstances. Their demeanor toward Louie was degrading, and they seemed to want to put him "in his place." Louie had no time for people like that, even if he was offered fifteen dollars a day to be their guide.

By the end of the second day of drinking, Louie was beginning to wonder whether the men had forgotten their original reason for coming to the small town. Quietly, he walked over to Harrison in a corner of the bar room and tugged on his shoulder.

"Tomorrow, I leave, me, w'en I wake up. If yo wan to come wid me, yo be ready w'en da sun she come up."

"Sure, Louie, we'll be ready," promised Harrison, a bit surprised. "We'll all be ready. We were just waiting for you, and all. The boys have been packed for three days now, and they're itching to get into the woods. We'll be here for breakfast and go after that."

Louie nodded once, then turned and headed up the stairs to his room. Even though he had drunk enough whiskey to float one of his canoes, he still managed to walk quietly and steadily up the wooden planks to the second floor. Harrison watched from below, anticipating the adventure that would soon follow.

Although Louie had told them to be there at sunrise, he was not surprised when only two of his new employers made it to the front porch of the hotel on time. Jerry and Bill Harrison were the only ones in sight, as Louie made the final adjustments to his pack load.

"The rest of the boys will be down in a few minutes," Harrison said, noting the annoyed expression on Louie's face. Once Louie was ready to go somewhere, he was like a skittish horse, pacing back and forth on a tether.

Zeke made his appearance within another few minutes, although it was a full half hour before Sheldon and Gerard strolled through the doorway. They looked as though they were enjoying a leisurely morning at home as they lazily traded a few last items between their two pack baskets. All the while, Louie eyed the activity while muttering under his breath.

"Where'd you find this guy, Bill?" asked Gerard. "Heck, where we come from, any guide alive would work for four dollars a day."

Sheldon quickly climbed onboard with the complaints. "And since we're paying him so much, why are we carrying all the heavy stuff? I say we let him take the cooking pots as long as he's the mercenary."

With that, Sheldon reached out and pushed two more objects into Louie's pack. One was a cast iron frying pan that had seen years of use. The other was a large chunk of salted meat that would serve as their evening supper. Louie never minded carrying the weight, as his strength had been built up by years of rugged activity carrying supplies for large parties. But he didn't enjoy the attitude these men displayed toward him, and he resented the very sound of their voices.

As they walked briskly out of town and into the hills north of the Corners, Harrison tried to converse with Louie, asking him about the landmarks they passed along the way. Louie was already into his woods mode, and wasn't interested in talking. For the most part, he either ignored Harrison's questions, or grunted single-word replies. Meanwhile, in the background, Sheldon and Gerard were doing their best to keep up, while overcoming their hangovers and complaining about their guide.

"Fifteen dollars a day!" Sheldon exclaimed. "Heck, for that he should carry my pack too! I think I'll give it to him as soon as we get over that next hill."

"Me too," laughed Gerard. "I'd like to see him carry all our packs right on through to the camp. Heck, the old man could probably do it without missing a step. They make those old Frenchies pretty tough, you know, because they're used to doing the cheap kind of work. They actually like it."

Louie heard that, and quickened his pace as he ascended the side of Page Hill. He decided that this was going to be a long week, but that he'd leave them if they became too raucous. He was no longer young, and just didn't need to put up with this kind of nonsense. Especially in his woods.

According to the maps and descriptions, Louie thought that they should head in the direction of his Pillsbury Lake camp first. Pillsbury, a body of water with several bays and inlets, was about a mile long depending on where you measured it. It was also a convenient stop because Louie had a well built camp on the lake, and he often had visitors stay at this location. The only detail that bothered both Louie and Harrison was the cave. Louie had lived in this territory for thirty years, and had never come across a genuine cave. Had the passage of time buried the entrance, or camouflaged it behind a wall of vegetation?

By five o'clock that afternoon, Louie was leading the men down the final straightaway to the camp. It had been a difficult day, with the two brothers needling Harrison about the fees being paid to Louie. Also, the steep uphill paths and the swarms of biting insects had exacted a toll from the weary travelers, and tempers were running short.

After supper that night, Harrison and Zeke retrieved the map from its sheath and spread it out on a plank bench.

"So what do you think, Louie?" asked Zeke, eyeing the representations of lakes and streams around Pillsbury. "Is there any place around the back of this lake where there might be either a cave or the remnants of an old camp? The original notes say that they could see the water from the cave. That means it's got to be pretty close."

Louie's eyes closed halfway as his mind recalled the topography around the lake. He had trapped the entire region, and his knowledge was encyclopedic.

"Ah been spend long tam on d'other side of dees lake, and I nevair see de cave. But 'morrow, we look at place where it might be. Ol' Louie take you der, ah do me."

"Yes, Louie, but are there any places where there are large rocks or boulders along the side of the hills over there? Places where there might be an opening into this cave?"

"Dat rock all over de place," Louie answered, pointing across the water. "We spend long tam looking, but we find it if it be der. Ol' Louie find it."

The next day, they worked their way around the north shore of Pillsbury, watching carefully for outcroppings within the first hundred feet from the lake. Jeremiah thought he saw an opening at one point, but it turned out to be an entrance to a shallow hollow in a jumble of rocks which had formed a small space of about thirty square feet. It looked as though some animal had adopted it for winter habitation, as it was littered with small bones and debris.

They also kept their eyes open for any remains of a stone building or wall, anything that would fit the words about storing the bags "behind fake wall in back passageway." It didn't make sense to Louie, but he would be paid regardless, so it mattered little to him.

By four o'clock that afternoon, they had covered most of the ground around Pillsbury and were thinking about moving over to Whitney Lake. By trial and error, they devised a method to quickly cover ground by breaking up into three two-man teams and forming search lines. Harrison said that he didn't think Pillsbury was the right location because the original notes described a much smaller body of water to the north of the first lake, but he wanted to check it out anyway.

Within an hour of returning to camp, Zeke and Jerry had managed to land four nice trout, which Louie cooked over an open fire pit. Meanwhile, Sheldon and Gerard broke out another bottle of whiskey and began playing with the fire as they drank.

"You suppose this entire thing is real, or just a myth?" asked Gerard.

"Well, I think that there was something there, once upon a time," said Sheldon. "But who knows if it's still here, or if it's buried so deep that no one could find it even if they knew where to look."

"That's kind of depressing," said Gerard. "Here we come back all this way, paying good money to this Frenchie, and he's gonna make more out of this week than we are."

"Shoot, I think Bill here could have brought us back here without hiring Lucy, and we could have saved all that money and probably found the treasure just as easy," said Sheldon as he poked a few embers back into the flames.

"Lucy?" asked Gerard. "Who the heck is Lucy?"

"French Lucy! That's our guide," replied Sheldon, gulping down another measure of whiskey.

The two men burst into hysterical laughter, while Louie turned away from the grill and walked back into the camp, muttering to himself. Jeremiah was chuckling too, although Harrison just looked at the two brothers with a stone-faced expression.

"If yo wan feesh for supper, yo can cook yoself. Louie no cook for dees men."

"Oh, come on, Louie," Harrison pleaded. "These guys are only pulling your leg. They don't mean nothing by it. Come on out and be a good sport and finish the job. Those fish are looking pretty good right now. We can't do it the way you do."

"Yeah, come on Lucy," repeated Gerard. "Only Frenchies can make fish that good. For fifteen dollars a day, you better be able to cook a damn fish!"

Upon hearing that, Louie stomped back inside and disappeared from view. The rest of the party gathered around the fire, alternately turning the fish and throwing down the booze. Everyone but Zeke was drinking; even Harrison took a few swigs from the bottle.

They were passing out the tin plates in preparation for dinner when Louie reappeared outside the camp. A pack basket on his back, he held a high-caliber rifle in the crook of his arm, ready for use. His face was set in a determined scowl.

Sheldon looked up from his seat and involuntarily jumped backwards. Gerard flinched as well, thinking that they had pushed the old man too far. For a moment, everyone froze, looking at Louie in a strained silence. It was very uncomfortable, and each of the men was justifiably scared.

Louie would never come right out and shoot a man, but they didn't know that. After staring at the company for a good five seconds, Louie turned left and walked out of the clearing, heading south and away from camp. They decided to let him go, hoping he would calm down in a few hours. However, Louie never returned that night. He must have decided to sleep somewhere else nearby, because as the sun set, they could hear no trace of anyone else on the lake. Louie had had enough for the day.

The next morning, late, Louie returned to find Harrison by himself outside the camp.

"Louie, I'm sorry about last night," he said, not waiting for Louie to walk by. "The boys had no right to treat you the way they did. And to show you how sorry I am, I'm going to pay you for your first two days right now. So here's thirty dollars," he said as he handed over some folded bills. "Please take this now, and if you don't want to come with us any further, I'd understand."

Louie reached out and took the money, looking slightly disgusted at the whole process. "Louie don understand dees whole ting. Yo come in dees wood to look for tings, yo don know what they be. Yo wan me to guide yo, but yo frens don wan me here. By da holy feesh, Ol' Louie don understand."

Bill Harrison was a man of many skills, and he gently persuaded Louie to continue the search, even though he strongly disliked the two brothers who seemed to spend more time drinking than searching. He didn't particularly want to continue in this role, but he had given his word that he'd guide them, and Louie never went back on a promise. He'd also never been paid anything close to fifteen dollars a day, and he appreciated the three ten-dollar bills that Harrison had just put in his hand.

The next day, Louie took them to the north and west, past the outlet of Pillsbury Lake and on to Whitney Creek. They spent some time walking the perimeter of Whitney Lake, although Harrison was convinced that they were off track.

"Louie, the stream that they talked about in the original notes flowed northeast. Are we going northeast?"

Louie shook his head. "No, dees here go west. We go on to Mud Lake from here. T'aint no water run northeast from Pillsbury."

"Well, how about this place called Cedar Lake, the one I circled on my map?" Harrison asked. "We're looking for a lake that's got an outlet running northeast, and it's also got a small pond about three miles to the north. We find that and I think we're on track."

Louie stopped to ponder that one for a moment or two. "Ah tink that mean one or two place," Louie replied. "Could be da Pillsbury Bay, dat stick out from bottom of da Cedar Lake. Mebbe he mix up da bay for a pond. Or mebbe he find Lost Pond, on t'other side of Cedar Lake. We go dere after we look other places."

By the end of the next day, they had search Whitney Lake, as well as the area up and around Pillsbury Bay, which was a lengthy extension on the south side of Cedar Lakes. Nowhere did they find the combination of rock formations and hills that Swain had recorded in his journal some hundred and thirty years earlier. It was as though the earth had been rearranged in that time, and the cave was lost for posterity. And Bill still couldn't figure out where the "fake wall" fit into the picture.

On the fifth day of the trek, they had rounded the eastern shoreline of Cedar Lakes and were approaching the headwaters of the Cedar River. Along the way, Gerard and Sheldon had literally tumbled into a small cave-like enclosure near the bottom of Goodluck Mountain. However, like the formation on Pillsbury, it was not a real cave, and they quickly ruled it out as a hiding place. Harrison stopped to look the place over, while Louie couldn't even be bothered to stop. If the two brothers were even in the vicinity, he would avoid the place like the plague. There was a lot of bad blood there, and the brothers didn't trust Louie when he had a gun in his reach.

Soon after crossing the Cedar River, Louie pointed to a flat stretch of ground near the water and suggested that they spend the night there.

"Dees spot, I catch mos feesh here, I do me. Yo do same lak me."

"You're the guide," said Zeke, slinging his pack to the ground. "If you say there's fish in this lake, that's good enough for me." He quickly assembled his rod and surveyed the weed-covered waterline.

Meanwhile, Harrison was gazing out across the lake, transfixed with the view.

"You know, Louie, this looks more like what we were reading about in that old record. This is what I was trying to tell you about the first time we looked over that topographic map. This lake is longer, and it's got several bays and coves jutting out. And it's in the right spot; it matches the whole description."

"Dat cave I tell you 'bout, de one where I make de camp, dat be at t'other end of dees lake, but she be far way from here," Louie said.

"Where are Beaver Pond and Lost Pond from here?" Harrison asked.

"De Beaver Pon, she be jus' little further up dees lake. She not be far," Louie answered. "Lost Pon, she be up dere, 'bout three mile. We go dere t'morrow."

"One last thing, Louie," Harrison asked. "This cave you keep talking about. The one at the other end of the lake here. Is there any chance that the notes in the ledger could have meant that cave? The one where you stay? Like, maybe if he got turned around and only thought he had headed north from here, but really ended up further down the same lake?"

Louie thought for a moment, then shook his head. "No, dat not de place, unless he bury it under de ground. Ol' Louie use dat for camp for long time, I do me, and I nevair did see nothing. Dat not de place."

Louie and the others spent a quiet night by the shoreline, cooking their meals and trading their stories by the campfire. Louie had put up a temporary shelter for the men, who had treated Louie better since the confrontation at Pillsbury Lake. But Harrison sensed that there was trouble bubbling up, an undercurrent of tension between Sheldon and Gerard and the old-timer guide. They were okay as long as the whiskey remained corked. But once they got to drinking, their tongues loosened and their natural tendency toward vulgar behavior came through. It was an unsettling peace that was bound not to last.

The next day the group walked around the large Beaver Pond extension on the north side of Cedar Lakes, keeping their eyes peeled for promising-looking rock formations. They found very little, even using their spread-out search line. By noon, they departed and headed even farther north.

"De Lost Pon, she be jus ahead, two, three mile," Louie promised. "Dat one small, we look dere for res of day."

"I've got it circled right here, Louie," said Harrison, pointing to his own map. "This might be the one. I've had this one circled all along. You just get us there."

The trip up to Lost Pond was relatively easy. Louie had trapped there as well, and he needed no assistance to point the way. They followed the contour of the hills north of Beaver Pond, winding their way counter-clockwise around the hillside and through the trees that bordered the small body of water. It didn't take long, perhaps two hours, before they were looking down on the small, darkly-colored ripples of Lost Pond.

Harrison was a bit unprepared for the diminutive size of Lost Pond. It was so tiny that the mere thought of putting a boat on the water seemed pointless. They could have walked around the entire shoreline in less than an hour. It was surrounded by a large area of mushy, marshy shallows that would make getting to the water somewhat messy. However, there were a few places where the ground next to the pond was slightly elevated, thus offering a dry approach to the deeper water.

Once they set their packs down on dry ground, Louie went to work constructing a small lean-to shelter, selecting materials that would keep the elements off them during the night. Jeremiah and Zeke set off to do a cursory examination of the immediate area, paying special attention to the jutting rock formations around the pond. Meanwhile, Sheldon and Gerard removed the cork from a bottle of whiskey, taking large swigs from the bottle. They had remained dry for the past three days, and they were ready for some refreshment. Louie eyed them disdainfully as he went about his work.

Even Harrison, who had grown short of temper on this trip, seemed to be tiring of the two brothers' taunting behavior towards Louie. He turned to Sheldon and addressed him scornfully.

"Why don't you try putting your energy to good use for a change. Go out and see if there's any fish in this pond. It'd be the first useful thing you've done all day."

"The first useful thing I've done..." Sheldon's voice trailed off, taken aback by the remark. "You look here, buddy boy. I've worked like a damn maniac all week, sweating through mud, bugs, rain, lousy food, and damn Frenchie guides who don't know a thing but still charge us fifteen dollars a day. And now you get mad at us because we want to relax a little with a drink at the end of the day? Well, the hell with you! We'll take our share of the gold as soon as we find it, or I should say if we find it, and then we're gone. You can keep these stinkin' woods. I wish we'd never come back here in the first place."

The remark made Louie quickly take notice. No one had ever mentioned the word "gold" before. He only knew that he was helping Bill Harrison search for his ancestor's belongings. This put a new twist on things. Still, he didn't let on that he had heard anything out of the ordinary, and he continued his task of lining the floor of the lean-to with cut balsam boughs.

While Harrison pored over his notes, Gerard took his brother by the arm and led him away from the campsite. Rather than taking along their fishing lines, Sheldon instead reached for his Winchester. Gerard carried his weapon as well, along with the newly-opened bottle of liquor. They headed across the clearing and into the woods, presumably to find something to shoot for dinner. Harrison looked up for only a second, not acknowledging them as they stomped away from the pond.

It was quiet for a few moments before voices were heard from the hill overlooking the campsite.

"Hey, Lucy! Where am I?" called out Gerard. "I'm scared of these big old woods! Would the old Frenchie guide help me for fifteen dollars a day?" It was followed by hysterical laughter as the two men downed more of the whiskey.

"Yeah, Lucy," shouted Sheldon. "Maybe if we pay you twenty dollars a day, we could get you to take a bath for once in your life. Do all you Frenchies stink like that?"

Suddenly, a shot rang out from their direction, followed by several more in rapid succession. A great scuffle in the brush was followed by a lot of whoops and hollering. The two men were apparently celebrating something that none of the others could see.

Harrison dropped his notes and sprinted across the clearing. Zeke and Jeremiah also came running from the woods where they had been searching. Only Louie did not react, simply turning to look in the direction of the shots fired from the woods.

When the men came upon Gerard and Sheldon, they were bending over the inert forms of a doe and two fawns. They were both laughing, slapping each other in congratulations, and celebrating with additional swigs of the booze.

Gerard yelled at his sibling, "Hey, you old buzzard, you're slow with the trigger! You only got that little one after I shot the first two!"

"You shot the first two?" Sheldon shrieked. "It was my shots that got 'em. You didn't hit nothin'! You couldn't ever hit nothin'."

Meanwhile, Harrison surveyed the scene, scratching his head in amazement. He wondered what they could possibly do with three deer, even if two of them were very small.

If Harrison was amazed, Louie was furious. Apparently, Gerard and Sheldon had shot the deer solely for the joy of killing. The doe and her fawns had been stirred from their hiding by the loudmouthed brothers, and were running for cover when they were blasted by the pair of rifles. There was no reason for the killing, other than to kill for sport. They had no way to preserve the meat of three carcasses, so most of it would go to waste. It made Louie's blood boil. He, who had killed hundreds of deer for subsistence, would never consider harming an animal for useless entertainment.

The slaughter of the deer had one other very negative effect. Zeke and Jeremiah were about two hundred yards shy of discovering the cave opening when the shots were fired. They dropped everything and deserted the search, not thinking to note their location as they ran. Had they remained dedicated to the task, they might have seen the opening in the rocks, still accessible, although shrouded in an even thicker cover of shrubs. When they resumed their search later that afternoon, they picked up in a different stratum of the rock, missing the cave entirely.

Harrison spent about an hour searching the ground north of the shoreline, focusing on some promising looking ridges with large boulders strewn about the ground. Time was running out, he knew, and this was perhaps his best shot at finding the cave.

Later, over the cooking fire, Louie turned the skewered venison meat slowly over the flames while the rest of the men sat on improvised seats fashioned out of large rocks. Harrison asked Zeke and Jeremiah for details of their search around the south side of the pond. Meanwhile, Sheldon and Gerard were polishing off the rest of the whiskey. It appeared as though they considered their role in the search for the gold to be over.

"Hey Lucy," said Sheldon, "how come you're the guide, but we're the ones getting us the meat? Ain't that part of your fifteen dollars a day?"

Louie ignored the remark, although he was seething inside. Today would be the last day of the search. He would tell Harrison the next morning that he was through. He wanted no part of these obnoxious, ungrateful upstarts who had come into his woods. He could live without the guiding fee. Heck, he wasn't even the one who had proposed that amount in the first place.

"And ain't a good guide always supposed to keep a sharp knife, Lucy?"

Gerard taunted. "This knife couldn't cut butter if it was heated in the fire!"

"I know! Let's try that out, by heck! Gimme that thing!" shouted Sheldon.

Louie turned around and glanced at Sheldon just in time to see him snatch his hunting knife out of Gerard's grasp. Then he took aim at the top log in the fire and let it fly. The knife fluttered over the fire and struck the rock on the back of the newly constructed fireplace, then ricocheted into the air, falling into the outer edges of the coals.

Louie was on it in a flash, kicking the blade out of the fire and away from the stones. Without stopping to blink, he then kicked the pile of burning wood toward Gerard, who fell backwards in his attempt to avoid the flaming debris. Sheldon made a quick move at Louie, who grabbed him by the arm and flung him on top of his brother, who both scrabbled to get away from the red embers.

Louie might have burned himself in the brawl, as he was just about to reach back and grab for his knife. But Harrison and Zeke both jumped up and grasped his arms, pulling him back from the brothers. Louie seldom cursed in the woods, but this was an exception. His profanities expressed the rage he felt towards these men, especially the two brothers who had made his life miserable for the past week.

"Louie, Louie, calm down, please," Harrison pleaded. "It's not worth it. Let me handle them. You just calm down and let me take care of it. I'll make sure they don't bother you any more."

"No. No more," Louie said through clenched teeth. "Tomorrow, we go out. You pay me for ma time, and you go home. Ol' Louie done with dees. I don't want no more of dees, by cripe."

Even Zeke, who had been the calmest and most objective member of the party, had to agree with Louie.

"Bill, I've got to admit, I've about had it myself. I don't know whether this gold was ever back here in the first place. But if it was, I don't think we've got a prayer of finding it after 130 years. It's either too well hidden, or someone's already walked off with it. I'm sorry."

Jeremiah, standing in the background, nodded his concurrence.

"OK, fellas, we'll go out tomorrow. I had hoped to search for one more day, but I'm out of ideas too. We've looked everyplace that I can find on the maps, and we can't find a trace of this cave. It's got to be back here somewhere. Maybe we're not even close. I don't know..." Harrison's voice trailed off into silence.

Louie gathered up his pack basket and his other belongings and walked briskly away from the lean-to. He wanted nothing to do with the rest of the expedition. Tomorrow he would walk them out of the woods. In the meantime, they could fend for themselves. He wouldn't even charge them for the day.

Without bothering to look back, Louie walked up the hill on the north side of the pond, the same one that Harrison had searched before supper. He cut a fresh supply of balsam branches and laid them on the ground, spreading his blanket out on top for bedding. Within fifteen minutes, he had erected a second primitive lean-to, just large enough to put a roof over his head, but not large enough to cover his pack. Still angry, he lay down on the ground and looked back over the pond, listening to the sounds of the men as they drank their whiskey and ate the venison. This being their last night in the woods, they all joined in draining the bottles, exclaiming loudly over the events of the week. To Louie, they represented everything that he disliked in "city folk." He was glad that he had chosen a life of solitary existence in such a beautiful environment.

For the next two hours, Louie watched and listened, fascinated by the change in hues of the western sky. While the other men paid no attention, Louie stared in wonder at the beauty of it all. The effect was hypnotic, and his nerves calmed as he gazed skyward.

Louie was on the verge of falling asleep when he saw something that made him catch his breath. It was an amazing sight that he had never before witnessed. From the hill on the other side of the pond came a black cloud. It was a solid stream of small black bats. Hundreds of thousands of them were flying up and into the air, following one another out of some unseen chamber. It was as though they had been kept inside a locked cage until the sun went down, and were now released simultaneously into the approaching night sky. The procession lasted at least ten minutes, with Louie marveling all the while at the sheer numbers of the nocturnal critters.

Because the other men of the party were gathered around the blazing bonfire, they neither saw nor heard the flock of bats. They were too engaged in their drink and merriment. Only Louie swatched, taking careful note of the exact cleft in the rock from which the bats emerged.

Smiling, the old timer shook his head and silently laughed to himself. "By da holy feesh," he said quietly. Then he rolled over and fell asleep.

The following morning, Louie packed up his things and walked back to the camp. Only Zeke and Harrison were awake. Jeremiah and the two brothers were still cocooned inside their bedrolls, loudly snoring off the previous night's alcohol.

"Yo tell yo frens dat we be leaving before de sun she go up high. Da walk to da Corners take whole day. Yo frens stay here if dey wan, but Ol' Louie go soon. Comprende?"

"Sure, Louie, we'll be ready soon. I'll get the guys up and fed, and we'll be ready to hit the trail in an hour," Harrison said.

Louie couldn't have known it, but Harrison wanted out as much as the rest of his expedition. He was wet, tired, and his feet were covered with blisters. Over the course of the week, he had been bitten by so many blackflies that he was bleeding from behind his ears. On top of everything, he felt as though he had accomplished nothing. For years he had read the family lore and studied the records. He had plotted the most likely locations of both treasures: the gold in the wilderness and the silver that had been dumped into the river. He had decided to go after the gold first because it represented over ninety percent of the legendary family treasure. But over the course of the week, he decided that maybe it would be an easier task trying to locate the silver that his great-grandfather had deposited into the waters south of Lake Champlain.

True to his word, Harrison had the rest of the crew up and packed within an hour, although Sheldon and Gerard were as disdainful as ever toward Louie. Now that their time together was coming to a close, they felt no need to cloak their hostility towards the old woodsman. Instead, they maintained a continuous diatribe of criticism and ridicule aimed his way as they wound their way back to civilization.

Louie ignored the verbal abuse over the course of the next several hours, increasing his stride to widen the distance between himself and the brothers. With relative ease, he paced himself to stay at least fifty yards ahead of his tormentors, who all the while hollered for "Lucy" to slow down.

At Louie's accelerated pace, it didn't take many hours for the group to return to Cedar Lakes and regain the main trail back to Blue Ridge. Then it was over Page Hill and down into the town of Newton's Corners. Louie had never been happier to see the clearings of the village, signifying that his duty guiding this group was over.

However, another unpleasant turn of events awaited Louie when they arrived at the Perkins' place in town, and Louie asked Harrison for the rest of his payment. Louie had spent seven days with the men and had already been paid for two of them. That meant that he was owed a balance of five days pay, or seventy-five dollars. However, some of the men were more willing to pay than others, and a heated dispute arose between them.

"He ain't led us to a single thing we were lookin' for," shouted Gerard, scowling at Louie. "And you want to pay him fifteen dollars a day? For what? I say he's been nothin' but a pain in the backside since we left here. I wouldn't pay him ten cents more than you've given him already."

"Dees b'tween Bill an me," Louie replied, looking at Gerard. "You no ask me to work. Bill ask Louie to work for heem, Bill pay me, he do me."

Harrison stood on the other side of Gerard, his hands out appealing for help. "Come on, boys, I don't have enough to pay him myself. That was part of the deal; you pay your way, and you get a share of the gold if we found it. A deal's a deal."

"That's your deal with the Frenchie, not mine," reiterated Gerard. "So if you think Lucy here was worth the price, then you pay him."Sheldon stood in the background, nodding in agreement. It was obvious that these two were not going to hold up their end of the bargain.

Harrison, Zeke, and Jeremiah all broke out their billfolds and collectively assembled fifty dollars, which was considerably less than what Louie had been promised. However, it was all that they could come up with between the three of them.

Harrison looked at Louie apprehensively. "I know this is a little short, but I can send you more once I get back home," he said. "There isn't much more that I can do right now."

Zeke and Jeremiah both seemed apologetic as well, as they felt bad about going back on the agreement with Louie.

"Tell you what," said Zeke. "I'm through with this forever. My treasure-hunting days are over. I never really wanted to spend so much time away from home in the first place, but it sounded like fun. Would it help you out at all if I left you my pack? It's gotta be worth a few dollars, anyway?"

The suggestion triggered a similar response from Jeremiah and Harrison.

"Good idea. Louie, you can have mine too. I'm never going to use it again," Jeremiah added. "You can keep the woods and the goddamn biting flies. I'm through with this stuff."

"Me too, Louie," said Harrison. "I rather enjoyed being in the woods, but I'm never using this thing again. You should be able to get something for it. I'll still send you some more money, though. I'm sorry, Louie."

Louie was angry, because he knew he wouldn't get much for the packs. They were small and of poor quality.

"Yo send Louie de money as soon as yo get home yo," Louie said. "Yo send Louie 'nother twenty five dollair. Louie be wait for dat."

Harrison agreed, and the two of them shook hands. As the five men of the search party turned and walked away, Louie bid them a silent "good riddance." He gathered the three pack baskets and tied them together with a length of twine. If nothing else, he should be able to get five or six dollars for the three of them.

All of the packs had some amount of trash and other materials left over from the journey, so Louie went through each, saving the bits of cloth and supplies that he might be able to use for some other purpose. When he got to Harrison's pack, he removed a pair of very wet and filthy socks, only to uncover a stiff leather binder underneath. Inside the binder were several documents, including the original notes from Thomas Swain, as well as the geographic map developed by Harrison. Louie looked for Harrison to return the binder, but he had already disappeared around the bend, presumably to catch the stagecoach home.

Louie unfolded the map and looked at the areas circled by Harrison. He had never learned how to read, but he did understand maps and the significance of Harrison's notations. For a full minute, he sat on his heels, his eyes set in an expression of deep concentration. In his mind, he was rolling back his thoughts to the previous day, as he sat on top of the hillside overlooking Lost Pond. He recalled the flood of bats that had poured up from the ground, practically urging him to explore the place again. This time he would go by himself, without having to endure the continuous taunts of the ignorant brothers. He didn't feel bad about this at all. After all, had they not mistreated him, he would have shown them his discovery and probably led them to their objective. But after enduring their abuse, he felt no remorse at all in not sharing his knowledge. Their loss was his gain.

Louie gathered up his things and strode off towards the Perkins' store. A trace of a smile crossed his face as he shook his head.

"By da holy feesh, I tink I go to Lost Pon soon. By da holy feesh!"

CHAPTER 7

August 15, 1903

It was two months later before Louie even contemplated making a return trip to the little pond north of Cedar Lakes. It wasn't that the distance was great, because Louie could cover that amount of ground in a matter of hours. But it was well out of the way, and Louie was a busy man. He often had a camp full of people to look after at his main retreat on West Canada Lake, in addition to his other interests and pursuits. It was a busy life for someone who had no official occupation or mailing address.

When Louie returned to the West Canada Lakes after his week with the treasure seekers, he found his garden overgrown with weeds and his camp in need of some work. He was lucky because his guests always paid for the use of his place whether he was in residence or not. Almost everyone who stayed with Louie had been there before, and they all knew how to look after themselves. They carried their own food into the woods with them, or they caught what they needed. They were, for the most part, professional people who needed little in the way of assistance from Louie. They were there to relax and enjoy the woods, as well as each other's company.

Louie spent several days in the garden, digging out the weeds and making repairs to his chicken coop. He grew a nice variety of vegetables, which he used in his meals or stored away for winter consumption. He was an efficient man, wasting very little of what he raised.

Once he had conquered the work around the grounds, he traveled to some of his other camps on Pillsbury Lake, on Whitney, and down the still waters of West Canada Creek. Louie had boats on almost all of these bodies of water, which he rented out for a fee to the various sportsmen. Some of them required work from time to time in order to keep them afloat and in good condition. It was an ongoing task that required his attention throughout the year.

By the time July rolled around, Louie was hard at work gathering building material for a new fireplace. He intended to build an addition onto his camp, with a great room that would provide more space for many more sportsmen. The centerpiece of this room would be a massive stone fireplace, around which the men could gather at night and swap tales of their experiences in the woods. Louie knew just what he wanted. He had developed a mental picture of the fireplace situated at the end of the room, dominating the interior space with its functionality and warmth.

Louie was able to find most of the rocks for his fireplace within a quarter mile of his camp. Since his place was virtually surrounded by lakes and streams, there was no shortage of gracefully-shaped, rounded stones that he could fit into the developing masterpiece. However, the long, rectangular rock he wanted for his mantelpiece came from across the lake. He had spied it while fishing for lake trout and decided to float it across the water in his large rowboat to use as the centerpiece in his creation. It turned out to be a perfect fit, as though it was formed for that very purpose.

Louie finished the fireplace within a few weeks, and then spent some additional time cutting and peeling timber that he would use in the construction. Most of this work he accomplished on his own. Others volunteered to help him, but Louie was an expert in using levers and other mechanical devices to lift the heavy objects on his own. He was a master of all trades in the woods, and he never called for help unless it was absolutely necessary.

After spending a few days guiding some newcomers around the upper part of West Canada Creek and Mud Lake, Louie decided to return to Lost Pond. He was not driven by the idea of monetary reward. In fact, Louie would not have known how much the gold was worth, nor did he care. His only interest in its value might have been in the number of drinks it could purchase for him and his friends down at the bars in Newton's Corners and Utica. But he had no interest in becoming rich. He had everything he could possibly want right back in his camps. Instead, this trip was motivated by his curiosity. He had done some trapping around Lost Pond and down Otter Brook. He wanted to know where those bats were coming from. And if there was a cave, why hadn't he seen it before?

As was his habit, Louie arose shortly before dawn and ate a solitary breakfast. Sitting on his bunk in the kitchen, he fried some potatoes in bear grease on the small wood-burning stove, and then he ate them with his fingers. Sipping his tea, he recalled the ledge where he had spotted the exodus of bats as they went airborne and wondered whether anyone else had ever observed that same event at the lonesome pond. It was not visited often, and even Louie could not claim the pond as part of his regular territory.

He left camp very early, before anyone else was awake. The red squirrels and tree swallows made a commotion as he trod past, his feet plodding down in his bearlike gait. Unlike many other travelers of the woods, Louie's eyes were always roving back and forth as he walked, missing almost none of the wildlife that hid in the undergrowth. He was as keen an observer as any man, and the years had done little to diminish his skills with the rifle. He could knock down a running fox at a hundred yards with a single shot. Old Louie was that good.

Louie passed by Cat Lake and Kings Pond in rapid succession before reaching the end of the third Cedar Lake. There he detoured slightly north, stopping at his camp on Cobble Hill to pick up some fishing line he had left there earlier in the year. He continued northeast, eventually passing around the back of Beaver Pond en route to the passage to Lost Pond.

It was mid-afternoon when Louie emerged into the clearing that encircled the small muddy pond. Looking around, he was surprised to see his small shelter from earlier in the summer still standing. With a grunt, he put his foot against the side of the structure and kicked it over. He wanted no reminders of that week with Harrison and the others. (He had received no notification from the post office saying that Harrison had ever sent the rest of his pay for the week.)

Louie worked his way around the outer edge of the clearing, slowly approaching the place where he had seen the bats. It didn't take him long to spot the darkened entrance to the cave. It was up the hill, about 150 feet up from the pond, and partially hidden behind some bushes and saplings, just as he had suspected.

The entrance had a natural walkway of almost evenly-spaced steps, which descended into the large outer chamber. Louie stepped cautiously over a boulder and down onto the gravel-lined floor below. Although partially lit by the slanted rays of the afternoon sun, it was still fairly dark inside the room, and he had to stop until his eyes became acclimated to the darkness. As he stood there adjusting to the conditions, more details began to appear. He noted a littering of small bones, as though a fox or other small predator had dragged game into the cave to consume.

Next he moved around the inside walls, noting the worn feel of the rock and the small tentacles of limestone that hung from the overhead ceiling. "Dat look like de icicle, but t'aint made of ice," he said to no one in particular.

After sitting down for a while to examine the place further, Louie noticed a long pile of rocks that sat in the middle of the chamber, piled in a regular pattern across the floor. "It look lak some one be here before Ol' Louie," he said, moving closer to the stacked rock.

Louie's curiosity was further aroused when he saw something protruding from one end of the pile. He began removing the rocks one at a time, stacking them against the wall behind him. It wasn't long before he uncovered a long bone that looked like it came from a human leg. Louie sat up and scratched his beard. He hadn't expected this, and he wasn't sure just what he wanted to do. Finally, his natural inquisitive nature took over, and he went back to moving the debris.

As Louie worked, more and more of the skeleton appeared before his eyes. Louie noticed several things about this body. First, even though some of the original clothing remained, he could tell that the person had died a very long time ago. The bones were devoid of flesh, although there was still some dried skin and hair left on the skull. Louie could tell that it had been a male, probably taller than average. He could also see that one of the skeleton's lower legs was badly smashed, although he wasn't sure whether that had happened before the man's death or after. Perhaps it had cracked when he was being interred beneath the rocks at a later date.

Another thing that interested Louie was the presence of the artifacts buried with the skeleton. There was a battered metal cup, which was of a very primitive design, sitting next to the right hand of the skeleton. Alongside was the broken barrel and part of the stock of an old muzzle-loader rifle. Louie had never seen anything like it, and he pulled it out for closer examination.

There were also a few shards of thick glass and two brass buttons which looked as though they had once belonged on the front of an old waistcoat or other outer garment. Louie looked at these closely before putting them back with the bones. After looking over the remains one last time, he replaced the stones until the skeleton was again concealed from view. While doing so, he worked with the utmost care to avoid damaging any more of the bones, which he could see had become brittle with age. Louie already felt his very presence in the crypt-like setting was irreverent, and he wanted to disturb as little as possible. He did, however, take the metal cup and the remnants of the muzzleloader and push them into his packbasket.

Louie next started exploring the deeper reaches of the outer room. So far, there didn't appear to be much to see in this underground formation. He wondered if maybe the bones belonged to Harrison's ancestor, and whether someone else had entered the cave and made off with anything that might have been of real value.

It really made very little difference to Louie, because he wasn't driven by the need to chase a treasure. As far as he was concerned, he had already succeeded in finding a new camp—a wonderful and permanent shelter that he could use year-round as he tended to his trap lines. Even in the coldest months of the year, he could dig down through the snow and burrow into this secure cave. With the aid of a small fire, he could skin his catch and stay dry until he decided to return home.

Louie finished his tour of the outer room and moved back into the narrower entrance to the tunnels. Here, the sunlight penetrated even less, and he found himself moving at a very slow pace. He followed one tunnel until it bent around a corner, finally giving way to complete darkness. To his left, he saw a glimmer of light, which he followed to investigate its source. The path joined a tunnel that went both to the left and to the right. The right fork would have taken him farther into the cave, whereas the left branch doubled back and rejoined the outer room. This was where the light originated, and Louie turned in that direction, using the dim rays of residual sunlight to navigate his way back to the main chamber.

As Louie's eyes became accustomed to the almost-dark conditions, he could see the outline of the rock surfaces that surrounded him. Shortly before he reemerged into the outer chamber, he had to duck his head in order to avoid bumping it on a low-hanging knob of overhead rock. As he hunched over, he noticed a glint of something metallic that happened to reflect light back from the cave floor. He kneeled down, eyes squinting, to sift through the soil and capture whatever it was that he had seen. He felt more than saw an object that was rectangular in shape, and had moving parts that swiveled around a shaft of some sort. He quickly decided that he was holding a buckle in his hands.

As Louie gazed at the object, he became aware of something else of interest. To his right was an accumulation of regularly-sized rocks that had been loosely stacked into a wall along the side of the passageway. Behind the wall was another pile of rocks that looked as though they had been intentionally arranged by some unknown hands. They were all too regular in size and shape to have been deposited by nature. Louie guessed that they had been used to bury another body, perhaps the bones of a friend of the man he'd uncovered in the front room. However, he quickly ruled out this possibility, as he discovered that the pile was simply a small mound of rock, perhaps three or four feet long and about as wide. In any case, it was not long enough to sufficiently cover any adult person.

Once again, curiosity got the better of Louie, and he began to pull rocks off the pile, setting them along the other wall of the tunnel. Within a few minutes, his hand felt a substance that was softer then rock, yet brittle and quite crumbly. He couldn't determine the identity of the object, but it had the feel of something that was old and decomposing, perhaps cloth or leather. If only he had a source of light, he could have illuminated the area and easily extracted the mass from the pile of rocks. Instead, he had to keep working, hauling the boulders away until the disintegrating bulk could be pulled into the center of the passageway. Even then, the mass was extremely heavy, and Louie had a difficult time managing anything but to drag it across the floor of the tunnel.

He was about to haul his find into the front chamber for a better look when he decided to have another feel to see if anything was left amongst the rubble. To his surprise, there was another large hump of material that felt much like the first, partially concealed under more rock. Another ten minutes of work was all it took for Louie to free this object and pull it alongside the first one. By this time he was breathing heavily, having moved several hundred pounds of large rocks plus the heft of the weighty objects, whatever they were. Louie rested on his hands and knees, look-ing down at the ground as his mouth hung open. He was no longer a youngster, and this kind of exertion affected him much more than he cared to admit.

After catching his breath, Louie shifted his position and moved in front of his first discovery. He grabbed hold with both hands and dragged it behind him, pulling it towards the daylight in the front of the cave. He felt particles coming off in his hands as the ancient artifact broke apart. But he maintained his grip, and within thirty feet he had enough light to fully see his discovery.

"By da holy feesh!" Louie said. "It look lak a saddle! What a man do with da saddle in da middle of dees here wood?"

Louie also couldn't fathom why a saddle would weigh as much as it did, even if it was waterlogged from years of sitting in the damp climate of the cave. Once again, he sat down to catch his breath, selecting a flat-topped boulder next to the wall of the chamber. As he sat down, something else caught his eye. He thought that it might be another buckle, which probably fell off the saddle. However, when he bent over to pick it up, he found himself holding onto something that was much more interesting. When he brushed away the dirt, he was staring at a large round coin.

At first, Louie thought he was holding a silver dollar. He had quite a few of those back at his camp, as some of his sportsmen visitors paid him for his services in the heavy silver currency. He levered himself to his feet and stepped out into the sunlight to have a better look. What he saw both excited and puzzled him. Louie had never seen a gold coin as large as the one he now held in the palm of his hand. At least, he thought it was gold. Nothing else really looked like this, and it was very heavy.

As he examined it closely, he noticed that the inscriptions on the piece did not appear to be in English. Even though Louie could not read, he could recognize English and French writing, and this looked like neither. It had symbols and a profile of a royal person who looked like a Spanish conquistador. Louie just shook his head and dropped the coin into his pocket, then turned and headed back into the cave.

Louie was as interested as anyone would be in seeing whether there were any more coins on the floor of the chamber. He looked around the area where he had found the first one, using his foot to move the dirt from place to place. However, his search was unrewarded, so he decided to move the saddle outside where he could look it over in the light of day. Due to its weight, he had to continue dragging it across the floor until he reached the natural steps leading upward.

Closing his eyes with exertion, Louie heaved upward on the rotting leather. The mass of the gold, which had been sewn into the weakened padding of the saddle, was too much for the material to hold. The seams that were so carefully stitched in place by Elinour Rowe 130 years earlier gave way in a sudden and complete split. Louie heard a muffled tear, which was followed by a massive cascade of coins and larger ingots of gold, which poured out of the saddle and onto the rocks of the cave floor.

Louie looked down, amazed and stunned, unable to make a sound. His heartbeat quickened as he took in the vastness of the treasure that lay at his feet. No wonder Harrison had spent so much time and effort trying to find it. It was obviously enough money to make one person very rich, although Louie did not pretend to know the value of the precious metal. For now, all he knew was that he would claim it for himself and move it to a more secure place.

Louie spent the next hour cleaning up the coins and bullion that had flooded the cave entrance. He moved most of it outside, using his pack basket along with some leather sacks as storage. It would be more than he could carry in one load, so he planned his trips as he worked. Perhaps he could take half the gold back to West Canada Lake tomorrow and then return later that week for the rest. But then what about that other saddle in the back of the cave? Was it stuffed with even more of the treasure? If not, why would someone hide the two of them together the way that they did?

Louie decided to find out right then and there. He retraced his steps into the back tunnel, finding his way until he once again grasped the other saddle. At least this time he knew what he was touching as he lugged the tack across the floor. But this time, the seams of the padding gave out even before he reached the rock pile in the middle of the floor. Louie listened as yet another river of gold coins spilled out onto the rock.

"Ba da holy feesh," said Louie, grinning from ear to ear. "Dat more dollair den Louie ever see, I did me," he exclaimed.

As it happened, it took Louie four trips to carry the gold from the site at Lost Pond to his lair on West Canada Lake. Had it been winter, he could have carried it in a single trip, loading it onto his wooden sled and dragging it over the frozen ground. But this was different. Not only did he have to carry the entire load on his back, but he had to make certain that not a single coin or piece of bullion fell out. Louie was afraid that if anyone found such a valuable coin around his camp, they would look for more, and possibly steal it all while he was away.

By the time Louie made it back to West Canada Lake with the last load of gold, it was early September. Already the leaves on the maple trees were turning a rich red, and a thin layer of frost coated the grass each morning. The change in seasons meant that his camp would soon be full with more sportsmen coming in to hunt deer and other game.

Louie was nervous about the gold, which he had hidden in buckets in the attic rafters of his camp. Worse yet, he was annoyed at himself for feeling nervous. Louie had never allowed money to control his life, which was the reason he'd hated having Harrison's group attempt to dictate his behavior for the exorbitant fee of fifteen dollars a day. Money was secondary to Louie, merely a way to pay for his semi-annual trips of fun and frolic in town. So why was he so bothered by the gold in his camp?

Louie thought that the attic was a fairly safe place to hide the treasure. But then again, that was the same place he stored his valuable collection of hand-drawn maps, which he had so painstakingly created from a quarter century in the woods. He knew that a few of the sportsmen would occasionally seek out the metal boxes in order to check out a fishing hole or the location of a nearby lake or trail. So instead, he decided to think of another place to conceal the gold, which would have to be moved within the next week to ensure that it was done in secrecy.

But where? Where could he hide the loot that no one would look? Louie thought of many possibilities, including the island in the middle of the lake in front of his camp. He also thought of burying it inside one of his outbuildings. But none of these were guaranteed to do the trick. After all, many people fished off the island or dived off the rocks that formed a ring around it. His outbuildings were often used by the same men who stayed in the main camp, so that was out. Louie tugged at his beard as he looked out the front of his cabin, gazing at the mountains across the lake. Then something caught his eye, and suddenly he smiled. The answer had been right in front of him all along.

Louie was indeed a richer man than he ever imagined, because he never needed to use any of the vast treasure that he had found. Content to live by his own rules, to hunt and fish and trap when he so desired, he more than paid his own way. The massive loads of furs that he sledded out each winter paid for his whiskey and all of his supplies, and he remained a respected and beloved citizen of Newton's Corners.

Within a few years, Louie would be getting too old to live by himself in the cold, hard climate of the Adirondack wilderness, although he would never admit that to himself. As it happened, he remained in his camp until the day before his death, on February 28, 1915. He preserved his self-sufficiency as a legacy that would live on in the hearts and minds of anyone who ever spoke the name "Adirondack French Louie." He also preserved the secrecy of the gold, until its existence no longer mattered to him.

Even then, he only told a single person of the tale that had its origin in the early days of the American Revolution. On a cold, snowy day, as he lay shivering in his bed, he murmured a description of the treasure to the only other person in the cabin. However, because of Louie's delusional state of mind, that person either didn't believe the story, or lacked the desire to chase the dream. It would take a miracle, plus the passage of another hundred years, for that dream to be realized.

PART III

MIRACLE AND A DREAM

CHAPTER 8

June 22, 2012

There was nothing smart about the ancient green Jeep that rolled up the switchbacked hill toward the Carey house. It was close to fifteen years old, and it showed every bit of its age in the flecks of rust that spotted most of the dull, forest-green exterior. The engine still sounded robust as it climbed the grade, but the transmission slipped from time to time, and the shocks were in serious need of replacement.

The owner of the vehicle seemed to notice none of this as he made his way up the final straightaway toward the driveway. A pair of stone gate mounts stood on either side of the drive entrance, although the gate was never closed. Without touching the brake, the driver spun the wheel to the left and "split the uprights" between the two posts without batting an eye. He kept the gas pedal depressed until the final thirty feet of driveway, when he punched the brake and sent the old four-wheeler into a sideway skid. His feet were touching the ground by the time the vehicle had fully come to rest.

Christopher Carey, Jr., was never a cautious driver, a fact that reflected his general outlook on life. Tall and athletic, with a dark complexion and a bushy head of curly, black hair, he seemed to run through most of his early life at a pace others considered to be maniacal. "Stuck in overdrive" was the description used by a college roommate, which was a fairly accurate description. Only twenty-four-years-old, he had experienced more in his life than many people twice his age.

In fact, the entire Carey family was full of Type A overachievers, and Chris was no exception. An honors graduate in accounting from Syracuse University, he was also captain of the lacrosse team and the bass guitarist of a college band. And while he always considered management and accounting to be his future profession, he also excelled in the rest of his academic subjects, managing a well-balanced curricula throughout his undergraduate years.

After graduation, Chris had completed a two-year master's degree in Business Administration, with a tilt towards accounting. This was not the course of study recommended by his father, Christopher Carey, Sr., who was an extremely influential Washington beltway attorney. Chris Senior had originally tried to steer his son into the legal profession with the idea that he would eventually take over his father's firm in D.C.; however, his son showed no interest in pursuing the same career path, and the friction between the two over this subject caused a rift in their relationship for a period of time. Thankfully, Chris's mother, Theresa, intervened on her son's behalf and halted the confrontation before it grew into a major schism.

Regardless of the dispute, the family remained close, although young Chris grew to become much more attached to his mother. This was primarily due to his father's business, which kept him in D.C. almost continuously, a captive of his own success. In fact, there were months when Chris and Theresa barely saw him. His law firm was a thriving entity that required constant oversight, and he was at the helm of this organization, along with his two partners, overseeing the work of over sixty of Washington's finest lawyers.

As a result of the firm's success, the family was able to afford both their huge home on a hilltop outside of Utica as well as Carey's luxurious brownstone house in the affluent community of Georgetown. Theresa had tried moving into the Washington home full time, but she soon realized that she was not cut out for the continuous hustle and bustle of life in the capital. Within a month of transplanting her life into the non-stop action of the beltway, she was pleading to return to their country estate, where she could feel at peace with the greenery surrounding her.

Theresa was standing on the front porch of the gracious mansion, watering the hanging pots of bright red geraniums, as her son's Jeep screeched to a stop in the driveway. She had expected him to stop by, so she continued her task without turning to say hello.

Chris bounded up the flight of six stairs in two great leaps, landing within a few feet of his mother. Putting an arm around her shoulder, he kissed her cheek before flinging himself into a white Adirondack rocking chair.

"So, how's Oneida County's finest horticulturist doing today?" he asked with a grin.

"Good morning, Dear," replied his mother as she continued to tend to the plants. "Does that mean you're asking me for a favor, or has your natural cynicism just gone on summer break?"

Chris threw back his head and gave a boyish laugh. He was used to his mother's sharp wit, and enjoyed her commentary, even when he was on the receiving end.

"Actually, I'm not even sure if I'm on summer break. I feel like I should be, but this job search business is more work than I anticipated. It's like finding a job is a full-time job."

"Welcome to the real world," Theresa replied. "It's like I told you before; the schooling was the easy part. Once you get that sheepskin and move into the nine-to-five routine, THAT'S when your eyes are opened. Relax son, you haven't even arrived yet."

"Great, Mom. Thanks for the dose of reality. It's nice to know that I've graduated from the frying pan and am ready to jump into the fire."

Despite the fake cries of despair from her son, his mother paid little attention. She knew that Chris's academic excellence and his résumé of extracurricular activities would guarantee a lucrative offer from either a Fortune 100 corporation or one of the Big Four accounting firms. His college transcripts and impressive recommendations would open doors in any major city. It would only be a matter of time before he was interviewed for the job of his choice. Chris seemed to sense this as well, and he was relishing his last summer of pre-career freedom.

"Oh, by the way, Sean called for you last night," Theresa said. "He wanted to know if you're doing anything next weekend."

Sean was Chris's best friend from his high school days. They had remained in touch through college and had chummed around together over summer breaks and winter vacations, sharing a love for music and the outdoors.

"Thanks, Mom. Did he say what he wanted?"

"Oh, something about getting off the beaten track and trying his hand at something new."

"Like what?" Chris asked. He knew that Sean was always trying new things, some of them more adventurous than others. He was always looking for Chris's company, especially in his crazier schemes. "He doesn't want me to go hang gliding with him again, does he? I'm just not ready for that."

"You're damned right!. Your father was ready to fly home and wring Sean's neck after that incident last summer. No, I think it was something much more docile. As a matter of fact, it had something to do with camping and prospecting."

"Prospecting!" Chris exclaimed. "As in spend a month in a cold stream being bitten to pieces to collect a gram of dust? No thanks! I think I'd rather spend a week studying estate tax law."

Theresa giggled as she put down the watering can. "Oh, you know Sean. He's a wonderful kid, but he falls in love with every newfangled idea that he reads about in the weekend section of the *Times*. Sometimes I don't know why he ever went into computers for a living. Somehow, he just doesn't fit the mold of your usual info tech junkie. He needs to be out exploring somewhere, carving out trails in the bush, knocking down hippos and boa constrictors with a machete."

Chris laughed, nodding his head in agreement, as his mom opened the screen door to the front foyer of the house.

"Anyway, Mr. prospective-accounting-firm president, come on inside and I'll pour you a glass of my homemade lemonade. I just made it this morning. It's enough to put three puckers on your face with a single gulp."

Chris followed his mother through the front entrance and into a two-story foyer with several doorways leading in different directions. To the left was a large sitting room with fine rustic furniture and oriental rugs. This room had another doorway, which opened into a large library containing thousands of volumes of legal and other varied texts. One entire wall was dedicated to the many pursuits that Chris had followed over the years, accumulating his own references that were now archived here.

The room to the right of the main entrance was a small sitting area for entertaining guests, which adjoined a formal dining room that measured a full thirty feet in length. The entire house, which had been built during the early days of the last century, was finished in dark wood tones, with intricate hand-carved doorways and railings throughout. Chris Senior and Theresa had pumped a lot of money into refurbishing the place when they moved in shortly after they were married, and they never regretted the expense and effort required for the restoration. He in particular was a staunch enthusiast of the "great camps" of the Adirondacks, and he wanted to emulate that general design as much as possible.

Theresa walked straight through to the kitchen, which was at the back of the house. Chris followed in her footsteps, sitting down on a tall stool next to the raised counter where he had often gulped his breakfast when he lived at home. As his mother opened the refrigerator door to retrieve the pitcher of lemonade, Chris looked around the kitchen at all the homey touches she'd added. Over the years, Theresa had made this room the center of the family's life. Even though Chris was a full-grown man entering the prime of his life, she still kept his childhood drawings hanging on the refrigerator door. She was too involved with him, too much the loving mother to ever bear removing them from her daily life.

Theresa dropped a few ice cubes into a pair of tall glasses and filled both to the top with the sweetly sour lemonade.

"So, are you thinking you might head out there with Sean for a couple of days?" she asked, taking a long swallow from her drink.

"Well, yeah, I guess that would be nice, depending on where he wants to go and for how long," Chris replied. "I don't have any interviews until the end of next week, and even then it's only for that firm in Albany. I'm not really interested in them, but I could use it for a practice run while I'm getting set for the important interviews next month."

"Just make sure that Sean doesn't do anything that will get the two of you thrown in jail," joked Theresa. "Your father would have a fit if he had to fly up here and make bail for you."

"Well, at least it would be nice to see him come up for something," Chris said sarcastically. "Maybe that's what it would take to get him to visit for more than a day. He could smuggle us some wire cutters baked into a cake and help the two of us bust out of jail!"

"Oh, come on, Chris," Theresa pleaded. "You know your father would like to be up here with us a lot more than he can. But he's a very important man, and his firm can't be as successful as it is without him being there full time. He loves you just the same. You know that, don't you?"

"Sure, Mom," said Chris, tipping back the last bit of the drink. "I don't begrudge him working the long hard hours and making a name for himself. It's great that we can afford the two houses and his boat on the Potomac. And I really appreciate having my degrees paid for without needing a loan. But don't you think it would have been nice if he had made it up to either of my graduation ceremonies?"

"Yes, dear, I do. But your college commencement fell on the same day as the merger with the Brockman firm, and your MBA ceremony was in the middle of that class action suit against the Texas chemical company. He couldn't have predicted that either of those dates would interfere with your special accomplishments, honey. He told you that, and he told me that as well. He was disconsolate about both, but he just couldn't get free for either. I'm sorry about that, and so is he."

Chris gave a non-committal shrug of his shoulders as he raised his tall frame off the kitchen stool. "I know, Mom, believe me. He's a busy man, and he always has been. I still love him as my father. I just wish he'd been around a bit more, that's all."

As he spoke, he ducked his head to inspect the tall cookie jar that sat on the end of the counter. "Are those your famous walnut chocolate chip cookies I see in there, or do my eyes deceive me?" he asked.

"Yes, of course. As soon as you told me you were stopping by today, I baked a batch."

"So," Chris said as he fished a pair of cookies from the jar, "did Sean say why he suddenly wanted to go prospecting—for gold, I assume—or anything else, for that matter?"

"No, but since when has Sean ever had to have a reason for anything? He just does as his impulses direct. And if I know him well enough, he'll find whatever he's looking for. He's always managed to court Lady Luck fairly successfully. He's the only person I've ever known personally to win anything in the lottery."

"Yeah, now that you mention that, he does seem to have the magic touch," Chris said, recalling the time his companion won over five thousand dollars on a single state lottery ticket. "And last time we went to the casino over in Niagara, he hit the slot machines for five hundred dollars twice in the same night. But finding gold, especially if we're working by hand, is an entirely different proposition."

"Oh, I know, it's a pretty small chance," his mother answered. "But maybe he's looking more for a relaxing few days in the woods than anything."

"You know, there have been a lot of rumors about different veins of gold and other commercially valuable minerals in the Adirondacks," Chris said. "They've mined garnets at various places within the North Country, and there was a large deposit of lead that was supposedly discovered by an Indian a few hundred years ago. But no one seems to know what happened to any of those mines."

"And you know about the early iron works that were established further north, back when Henderson had his operation going up in Essex County, right?"

"Sure, everyone knows the story of Calamity Pond and the monument they put up where he was accidentally shot," Chris said. "But I'm not interested in that, Mom. I'm only interested in the good stuff: gold! If I'm going into the woods for a few days of panning with Sean, that's what I'll be looking for. You know, there are some people who believe that there actually is a hidden jackpot of gold somewhere in these mountains. And with the price of an ounce of gold going up over a thousand dollars, it wouldn't take much to make us very rich men."

"Oh, listen to you," Theresa laughed. "Ten minutes ago you didn't want to call Sean back. Now, you sound as though you're ready to start crushing your first ten tons of ore! I think Sean has more of an influence over you than you know."

"No, I wouldn't be doing this under any false illusions," Chris replied. "The chances of finding anything much beyond a large flock of mosquitoes and blackflies is pretty remote."

"Unless, of course, you enlist the help of your grandfather," his mother said. "Maybe he can steer you in the direction of the legendary Adirondack treasure."

"The what?" Chris asked, his face registering his surprise.

"There's a legend about lost Adirondack treasure. It's a tall tale that was passed along from generation to generation, although no one really knows where it started. The treasure was supposedly carried into the hills at the time of the Revolutionary War and buried somewhere for safekeeping. Some time after that, information about the location of treasure was lost, and it was never recovered."

"That sounds just like a thousand other fairy tales about lost piles of gold and silver," said Chris. "As long as there have been men looking to make a quick buck, treasure seekers have chased fables around the seas and over mountains to the end of the earth. But no one ever finds anything because none of these lost fortunes really exist."

"Well, you know, this story does have a family tie," Theresa said with a smile. "Rumor has it that an Adirondack hermit stumbled across the loot long after it was hidden. No one knows what he might have done with it, but your great-grandfather, Calvin Carey, knew the guy personally. He was a recluse who lived north of here, in a place in the middle of the woods, somewhere north of Piseco, in Hamilton County. Calvin used to stay at his cabin sometimes while he hunted deer up that way."

"What was the hermit's name?" asked Chris.

"His name was Louis Seymour. There's a book about him in your father's library."

"Louis Seymour? That's Adirondack French Louie! Yes, I know all about him, and I read the book. I've even been to the place where his cabin used to sit, up on the shore of West Canada Lake. It's right on the Northville-Lake Placid Trail that I hiked back in high school!"

"Well, if you read the book, then you should know the story," said Theresa. "Except that I'd imagine every dreamer with a local history book and a metal detector has probably gone through the area by now."

Chris, sat for a few moments, lost in his thoughts. "That's a long way to carry a metal detector, Mom. And you know, I don't remember anything in that book about Louie finding a treasure—or even looking for a treasure. As a matter of fact, this is the first time I've heard about it. I think it's another tall tale of the woods. But like you said, it's an interesting proposition."

"I don't know, Chris. I have a hard time believing in treasure stories myself, but Calvin spent his whole life wondering about that stash, which was supposedly quite a pile of gold. Your grandfather, Denny Carey, mentioned it on several occasions, saying that his dad had some clues that it really existed. But no one in the family ever took it seriously enough to search for themselves. Either they were too busy or they didn't have enough faith in the fable."

"Huh, funny that he's never mentioned anything to me," said Chris. "And I've talked with him a lot over the years. If he really had anything concrete, I'd think he would have said something."

"Well," said his mother, putting the lemonade pitcher back into the refrigerator, "Denny's always been a pretty busy man, even in retirement. He might have thought you wouldn't be interested. And then again, maybe he just forgot. You know, his memory hasn't been the best lately, and he's not getting around too well these days. It's probably been forty years since he told me that story about French Louie, so Lord only knows what he remembers of it today."

Chris nodded, already thinking about a possible camping excursion with his friend Sean. "Well, I'm stopping by to see Gramps sometime later this week. Maybe I'll ask him about it. But in the meantime, did Sean say when he wanted to head into the woods? I can spare a few days after the weekend, but I want to get some letters out before my interview next week."

"No, he didn't say when. He just asked you to stop by or give him a call when you had the chance. He said he'll be around most of the day today."

Chris leaned over and kissed his mom on the cheek. "Well, I guess I'd better hit the road if I'm going to catch Sean before he takes off for Albany. He's got a contract there with some insurance company's IT department, and I think they're doing some kind of upgrade thing this week. He's been down there every night this week. I'll call you in a couple of days, OK?"

"Sure, dear. I'm usually home."

"Oh, by the way, would you mind if I borrowed Dad's copy of that book on French Louie? I wouldn't mind having a look through it one more time."

"Sure, help yourself," Theresa said. "Your father's New York books are against the back wall, over the top of his desk. But just don't go getting yourself lost in the woods, OK? And make sure you keep Sean out of trouble too. He's the only kid in your entire high school class who was more forgetful than you!"

As Chris backed out of the driveway and turned right onto the hilly lane, he reflected on his mother's observations about Sean. The truth was that Sean was a very bright individual who had taught himself about the inner workings of computer networks and information security. Naturally gifted, he effortlessly cruised through college with a 4.0 grade point average while starting up his own IT contracting business. He maintained that business even after graduating summa cum laude, choosing to turn down several lucrative job offers from major corporations. The confines of a cubicle and a nine-to-five job never interested him. He needed the freedom to pick up and leave whenever he so desired, and to operate by his own rules.

The friendship between Chris and Sean had originated back on the playgrounds of elementary school. They had been together on the same Little League team and had shared many of the same classes in the Utica school system. They had even double dated for a short while, until Sean moved west to attend college while Chris got an apartment near the university in Syracuse. Even after that they had remained in constant touch with one another, and continued to enjoy sharing their free time as they pursued a variety of outdoor adventures. Chris still lived in his small Syracuse apartment, while Sean now rented a small cottage on the edge of a golf course in Little Falls.

Chris's thoughts wandered as his Jeep rolled along the curves of Route 55. He could have made better time on the Thruway, but he never was one for following the straightest path between two points. On the highway, as in life, Chris had always favored the more unconventional routes, which resulted in his unique outlook on events. His ability to think outside the box had distinguished him throughout his educational years, attracting the attention of many of his professors.

It was still early afternoon when the Jeep turned off the gravel road into the dirt-packed driveway of the small white cottage. Since he had already called ahead, he didn't bother ringing the doorbell of the house. Instead, his long strides took him down the path leading to the back of the building, where a row of twenty-foot evergreen trees shielded the edge of the golf course on the eleventh hole. The house was so close to the fairway that it was occasionally struck by errant tee shots.

Through the limbs of the trees, Chris could see the white shirt and tan shorts of his friend as he lined up a shot to the green. Sean stood a full head shorter than Chris, with a slight build and closely-cropped, sandy-colored hair. His concentration was total as he addressed the ball, pitching wedge in hand. Chris chose not to announce his presence as he approached stealthily from the rear.

"FORE," he called out, just as Sean's club came down and through the ball.

Sean never flinched as he followed through, the club head coming up in perfect form as the white ball flew straight at the pin. After a bounce and a lengthy roll, it came to rest a mere twenty-four inches from the hole. A collection of three other balls, all within six feet of the cup, testified to the fact that he was accurate with the chip shot.

"Nice shot! You do that often?" questioned Chris jokingly. He was well aware of his friend's prowess on the golf course, as well as his eight handicap. Sean had golfed since he was in grade school and fared well in the local tournament scene. He further refined his skills by popping outside and lining up shot iron shots when no one was looking. He had befriended Maggie, the course steward, who looked the other way whenever she drove by in her golf cart. She knew Sean had the common sense and courtesy not to interfere with the club members, who seldom saw him on the course.

"Thanks. And you can forget trying to surprise me with the "fore" bit. I heard your jalopy coming up the driveway. I would have heard that thing from a mile away. You'd never make it as a private investigator."

"Remind me to have the engine tuned," Chris said, smiling at his friend. "So Mom told me you said the magic word—camping—and my ears perked right up. You want to go in and spend the weekend up in the woods? And what's this about prospecting? I didn't think you were interested in such mundane activities."

"Well, first of all, I can't go this weekend," said Sean. "I've got a big software upgrade to do for a new customer in the city on Saturday, and I've also got a couple of meetings on Monday that I need to prepare for, so I'm working the entire weekend. But I was thinking the week after next, maybe we could poke around some formations that look promising in the central Adirondacks."

"Promising formations?" Chris asked. "What do you mean by that? Gold? Iron? Gem stones? What's the prize here, and what made you decide to spend a week of your life chasing it?"

Sean laughed as he walked across the green and gathered up his golf balls. "No, there's no pot of gold at the end of the rainbow, at least not all in one place. But I have been reading about small deposits of gold being located in various stream beds during periods of high water, and I just got curious. I thought I'd call on your encyclopedic knowledge of geology to steer me in the right direction."

"My WHAT?" Chris replied, much astonishment in his voice. "I haven't studied geology since Mr. Gilbert's ninth grade Earth Science class, so I hardly qualify as an expert in the field."

"Well, you got an A, didn't you?" Sean said. "Then again, you aced just about everything in high school. But you cheated: you actually read the text book in those days!"

"Nah, that was just an ugly rumor. I've always flown by the seat of my pants in school. I never could see the point in studying. It just keeps you away from the fun stuff in college, like the girls and the beer."

Sean laughed, recalling his friend's reputation as a devotee of the "work-hard, play-hard" school. He knew that Chris worked hard for every grade he achieved and was fiercely competitive when it came to his class standing. It was part of his nature, and Sean had always admired that in his friend.

"Anyway, there are a few records from the 1800s that mention some early explorers found small amounts of gold in remote locations throughout the territory now enclosed inside the Adirondack Blue Line" Sean said. "Two of the references talk about caves, which supposedly contained gold, silver, and lead deposits. I thought that you, with your demonic love of the underground, would enjoy chasing them down with me."

"Ah, now the truth comes out," said Chris as he followed Sean through the screen door leading into the cabin. "So the only reason you wanted me for this excursion was for my troglodyte tendencies, huh?"

The friends laughed as they collapsed onto some old wicker chairs on the screened porch. Sean knew that Chris was an avid spelunker, although his busy schedule had for the most part preempted his caving activities over the past several years. Still, he had managed to make exploratory trips through a number of cave systems across Pennsylvania and Virginia in the past two years, and he was always looking for a new underground challenge.

"Well, you gotta admit, your eyes do light up a bit whenever someone brings up the subject," Sean said. "And as long as there might be some profit to be had if we find the mother lode, that makes it all the better."

"And you know where these hidden caves are located from your readings of early Adirondack literature?" asked Chris, warming up to the subject.

"No, not exactly."

"How close could you put us?" asked Chris, pushing his companion for details. "Could you at least find the right US Geological Survey quadrant map, or is this a complete wild goose chase?"

"No, of course it's not a goose chase," replied Sean, displaying fake indignity. "I know for a fact that it's inside the blue line in the southern part of the Adirondacks. I read it in the *National Enquirer*."

Both men burst into another round of laughter at that remark.

"Oh, I see, so you've got it narrowed down to a mere three million acres of heavily wooded territory. It shouldn't take us more than a couple of centuries to locate. We'd better get started right away!"

Sean stood up, followed by Chris, and led the way into the small dining room. Chris always marveled at his friend's choice of décor, as the walls of the cramped living space were almost completely covered with mounted animal heads of various different sizes and shapes. Many of the specimens boasted trophy-sized antlers, while others were less impressive specimens. What made the display even more improbable was the fact that

Sean was not a hunter. He had never hunted and had no interest in learning. He inherited the collection from a deceased uncle who spent much of his later years traveling around the world on hunting safaris. In addition to the genuine examples of game, Sean had added his own whimsical bits to the collection. These included a singing fish which was mounted on a walnut plaque and a fake elephant head that shot peanuts out of a rifle-barreled trunk. It never ceased to amuse Sean to take target practice with the peanut gun, aiming at a wastebasket on the other side of the room.

"Here, let me show you something," said Sean, motioning Chris to have a seat in front of a widescreen computer monitor. "I've been in touch with a geology professor down at Cornell who said he has some leads on where caves might be in the Adirondacks."

As he spoke, he opened a document showing a map of the southern Adirondacks with several areas shaded in red and blue. He used the cursor to point out the most promising locations.

"He's quite honest about it; he says he can't guarantee anything. But he also says that he's been able to track some of the possible routes used by the Indians mentioned in the local folklore and match those up with some of the known geologic formations in the region. It raises some interesting possibilities, assuming that someone is willing and able to take the time to find them. It's pretty remote territory, and there aren't any trails in these places. You feel up to it?"

Chris inhaled and let out a long sigh. "Well, I agree, it's an interesting proposal. To tell you the truth, I'd consider going down there and talking to this professor just to find out more about these caves. I have a hard time taking the whole gold thing too seriously. I told my mom the same thing this morning. But finding a new cave that no one's ever been in before, or at least in a couple of centuries, now that's a different matter. I can picture it now: 'Chris' Caverns!' Tours given daily, admission price thirty dollars!"

Sean rolled his eyes in mock dismay. "You mean, 'Sean's Cavern and Sports Bar'—no cover charge except on weekends! No, seriously, he thinks that he's got a pretty good idea where this thing might be, at least down to a few strong possibilities. And even if we don't find the place, we'll still have a blast looking. I'll even teach you how to pan out the debris and silt to see if you've got anything. But I won't have time to make it down to Ithaca to talk to this fellow before we leave. You feel up to it? His name is Dr. Earl Meyers. He sounds like a real nice guy, and he's pretty well respected in his field. Heck, you'll have a blast talking to him, because he's another speleologist. The rest of the faculty can't keep him away from his spelunking. If he goes missing from campus for too long, they send the Saint Bernards into the nearest caves to find him."

Chris closed his eyes for a moment and thought back over his schedule for the coming week. His interviews were still over a week off, although he had some preparations to do before he walked in for his first meetings. Also, he had some work to do on his Jeep that he had been putting off for some time.

"I could probably squeeze in a little time early next week. It only takes me about an hour to get down there from home. I'll try to give him a call tomorrow morning and set something up. Where do you know this professor from, anyway?"

Sean answered as he opened more files on his computer desktop, still trying to locate the document he wanted. "I met him on a canoe trip a couple of years ago up on the Fulton Chain in the park. That's the one where you couldn't go because you were taking that barmaid friend of yours to the spring ball up in the Syracuse," he said, referring to a college formal dance. "We spent the night in a lean-to up on Eighth Lake, and he turned me on to a few hiking trails I never knew existed. But he was really into the caving thing, and he had all kinds of theories about lost cave systems in New York State. You'll enjoy talking to him. But one word of warning: you might not be able to shut him up," Sean chuckled, recalling his own conversation with the professor. "The guy does love to talk."

Sean's search was finally rewarded, and he reviewed a two-page document before sending it to the printer. "This is a list of questions that I wanted to ask Dr. Meyers about the possible cave locations. Any chance I could ask you to bring these along and have him take a look? I'd like to have as much detail as possible before we head in there."

"Ah, I see you trust me about as much as usual, my worrywart friend."

"Trust has very little to do with it. The professor mentioned some specific characteristics of the land back there where he thought he might find something. I've taken it a step further and gathered some satellite imagery, which I pieced together into a patchwork map of the area. I just want to ask him about some features I've seen that appear to differ from his observations."

"OK, OK, sorry I voiced my concerns," said Chris as he rose to leave. "But you're right; I know very little about the geological aspects of cave formation or the historical background of forgotten caves in New York State. I'll bring along your list, and then I'll call you next week to compare notes. In the meantime, I'll block off a few days for the week after next, and maybe we'll go in and start with the Siamese Ponds area. Perhaps we could even find time to drown a worm or two."

"I'll renew my fishing license," promised Sean, yawning as he stretched out his compact frame.

As he walked towards the door, Chris noticed a shallow, dull metal pan on a side table. He lifted it to the light for a brief inspection.

"Unless I miss my guess, this is what you call a gold pan, correct?"

Sean nodded. "Yup—that's a genuine fourteen inch panning dish. I bought it from a guy who used it up in Alaska last summer. He showed me how to work it, but I haven't had the chance to try it out locally."

Chris tipped the dish sideways, then tried swirling it in the typical circular motion, just to get the feel of it.

"This thing could give you a real workout, manhandling pans of silt all day long, couldn't it?" he asked, looking at Sean inquisitively.

"I don't know. I guess so," Sean replied absently. "If we don't find anything at all within the first couple hours, I don't intend to pursue it much further. I'd really like to spend a good part of our time looking for signs of that cave, if it exists. Actually, the legend says that the cave will lead us to the gold, so we might not need to prospect after all. That's why I'm so interested in what you can learn from Dr. Meyers."

"Sean, I hope you realize that we're probably not going to find a thing. If the Adirondacks contained any commercially valuable supply of precious metals, there would be all sorts of people back there right now, doing just what we're planning. I mean, exactly what do you expect to find?"

Sean thought a moment, a grin coming over his face. "You mean, if we get really lucky and hit it big?"

"Yeah—something like that," Chris answered, expecting just about anything from his friend.

"Oh, maybe a fraction of a gram. No more."

"And at a sixteen hundred dollars an ounce, how much would that fetch us in exchange?" asked Chris.

"About enough to buy us each a corn dog and a drink at Shifties," laughed Sean, referring to a popular old hangout they had frequented in their college days.

"Will there be enough left over to throw in an order of fries and a malted shake?"

"Sure," said Sean. "If not, I'll make up the difference."

"You're on." exclaimed Chris as he let himself out the porch door. "I'll call you when I get back from Cornell. You'd better have that corn dog waiting!"

CHAPTER 9

June 27, 2012

Chris' mind was pleasantly blank as he stepped out of his lofted A-frame apartment on Friday morning and settled himself behind the wheel of his Jeep. At six feet two, his wiry body didn't have much extra room in the driver's seat. However, years of running sprints on the lacrosse field had yielded him a very limber body, and he coiled effortlessly into the small seating compartment.

The Jeep rolled through the Syracuse rush hour traffic before merging onto Interstate Route 81 South, which took him through the Onondaga Indian Nation Territory.

As he drove, his thoughts meandered over the events of the past couple days. He had used Google to search online references to both New York State gold strikes and legends of caves, although none of it led to anything of interest. There were a few stories about a pair of prospectors from Colorado who found some promising samples of ore before getting lost and succumbing to the elements. But nothing pointed to a mine that the Indians, or anyone else, had claimed, or even located, inside the Adirondack Park. Chris was ready to conclude that the tales of the rich vein were just that: so many fairytales.

The new spring foliage made for spectacular scenery as he exited the interstate at Cortland and turned onto Route 11. From there, he followed country roads through Tompkins County before finally merging onto Route 36, which became Dryden Road in Ithaca. This street took him directly to the Cornell University campus.

Chris wasn't sure what to expect when he called Professor Meyers' phone the previous Wednesday. For all he knew, the learned geologist might not have even remembered meeting Sean on his canoeing trip, much less extending an offer for free consultation. Also, Chris knew that many people had probably searched for the same elusive mother lode in the past, so he might not be the first person to approach the doctor for advice.

Instead, he decided to focus their conversation on the caves themselves, and to find out what the doctor actually thought about their probable locations. He could pose the question as an interested spelunker, although he didn't want to appear as though he'd take sole credit for finding the caves, assuming that they did exist.

He turned this over in his mind while driving through the picturesque campus. Since it was late June, most of the students had already headed home for the summer; those who remained were busy with summer courses or research work. Chris watched them with a mixture of emotions. He loved being part of the academic scene, and he had enjoyed his six years on the Syracuse campus, yet he didn't miss the late nights and endless caffeine binges while cramming for tests and typing lengthy term papers.

Following Campus Road around the engineering quad, he finally pulled up in front of the modern architecture of Snee Hall, home of the Department of Geological Sciences. It was a very impressive structure, with an exterior that curved away from the hillside. A natural sand-colored stone finish adorned the outside of the building, with long stretches of glass windows along the sides.

He entered the front door of the building and raised an eyebrow at the expansiveness of the space. The entrance was four stories high, enclosing a glass-ceilinged atrium. Inside the showpiece foyer were numerous exhibits related to the sciences of geology and paleontology, including displays of dinosaur footprints, a life-sized Plesiosaur, and even a continuously operating earthquake-recording seismograph machine.

Dr. Meyers had instructed Chris to call him on his cell phone if he arrived before ten in the morning. Glancing at his watch, he noted the time, which was roughly half past nine. He took his cell phone from his belt carrier and entered the number he'd been given. The professor answered on the second ring and promised to be down to meet him within a few minutes.

While he waited, Chris looked further at the exhibits. He then wandered over to a wire rack offering university literature, with separate brochure holders for some of the many schools and degree programs. He pulled out a glossy tri-fold publication advertising the Weill Cornell Medical College of Cornell University. Quite a mouthful, he thought to himself as he put the document back in its place.

Just then, he heard light footsteps approaching from a wide hallway. He turned in time to see a middle-aged man approaching, wearing a button-down shirt underneath a brown tweed jacket. He was of medium stature, with thinning brown hair that was tinged with flecks of grey throughout.

"You must be Chris Carey?" the man asked, extending a handshake.

"Yes, that's me. And you are the sought-after Dr. Meyers, I assume?"

The doctor laughed and shook his head. "Well, sought after, maybe. But they always want me for all the wrong reasons. Whenever one of the administrators wants a new project started or a grant proposal written, they seem to find me. I'm lucky I still have time for my graduate students."

"You should take that as a compliment. The best people will always have a full plate, because others recognize their ability to get results. It's the same way in the corporate world. Steer clear of employees with little to do, because they probably aren't very good at their jobs."

"Well, thankfully, I've been able to avoid the corporate jungle. I'm not sure I could survive the daily competitive grind, although the academic world probably isn't far behind."

Dr. Meyers motioned for Chris to follow him into a nearby elevator. "We'll go up to my lab on the third floor and talk up there. You'll have to excuse me for not offering my office, but they're tearing the back wall apart this week to hook up the electrical supply for a new electron microscope in the adjoining room. For the time being, the lab's the best I can offer."

"I'm sure it will be fine," Chris said, watching the panel lights indicating that they had stopped on the third floor. "Hopefully, I won't take up too much of your time. I really appreciate you carving out some time to see me this morning."

They stepped off the elevator into a brightly lit hallway. The professor led the way down the corridor, stopping by his office to pick up a large parcel of bundled documents. They then proceeded farther down the same hallway before stopping outside the door of a spacious laboratory. Dr. Meyers opened the door and guided them into the room, which was filled with black, resin-topped lab desks. The perimeter of the work area was lined with deep sinks, ventilation hoods, and scientific equipment. Several students were collaborating on a project at the far end of the room, all wearing white lab coats and protective eye goggles.

"Please, have a seat," said the professor, pulling out a chair next to the front desk. "Since we're seated away from the chemicals, I guess I can permit you to go sans goggles." Meanwhile, the professor sat down on the other side of the lab desk.

"Thanks, Doctor. I always found a way to fog those things up pretty quickly. That's why I didn't like chemistry labs; I could never see what I was doing."

Dr. Meyers laughed, his face reflecting a naturally jovial personality.

"So, please, tell me, what can I do for you? Your friend tells me that you are looking for caves, or gold, or both. Sounds like fun. Could I come along too?"

"Ha! You'll have to excuse Sean," said Chris. "He gets overexcited about things, and this week the topic is prospecting. He's got it in his head that we should go panning for gold. In the Adirondacks, no less! I've tried telling him that there is nothing worth looking for inside the park, but he's psyched to give it a shot. He's got some notion about finding some supply that was originally worked over by the local Indians of the 1800s. Oh yes, and there's the rumor of a cave, too. He wants to find a cave that no one has been able to locate in over two hundred years. Now you see what I'm up against?" asked Chris, rolling his eyes.

"Yes, I do," chuckled the professor, placing his hands behind his neck. "I only spent one night with Sean. My wife and I were paddling the Fulton Chain of Lakes a couple years ago, and we stopped overnight on a small island on the west side of Eighth Lake. It was a beautiful lean-to, but cold as bloody hell that night. Chris was there with a friend who was a self-professed woodswoman. But between the four of us, we couldn't seem to get a fire going. Finally, this lady took half a pint of white gas and poured it over the wood we had in the fireplace. It practically blew the fireplace apart!"

"OK, that would be Amanda," said Chris. "She's an avid canoeist, biker, hiker, and raging pyromaniac. She's also Sean's sister, which explains why she's the only female in North America who would trust Sean in the woods for a week."

"Too funny, too funny," said the professor, lost in his laughter. "I'm glad the two of you don't work in this department. I'd never get any work done." Then, settling himself, he got back to topic. "Sean and I got into quite the discussion that night. He was talking about trying his hand at prospecting; he wanted to check out some of the old California claims that had shut down when the gold ran out. His thought was that the companies that had mined there couldn't remain in existence because they required a fairly large output to justify their expenses. He thought that if it was only him, he'd be able to support himself on very little gold. That was his whole idea: capitalize on the bits and scraps that were left over when the big guys moved out. But then I told him that he didn't have to go all the way out to California, or to Alaska, for that matter, that there is gold right here in New York State, if you are willing to look and work hard enough."

"And that's what you believe, or what you know?" asked Chris. "That there is gold to be had right here in the central part of the state?"

"It's here, but it's in very small quantities, and it's not found everywhere. But there have been several claims staked across the state over the years, including ones made in Saratoga, Warren, Jefferson, Oneida, and

Hamilton Counties. Whether those panned out, please excuse the pun, was another matter."

Chris tossed that around for a moment, mentally plotting the positions of the counties mentioned. "And were any of these claims made in recent years, or were they in the same era as the Western gold rush days?"

"Good question," answered Dr. Meyers. "Most of the New York claims were filed within a few short years, around 1897 or 1898. I think there was one big claim staked right inside the city of Binghamton as late as 1910. As you know, that's well after the heyday of the California gold rush, which started in 1849 and lasted through about 1855."

"So what you're saying, if I understand it correctly, is that no one has really found anything in about a hundred years, right?"

The doctor twisted in his chair, looking for words to explain his thoughts. "You have to be careful about what you mean by the word 'nothing.' Gold is a natural element, and it exists to some degree almost anywhere. But you also have to understand that there are several different kinds of gold deposits, and not all of them exist in quantities worth mining."

"The theory of diminishing returns, right?" asked Chris.

"You get an A for interpretation," replied the professor. "You see, most of the people who go searching for gold are looking for a form called 'placer gold.' This is the stuff that is found in small flakes in the bottom sediments of streams and rivers. It has been washed downstream as a result of erosion, which removed it from its original housing in the soil or rock. Your weekend recreational prospector, armed with a gold pan, can sift through the stream sediments and maybe end up with a few flakes of the real thing. But it's a slow and tedious process that takes a lot of time and patience. It also takes a lot of practice, or you'll end up discarding the gold along with the sand."

"Dr. Meyers, just how much of this stream sediment material can a single person sift in a day? It sounds very time consuming."

"It is, it is," replied Dr. Meyers. "I'd say that even a very experienced prospector could process perhaps a cubic yard, maybe even a little less, in a full day of grueling work. That's why most people who arrive with gold fever in their eyes are gone within a few weeks. It's hardly the easiest way to make a quick buck."

"But there are other forms of gold, right," asked Chris, "the larger nuggets that you always see in the old movies?"

"Yes, but now you're getting into a whole different category," said Dr. Meyers. "That's what you'd consider lode gold, which is when the metal is found inside the original solid rock material. That's where the real money was to be made. Once a high grade gold-producing ore was discovered, they would mine the ore and crush it, then extract the gold and melt it down into its pure form. It's a mechanized process that requires a lot of heavy machinery, not to mention the mining rights to work the claim. It's also tough because much of the land where there was any promise of finding gold was picked over a hundred years ago. The chances of finding a new mother lode, especially in the East, are about nil."

"Could we change topics here, at least for a bit, and talk about caves?" asked Chris. "It's a topic that's always intrigued me. I don't know if Sean mentioned this to you, but I'm an amateur spelunker myself. I try to do a trip or two every year if I have time."

"Certainly!" replied the professor, his eyes aglow with excitement. "That's one of my favorite subjects. Some of my colleagues around here think I move underground in the summer months."

"That's the main reason why I'm here," said Chris. "Sean said that you had already done a lot of research into the rumors that the local Indians had located some caves in the central Hamilton County area. Some of those caves supposedly contained mines."

"That's right," said the doctor. "Not only Hamilton County, but other places across the southern and central Adirondacks as well. But most of these supposed mines you mention weren't gold mines. As a matter of fact, I believe that several of the legends were linked to lead, which they used a lot more then than they do today."

"Don't you think it's a bit odd that no white man ever saw any of these places?" asked Chris. "I mean, there was an awful lot of activity that took place in those woods. Most of the Adirondacks were logged over completely at least once, maybe more. There were also some pretty big fires in the early part of the 1900s that burned a lot of forest back to nothing. I find it highly improbable that there are any secret caves back there, waiting to be discovered."

Dr. Meyers listened thoughtfully, nodding as Chris spoke.

"You may be right, but you've got to remember a couple of things. First, not all of the Adirondacks were clear-cut. It's true that most of it was logged, but a lot of that was selective versus clear-cutting. So the early loggers may not have had the opportunity to come face-to-face with a cave opening if there was no large timber nearby to attract their interest. Also, not all caves have big openings. You know, when we say the word cave, people seem to imagine a majestic cavern, with a gaping hole in the bottom of a cliff, with an overhanging archway that is sixty feet high and fifty feet across. The truth of the matter is that a lot of caves may have entrances that are no more than a simple hole in the ground. Finding them is a matter of luck more than anything."

"OK, I'll buy that," said Chris. "Sean said that you've actually been able to correlate some of the folklore to geographic features using satellite imagery. Is that true, and would you be willing to share any of that information?"

"Yes, and yes," replied Dr. Meyers. "I have done some initial research in this area, and I would be willing to share my thoughts with you. But I have some conditions that I want you to agree to before I spill the beans, OK?"

"Of course" said Chris. "We appreciate anything that you can give us, whether it's on the subject of either gold or caves."

"Let's take a look at a few of these maps I've brought along. We can spread them out over the desk and look at some of the more promising areas."

Chris helped the doctor remove the documents from the large portfolio binder and spread them out across the lab table surface. He noted that several of the maps were overlaid with different colors of shaded marker.

"I want you to look at two areas that are especially promising," said the doctor. "I'll show you everything I've got, but then I want to discuss my conditions."

Chris agreed once again to abide by whatever stipulations Dr. Meyers made. They pulled two maps out from the stack and laid them on top.

"This first map shows an area on the eastern side of the Adirondacks, around the west side of Lake George. Everyone thinks of that area as being very built up, yet there are places where it's still heavily forested and remote. A bunch of hunters in the 1880s were offered samples of rock to purchase from an old Iroquois who claimed he had an unlimited supply. The rock was studded with a metal that looked like gold, and it tested to be fairly high quality ore."

"Did the hunters ever see the mine itself?" asked Chris.

"No, they tried following the Indian, who claimed that he had a discovered a cave with tons of gold and silver just like the sample. But before they could find the cave, he simply vanished into thin air. They never saw him again. They did stake a claim with the State of New York that covered almost a square mile around the place where they last saw the Indian, but nothing ever came of it. I've looked at the rock strata and the surrounding topography and marked up this map to show the areas most likely to contain caves of any size. The only problem is that the area is so remote, with no roads or trails going in there. I'd say the chances of me ever seeing that territory are pretty small. That's why I'd be interested to see if the two of you can find anything."

Chris noted the coordinates on the map, jotting them down in a loose-leaf notebook. As he wrote, he cleared his throat in a nervous sign of anticipation.

"Let me guess," he said. "This is where your conditions come in, right?"

"Right," said the professor, the smile returning to his face. "Actually, they're not that restrictive, considering that my information could bring you to the doorstep of a major discovery. Or maybe I'm just being overly optimistic."

"You want half of the total value that comes out, regardless of how long or hard we have to work doing it, right?"

"Ha! That's a good one," said the professor, thumping the table with glee. "I can see that you don't understand the ground rules here. If you do happen to find any gold or silver worth mentioning, neither of us will get to keep it, much less profit in any way."

"How's that?" asked Chris, putting down his pen and pad. "Isn't it a case of 'finders keepers,' or don't those rules apply in the Adirondacks?"

"It's not just the Adirondacks, I'm afraid. This state gets you coming or going. It's covered in a catch-all provision called Article 7 of the New York State Public Land Laws. Basically, it says that any gold or silver found on public or private land becomes subject to State ownership. So you can dig all you want, and you can find all you want. But you can't keep any of it."

Chris was disappointed, but not crushed. "Well, we're probably not going to find enough to make it worth anyone's while. And there's no law against doing some panning on State land, is there?"

"No, you are allowed to pan for anything your heart desires. But another clause of the law reads that 'the use of State forest preserve land, or any improvements thereon for private revenue or commercial purposes is prohibited.' So that puts you right back where you started."

Chris sat back in his chair, thinking about the dim prospects of finding anything besides a few pyrite crystals, particularly in light of the restrictions tacked on by the State government. He felt much less enthused about the upcoming venture into the woods than before meeting the geologist.

"What about the second area?" Chris asked. "Is that in the same part of Warren County?"

"No, as a matter of fact, the story surrounding that comes to us from the middle of Hamilton County, in the territory around Indian Lake. It's another bit of folklore, about an Indian up in those parts who was able to access lead and other ores from a mine that was supposedly inside a cave.

This Indian sold chunks of the metal to other early settlers, who also tried following him into the woods. But this story had a different ending, one which you may find amusing. The story goes that two trappers tried following the Indian with the thought that he'd lead them to his mine. They dropped a trail of white beans behind them, in order to find their way back out of the woods after they located the mine. But the Indian knew that he was being followed, and he in turn had his wife following the hunters, picking up the beans as she went. Finally, after about three miles of doing loops in the woods, the Indian announced he would shoot the two hunters if they followed him any further. His wife then gave them back their beans and escorted them from the woods."

"So they never found that cave either?" asked Chris.

"No, they never did," replied the professor. "But once again, I have been able to correlate the route used by the Indian in the stories with local features around Indian Lake, and I've placed markers on this map with the locations of landmarks and promising rock formations. If you can make it back there, you just might find what you're looking for."

As the two men talked, a pair of women in white lab coats approached, carrying stacks of trays and placing them into a deep sink nearby. Dr. Meyers turned and smiled, offering an introduction.

"Ah, Chris, as long as we're speaking of caves, there are a couple of people here I'd like you to meet. Maybe they could shed some additional light on the subject of local caves in your area. May I present Maria Gonzales and Kristi Kincaid, both in our graduate program. Maria and Kristi, this is Chris Carey, from Syracuse."

Chris stood up as the doctor introduced the two women. He extended a handshake and a warm smile.

"Hello, Chris," smiled Kristi, a tall, thin young woman with long dark hair and a dazzling smile. "It's always nice to meet another enthusiast, especially one who shares the same interest as our esteemed advisor."

Both Chris and Dr. Meyers laughed at the flattering compliment about her professor.

"Thanks, and nice to meet you too," said Chris. "I sure wish I knew as much about cave formations as you all do. It would be so helpful in our upcoming venture. At least I'd know what to look for."

"Oh, so you're actually going to be his guinea pig and follow the yellow brick road?" asked Kristi, her brown eyes showing the same enthusiasm as Dr. Meyers' had.

"Yes, that's the idea," said Chris, looking from one woman to the other. "Dr. Meyers has graciously given us recommendations for narrowing our search sector. But it'll be tough, because we're looking for something that may not exist. Exciting stuff! I've been spelunking for about five years now, and I've always wanted to find and explore a cave that's never been seen before."

"Ah, yes," said Kristi, "that's every cave explorer's fantasy. Just make sure you know what you're doing and don't get yourself turned around in there. I'm sure the doctor would hate to hear that you got lost and couldn't get yourself back out."

"I promise to bring along an extra supply of bread crumbs," said Chris.

As the two students said farewell, Chris turned back to the professor and asked "So what were those conditions you wanted to discuss. We never did get to that."

"It's really no big deal," said Dr. Meyers. "But if you do find something, large or small, I'd like you to keep it quiet until our department gets a chance to put a team back there and do the geological survey on the place. Even if it's a just single chamber, it's still a find that we would take pride in, and you never know what you'll find—it could be something more. That's all I want out of this."

"Of course, Dr. Meyers, you have my word on it. And I appreciate your confidence in us. I hope to be able to announce the discovery of 'Meyers' Caverns' to your department within the next month."

Dr. Meyers roared with laughter. "Oh, no you don't! With my luck, there will be a curse attached to the place. Better I leave this planet quietly someday rather than leave behind a permanent reminder."

Chris put his notes into his binder and prepared to leave.

"I appreciate your time, sir," he said as he stood up. "If nothing else, we'll have a good time hacking around the brush looking for phantoms. And I think we'll pass on the gold entirely. The only pan I'll be using is for the trout!"

"That's not a bad idea," said Dr. Meyers. "I think you could pan all year long in most of the state and still not come up with enough gold to buy yourself a bottle of good beer."

"How about a corn dog?" asked Chris, referring to the comment made by Sean earlier in the week.

"Excuse me?" the professor said, looking at Chris with a quizzical expression.

"Never mind; it's an inside joke," said Chris.

They stepped into the elevator and started down to the lobby. The professor looked at Chris with an amused expression.

"You know something, Chris. If you wanted to look for gold in any quantity, it would make more sense to go after one of several buried treasures that have reportedly been lost over the centuries. There are several in this part of the country, you know, and some of them probably do exist. I read an interesting book a few years ago that said there are all kinds of stashes that have been hidden and lost to the ages."

"Yes, I know," said Chris. "Coincidentally, I had this discussion with my mother just last week. It turns out that our family is linked to one of those mysteries."

"Really!" said the professor, motioning Chris out of the elevator on the main floor. "Is this a story that has been known for a long time, or is it a newer tale?"

"It's one that's been around for at least eighty years," said Chris. "But I just learned of it this past week. Still, it's nothing I'd choose to pursue because it's probably all hearsay. Even worse, it's four generations of hearsay, making it even more unlikely that anything would ever come of it. Why do you ask? Did Captain Bluebeard come ashore in the middle of

New York and hide a treasure under the State Thruway?"

"Nothing quite so romantic, I'm afraid," said Dr. Meyers. "Most of the well-known treasure stories either date back to either the Revolutionary War or are associated with one of several notorious gangsters of the last century. Two of them took place in areas that border the Adirondacks. It might be fun to check them out some day."

"Could you give me the Cliff's Notes version of either one in thirty seconds or less?" asked Chris.

"Well, as I recall, one was a cannon full of gold coins buried in the Oswego River by a group of Frenchmen sometime in the 1600s. The other was a huge load of bullion dumped into the south end of Lake Champlain about a hundred years later by a Loyalist named Robert Gordon. Both were left behind as groups fled for Canada, although during different wars. There's no proof in either case that those treasures still exist, if they ever did. Many people have spent a lot of time and effort over the years looking, and lots of rumors abound about partial finds. But in all these years, nothing has ever come of it. Still, it adds color to the area, sort of like stories of the Loch Ness Monster do."

"Yes, I think you're right," laughed Chris. "And they're just as likely to be real."

Chris turned to face Dr. Meyers as he got ready to depart. "Thank you so much for your valuable time. And you have my assurance that if we find anything, you'll be the first one I call."

"You'd better have my cell phone on your speed dial list. I'll be waiting for the call."

"You wouldn't happen to have a business card with your e-mail address, would you?" asked Chris.

Dr. Meyers reached into his jacket pocket and extracted a neatly printed card with the university logo. "Here you go. I've even put my private cell phone on this one, so you've got no excuses. Call me if you need me."

As Chris looked at the professor's e-mail address, he suddenly remembered that he was supposed to check his own e-mail for an update from

Sean regarding the upcoming week. He asked his host if there were any public access computers within walking distance on campus.

"We can do better than that," replied Dr. Meyers. "Follow me and we'll get you hooked up in this building."

Chris followed the professor a short distance down the main hallway on the first floor to a student lounge filled with comfortable chairs, a few snack machines, and tables full of scientific journals. Along the far wall was a workbench with three desktop computers, each hooked up for internet use.

"Thanks again, Dr. Meyers," Chris said. "I'll be in touch as soon as we leave the woods, even if we only come out with mosquito bites."

After they traded handshakes, Chris sat down at the nearest workstation while Dr. Meyers turned to head back to his lab. Interesting morning, Chris thought to himself as he brought up the web browser and typed in his Yahoo! e-mail address.

As he waited for the login screen to appear, Chris closed his eyes, recalling everything he was supposed to do the following week. The camping trip with Sean would be fun, but he had more important things to think about. He had two job interviews that would both require extensive research which he hadn't even begun. A firm believer in arriving prepared, Chris had perfected an approach to interviews that never failed to impress his prospective employers. Regardless of the opportunity, he tackled each appointment with a degree of preparedness and confidence that gave him a competitive advantage over his peers.

Deep in thought, Chris never noticed the figure that passed in back of him as he logged into his account. He vaguely heard the jingle of coins dropping into the soda machine, followed by the sound of a bottle dropping into the bottom tray. But he never noticed the eyes roving over his keyboard as he tapped in his user name and password.

Username: chriscarey1986
Password: misterchips

Chris had used the same password for a few years. "Mr. Chips" was the name of his childhood pet, an old Scottish Terrier that had lived with the family until Chris was in high school. Once he entered college, he found the name conveniently easy to remember for all his student accounts.

As Chris sat there, looking through his inbox, the silent visitor in the lounge stepped away from the drink machine and passed back through the room. Chris quickly deleted a few messages and chose to reply to some others. Then he wrote a quick note to Sean, which read:

Hey, slacker! I just wrapped up talking with Dr. Meyers. Nice to know I'm doing your dirty work while you're making the big bucks playing the high-priced consultant. I ought to charge you for my time. Seriously, though, this was a good idea. He gave us two great places to search, and I've got the maps to prove it. Probably no prospects of finding your gold, but at least we can have fun looking at the furry little bats with my headlamps. I know you're looking forward to that! Talk later, dude. Out.

After finishing the e-mail, he logged off the computer, still smiling to himself about the bats. Sean hated bats with a passion, and most caves served as a residence to the winged animals. They were one of the main reasons why he had resisted Chris's offers to join him on most of his explorations. It was another inside joke, one of many shared between the two friends.

Chris then tucked his notebook under his arm and exited the lobby door for his Jeep. He was excited, invigorated, and completely unaware that they now had competition in the race that had just begun.

CHAPTER 10

July 17, 2012

The small, cozy A-frame sat up on a hill on the north side of Syracuse. It was close to the city while still retaining a secluded atmosphere. Located at the back of a dead-end dirt road, it received little or no traffic except for the familiar green Jeep of the tenant.

Chris's only roommate had moved out after the winter semester, leaving him as the single occupant. Even though the bottom floor of the house was now vacant, he still slept up on the loft, leaving most of the open space below with bare walls and floors. The first floor also contained a small kitchen area, with an L-shaped counter and a small dining table. Neither Chris nor his roommate had been extraordinary chefs, so the kitchen was sparsely stocked with cans of ready-to-eat soups and vegetables, along with the obligatory bachelor's supply of ravioli.

The rear interior wall was lined with red brick, which added warmth and character to the room. However, now that Chris had the house to himself, he discovered a new use for the brick surface. Whenever he needed time to think about events in his life, he would absentmindedly grab one of his lacrosse sticks and toss a ball against the wall, using it as a rebounder. The high, open ceiling of the main room allowed him the freedom to swing the stick without wreaking havoc with the lights or overhead fan.

This particular afternoon, the walls echoed with the repetitive "thump-thump, thump-thump" as the heavy rubber sphere short-hopped off the wall and floor of the old A-frame. With little thought dedicated to his movements, Chris mulled over the events of the past two weeks. His interviews had gone off without a hitch, and he was expecting a call-back from both companies. The trip into the woods had been put on hold, as Sean had been called in repeatedly to troubleshoot some network issues for a few of his ever-expanding list of client firms.

Chris had used the Fourth of July break to spend some time at home during a rare visit from Chris Senior. He had flown up from Washington to spend the holiday with the family and visit his father, Dennison "Denny" Carey, who lived outside of Utica in a home not far from the house where Chris grew up.

Chris had also used the time to complete some work on the Jeep, replacing both the brakes and the rear shocks. He had converted the garage in back of the house into a makeshift repair shop, in which he performed most of his own auto maintenance and repairs. Over the past several years, he had spent many hours inside the small outbuilding, tinkering over the aged machine. It had become almost a home away from home, even containing a small refrigerator in which Chris kept a supply of cold drinks for the summer months. More often than not, Sean looked for him inside the garage before he ever bothered trying the house.

Chris put down the lacrosse stick and paced the floor, feeling a bit like a caged animal. The meeting with Dr. Meyers was still on his mind, and he was eager to get into the woods to commence the search. He was also feeling badly about not stopping in to see his grandfather over the Fourth of July break. At age ninety-two, Denny Carey was becoming frail, and he needed help getting around. Chris had always been diligent about visiting when he was in the area, but he had found it more difficult to carve time out of his schedule these past several months. Resolved to remedy the situation, he pulled out his cell phone and quickly punched in a number.

The phone on the other end rang six times before it was lifted off the hook. Chris smiled, because he knew that his grandfather never believed in answering machines. "If they want me bad enough, they'll call back," he was fond of saying.

"Hello," came the gravelly voice from the other end.

"Hi, Gramps, it's Chris, just calling to say hello. It's been a while, and I thought I might like to stop by and see you, if you don't mind."

"Mind? Why would I mind? It's always good to see my favorite grandchild, you know that." It was an old joke, because Chris was the only grandchild to be born into the family, and he had always had a warm relationship with the Carey patriarch.

"That's great, Gramps. I'm moving a bunch of books and things down to the house the day after tomorrow, so I'll be near your place around noon. How about I pick up lunch, and we can chat for a while?"

"Sounds good," said Denny. "But why are you bringing things to your mom's place? Shouldn't you be bringing them to your own house, wherever that turns out to be? After all, when you and that lovely girl—what was her name again, Martha?—get married, you'll need a big house and lots of space."

Chris chuckled as he answered his grandfather's question. "No, Gramps, her name was Melissa, and we're not getting married. As a matter of fact, she's moved back to Chicago. So you can call off the wedding bells."

"Too bad for you," said the grandfather. "She was a nice girl. Damn good looking, too, if I must say so myself."

"I didn't know you still noticed things like that, Gramps."

"Just wait until you get to my age. You'll see that you never stop looking. It's just that fewer people think you are!"

Feeling that they'd exchanged enough small talk, Chris broached the topic for his call. "By the way, Gramps, I wanted to ask you about something. I was down visiting Mom a couple weeks ago, and she said that your dad knew Adirondack French Louie. Is that right?"

"I can't believe your mother remembered that," said Denny, the surprise evident in his voice. "Yes, he used to stay at Louie's camp on Pillsbury Lake when he went into the woods to do some winter fishing. He hunted there a bit, too, but not very seriously. My dad wasn't the best hunter in the woods."

"Well, Mom talked about him a little bit, and she made a reference to a legend about some treasure that Louie had found, or hidden, or something like that."

"Yep, that would be the mysterious pile of gold that Louie supposedly dragged into the woods and buried," said Denny. "I got the story from my father, who gave me a few bits and pieces that were supposedly clues. He passed them along to me when he found out that he was dying, back around 1975. I looked at them a bit back then, and I tried to figure out what they meant, but I couldn't make heads or tails out of them. I even had two of the items examined by the curator of the State Museum in Albany. She gave me some interesting information about them, but nothing that ever led me to the supposed pot of gold."

"It doesn't sound to me as though you believe in it yourself."

"Well, Chris, you've got to understand that I never met Louie myself. I went into the woods with my father once I was old enough and could handle a gun. But Louie had been gone for a good ten or twenty years before I ever set foot in the West Canada country."

"So we don't really know anything one way or the other," said Chris.

"No, I supposed we don't," said his grandfather.

"Anyway, I'd love to see you to catch up. So is noon on Thursday good for you?"

"Sure," said Denny. "I'll make sure to keep a cold one in the fridge for you."

"Sounds great, Gramps! I'll see you at twelve on Thursday. I'll bring roast beef subs."

Chris heard his grandfather laughing as he hung up the phone. Despite his advanced age and his decreased mobility, Denny Carey was doing well for someone of his years. He still enjoyed a good meal, and his appetite for "all the wrong things" had apparently not affected his longevity.

Just before ending his conversation, Chris had heard the quiet "beep" on his phone indicating that another call had come in. He accessed the menu for "calls received" and saw that Sean had tried to reach him a minute earlier. Despite pressing the "Recall" button immediately, he found that Sean was already on another call, but he'd sent a text message.

Seem to have missed you again. I'll call back tonight. Let's plan on the camping trip next week, if you can still make it. Talk later.

Chris was surprised. His friend was normally extremely brief with his words. This message was more loquacious than most. He made a mental note to block off part of the following week for the excursion. In the meantime, he wanted to find out exactly what it was that his grandfather had kept for all those years, passed along from his father. It sounded intriguing, and he found himself looking forward to the trip.

Before leaving for his afternoon run, Chris logged onto his computer and opened his e-mail. He deleted a bunch of spam messages, annoyed with the amount of junk that got past his filter. He then noticed that Dr. Meyers was online, his name appearing in Chris's instant message list. As an afterthought, he tapped out a quick message:

> **chriscarey1986:** Good afternoon, Doctor. We still haven't made our trip yet, but we're planning on it for next week. I'll be sure to e-mail you as soon as we're back. Thanks again for your help.

The reply came back almost immediately:

> **Cave_dweller_DrM:** Thanks for the update, Chris. It was a pleasure to meet you. I look forward to hearing what comes out of this. Bye.

Thursday morning was a dreary, rainy day. Chris had a few errands to run before departing for the quick trip over Route 90 to Utica. Still, he was able to leave his house by ten forty-five, and he made good time on the Thruway.

Chris pulled into the Subway shop nearby his grandfather's street exactly one hour later, which was perfect. His grandfather had always been critical of those who were not punctual, and he expected visitors, even those who were family, to be on time. It was an odd quirk in an otherwise very relaxed personality, but Chris had always attributed it to his grandfather's Army days. Denny had been a Lieutenant in the European theatre and had served under General Patton. His Bronze Star and Purple Heart still hung proudly on the wall of his house.

Chris picked up a pair of roast beef subs, remembering to add extra horseradish to his grandfather's roll. "I like my food to bite me back," he was always fond of saying.

The Jeep pulled into the driveway at one minute to noon. As Chris knocked on the door, he could hear his grandfather's clock chiming in the background. He heard footsteps approaching, and the door swung open.

"Hello, Emma," Chris said to the pleasant-faced woman who stood before him. "Nice to see you. Would you mind putting this in the refrigerator?" he asked as he held out the bag with sandwiches.

"Well, hello, Chris," smiled the housekeeper, taking the package from him. "Your grandfather's been looking forward to seeing you. He's been talking about you ever since you called. Please come in."

Chris walked into the small living room of the Cape Cod home that his grandfather had occupied since the 1970s. After his wife passed away, he had lived alone and without assistance for many years, until he finally became too old to properly care for himself. Since Chris Senior was living in Washington, Theresa tried to help all she could, but she found that the day-to-day routine required more time and energy than she could muster. To help cope, the family had hired Emma, a local retired healthcare provider, to stay with Denny through the daytime hours and look after his needs. It was an equitable arrangement, and Emma had become almost like one of the family.

As Chris stood looking at a high school photograph of himself on top of an old piano, his grandfather shuffled out from the kitchen. Despite being slightly hunched over, he still stood almost six feet tall.

"Well, well, look who decided to drop by," said Denny, reaching out to take Chris's hand. "You're looking good these days!"

"Hi, Gramps! Thanks," said Chris, returning the handshake. "I'm glad to hear you've been behaving yourself."

"Well, it's hard to get myself in trouble with Emma watching me all the time," he said, smiling at his aide. "She keeps a pretty tight set of reigns on me most the time. I'd set up a date with the pretty blonde next door if it weren't for the fact that I'd have to crawl out the window to get away."

Emma and Denny both laughed. Chris could see that there was a compassionate friendship built up over the years that meant a lot to both of them. Emma, too, was a senior citizen, although she was over twenty years younger than Denny.

His grandfather looked up at Chris and preemptively asked the question. "So what is your interest in old French Louie, and how can I help you?"

"Well, Gramps, as I told you over the phone, Mom mentioned the family legend about Louie and a treasure, although that's not our main reason for exploring the area around his original homestead. We're interested in the possibility of finding an old mine that was supposedly located in a cave up in the same territory. We're not sure whether there was gold there, or some other mineral. But the story goes that several Indians had located caves in the region west of Indian Lake, as well as in the Lake George region."

Denny listened thoughtfully, squinting his eyes as he recollected the facts from decades before.

"I'm sorry, son, but I don't know whether I can help you with that. That's a big country up there, and the caves you're looking for could be almost anywhere. Louie mentioned caves to my father when he tried telling him where to find the gold, but those sound like different caves. I doubt there's any connection there at all."

Chris looked somewhat disappointed, but he was not to be deterred. He would follow all leads and see what became of them.

"Anyway, how did your father come to possess those things you spoke of, these clues that Louie gave him before he died? And why would Louie pick him, of all people, to tell?"

"Well, according to your great-grandfather, Louie had no family to speak of," said Denny. There was one young lad who used to come and visit him a lot. Some kid named Haskell, if I'm not mistaken. They were real friendly with one another, but Louie had no children. So who else could he trust with his secrets? My dad was pretty close with Louie too, or at least as close as Louie was with anyone."

"When did all this happen?" asked Chris. "When did Louie tell your father the story?"

"That would have been sometime in late 1914. I know that because it's the last year my father ever saw him. I've got pictures of his cabin up in the attic, and some of them have dates written on the back."

"Could I see the things that Louie gave him that last year?" asked Chris. "And do you know what he told him that might be useful in finding this cave, or wherever he might have buried this supposed treasure chest?"

"There's not much, Chris," said his grandfather. Remember, this happened almost a hundred years ago, and sometimes I can't remember what I had for supper yesterday. But come into the back room and I'll show you what I have."

Chris followed his grandfather into a dimly lit dining room, which was thickly covered in a deep Oriental carpet. One entire wall was lined with mahogany shelving, which housed almost two thousand books.

"My balance isn't what it used to be, lad. Would you please grab the step ladder and bring down that box on the top shelf?"

Chris looked up and saw the ornately carved wooden box near the top of the bookcase. It was large, approximately two feet long by one foot wide, and several inches deep. It looked heavy. Even though he could probably reach it without the ladder, he did as he was told and used the steps, carefully lifting the box from its resting place.

The wooden container was a thing of beauty, made of an undetermined wood with dark heavy grains. The sides were etched in deep relief patterns, while the top cover was a much simpler design of geometric figures. A hinge on the side of the cover allowed the top to fit perfectly onto the rest of the box, forming an almost airtight seal.

"This is beautiful!" exclaimed Chris, running his hand over the exquisite wood. "Did Louie give your father this box, too?"

"No, no, that box belonged to your grandmother," replied Denny. "It's definitely an antique, because I believe her mom gave it to her. I don't think it's been opened in at least thirty years."

Chris felt his heart beating faster as he set the box on the dining room table. He brushed a thick layer of dust off the top, exposing even more of the hand-carved artwork. Next, he pulled back the metal clasp on the side of the box and lifted the lid.

Inside the box were a few items, all of which looked very, very old. A simple metal drinking cup, ringed with thin lines and sporting a looped handle, sat on one side of the box. It could have been made of pewter, although Chris guessed that it was probably forged from tin. The box also contained the remains of a rifle stock, which had partially decayed and provided few clues to identify the original weapon. Neither of these two items seemed to be of any particular importance to Chris. He gently set them aside and continued to explore the bottom of the box.

Underneath these two items was a large leather sheath made for housing documents. It was almost as wide as the box, and Chris had a difficult time reaching around its sides to remove it from the wooden container.

"What's inside this cover?" he asked, looking at his grandfather for permission to move ahead.

"Some papers and a map, as I recall," said Denny, looking over Chris's shoulder. "Go ahead. Take a look for yourself, and then after you're done I'll explain what you've seen."

Chris took the darkened leather binder out of the box and set it on the table. He lifted the cover, allowing the front to rest open against the side of the wooden box. As he did this, he noticed that small particles of the ancient leather broke off and lay like crumbs on the table surface.

Inside the binder lay several documents, stacked on top of one another in a neat pile. The top paper was the smallest and was relatively square, about six inches on each side. It was a rather basic drawing featuring a collection of irregular shapes, most of them either circular or slightly squared. They formed a loose pattern, as though they were part of a larger shape that was also irregular in design. A series of wavy lines ran out from the shapes along one side of the drawing. An arrow had been drawn to point out some feature of importance to the original creator of the document, although Chris could not determine its meaning on first glance.

The next article in the portfolio was a map, which had been folded into a rectangular shape about six inches by four inches. Chris carefully removed and unfolded the document underneath the overhead light. It was an aging topographic map from 1903 showing much of the West Canada Lakes territory. At some time in the past, an unnamed author had recorded a great many notes and coordinates directly onto the surface. Entire areas surrounding lakes had been shaded in colored pencil, with arrows and numbers recorded next to each. In the top right corner, someone had neatly penned the name "W.J. Harrison" in black cursive characters.

Poring over the map, Chris noticed that most of the lakes in the center of the region had shaded areas marking the boundaries, including Indian Lake, Cedar Lakes, Pillsbury Lake, Lost Pond, Whitney Lake, and Mud Lake. Numbers appeared along lines between the bodies of water, but they had no apparent meaning. Chris guessed that the map had been used either as a tool for searching, or for planning a search.

There was one other set of notes on the map, and these were centered alongside a single transect line. Someone had taken a fine lead pencil and laid down a track that ran from east to west across the right half of the map. Inside the right margin of the large document, the hand written notes read: 5/28: 12/265, 5/29: 10/265, 5/30: 8/265, 6/1: 13/265, 6/2: 2/285, 3/005, 6/3-6/4-6/5: 0. The track did not appear to have a destination, and it ended in the middle of nowhere, not far north of Cedar Lakes.

After about fifteen minutes, he set the map aside and retrieved the last item from the bottom of the box. It was a small card with a few lines of handwritten text. They read as follows:

The cup and the stock came from the man in the cave.
You find the gold where I show you. This picture show you.
You use the gold to take care of this place.

The date "December 10, 1914" was written on the bottom of the card.

Chris turned the card over in his hand to look for inscriptions on the back, but there was nothing. He put down the card with the other two papers and looked at his grandfather.

"OK, Gramps, what do you know about these? About all I can tell is that they weren't all written by the same person."

"Good observation," nodded Denny. "As a matter of fact, all three of those were written by different people."

Chris picked up the map noting the various shaded areas.

"Whose markings are these, and what were they used for?" he asked.

"That's a map that was annotated by an early treasure hunter to localize the site where the gold was originally hidden. My father spent quite a bit of time trying to figure out those numbers, but he never cracked the code."

"Do you think Louie made this map?" asked Chris.

"No, according to my father, Louie couldn't read or write. If someone wrote him a letter, he had to wait until someone read it to him. He could draw, but he couldn't do much more than that."

"How about the name up in the corner here, W.J. Harrison. That mean anything to anyone?"

"I'm afraid he never figured out that riddle either. He went as far as looking up the name in most of the phone directories of the major cities of the day, but he kept coming up empty."

"You're kidding, right, Gramps?" Chris asked, his face registering surprise. "I wouldn't have thought that they had phone books in that era."

"Oh, you'd be surprised," said his grandfather. "Some cities had listings of local numbers before the start of the twentieth century. By 1900 or 1910, most of the major cities had their own phone books. But it mattered little, because most people didn't have a phone in their house for many years after that. Apparently, Mr. W.J. Harrison didn't have a phone either."

Next, Chris picked up the small card and scanned the lines.

"Who wrote this? It appears to be just a collection of quotes."

"My father used that to record some of the things that Louie told him during his last visit," said Denny. "Louie was very sick by that time, confined to his bed because he couldn't walk well. My father told me of how he found Louie during that trip, all alone on the cot in his kitchen. He was in some pain, and he didn't seem to be completely lucid. He was mumbling about 'finding the gold,' and 'taking care of the place.' It's almost as though he knew he was going to die soon."

"And did he?" asked Chris.

"Yes, as a matter of fact, my father said that he only lived until the middle of the winter, although no one could say what he died of. Some suspect that it was cancer because of the pain that he had in his side, but there was no way be sure."

"So Louie died sometime after your dad spoke with him in the winter of 1914–1915. But what led your father to think that Louie was referring to a *sizeable* sum of gold, whether in a mine or any other form? I just don't see the connection here."

"Well, that's where the other paper comes into the picture," said Denny. "He told your father that he would find the gold buried 'right where I showed you.' The drawing, which is a crude map, shows a collection of lakes with their associated outlet streams. It's a very rough map, but that's the way all of Louie's maps were drawn."

"And I assume that the arrow on this map was drawn by Louie too?" asked Chris.

"Yep. That map is exactly as it was when Louie gave it to my dad in 1914."

"Hmmm, not a lot to go on," said Chris, turning it over in his hands. I can't think of anyplace along the route through the West Canadas where the lakes are this close together, or even this shape. As a matter of fact, it doesn't make much sense to me at all. And on top of that, there are streams drawn in all over the place, all running north-south. Most of the streams and rivers I can think of back there run east-to-west."

"Well, at least I can help you with that one," said Denny. "Louie was known for drawing very crude maps that didn't accurately represent size or shape. As a matter of fact, he drew most of his lakes round and about the same size, regardless of their actual proportions. Even the distances between the lakes on his maps weren't proportionate. He just wanted to show general direction between any two points, with little reminders of where he had set a trap or hidden a boat. They were certainly not a thing of beauty, but they worked to get him around the woods, and that's all he cared about."

"That's great for old Louie, but it didn't help your dad, and I don't think it's going to help me much. But that's OK, Gramps. It still makes for a great story, even if it's only just that."

Chris' grandfather fixed him with a solid stare, his eyes reflecting his curiosity. "So what do you think it is, young man? Fact or fiction?"

"If I had to venture a guess, I'd say that the bit about the Indians having a hidden mine in the area might be real. There are too many references to that to ignore, although we may never find out whether it's commercially viable. But I don't buy that there's a treasure chest full of gold. There are too many similar tales spread around the country to believe in that one."

"Then why are you interested in these artifacts?" asked Denny.

Chris laughed, nodding his head in understanding. "OK, Gramps, I guess you got me on that one. I am curious, I'll say that much."

"I thought so," smiled his grandfather. "You've always had too much natural curiosity in you to not bother looking under the hood. But now, what comes next?"

"Well, what I'd like to do, Gramps, is to ask if I can borrow these items. I'd like to copy the papers and run the rifle stock and the cup by some museum folks and see if they can shed any light on their origin. If you don't mind, I'll take them for a few days. I promise I'll return them in pristine condition within the week."

By the time they had finished their examination of the box, it was nearly one o'clock. Chris's grandfather looked at his grandson with a peculiar expression on his face. He tilted his ear up, as if listening to a very faint noise.

"You hear that?" he asked, concentrating on an inaudible sound.

"No, Gramps. You must have better hearing than me. I don't hear a thing. What is it?"

"It's the sound of my stomach aching for that roast beef sub you promised me! I'm starved."

Chris threw back his head and laughed. "Well, I see your appetite hasn't been affected by the passage of a few short years, has it? And as long as we're discussing the topic, yes, I did remember the extra horseradish. You've got enough on there to choke a mule."

"Good. Just the way I like it," said Denny, anticipating the treat.

The two men moved into the kitchen for their meals, and the topic of conversation moved on to more mundane matters. Chris stayed for another hour, eating and talking with his grandfather, before borrowing a plastic storage bin so that he could carry the papers and other articles without having to take the heavy wooden box, and reluctantly taking his leave.

After saying farewell to his grandfather and Emma, Chris backed out of the driveway and turned down the road towards town. He pulled off onto a sandy parking lot before reaching the next stop sign. Grabbing his cell phone, he called Sean to find out where he'd been. His friend answered on the first ring.

"Hey, I thought you were going to call me back a couple nights ago," said Chris. "What happened? You fall out of Windows XP?"

Sean laughed, even though he'd heard Chris use that line before.

"Hardly. I apologize for going silent, but I've been up until almost one o'clock the past two nights. It's been pretty busy, and I've had to put some work on hold. I think I need to hire some help."

"Sounds like you've got your hands full," said Chris. "I was going to ask you if you had time to do a favor for me."

"Of course I do," said Sean. "But you better not need me too early in the morning. What's up?"

"I need to meet up with you for a few minutes this week, just enough time to give you something to take to the curator at the museum in Albany. I'll set up the appointment for you so that all you'll have to do is show up and meet him with the stuff."

"What stuff?" asked Sean. "I don't know what you're talking about."

"It's a couple of items that my grandfather gave me to look at. They came from an old hermit named Adirondack French Louie, who lived up in the West Canada Lakes territory north of the town of Speculator. You want to find gold, I may have a lead on some. But finding it is going to be tough."

"Wow. You've got my attention," said Sean. "Can you give me any more details than that?"

"Only that Louie gave a deathbed statement to my great-grandfather that he had found some amount of gold that he'd buried somewhere in the Adirondacks. How's that for a small search area?"

"Care to speculate on where this pot of riches might be?"

"Not now," said Chris. "Sorry, but I've got to get back and set up a few appointments of my own. I'll hit you with an e-mail and explain as much of this as I can, OK? Then, we'll meet up sometime tomorrow or Saturday, if you can fix it so that I can work my way into that schedule of yours."

"Where are you going to be while I'm talking to the curator in Albany?" asked Sean.

"I'm going to head north to the Adirondack Museum at Blue Mountain Lake. Assuming that I can get in the door there, I think it might be valuable to take a look at old Louie's things. Maybe he left behind some clues in his other possessions that are part of their collection. It can't hurt, anyway."

After hanging up the phone, Chris paid a quick visit to his mom, then drove back to his house in Syracuse. He stopped at a commercial print shop along the way so that he could make a couple full-sized copies of the documents he'd borrowed from his grandfather. The attendant inside the print shop looked at the extended map as he placed it onto a large-format scanner.

"This thing looks pretty old," he said. "What are all the markings on it?"

"That's from an old friend of mine up north," replied Chris. "He's an avid fisherman, and he's marked out all the old spots where the trout fishing used to be good. Not much left there anymore, though."

"Ain't that the truth," said the worker. "Must be the acid rain. The place is going to hell in a hand basket."

Chris walked in the door of his A-frame late that afternoon and went straight to his computer. He set the plastic box of artifacts on the floor and pressed the power button. While waiting for the machine to come online, he placed a bag containing some of his mother's home-made meatloaf into the refrigerator and then grabbed a can of Pepsi from the top shelf. His mother was a wonderful cook who worried about her son's spartan eating habits. Whenever possible, she loaded him up with bags of "take out" to stock his kitchen.

Among other personal emails waiting for Chris was one from Dr. Meyers. He opened that one first and scanned the contents:

Chris—I found another reference to the story of the Indian cave we talked about when you were here. It was in an old *Field and Stream* issue from 1918. I scanned in the article and attached it to this email. Looks like it concurs with the map I showed you. Sounds interesting. Happy Hunting!

Chris typed in a brief reply, and then opened the attachment. It was a story of another Indian who lived below the village of Indian Lake, and who regularly carried small nuggets of gold from a purported cave in the woods. Unlike several of the tales in circulation about such finds, this one contained a small photo of a notarized letter certifying an assay on the quality of the metal. It looked authentic, but it represented yet another "goose chase" opportunity for Chris's overburdened schedule.

Also in his inbox was an e-mail from his father. Chris Carey, Sr., seldom used his e-mail account. He had secretaries who handled all his administrative affairs, and junior attorneys who wrote most of his professional correspondence. As a result, he found that he had little time or patience for sitting in front of a computer. His valuable time was much better spent meeting with clients or finding new ways to expand the business.

Chris opened the e-mail and found a quick note about his job search efforts. It read:

Chris—keep me posted on the job prospects up north. If it doesn't work out, I know I can pull a few strings down here and get you into a half dozen D.C. firms—management, top dollar, company car, and all the benefits. Just say the word. Great seeing you on the Fourth! Talk soon. Love, Dad

Chris closed the e-mail without responding. His father would have gladly hooked him up with one of his Washington cronies to get him to move down to the capital. But Chris, like his mom, had no interest in living there—too many cars, too many people, and too much hassle. He'd told his father that before, but to no avail.

Next, he started a new e-mail to Sean, in which he described the conversation with his grandfather. He told him about the documents showing the search pattern around the West Canada Lakes and described the drawing made by French Louie showing the various bodies of water. He continued:

The whole search seems to focus on the area from Cedar Lakes to West Canada Lakes, which are both in the West Canada Lakes Wilderness Area. Our primary search box is shaped like a rectangle that is about eight miles wide and six miles high. Almost all of the references to the Indian caves fall inside this fifty-square-mile box. We need to narrow this down some before we search. I also have some new material that talks about French Louie finding buried gold, but that's an unrelated story. Could I swing by your house tomorrow morning, around 10? I'll bring those two things that I'd like you to take to the museum.

Before sending the e-mail, he retrieved his digital camera from the loft and snapped a couple shots of the drinking cup and rifle stock from his grandfather's house. He downloaded the photos to his PC and attached the files to the e-mail. Sean should have them within a few minutes of logging on, whenever that might be.

Chris hit the "Send" button and then rose from his seat. He prepared a meatloaf sandwich from his mother's package, and then flopped down on a chair in front of the wide screen television. He used the remote control to settle on a Red Sox game, where Boston was in the process of defeating the Yankees for the third consecutive game. A huge Sox fan, Chris allowed an involuntary cheer to escape as he settled in to watch.

He had barely finished the last bit of his sandwich when his cell phone began playing the theme song from "The Adams Family," which meant that Sean was on the line. He answered it without bothering to say hello.

"Jeez, bad news sure travels fast. You don't waste time, do you?"

On the other end of the line he could hear his friend laughing. "You know me: 'answers in an instant.' I just figured I'd call you instead of going back and forth with another four rounds of e-mails."

"Thanks," said Chris. "It shouldn't take more than a minute or so. And I've got one other favor to ask of you that you can do from right inside your house."

"What's that?" asked Sean.

"I'd like you to use your computer savvy to conduct an all-out blitz search for someone by the name of W.J. Harrison. His name is on an old map that I pulled out of my grandfather's house. That map once belonged to French Louie, but it's got cryptic notes written all over it, none of which make sense to me. Regardless, the notes on the map match the handwriting that did the name, so whoever this Harrison fellow was, chances are pretty good he was searching for the same thing as us. Anything we can find on his background might be useful."

"I take it that he's not still living amongst us, then?" asked Sean.

"No, that's a pretty good assumption," answered Chris. "My guess is that he made the notations on the map sometime between the years 1903 and 1914."

"And what, Mr. Sherlock Holmes, leads you to that conclusion?"

"It's elementary, my dear Watson," replied Chris, following his friend's lead. "The map itself is a U.S. Geographic Survey map that was issued in 1903, so we know that it was used sometime after that. Also, the map ended up in the hands of Louie, who passed it along to my great-grandfather in 1914. Soooooo," he let his voice trail away, waiting for a response.

"You want me to look into every genealogical database I can find to try and find W.J. Harrison, even if I have to hack my way in. Is that the idea?"

"I love it when you talk like that!" said Chris, using his most villainous voice. "Make sure you're awake when I stop by tomorrow morning. I'd hate to be arrested breaking in through the front window."

"See you then. I'll have the coffee pot going when you get here."

Chris looked up at the clock over the kitchen sink and noticed it was after four-thirty. Since it was so late in the day, he doubted that anyone would still be working at the Adirondack Museum in Blue Mountain Lake. But rather than put it off, he decided to give it a shot. He called information, which provided the phone number and connected him to the museum. Someone at the main desk answered the phone and offered to put his call through to the curator.

"Hello, this is Deborah Santori," said a pleasant-voiced woman. "How may I help you?"

"Hello, Deborah, my name is Chris Carey. We don't know each other, but I'm writing a book about some of the famous woodsmen of the Adirondacks, and I'm trying to learn more about one particular French-Canadian who lived in the southern-central area of the park about a hundred years ago."

"And that would be?" asked the curator.

"A man named Louis Seymour, although everyone knows him by the name 'French Louie.'"

"Of course," said Deborah, sounding somewhat triumphant in her response. "Everyone knows about Louie. We've had exhibits about him here in the past. He was a very popular fellow, you know."

"I read about him when I was a kid," said Chris. "To tell you the truth, he's one of the main reasons I started thinking about doing the book," said Chris. He felt rather bad about having to make up a story, but he knew that he'd have to pose as a researcher in order to gain access to any of Louie's belongings that were not on display. It was the best story he could come up with on short notice.

"Well, Mr. Carey, we do have a lot of the original items that were brought out of his camps after he passed away. Other items still reside in private homes and collections, I'm sure, because we didn't have a museum building until 1957. But every once in a while, people do bring in things that they find in their attics, and we categorize and store them for future use. We have many buildings full of items that have never been on display."

"I'm going to be up that way tomorrow afternoon. Would it be possible for me to stop by and have an hour of time with either you or an assistant?" asked Chris.

"I'm sorry, but that would be impossible, at least for tomorrow. I'm busy with two school projects, and my other material handlers are setting up a new exhibit on early immigrants. I might be able to spend some time with you next Monday, but that would be the earliest. Sometime in the early afternoon would work."

"I'll take it," said Chris, grateful for the opportunity she extended. "I thank you for your offer, and I'll try to make the best use of your time."

"It would be my pleasure," said Deborah. "And I'd love to have an autographed copy of your book once it comes out."

"You got it," said Chris, now feeling even worse about the fib.

Chris coordinated the time of the meeting with the curator, and then exchanged phone numbers. He wasn't sure whether the visit would be worth his time, but he knew that he needed to find out more about Louie and his territory. He also wanted to see if any of Louie's other hand-drawn maps existed, as described by his grandfather. And if so, did they contain notations that might provide clues to the gold or a cave? Those questions would have to wait until the following week.

It was almost ten fifteen on Friday when Chris knocked on Sean's door in Little Falls. Not waiting for an answer, he walked in and immediately detected the smell of bacon and eggs coming from the kitchen.

"Hello, anyone home? What's a person gotta do to get some breakfast around here?"

Sean walked in from the back room, plate in hand, still chewing a piece of toast.

"I already offered you a cup of coffee. If you had wanted breakfast, you should have called ahead with your order. Sorry, but the kitchen's closed."

"That's OK. I'll settle for the caffeine, thanks," said Chris.

The two of them sat down at the kitchen table and Sean poured the coffee. As he did, Chris opened the plastic box and withdrew the rifle stock and the cup.

"Here you go: these are what you're going to take with you to Albany. Think you can do that without losing them?"

"I'll do my best," said Sean, examining the artifacts. "I was looking at the photos you sent last night. You know, the rifle stock looks even older when you're holding the real thing. This has been around for a while. Where did it come from?"

"I have notes written by my great-grandfather that say these 'came from the man in the cave.' It doesn't specify what man, or what cave. So that's a mystery."

Sean turned the cup over in his hands, examining the bottom of the vessel for markings, then the inside. There were some letters stamped into the bottom surface, but they were too lightly engraved and worn to read.

As Sean continued to study the drinking receptacle, Chris began unfolding one of the large copies of the map he had borrowed from his grandfather.

"As long as we're talking about caves, I'd like to show you a copy of that old map I was mentioning, the one that my great-grandfather had been given by French Louie. You can keep this one and try to figure out some of these notes. I think it's a pretty safe bet that whoever was using it was looking for something pretty important."

Sean scanned the reproduction carefully, studying the lines and shaded areas, with the figures recorded next to each. He also noted the name written on the top of the map.

"There's our esteemed colleague, W.J. Harrison. I wonder what his part was in this whole scheme?" asked Sean.

"We may never know the answer to that question. But I'm hoping that the folks at the State Museum can look at those artifacts and at least put us in the ballpark with respect to the year they were used. Anything above that will be gravy."

"So what questions do you want me to ask the museum people when I get there?" asked Sean.

"First of all, you'll be looking for a Dr. Simon Rehnquist, who is an expert on the period from the French-Indian War through 1800. He'll meet you in his office on Monday morning at nine-thirty. Once you meet him, just let him look over these two items and see what he's got to say. Primarily, I'm interested in learning how old they are, and where they likely originated."

"Anything else?" asked Sean, polishing off the rest of his breakfast.

"If they pre-date the Revolutionary War, I'd be interested in hearing Dr. Rehnquist theorize on how they may have come to be in Louie's possession. But I doubt he'll have much to say on that topic."

"OK then, I can handle this. I'll have a full report to you by Monday afternoon," said Sean with a mock military tone to his voice.

"Don't worry, I'll still be on the road from Blue Mountain Lake by then," said Chris. "I had to pose as a researcher to get in the door there, but I managed to pull it off. I probably won't make it back until Monday night."

"Sounds good. Maybe we'll talk next Tuesday instead. In the meantime, I'll try to get around to that Internet search this weekend. Maybe I'll have news for you regarding the infamous W.J. Harrison."

"I'll look forward to it. And now, my friend, I'll perform another magic act for your viewing pleasure. You're about to see the Great Carey disappear. Go forth and do great things!"

The two said farewell, and Chris headed back to Syracuse. En route to his house, he stopped into the Syracuse University library and sat down at a public access computer. He quickly checked his e-mail. Finding nothing of interest, he then searched the library databases for "gold" and "New York treasure." The resulting list contained a half dozen titles, many of which were old references inside magazines and journals. He made copies of some of these and checked out a book about buried treasures thought to exist throughout the mid-Atlantic states, including New York. Included in the text was a short chapter on Robert Gordon and the legendary cache lost in Lake Champlain. He then headed back to his house to relax and look at the library material.

Since it was the start of the weekend, Chris had very little to do that evening. He had been asked by some of his old lacrosse teammates to join them in a pickup game on Saturday afternoon, but other than that the weekend was empty. On the way to the refrigerator, he reached out and turned on the computer. It was an automatic motion; a self-admitted "info junkie," he needed to be connected to his network in order to feel comfortable. He also wanted to send a quick note to everyone he had listed as a reference during his recent interviews. He had been told that they would be contacted, and he always liked to let those people know in advance so they would be expecting the calls.

Functioning on autopilot, he opened his Yahoo! e-mail login window and typed in his password:

Username: chriscarey1986
Password: misterchips

However, instead of opening his account, he received an error message that read:

Your Yahoo! mail account is still open on another computer. Do you wish to continue?

Chris looked at this for a moment trying to digest the meaning. He was already online? How was that possible? Thinking back, he recalled logging into his e-mail account at the Syracuse library within the past hour. Had he failed to log out of his account? It was the only possible explanation, and he found himself cursing his forgetfulness.

Rather than drive the hour-long round trip to the library, Chris picked up his cell phone and called the university switchboard. They connected him to the reference desk, which was located near the computer bank. He spoke to a computer-savvy librarian, who volunteered to check the workstation that Chris had used that afternoon. She was back on the phone within three minutes.

"Yes, honey, someone was on that machine, but he wasn't online. He was only looking up periodicals in our extended database. I even went online and pulled up the Yahoo! e-mail logon screen to see if you had accidentally asked the computer to remember your password. You hadn't, so you should be safe."

Chris thanked the librarian, and then returned to his computer, dismissing the incident. He selected "Yes" to log on, and then opened his e-mail. After taking care of his business, he logged off and called it an evening. It had been an eventful week.

CHAPTER 11

July 23, 2012

Normal people are still in bed at seven. That was the thought running through Sean's mind as he maneuvered his tan 1966 Mercedes-Benz 250S along US Route 20, which would become Madison Avenue in Albany. Keeping his appointment with the curator of the NY State Museum meant setting his alarm clock for an hour that he considered to be obscene.

Taking a chance, he pulled into the small parking lot near the side of the museum, which was normally full by that hour. However, Lady Luck was on his side this morning, as he immediately noticed an SUV pulling out of a parking space. He parked, jumped out of the antique car, and inserted his key into the trunk. Inside the cavernous compartment sat the plastic box with the rifle stock and the cup.

Sean entered the main lobby of the museum and looked up at the massive skeleton of the woolly mammoth that dominated the room. The sheer size of these prehistoric behemoths never failed to astound him, and he often wondered about the environment in which they lived.

Glancing at his watch, he noticed it was still about ten minutes before he was to meet Dr. Rehnquist. Rather than interrupt the curator before he was due, Sean decided to wander about the first floor of the museum. He strolled through exhibits on the Adirondack logging industry, mining, and the rocks and minerals of New York. He was impressed with the quality of the layout. Like most state residents who lived within driving range, he had never taken the time to visit the facility.

By the time he walked back to the lobby, it was almost nine-thirty, so he decided to head up to the second floor to find Dr. Rehnquist. Sean used the main elevator, stopping at the next level. He followed the signs to the Administrative Office and Curator and soon found himself inside a brightly-lit central area, surrounded by a lot of cubicle-style offices with glass partitions that extended to the ceiling. Several office workers walked past him from various directions, although no one seemed particularly interested in determining his identity or destination. He managed to attract the attention of one female administrator who directed him to a section of offices on the other side of the hallway. There, he found a small office with a plain nameplate on the door that read "S. Rehnquist."

Sean knocked on the door, prompting a monotone "hello" from the other side. He pushed the door open and peered into the room, where a balding middle-aged man sat behind a desk that was loaded with papers and files. The doctor looked up at Sean through black frame bifocal glasses, his face devoid of any emotion.

"Dr. Rehnquist?" asked Sean.

"Yes, that would be me," said the man, again without changing expression.

"Hi. My name is Sean Riggins. I had an appointment to see you. I hope I'm not disturbing you?"

The doctor looked at Sean for a full five seconds without saying a word. He then looked at his wristwatch, then back at Sean.

"I'm sorry. I didn't have this on my schedule. Did you speak with me personally?"

"No sir, my friend, Chris Carey, called last week and set this up. I'm sorry for the confusion."

Dr. Rehnquist didn't look as though he appreciated the intrusion, but he still managed a polite response.

"I have a meeting with the exhibits specialists in a half hour. But I can spare a few minutes, if that's all you need. What can I do for you?"

Sean smiled and nodded his thanks as he moved into the office and placed the plastic box onto the curator's desk.

"I have a couple of items that are pretty old, and I'd like to find out when they were produced and used. I heard that you are a specialist on old Americana and that you might be able to enlighten me on their origin." As he spoke, he lifted the lid of the container and exposed the wooden stock and the drinking cup.

Dr. Rehnquist never batted an eyelid as he reached into the box and lifted the cup to eye level. Before he even had a chance to examine it, he asked Sean where the items had been obtained.

"My friend's great-grandfather was given both of these by a hermit who lived in the Adirondack Mountains. But we don't know where that individual obtained them, or whether they had originally belonged to him or not."

"A hermit?" repeated the doctor, sounding as though he needed to confirm what he had just heard.

"Yes, Sir. Actually, I guess it would be more accurate to say that he was an early woodsman in the Adirondacks."

"Would you happen to know when this man lived?" asked Dr. Rehnquist, his hands examining the upper and lower lips of the vessel, "perhaps a period of years that I could work with?"

"We know that he died in 1915," replied Sean. "We don't know when he was born. I'm not sure that anyone does. We do know that he lived in the central Adirondack region for about forty years, from around 1870-something to 1915. Sorry I can't be more precise than that."

The doctor fell silent again, still looking closely at various aspects of the cup.

"One thing I can tell you for sure is that this wasn't new when your hermit friend got it."

"You mean it probably pre-dates Louie?" said Sean.

"Louie?" asked Dr. Rehnquist, looking up over his glasses.

"I'm sorry. Louie is the name of the hermit who gave my friend's ancestor these items."

"Yes, I'm certain of that," replied the doctor. "This cup is a nice but very common example of the simple drinking vessels used during the Revolutionary War. Actually, they were used in this country from the middle 1700s right up through the 1820s. The cups were easy and inexpensive to make, and they were issued to almost all foot soldiers throughout the war. There are a lot of variations on the theme, but most of them are relatively similar, with the straight sides and the simple handle attached by a pair of rivets. Also notice the rolled lip on the top, which protected the soldier's lip from the sharp edge of the cut metal. Sometimes they just made a simple hem on top by folding the metal down around the rim and pressing it flat."

"What metal is this made from?" asked Sean, pointing to the interior surface of the cup. "It's a different color on the outside than it is inside."

"That's the standard construction of the day," replied Dr. Rehnquist. "The body of the cup is made of copper, although the inside is lined with tin. There's nothing unusual about this one, although it's a nice example of the soldiers' everyday mess gear."

The doctor returned the cup to the box and lifted out the rifle stock. He moved in for a very close look at the wood, examining the grain through the bottom of his bifocals.

"Did this come from the same place as the cup?" asked the curator, still making observations of the weathered surface.

"Yes, it came from the same person," replied Sean. "We don't know the circumstances, but it's possible that they were both stored in a cave for many years."

"A cave?" said Dr. Rehnquist, his eyebrows moving up his forehead. It was the first sign of emotion he had displayed since Sean had entered the office.

"Yes, Sir, according to the notes we have from my friend's great-grandfather, although we can't be sure, because no one seems to know where this cave might be. I know it's a rather convoluted story, but we're trying to get it sorted out. That's why we wanted to see you."

The doctor took another minute with the stock, rotating it lengthwise as he made a series of silent observations. He then set it back into the container with the cup.

"Do you know what it is?" asked Sean.

"Yes, but I'm afraid that the answer probably isn't as exciting as your story that goes with it. It appears to be the stock off a British muzzle-loader known as a Brown Bess, which was the most common long gun of its day. It was first produced in 1722 and used throughout most wars right up into the 1830s. There was supposedly even one used in the Civil War. It's a very common gun, as millions of them were made."

"So it was used by the British against the American colonists?" asked Sean.

"Actually, the gun was sold to many different countries, and it ended up in the hands of the colonists as well. So they probably ended up in skirmishes where both sides were using the same weapon."

"Is there any way to determine how old this particular piece is?" asked Sean.

"No, only to say that is was probably manufactured sometime during the middle of the 1700s. Also, I can tell you that this stock was exposed to the elements for a very long time. The wood is extremely weathered. Normally, the walnut grain retains its deep color better than this piece. Chances are it was either discarded at the time of a battle, or perhaps lost when its owner was killed. Whichever, it likely sat outside for a number of years."

Sean twisted uncomfortably in his seat. He wanted to obtain more information regarding the age of the items, but the doctor seemed unable or unwilling to provide this information.

"So, Dr. Rehnquist, would you say that these two items might possibly have been used by the same person, at the same time, perhaps during the middle of the Revolutionary War?"

"That's a distinct possibility. But it's not something that I could state with any assurance. You see, whenever you have two such common items that were used over such a lengthy period of history, it becomes pure speculation as to whether they 'co-existed' at any given date. Yes, they may have. But either one may have been in use as early as 1720, and as late as 1830. I'm afraid that's the best I can give you."

Sean nodded his head, realizing that the two relics would be of little use in their ongoing search. He stood up to go, and thanked the doctor for his assistance. Without asking, he helped himself to a business card from the man's desk. He then extended his arm to offer a handshake, but the doctor was already reading the next paper on his desk.

Back in Syracuse, Chris was having a much different kind of day. More of a morning person than Sean, he arose with the first rays of sunlight, and was out the door running by seven. He poked fun at Sean whenever he could because of his friend's late nights and even later mornings.

Chris returned from his run forty-five minutes later, then showered and sat down for a quick breakfast. He poured a glass of milk over a bowl of cereal, only to find that the milk had gone sour over the previous week. Instead, he settled for a frozen bagel and a glass of orange juice.

He quickly booted his computer and logged in to his e-mail account. However, before he could open any of the new correspondence in his Inbox, an Instant Messenger window appeared asking him whether he wanted to reply to a message from dr_galloway_cornell. Normally, Chris would shun instant messages from unknown senders, as most of them were spam. But he quickly accepted this one because it sounded as though it was from a member of the Cornell faculty.

The conversation developed rapidly:

chriscarey1986: Who are you?
dr_galloway_cornell: This is Dr. Gene Galloway,
Anthropology Department at Cornell. My associate Dr. Meyers
gave me your email. Good morning.
chriscarey1986: Good morning, doctor.

dr_galloway_cornell: Dr. Meyers told me he provided you with search tips for Adirondack caves.

chriscarey1986: True. We've been trying to get in to explore, but schedule was pushed back. We should be going in soon. What is your interest in this?

dr_galloway_cornell: My focus is the Six Tribes of the Iroquois Nation. I'm trying to find evidence of early Indian use of caves in New York State.

chriscarey1986: Sounds interesting.

dr_galloway_cornell: Which site do you plan to search first?

chriscarey1986: South-Central Adirondacks; West Canada Lakes region.

dr_galloway_cornell: That's a big area. Could you narrow that down a bit?

chriscarey1986: I'll know more after today. Going to Adirondack Museum to chase a few leads. Could I get back to you next week?

dr_galloway_cornell: Certainly. I appreciate the assistance.

chriscarey1986: Thank you. Nice chatting. Take care.

dr_galloway_cornell: You too. Bye.

After answering a few more e-mails, Chris shut down his computer and pushed his feet into a pair of Docksiders. He planned on a slow and leisurely drive up to Blue Mountain Lake, which should take him about three hours. Assuming that he stopped for lunch, he should be able to make it to the museum by one.

Chris's estimation was only off by about fifteen minutes, his drive slowed by the traffic in Old Forge and the other resort villages. Upon arriving he went directly to the museum office. There, he was greeted by a receptionist who used a digital pager to contact the curator.

Deborah Santori appeared within three minutes, neatly adorned in a red and white summer dress and a wide-brimmed straw hat. She greeted Chris enthusiastically and offered him a drink before they moved back into the research library. When she asked Chris if he was only interested in French Louie or whether he wanted to see material on the many other famous woodsmen and loggers who appeared throughout their collections, Chris had to mentally replay their conversation of the previous week to accurately remember his own story.

"Thanks, Debbie, but I think for today I'll just focus on Louis Seymour. If I get through everything you have on him, I might move on to some of the other famous names of the day. And I'd love to see a complete listing of your logging exhibit material, even if we'd never have a chance to see it."

Debbie laughed as she motioned for Chris to walk through a back doorway.

"You have no idea about the extent of our collections," she said. "We've been open for about sixty years, and still we're given new items every year. Books, diaries, town records, artifacts; it seems to come out of the woodwork. I'm already about three years behind in processing new acquisitions, and it's coming in faster than we can handle it."

As they talked, they walked along a paved pathway that took them to a main building, which was located behind and to the left of the visitor's center. This building housed not only the Lynn Boillot and Living with Wilderness Art Galleries, but also the photographic collections and research library. A separate area of the building that was not open to the public also served as the museum's warehouse and storage facility.

"In addition to the documents, would I be able to see some of Louie's actual possessions, including any articles that were brought to you from his various camps?"

"We could arrange that, assuming that I could locate all of it at one time. Some of it may be spread across a few different storage rooms. We'll see how much time we have."

The curator brought Chris into a temperature- and humidity-controlled room and showed him to a wide work table that already held a stack of books and periodicals of related materials, with pages flagged indicating references to the famous hermit. Chris was able to leaf through those documents quite quickly, as none of them would contain anything that would help them on the search.

"How about any of the maps and drawings that Louie made himself?" he asked. "Do you have any of those documents that might have come directly out of Louie's cabin?"

"As a matter of fact, we do, and some of those are stored right here inside this very room. Let me see what we've got."

Debbie tapped a few keys on a reference computer and printed out a listing of all items under "French Louie" and "Seymour." Then she moved to a file cabinet about halfway down the aisle and opened a heavy metal drawer. From inside, she removed two thick files and an old metal box. These items she placed on the table in front of her visitor.

"OK, now you remember the rules. The Disclosure Agreement you signed states that you may not remove any documents from this library and that you must have our permission to make copies of anything in the collection. If you decide that you do desire copies, you will let me know, and I will produce them for you. There will be a nominal fee for copies, which you will pay before leaving. You understand?"

"I understand. Thank you," replied Chris. "I'll try to get through these within an hour or two so that I'll have time to look at some of his other belongings."

"OK, I'll be in the adjoining office if you need anything. Good luck."

The curator left Chris alone in the room with the folders and the metal box. He knew these documents had already been viewed by many other people; however, none of those prior viewers were looking for the same clues regarding a link to a past treasure, so he wasn't certain what he'd find. As far as he could tell, no one outside of his family besides the mysterious W.J. Harrison knew anything about a hidden stash in the Adirondacks.

Chris started with the first folder, which was packed full of original documents from the early days of Louie's time in the West Canada Lakes region. Much of it appeared to be mail, which he had saved in his cabin for some unknown reason. Since Louie could not read, he may have kept everything that was sent to him, reasoned Chris, in case it was needed at a later date. Some of these letters were from hunters wishing to secure his services as a guide, while others were from tanneries with which Louie conducted fur and hide business. Nothing inside the cardboard folder was of particular use.

The second folder contained more correspondence, including a couple of wonderful photographs of Louie that had been made into postcards. A hand-drawn map in Louie's own primitive style attracted Chris's attention momentarily, although he quickly deduced that it was used to denote the positions of traps on a winter trap line. Within forty minutes, he had finished emptying out the second folder.

The last item on the desk was the metal box, which once contained hard candies. It was a rather plain design, except for the painted name and logo on the top cover. Chris noticed that the advertising print had been mostly worn off the lid, indicating that it had seen significant use after the original contents had been emptied.

He used his thumbs to pry the cover off the box then set it aside and pulled out the stack of papers from inside. They were similar to those inside the first two folders in appearance, with pages of different sizes and shapes arranged in random fashion. However, several of the top pages were maps from Louie's personal collection. This is what Chris was hoping to find, and he examined each one in minute detail. As his grandfather had told him, Louie had a unique method for representing lakes and other geographic features. All bodies of water were drawn as round shapes, and each was the same size as the next. He reviewed each map to determine whether any unusual notations appeared that could indicate something out of the ordinary, such as a cave or some other "find." He found maps covering the Indian River, the West Canada Creek, and the Moose River, but none of these contained anything unexpected.

Underneath the aforementioned maps was another cartographic representation that was labeled "Otter Brook" in pencil. Chris wondered who had labeled this map, because the handwriting was neat, even ornate. The map was folded in half over a stack of about a dozen very worn and yellowed pages. These papers had obviously been exposed to water at some point, as the ink on the front page was somewhat smudged. The pages that were behind the front leaf were in worse condition, and a few of the sheets were stuck together. They made an audible crackling sound as he unfolded and flattened them on the table.

As Chris's eyes scanned down the page, he felt his heart begin to flutter. The first thing that caught his attention was a line that appeared on the top right corner of the document. It read, "Property of William J. Harrison." The handwriting looked identical to the writing that appeared on the map from his great-grandfather. The rest of the front page contained entries of what looked like a diary.

> May 26—departed Red Barn at first light. Bid farewell to Robert and Rose. Each with our share of the metals, we did commence our journey. Ours west, theirs north. Went we with Godspeed. Traveled first south, over Skenes Road. Avoided fort, observed soldiers on trail to lake.

Chris looked at that entry long and hard. Unfortunately, there was no year recorded on the entries, only months and dates. But yet the names seemed so familiar: Robert and Rose. There were no last names given, but Robert and Rose...so familiar.

> May 27—attained southernmost point of Lake Champlain, began journey northward and west. Must locate shallows to cross Hudson and gain woodlands for protection. Guides leading up to promised crossing.

Chris followed the log entry to the bottom of the page, where it concluded with an abbreviated signature: "T. Swain," a name that Chris did not recognize.

Chris gently teased the next couple of pages away from one another, cautious not to rip the aged fiber as he lifted one sheet from the next. Much of the writing was blurred, and some of it was completely illegible. He was able to discern the signature of T. Swain on two more pages, after which the handwriting appeared to switch dramatically; it seemed the second half of the recordings were made by a different person than those in front. The final three pages of the stack were irretrievably affixed to one another.

There was something else that Chris noticed about this document. There was a separate set of notations recorded down the right margin of each page. It was in a different color ink, and it stood out as though it was written considerably later than the original writing. Each of these notes provided a simple distance in miles and a direction, which Chris guessed was a summary for the travelogue of that day. By comparing these figures with the handwriting, Chris concluded that they were written by William J. Harrison.

So far, the ledgers appeared to raise more questions than they answered. Exactly what event did this record document? Chris could not tell, yet he couldn't dispel the notion in his mind that this was a key piece of the puzzle. What were "the metals" that were carried by this man Swain, and who were Robert and Rose? Also, Chris knew that the "Red Barn" was an important setting but he couldn't recall from where.

Rather than call attention to the document by asking for a copy, Chris decided to play it safe. He quietly lifted his cell phone from his packet and used it to snap off a quick series of photos of the front three pages. They wouldn't be as high resolution as he would have liked, but they would suffice for his purposes.

The bottom few documents in the tin box were letters to Louie from a logging firm, asking him to serve as fire warden in the area around the West Canadas. Chris quickly placed these and the rest of the stack of papers, including the ledgers from T. Swain, back into the box and replaced the lid. In order to disguise his intent, Chris decided to ask the curator for copies of a couple letters from the first folder. Meanwhile, the important discovery of the day was re-interred inside its original container, perhaps never to be viewed again.

As Deborah made the copies, Chris jotted down a few notes in his pad and looked at a map of the museum. His next task was to see if the museum held any clues in the form of items that had come from Louie's cabin.

"There you go," said the curator as she placed the photocopies of the letters in front of Chris. I hope these help. Before you leave, I'll have to collect the fee for the copies, which is a whopping seventy cents. Think you can afford that?"

"It might be tough, but I think I can scrape up that much cash."

Chris pulled out his wallet and extracted a twenty dollar bill.

"As a matter of fact, please keep the change and donate it to your wonderful facility. This has been very helpful."

"My, my," said the surprised curator. "We need to have you come by more often! Is there anything else I can offer you?"

"As a matter of fact, there is," said Chris, taking advantage of his host's offer. "I'd love to see anything else that you might have of Louie's, unless it's already on display. You mentioned that you have a few of his things in your storage facility?"

Debbie nodded and looked down at the document she had printed from her computer search. Louie's possessions took up a full page on the printout, although many of the items were stored in the logging exhibit on the other side of the museum grounds.

"We have two pallets of items removed from his cabin inside the storage warehouse in this building. We also have several of his tools, including things like axes, wedges, saws, and log peelers over in another building. Which would you like to see first?"

"Could I start with the pallets you have in this building?" asked Chris. Then we could move across to the other building if we have time."

Debbie held up her wrist and looked at her watch.

"That might be getting a little tight. It's close to three already, and we close at five. Also, I've got a meeting with our director at three-thirty, so I won't be able to stay with you long. But I'll let one of the other staffers know that you're looking at some things, so you should have at least an hour before we start packing up for the day."

"That's very kind of you, Debbie. Thank you for everything you've done for me. I'll make sure to acknowledge your contributions in the book credits."

"That's OK. It goes with the territory. Just remember that everything I have from Louie's exhibit is at least one hundred years old, so please treat it gently. Nothing here can be replaced."

"I promise to treat it with kid gloves," said Chris.

Deborah led the way past the reference library and through a heavy locked door. She then used a key to open yet another door which led into a large, darkened room. Once she turned on the light switch, a long row of overhead fluorescent bulbs illuminated a neatly organized but very full warehouse. Row after row of pallets was stretched out in linear fashion. A heavy-gauged metal shelving system allowed the materials to be stacked to a height of eight feet, which greatly increased the capacity of the warehouse.

The section containing Louie's belongings was located at the far end of the room. The two pallets of materials were sitting on the floor, side by side. Chris was glad to see this, because he didn't know how he could have effectively searched a pallet that was stored on the second shelf.

"As you can see, each pallet has an inventory list, so please make sure you replace everything where you found it. Otherwise, we may not be able to locate it again for years."

Chris thanked Deborah for her time, after which she departed for her meeting. He then dug in, lifting artifacts from the first pallet and examining each one by one. Several of the first boxes contained outdoor clothes, which were all in extremely poor condition. Ragged and worn, Chris could hardly picture anyone still using garments such as these for anything but rags. Although he felt self-conscious doing so, he felt through each of the pockets, looking for anything that might have been overlooked by the museum curators. He came up empty each time.

The remaining boxes on the pallet contained cooking utensils, glassware, and other items that came from Louie's pantry. None of these would provide any clues to his secrets, so Chris carefully repacked the boxes and moved on to the second pallet.

Looking over the inventory list attached to the front box, Chris noticed a few items of historical interest in this portion of the collection. He looked at a knife that Louie had used to skin the mink and otter from his trap lines. It thrilled him to know that he was holding a piece of Adirondack history in his hands.

The back half of the second pallet was taken up by a large wooden chest. It was very old, covered with marks and gouges from being transported on rickety horse-drawn wagons. Chris noticed that the chest had its own inventory list taped to the top cover. Since the top of the chest would not open without hitting the upper shelf, he had to pull the entire pallet out from the storage bin. After doing so, he was able to open the cover and fully view the contents of the chest.

The first thing that Chris noticed was a heavy medicinal smell. Louie was known to have had homemade remedies inside his cabin, and several of the bottles containing these were saved within this collection. Also inside the wooden container were two heavy woolen blankets, a pack basket, a kerosene lamp, and a few old editions of *Field and Stream* magazine. He also found a strange, unusual article: a cigar box which had served as the base for a makeshift fiddle. Chris wondered if Louie had made that device himself. Absentmindedly, he plucked a string or two and was surprised to find that it was capable of producing a musical note.

Working as quickly as possible, Chris continued unpacking the chest while checking off the items against the list on the pallet. It matched completely. When Chris reached the bottom of the chest, every item on the inventory card had been accounted for. There were no surprises, and every item was exactly as described. It was disappointing, although Chris knew that the document he had discovered earlier was, in itself, worth the time and effort spent to make this trip. It provided one more link between W.J. Harrison, who was seeking the treasure, and French Louie. Chris only wished he had some proof that Harrison wasn't just another delusional treasure-seeker with a case of gold fever. In other words, there was no proof that any gold existed other than the words in the fables of folklore.

Chris rested on one knee, his arm on the top edge of the open chest. The overhead lights provided a shadowless view of the inside of the large container, which Louie had probably inherited from one of the logging camps. The inside was constructed of horizontal side boards which were attached to horizontal struts. The bottom boards were sturdy planks which were wider than the side boards, and slightly darker in color. Chris wondered whether perhaps they were added later, to shore up the strength of the chest bottom. He reached down and felt the edge of one of these boards, which was about a half-inch thick. When he did so, he was surprised to feel it slide back and forth under the pressure of his grasp.

His curiosity aroused, Chris reached underneath the board and pulled it to the center of the chest. After doing so, he was able to lift it up and away from the lower surface. This exposed the other bottom plank, which it overlapped to cover the rest of the chest bottom. He repeated the process, pulling up the second board, beneath which lay the original bottom spars of the chest.

What Chris saw took his breath away. There, between two of the rotting original ribs of the chest, lay two coins which glittered like the day they were minted. They were large, and gold, and extremely beautiful. He lifted them out of the chest and examined them, one by one, first the front, then the back. They were identical in almost every regard. The front of the coins depicted the bust of a man who was obviously royalty, most likely a king. The name, which appeared on the left side of the subject's face, read "Carol III." He wore long hair that was pulled back, with locks that hung well below his ornate collar. Chris also noticed that he had a curving, beak-like nose that rendered his facial features somewhat comical. The writing on the front appeared to be in Spanish. The back of the coin was a heavily patterned shield or crest, with a crown on top and more Spanish inscriptions around the edge. The outside of the coin was thickly rimmed on both front and back. The year 1773 appeared on the bottom of the front side.

Chris realized immediately that the coins had been hidden beneath the planks, most likely by Louie, long before the chest had been brought to the museum. He also knew that the museum staff must never have known about the existence of the coins, or they would have caused an uproar from treasure seekers everywhere.

He sat there on his knees, wondering what to do next. The logical and honest thing to do would be to call the curator immediately and point out the new discovery. However, Chris knew that that would almost certainly spell the end of their quest to find the answer to this mystery. He could not simply hand over the two gold coins without stirring up a hornets' nest of public interest in the lost gold. He also knew that the scenario had changed. Somewhere, somehow, Louie had become mixed up in the search for a load of gold from an earlier day. And from the looks of things, he had probably located it.

Chris pulled out his cell phone and used the camera to snap two photos showing the coins resting in the bottom of the chest. Then, he quickly palmed the coins inside his right hand while he pulled a handkerchief from his rear pocket. He folded the coins, one at a time, into the material so they wouldn't jangle against one another. Then, he pushed the handkerchief back into his pocket, all within a span of fifteen seconds. He promised himself to return the coins after he could have them identified, knowing that they would have to remain in his possession until their search was complete. He felt little remorse in the deception, since the museum never knew of their existence.

It took Chris ten minutes to reinsert the bottom boards into the trunk and fold and replace the remaining blankets and other articles. By the time he heard footsteps approaching, he had cleaned up the area and pushed the pallet back into its original position beneath the metal racks.

The footsteps belonged to a young male assistant, who had been asked by Deborah to make sure that the visiting researcher had finished his work and exited the archives before closing time. The fellow, who introduced himself as Dave, asked if Chris had found what he needed.

"Yes, it's been a very helpful day," replied Chris. "I've learned a lot about French Louie's life and times. I should be able to use a lot of this in the book I'm writing."

"That's great. I'm glad your time here was well spent. And now, please follow me and I'll walk you back to the gate."

Chris exited the museum gates and walked back to his Jeep, all the while refraining from an outward show of glee. The trip had provided more than he ever dreamed. He now knew that a cache of gold almost certainly did exist, and that Louie had somehow had his hands on it, or at least part of it. Now he was ready to tackle the rest of the riddle.

After sitting down in the driver's seat, Chris pulled out his cell phone and dialed Sean's number. He let it ring five times until it was finally answered by his machine. Unlike many people who have "cute" messages announcing their absence, Sean's simply said: "This is Sean. I'm not here, so leave a message and I'll call you back."

"Hey, Chris here. I just wanted to find out if you've had a chance to do a search on that guy Harrison yet. Oh, and by the way, W.J. Harrison is William J. Harrison. I don't know if that will buy us anything, but at least it's a little more to go by. Oh, and one other favor I'd like to ask of you. I have a couple of names for you to check out: 'A. Smith' and 'T. Swain.' You can try running them through on your online search programs, but I doubt you'll find anything there. These were minor figures who were involved somehow with Robert Gordon and his money. Maybe you could contact the Skenesborough Museum or the Washington County Archives Department and have them check the register of local names from 1774 to

1777. My guess is they'd turn up there somewhere. OK, I'll probably be getting back late tonight, so let's touch base tomorrow morning and compare notes. Talk to you then."

Chris pressed the disconnect button to end the call, and then inspected the traffic on the busy stretch of Route 30 outside the museum. Ensuring that the road was free of oncoming traffic, he turned the wheel and made a sweeping U-turn that faced the vehicle downhill. The excitement of the afternoon's discoveries coursed through his veins, and he mentally plotted out his next course of action. There was so much to do now that he knew that the legend was genuine. He couldn't wait to get together with Sean and show him the coins. The suspense was almost overwhelming.

As he rolled down the steep hill into the village of Blue Mountain Lake, Chris decided to stop for a quick bite to eat. He hadn't had much for lunch, and his stomach was growling audibly inside the compartment of the vehicle. He hadn't had a very active day, but the nervous tension had revved up his system and put his digestive tract into overdrive. A shop advertising submarine sandwiches attracted his attention, and he quickly pulled into the parking lot.

Chris asked for his sandwich and drink to go, got back into his Jeep, and headed south of town a short way. When he found a parking lot with a scenic view of the lake, he pulled in and got out of the vehicle, taking along the bag with his food. The rest stop had picnic tables, so he sat down to eat while watching the sunlight of the early evening ripple on the wavelets of the lake. He always found that the sound of water lapping against a shoreline enabled him to better think through a problem.

While consuming his roast beef sub, Chris suddenly had an idea about the drive back to Syracuse. On his way south, he could stop in and see his college buddy, Eddie Griffith, who lived in the town of Boonville. Eddie had been another one of Chris's teammates on the Syracuse lacrosse team, and the two had grown to be friends over the course of the two years they spent together on the field. He had even moved into Chris' house for a short period while looking for an apartment in the city. They had kept in touch via e-mail, although they rarely had the chance to visit.

Chris found Eddie's number on his phone directory and pressed the "Call" button. It rang about five times before a voice came on the line.

"Griff's Auto, Griff speaking." Eddie had taken over his father's automotive repair and body shop business and had never bothered getting a second phone line for his residence. Every call was answered using the business greeting, which drove his family crazy.

Chris spoke without introducing himself.

"Hello, I have a special paint job I'd like you to do for me. I'd like to swing by in about an hour, and I'd like you to paint my Jeep a bright shade of pink. Could you do that before closing time today?"

"Chris! How the heck are you?" Eddie boomed over the phone. "Of course—I'll paint your Jeep pink, if that's what you want. Come on up!"

Chris was flattered by the enthusiasm of his friend's response.

"Actually, I'm about an hour north of you, in Blue Mountain Lake. I'm heading south, right past your place. I could be there in an hour, if you have a little time to spare for your kid brother." It was an inside joke, as Eddie was two years older than Chris, a fact that he harped on as he did his best to make Eddie feel old. He had even gone as far as sending him a bottle of geriatric supplements one year at Christmas.

"Sure, swing by. I'd love to see you and show you some of the changes we've made around here in the past two years. Plus, I've gotta show you something you won't believe."

"What's that," asked Chris, "another picture of you scoring that goal against Johns Hopkins?"

"No, it's even better. Well, maybe not better, but certainly more valuable," said Eddie. "I've got a 1949 De Soto DeLuxe 'Woody' in the shop for some detail work. It's to die for. It still looks like it rolled off the line yesterday, and it's got most of the original parts. The owner shows it all over the country."

"Sweet," said Chris. "You ought to buy it."

"Not unless I can find six figures of bills in my dresser drawer anytime soon," said Eddie. "Anyway, it's inside the shop. I'll show you when you get here. Ciao!"

Chris took his time finishing the rest of his supper before loading himself back into his aged vehicle. It took him almost exactly an hour to motor down the winding pavement of Route 28, through Raquette Lake and Inlet, before turning right at the tiny hamlet of Woodgate. From there, it was less than ten miles across Hawkinsville Road to the junction of Route 12, which he followed into Boonville. His friend's shop was on Ford Street, on the back end of the tiny town.

Chris pulled down the small driveway that ended in front of the old, white building housing the auto business. Eddie was out of the house and alongside the Jeep before Chris had time to turn off the engine. A great big bear of a man, Eddie stood a shade over six foot six, towering over his friend. He had put on a bit of weight since his college sports days, and his imposing frame would have appeared menacing on a less friendly person.

The two shook hands, and Chris patted Eddie's growing stomach through the open car window. "Looks like the auto business doesn't cut into your dinner hour, does it?" he asked jokingly.

"Yeah, I've got to admit that I'd hate to have to do one of our full-length workouts today," said Eddie, pulling his friend from the front seat. "It seems like the business keeps me going twenty-four hours a day. I hardly have time for exercise at the end of the day. So tell me, what brings you by here like this in the middle of the work week? You working some kind of sales job?"

Chris explained that he was interviewing for jobs while also chasing down a story about the famous Adirondack woodsman. He told Eddie about his day up at the museum in Blue Mountain Lake, although he prudently left out the part about the gold. He felt no need to disclose that information to anyone but Sean.

Eddie took Chris into the garage and showed him the equipment he'd purchased to upgrade his father's business. He was trying to expand the operations of the auto shop by providing a greater range of services, while also using a radio advertising campaign to publicize their facility. It appeared to be working, as he'd already had to hire two new employees to keep up with the increased business.

"Look at this," Eddie said as he swung open a wide door to a rear area of the garage. "Feast your eyes!"

Behind the gate was the sparkling DeSoto, its front chrome grillwork glittering underneath the lights of the garage. Chris was amazed at the luxurious finish of the wood-grained doors, as well as the quality of the newly refinished interior upholstery. He had never seen an antique classic refurbished so completely. "This looks even better than new," he exclaimed.

"In some ways, it is better than new," said Eddie. "The inside has been refinished with leather upholstery that wasn't part of the original package. The owner has also added some nice touches of his own, such as refinishing the woodwork and adding halogen lamps to the front end. It's hard to believe that this car sold for $2,959 in 1949, but you'd have to pay about forty times that much to buy it today."

"Is it particularly rare?" asked Chris.

"Oh, yes," replied Eddie. "DeSoto stopped making 'Woodies' in 1950. There were only 850 produced. Of that, there are fewer than a dozen survivors, probably none nicer than the one you're looking at now. I wasn't kidding when I told you that it would cost over 100K to buy this thing. And that's if the owner would sell it."

"I take it he's not exactly on food stamps, then?" said Chris.

Eddie rolled his eyes. "No. Not even close. He owns half the dry cleaning businesses in eastern New York."

After turning out the lights, Eddie locked the garage, and the two friends went into the house. They talked for a couple of hours, looking at pictures from the old days and laughing over each other's stories. Before Chris knew it, it was past ten and time to depart.

After saying goodnight to one another and promising to meet at year's end for dinner, Chris climbed back into his Jeep and pulled out of the yard. It was late, and he had the better part of two hours driving left ahead of him.

He drove through the quiet streets of Boonville without seeing a soul. The sleepy town, as with many small villages, tended to roll up its sidewalks soon after dark. The local roads were similarly devoid of auto traffic. A quick jog to the left, then another to the right took him to the junction of Route 12, where he turned south. From Boonville to Alder Creek, where the road merged back into the larger Route 28, was barely six miles.

He almost made it.

About a half mile before the merge point, a small road entered Route 12 from the left. Chris's attention was drawn down that street when a large deer appeared out of nowhere and sprinted across the road directly ahead of the Jeep. Chris jammed on the brake and swerved to the right, narrowly missing the animal's hind quarters. However, he never had a chance to breathe a sigh of relief, as two smaller does dashed out of the same thicket of trees and brush, following the buck.

This time, the collision was unavoidable. Chris made a valiant attempt to again steer clear, turning the wheel even further to the right. However, he had been doing fifty-five miles per hour before hitting the brakes, and he was still registering over forty when the second deer smashed against the front grill of the Jeep. Unable to control the skid, Chris felt the vehicle veer off the road and wildly bounce over a large log, sending it careening towards the woods at a sharp angle. The wheels on the right side of the Jeep were completely off the ground by the time the front corner of the hood smashed into the first tree. The vehicle ricocheted off the trunk and plowed through another row of saplings before ramming straight-on into a white birch tree.

The sound of breaking glass and twisting metal seemed to take a long time to subside. Then, all was quiet.

CHAPTER 12

Sean had come home from work early. He had made excellent progress in installing the new file servers into an insurance company's headquarters building, and he expected to wrap up the following morning. He knew that he should probably hire a few other people to work with him so that he could avoid the crazy hours. But he reveled in being a one man show, with no one to count on but himself.

He walked in the door of his course-side shack in time to catch the end of the late news, which he watched while devouring an oversized burger from the corner fast food joint. It wasn't his idea of a good meal, but he wasn't in the mood for cooking, so he settled for easy.

Noticing that the message light on his phone was blinking, he pressed the button and listened to his calls. Chris's was the only message on his recorder, as most of his business clients called him only on his cell. He made a mental note about William J. Harrison's full name, then went back to finish his drink. He had wanted to get started on the Internet search for Chris over the weekend, but he hadn't found the time to do so. The only time he had found himself with a spare moment was on Saturday afternoon, but then Maggie appeared in his small back yard, looking very official in her course-owned golf cart, with a foursome of cold beer bottles. They killed the next two hours making small talk and watching an array of golfers find the sand traps beside the eleventh hole.

After finishing the last of his meal, Sean settled into the swivel chair in front of his computer. He accessed a number of his favorite web-search tools and prepared to commence his hunt. A scrap of paper next to the monitor held the name W.J. Harrison, with the first name William scratched on top in red ink.

Instead of relying on a simple search utility, Sean preferred to use his knowledge of multiple applications and Boolean operands to increase his flexibility and number of "hits." He started with the names W.J. Harrison and William J. Harrison, and worked outward. He then added the words "Adirondack," "cave," "gold," and "treasure" in various combinations, each time testing and comparing the returns. His queries returned thousands of results, most of which he could quickly discredit due to the location of events or the age of the subject.

After reading a few of the more interesting search results, Sean tapped into a database that tracked the ancestry of millions of people in both the U.S. and Canada. He was looking for links between any of the "Harrison" combinations and the descendants of anyone linked to the exploration of treasure in New York State. He had created a spreadsheet that listed all of the famous missing treasures over the past three hundred years. He also entered the names of the places across the northern portion of the state where gold or other precious metals were rumored to have been found. Not expecting to find anything, he pressed "Enter" and waited for the results to appear.

The computer flashed up the results of his search in 0.27 seconds. There was but a single listing, which came from a magazine article on treasure hunters of the previous century. The extract from the article read:

> Search for historic silver bullion in Lake Champlain: The search party led by William J. Harrison, of Quebec City, Canada, searched for the chest supposedly left behind by his great-grandfather, Robert Gordon of Skenesborough (now Whitehall, NY), prior to the Revolutionary War. For two weeks in the spring of 1905 the group trolled the shallow waters and swamps west of

Benson and West Haven, Vermont. Nothing was found on the search, which was disbanded permanently in June of the same year."

Sean looked at that paragraph repeatedly, wondering out loud about the particulars. The names were correct, but the location seemed to be wrong. If this was the treasure that Louie had helped to find, how would that explain a search that focused in the swampy waters of a creek between New York and Vermont?

Next, he used a simple Google search for the name "Robert Gordon," which provided insights into the famous merchant of Skenesborough in the 1770s who escaped to Canada after dumping his gold into the lower reaches of Lake Champlain. But…gold. Not silver. Why did the search change from gold to silver, and where was the gold if it wasn't sunken below the waters of the lake?

Sean printed out what he'd found, and then tried a few more searches, all without further success. He also located a slew of articles and references to caves and mines, but none which would be useful in their trek of discovery. Each time he located a reference to an Adirondack cave, it turned out to be either a well known attraction, or a mythical Indian location that was unseen by any white man. Each one ended in a dead end, and Sean eventually grew tired of looking. It was over two hours since Sean had started his search when he finally pushed his chair away from the computer. He rubbed his eyes, which were slightly bloodshot from concentrating on the monitor without the benefit of a break. He was puzzled at the new bits of information, although he felt satisfied with his early progress.

He was about to get up to clean up his trash from dinner when he noticed the icon in his "Contacts" list that indicated that Chris had logged onto his own computer. He decided to send him a quick instant message to report his findings:

Sean-Riggins-IT: Hey Chris. How goes? I had a good day,

although the trip to the museum didn't turn up much. You have time to chat?

Sean waited for a response from his friend, but it never came. As he watched the monitor for another sixty seconds, Chris's name suddenly vanished from the "Contacts" list. He had logged out without responding.

Sean furrowed his brow as he looked at the display. Why hadn't Chris at least dashed off a line or two saying that he'd be back in touch? He must have been in a terrible rush, but yet he knew that Chris wanted to talk to him. He looked up at the clock on the wall and noticed that it was ten thirty-five. Even with a late return, his friend should have been home by now. As a matter of fact, he had to be either home or someplace with computer access.

Rather than wait, he decided to reach Chris on his cell phone. Even if he had just logged off his computer and dashed out of his house, he'd have his cell phone in his car, assuming that's where he was. Sean entered Chris's number and waited for the response.

The phone rang a half dozen times, and then went to his answering machine. This was truly puzzling.

"Hey, Chris, it's me," Sean said to the recorder. "I've got a lot of interesting news and info to pass along, so give me a shout as soon as you can. I know you must be in a hurry, because I saw you log in for a minute tonight and then log right back out. Don't worry about it. Just call me when you can. Later!"

Rather than harp on his inability to reach Chris, Sean decided to take a look at the map his friend had given him. Everything marked on the map was east of Indian Lake, which was in the central part of the Adirondacks. And yet the article he found online said the search by William J. Harrison was conducted entirely inside the narrows of Wood Creek and Lake Champlain. What was the connection? Or was there a connection at all?

Sean folded the map and placed it on the shelf above his desk. After all, if Chris was off having fun somewhere, too busy to answer an instant message, then he couldn't see the urgency either. It could wait until tomorrow.

CHAPTER 13

Chris wasn't sure exactly how long he'd been sitting in the wreck of his Jeep. When he opened his eyes, it was completely dark except for the little bit of moonlight that filtered down through the trees. The engine was off, as were the headlights. Had he turned them off, or had they been broken as the vehicle crashed through the underbrush, he wondered?

For a moment, he couldn't remember how he had ended up parked in the middle of the clump of spruce trees. Then, he remembered the deer and the swerve and the collision with the first tree. That was all he could recall of the accident.

Taking stock of his situation, he realized that the Jeep was still upright, although it appeared as though the front end was wrapped around a large spruce tree about eighteen inches in diameter. He could hear a hissing noise, and he detected a smell of some type of fluid, possibly water escaping from a ruptured radiator. The front windshield was shattered, and bits of glass were scattered across the front seat.

Slowly, Chris began moving his body parts as he checked himself for injuries. He found that he could move his toes, feet, and legs without pain. Likewise, his arms and hands functioned normally, although he found that the back of his right hand was sore and bruised, and the ring finger on the same hand may have been hyper-extended.

It was when he placed his hands on his head that he discovered his biggest concern. There was a spot on the left side of his forehead that was tender, and it felt swollen to the touch. It didn't feel as though there had been any major damage, but it still needed to be checked out. Chris theorized that a defect in the Jeep's old airbag was responsible for the wound. He must have been thrown forward so that his head hit the steering wheel, which probably knocked him out. Or possibly his forehead smashed against his hand, which was what caused his other injury. Regardless, he knew that he wasn't going to drive his vehicle out of there. It was probably totaled.

Chris felt around for his cell phone, which remained clipped to his belt holster. Rather than call 911, he decided to call his friend Eddie first, just to get his bearings. As he pulled the phone out of its holder and flipped it open, he noticed that Sean had called at ten thirty-six. It was listed as a missed call, although he had never heard the phone ring. The time showing on the bottom of the screen was ten forty-two, which meant that he had been unconscious for at least six or seven minutes, and probably longer. He had no feel for the passing of time since he ran off the road. His only sensation was the bruise to his head, accompanied by a slight grogginess as though he'd been awakened from a short nap.

Still sitting in his wrecked vehicle, he punched in Eddie's number from his phone directory list. This time it was Angela, Eddie's wife, who answered the phone. Rather than try to explain anything to her, he simply asked for her husband. His voice came over the phone a moment later.

"Hey, I didn't think I'd hear from you so soon! You must have missed me so much you decided to stay for a few days, right?" Eddie said jokingly.

"Missed you; no, not yet. Stay for a few days; maybe," said Chris. "Any chance you could come and get me? I'm about five or six miles down the road from you."

"Oh no, man, you break down on the road?" asked Eddie. "I could tow you back to the shop and fix you up tonight, depending on what needs fixing. It's probably nothing major."

Chris wasn't sure how to answer that question without alarming his friend, but at the same time it seemed a bit funny, given the circumstances.

"OK, as long as you're going to 'fix me up' tonight, I'll give you a choice. Would you like to start by extracting the deer from my front bumper, or by unwrapping the rest of my car from around this fine spruce tree? It's your choice."

There was a silence on the line, during which Chris could almost hear Eddie trying to determine whether he was kidding.

"Tell me you didn't hit a deer?" Eddie asked.

"I not only hit one, and possibly a second, but I drove my Jeep at fifty miles per hour well into a grove of trees. I'm still in here, and I'm not sure that I can even describe where I am."

"Are you hurt?" asked Eddie, alarm registering in his voice.

"I don't think I suffered anything worse than a few bumps and bruises," answered Chris. "I still haven't moved out of the wreckage, though. I think I blacked out for a while after I hit the tree."

"Hang on while I call the police, and then I'll come to find you," said Eddie, as he put his friend on hold and raced across the kitchen and headed towards the door. He quickly made the emergency call and returned to Chris. "Could you tell me the last thing you saw before you went off the road? That should get me close. Then you can talk me in using our cell phones."

"Well, I was driving along Route 12 heading south, and I was within a mile of Route 28, maybe even closer than that. The last thing I saw, I think, was a road coming into the highway from the left side. It was a smaller road, and it had a pretty good-sized building on the corner; it could have been a school."

"That sounds like Taylor Road," said Eddie, already in his truck. "I'm heading down there now. I shouldn't be more than about ten minutes. Just stay on the phone with me and keep looking for my truck with the big yellow flashing lights on top. Let me know when you see them."

Eddie violated half the motor vehicle laws of the state as he sped through the empty streets of Boonville at twice the speed limit, all while maintaining an open line with Chris. Once he hit Route 12 south of town, he accelerated his big Dodge Ram truck to eighty miles per hour, determined to get to the crash site as quickly as possible. When he was within about a mile of Taylor Road, he turned on his powerful emergency flashers. Within another twenty seconds, he heard his friend's voice again on the phone.

"OK, I think I see you. You're still coming in the right direction, but slow down. You're almost on me," Chris said.

Eddie slowed his vehicle to a crawl and peered into the woods.

"Oh, my...in case you like venison, I've got about 120 pounds of it here on the shoulder for you. And I think I see the back of your Jeep," said Eddie into his phone.

"That's OK. You can keep the deer. Any sign of the police yet?" asked Chris.

"Nope, not yet. But they should be here soon. They've got a substation just about five or six miles south of here, in Remsen, so they won't have far to come. Anyway, just hang on. I'm coming in to get you now."

Chris waited as his friend turned his truck to point his headlights into the woods, illuminating the area around the crash site. Soon, he could hear the sound of heavy footsteps making their way through the undergrowth. They were accompanied by the dancing beam of a powerful hand-held lantern.

"Well, well, we have to stop meeting like this," said Eddie, shining his light into the open front door of the Jeep.

"What took you so long?" asked Chris. "I was about to send out for a pizza."

Eddie chuckled at his friend's irrepressible sense of humor as he surveyed the scene.

"You really weren't kidding when you said you went 'into the woods,' were you? I don't see how you made it as far as you did without hitting another tree. I'd say you were lucky, because you had probably lost a lot of velocity by the time you collided with this one."

"That's OK. I hit pretty hard as it was. I think I wrecked the whole front end."

Eddie looked around the front of the vehicle as they waited for the police and emergency vehicles to arrive.

"I'd have to agree with you, my friend. I can also tell you, as an automotive repair guy, that this vehicle has driven its last mile. The only thing you're going to do with it is let me tow it to the junk heap. I can already see that you've bent the frame, not to mention damaged over half the exterior."

Chris groaned, thinking about the headache involved in purchasing another car. Never mind that the Jeep was held together by rust and duct tape. He had driven it since he got his license. It had become a part of him, and he couldn't picture himself behind the wheel of anything else. He also couldn't afford to buy a car until he had accepted a job and started working.

As he sat there thinking about all of these variables, Chris heard the first distant whine of a siren, which was soon joined by a second. Within a couple minutes, the site was teeming with two state trooper cars, an ambulance, and assorted emergency personnel.

Considering everything that needed to be done, the rescue process went fairly smoothly. A concerned and caring trooper named Sergeant Hinds asked Chris a multitude of questions while the ambulance EMT examined his wounds. They walked on either side of Chris as he was carried out of the woods and into the open back of the ambulance. Chris was adamant about not wanting to go to a hospital, but the officers and EMT insisted.

"At the very least, sir, you need to get an X-ray to see if you sustained a secondary injury when you hit your head. It's better to check it out now than to find out you've got some damaged neck vertebrae later. That's our standard procedure, and I'm afraid it's not optional."

Once the officers had finished their paperwork, the ambulance departed for Faxton-St. Luke's Hospital in Utica. Eddie followed the emergency vehicle in his truck after promising the troopers that he'd personally tow Chris's Jeep out of the woods the following morning.

Even though it was now almost midnight, Chris decided to call his mother and tell her that he would be coming by the house to spend the night. He wisely decided to hide the reason for his visit.

"Sorry for calling so late, Mom. I hate doing this. But I've been up in Blue Mountain Lake all day, and I'll be passing through in a few hours. I might stop in and sack out for a few hours, if that's alright with you."

Chris heard the combination of sleep and surprise in his mother's voice.

"Of course, dear. You have the key; just let yourself in whenever you get here. I probably won't get up. I'll see you in the morning."

Sensing that his mother was still mostly asleep, he decided to say no more. He would have to explain the bruise on his head the following morning anyway, so there was no point in having her worry needlessly tonight.

Chris had never before ridden in an ambulance, much less lying on his back, so it was a new experience for him, although not one he would treasure. He passed the time by trading stories with the EMT about sports injuries, of which he had seen many while playing lacrosse for Syracuse.

It took less than thirty minutes to get the rest of the way to Utica, although it was already late by the time Chris was checked into the emergency room. Another hour was spent going through a brief exam given by a young intern, followed by a pass through the x-ray lab. Finally, an older physician came into the examining room where Chris and Eddie had been sitting, awaiting news. The doctor was tall and slender, with grey hair that was thinning across the top. He appeared to be in good spirits considering the hour.

After reviewing intern's notes, the x-rays, and a copy of the accident report, he looked up at his patient, sizing him up. "So, Chris Carey, Jr., from Syracuse, you look a lot like the Chris Carey I know from Utica. By any chance, is he your father?"

"The Washington attorney?" asked Chris.

"As a matter of fact, yes," said the doctor.

"Yup, that's my dad," said Chris. "How do you know him?"

"We were both on a board together for a couple of years, but that was back in the 1960s. We used to play golf together, too, before he decided that Upstate New York wasn't big enough for him." The physician shook his head, thinking of the old days. "Your father sure does have a lot of energy."

"Yes, he does," said Chris, somewhat wearily. "Lord knows I've never been able to keep up with him."

The doctor looked at Chris questioningly, as if trying to determine whether his response was indicative of a family problem.

"Well, anyway, please say hello when you see him, OK? Tell him that Dr. Anthony Morelli said hello."

The doctor quickly examined Chris's head and hand bruises and advised him to get some extra rest over the course of the following days. By the time he was given a clean bill of health and permission to leave, it was almost three. Eddie stayed with him the entire time so that he could drive him to his mother's house in Utica.

"I owe you big time, buddy," said Chris as they heaved themselves up into the elevated cab of the truck. "I don't know what I would have done without you tonight. You're going to be pretty beat for work in the morning."

"Nah, not a problem," said Eddie. "And you don't owe me a thing. Heck, the only reason you ended up running into Bambi back there was because you came out of your way to see me. I feel guilty as hell."

"Well, at least let me give you some money for gas," said Chris as he reached around into his rear pocket. As he did so, his hand brushed over the folded handkerchief he had placed there the previous afternoon. He smiled to himself and shook his head; his visit to the museum already seemed like the distant past. He squeezed the material to ensure that the coins were still inside. After confirming that they were safely stored, he extracted a twenty dollar bill from his wallet and passed it to his friend.

It was only a ten minute drive to the Careys' hilltop home. The two spent the entire time discussing the logistics of getting the Jeep out of the woods and back to Eddie's shop.

"Don't worry about a thing. I'll keep it stored there until your insurance adjuster can get out to take a look at it. I'm sure he or she will total it, and then you should be able to have it hauled off to the junkyard."

Chris didn't like hearing that, even though he'd known that the vehicle would definitely have to be scrapped. It had no remaining book value, and hadn't for years. But the sentimental value was great, and he would miss the old clunker.

"Sounds like a plan. Hey, I want to thank you again for staying with me tonight. You have no idea how much it's meant to me."

The two said goodbye as Chris climbed out and headed up the driveway to the house. It would be light in another two hours, and the only sleep he'd had was a result of being knocked on the head. He'd had better days.

The door to Chris' bedroom swung open at noon. His mom looked curiously at the long, lean shape that filled the bed. Since the time he'd been in high school, she couldn't remember ever being awake before her son.

"Hey, sleepy bones. I thought I was going to feed you breakfast this morning, but if you don't get up soon, you'll miss lunch."

Chris' eyes fluttered open and he looked around him.

"Oh, sorry mom. It was pretty late when I got in," he said as he sat up. "I guess I was more tired than I thought."

"GOOD HEAVENS!" shouted Theresa, staring at the dark bruise across Chris's brow. "What happened to you? You look like you've been smacked with a baseball bat."

"Worse than that," said Chris. "I got beat up by my steering wheel. I did a bit of a number on my right hand, too."

"You were in an accident?" asked his mother. "I was wondering where your car was when I didn't see it in the driveway this morning. I had to look in your room just to see if you were here."

"What's left of the Jeep is wrapped around a tree near Boonville. If you'd arrived when it happened, I could have offered you some nice venison steaks. But the meat's probably spoiled by now."

As he spoke, he arose from the bed. His mother was surprised to see that he'd slept in his clothes.

"I'm sorry to hear about the Jeep, but at least you seem to be OK. Did you see a doctor? Come downstairs and tell me about it while I fix you something to eat."

Over the course of the next hour, Chris filled his mother in on his experiences of the past week. He told her about the leads he'd received from his grandfather, as well as his visit to Dr. Meyers at Cornell. As she listened, she noticed the gleam in her son's eye.

"If I had to venture a guess, I'd say that you've been bitten by the treasure bug. The last time we talked, it sounded like you didn't believe the story."

"Mom, I honestly don't know what happened, or when. But one thing I can tell you is that at some time in the past, there were some valuables that were carted into the middle of the Adirondacks by someone, and then left there. Believe me, it's not something that I started out hunting. My whole interest was finding a new cave that was supposedly discovered by Indians back in the 1870s. That's it. All I wanted was a new place to explore. But it's changed since then."

"Honey, with all the treasure hunters in the world looking for the elusive pot of gold, why do you think you're the one who is finding the keys to the jackpot first? You've got to admit, it is a bit improbable."

"I know, Mom. It's pretty wild. But you've got to remember that the main character in the plot is Adirondack French Louie, who told grandpa's father about a pile of gold he'd located and then hidden. Think about it, Mom. He told Calvin Carey about that when he thought he was on his deathbed, and he died within a matter of months. It's quite possible that no one else ever knew that Louie had possession of the gold."

"That is, assuming there was ever gold in the first place," said Theresa. "Remember, the only one who was there to hear about it was your great-grandfather, who's been gone for years. Your grandfather never thought enough of it to really look into it seriously, and your father never even wanted to hear about it. The reason why, in my opinion, is that they didn't honestly believe the words of a man who may have been delusional in his final days. And even if he was telling the truth, honey, how would you know someone else hasn't already uncovered the bullion in the last hundred years?"

Chris was trying to suppress a smile the entire time his mother had been speaking. While she had some powerfully logical reasons why Louie may not have had possession of the gold, he held the trump card in his back pocket.

"Mom, if I show you something, could I get your solemn promise that you won't tell anyone?" he asked.

"Of course, you know that," his mother answered. "I'd never tell anyone something if you asked me to keep it a secret."

Chris placed the handkerchief on the table and began unfolding the dark blue material. He performed this motion slowly, as in a ritual, to increase the theatrical effect. Then he reached inside and removed the two gold coins and placed them on the mahogany tabletop. The darkness of the wood added extra emphasis to the shiny gleam of the coins.

Theresa's eyes grew wide as she reached a shaking hand out to the ancient doubloons. Lifting them up as if they might break, she turned each over, looking at the detail engraved into each side. She cradled them in her fingers as though she was mentally weighing each coin.

"Where did you get these?" she asked, her voice barely above a whisper.

"I found them in a hidden compartment of a chest that had been owned by Louie," said Chris. "They were in the museum at Blue Mountain Lake, although their staff never realized that the coins were in there. I'll return them, but first I want to have them identified. They may provide some clues as to where the gold came from and where the rest of it is stashed."

For once, Chris' mother was silent, stunned by her son's discovery. Finally, after about thirty seconds of thought, her voice returned.

"I think you've missed your calling, Chris. It appears as though you have developed into quite the detective. Now I understand why you wanted me to keep quiet on this. If anyone found out that there might be more of these buried somewhere in old Louie's woods, half the state would be out there with shovels."

"I've got to admit, Mom, I was a bit lucky to find this. And I still don't know where the stash of gold came from in the first place, assuming that there is more. But hopefully I can start piecing together my own discoveries with whatever Sean has been able to uncover, and we'll have a few more answers."

"Oh, speaking of Sean, I forgot to tell you; he called twice this morning. He said he'd been looking for you, and I told him that you'd give him a shout at around ten. I guess it's a bit late for that, though."

Chris suddenly remembered that he had not returned Sean's call of the previous evening. He hoped that it wasn't critical, and that he'd still be able to catch him on his cell. He walked out onto the front porch and dialed Sean's number, hoping to be able to talk his friend into a ride back to Syracuse. Sean picked up on the second ring.

"Well, well, I see you finally saw fit to return my call," said Sean. "I'm happy to see that I'm so high on your priority list."

"Sorry about that, guy. It's been a rough twenty-four hours, including totaling the Jeep. I was in a wreck up north; I was coming back from Blue Mountain Lake when I ran into a deer while I was doing fifty-five miles per hour. The Jeep ended up in the woods, and I ended up in St. Luke's."

"Oh my God," said Sean. "I'm sorry I kidded you about it. I had no idea. Are you OK?"

"Yeah, they took me in for x-ray and to check me out for any other injuries. But outside of a bump on my head and a sore hand, I'm good to go."

"So how did you make out at the museum up in Blue Mountain Lake?" asked Sean. "You find anything worthwhile?"

"You bet," answered Chris. "I now know that we're really onto something here. You're interested in gold, I'm interested in caves; I think we've got at least some of each. I can't wait to show you what I found."

"It sounds as though you did better than I did," said Sean. "The curator in Albany gave me some interesting information about the old cup and the rifle stock, but nothing that will help get us to a cave. I hope you've got a good roadmap for that, because I think I struck out."

"I tell you what, old pal, old buddy. How would you like to fill me in while driving me back home to my house? I'm stuck at Mom's with no way to get home."

"Sure, I can do that. I've got a break in the schedule, if only for a day. When do you want me to swing by?"

"How about mid-afternoon, maybe around three? We'll make it back to my place in time for dinner. I'll even spring for it."

"How can I resist?" asked Sean. "Good news and good food. What a combination!"

"The only food you'll get at my house right now is out of the freezer," said Chris. "We'll stop when we get into town and pick up something to take out."

"Sounds great. I'll see you in a couple hours."

Chris hung up the phone and walked back inside. His mother was just cleaning up a few things and preparing to leave the house. She served as a volunteer driver twice a week for a bus that transported people with disabilities around the city. It got her out of the house and gave her something to do. It also made her feel good to know that she was helping the community.

"You can stay here as long as you like," said Theresa. "Just make sure you lock the door on the way out, and make sure the cat doesn't follow you."

"Sure, Mom," Chris laughed. "Don't worry about that. He's never liked me much anyway." Then, as an afterthought, he called out to her again. "Mom, as long as you're going out, would you mind if I went online from your computer and checked my e-mail?"

"No, of course not," she called out as she pushed her way out the front door.

"What's your password?"

"T-H-E-R-E-S-A," she called out. "Think you can remember that?"

Chris rolled his eyes at her, and then she was gone.

Considering the fact that he had been away from his account for over a day, he had very little in the way of new mail. There was one from St. Luke's asking him to complete an online survey. He also saw an e-mail from Eddie saying that he had successfully pulled the wrecked Jeep out of the woods. The entire chassis had been bent, and the rear axle was severed in half where it had smashed into a boulder. The engine block was cracked as well, which may have caused the hissing noise Chris heard when he came to. He was just about ready to reply to Eddie's note when an instant message window popped up onscreen.

dr_galloway_cornell: Hi Chris. How was Blue Mountain Lake?

chriscarey1986: It went very, very well, thank you.

dr_galloway_cornell: Sounds like you had a big day.

chriscarey1986: Sure did. I think I found proof that Adirondack French Louie did find a hidden treasure of gold somewhere within his guiding range of the central Adirondacks. Unless I miss my guess, that means the presence of a cave that may never have been visited by any white man.

dr_galloway_cornell: Now THAT would be big news. I'll be interested to see it myself, and perhaps be involved in the carbon dating process.

chriscarey1986: Assuming that we do find the cave, or caves, would Dr. Meyers be working with you on that?

dr_galloway_cornell: If he's interested, then yes, although it's really more of an anthropological study than geological. But you know how Earl loves his caves. I'd probably be stuck doing all the hard work while he was down there exploring.

chriscarey1986: Could be. You know him better than I do.

dr_galloway_cornell: Do you know yet when you're going in looking?

chriscarey1986: Not yet. Sorry. We've been trying for at least a month now, but things keep getting in the way.

dr_galloway_cornell: Where do you intend to search first?

chriscarey1986: I want to start off by looking at a couple things around Louie's site on West Canada Lake. I'm also going to run a metal detector over his cave camp at Cobble Hill, north of Third Cedar Lake. We should be able to cover both of those in two days, and then move up to the area around Lost Pond, which is "ground zero" for my search. If we don't find anything there, I might even look as far north as Little Moose Lake.

dr_galloway_cornell: Sounds like a good plan. Keep me posted, and I'll try to forward you anything I come across that might be useful.

chriscarey1986: Thanks, Dr. Galloway. I appreciate that.

dr_galloway_cornell: You bet. Take care.

<dr_galloway_cornell has signed out>

Chris was sitting on the front porch with his feet up when Sean pulled into the driveway. The beautiful luster on his Mercedes and the soft purring of the engine made it hard to believe that the car was almost a half-century old. It was Sean's pride and joy, and he kept it in immaculate condition.

"Taxi!" Chris called out, raising his arm and waving his friend to a stop. "Do you have room for a free ride today, Sir?"

"Shut up and get in the car, clown," said Sean, laughing. "And you'd better be nice to me or I'll sock you right on top of that ugly oozing mess you've got up there." He looked up at Chris's head, pretending it was even worse than it was. "Ugh—that must have hurt."

"Actually, I was asleep at the time. Let me tell you about it."

As they drove along the Thruway back to Syracuse, Chris described the accident that had sent his Jeep crashing into the woods. Sean agreed that he was lucky to have escaped a more serious injury.

Chris then described his visit to the Adirondack Museum, starting with the discovery of the journal that had William J. Harrison's name on top.

Chris heard his friend gasp. "You're kidding me?" he asked, barely hiding the excitement in his voice.

"No, whoever Harrison was, his name appeared on both the trip journal at the museum as well as the map owned by my grandfather. Although I must admit, I don't think that he was the one who originally wrote the journal. His name is written in a different ink, and that document appears to be quite a bit older. Why do you ask?"

"I'm going to defer on that question for just a couple minutes," Sean said. "I'd like to first hear your theory on why your last statement is important to us."

"Well, it looks to me that this Harrison fellow owned both of these documents, at least at one time or another. And since we know that Louie ended up with one of them, I'd have to guess that Louie and Harrison probably met at some point."

Sean listened, obviously excited with the news. Without saying anything, he pulled his car off the road and into a small rest area.

"Whatcha doing?" asked Chris, who was unfamiliar with the turnoff.

"What I have to tell you deserves your full attention. I want to be able to see your face when I tell you what I found out from my Internet search."

Sean pulled the car into a space, and the two of them walked over to a picnic table.

"It wasn't easy to find our specific W.J. Harrison. As a matter of fact, if you started with a simple Google search on that name, including the initials, you'll get a list of over ten thousand listings. But by narrowing my search and bringing in multiple databases and search parameters, I was able to zero in on one specific individual. And I think you're going to be excited when you find out who he was."

"Go ahead," urged Chris, a bit impatiently.

"William J. Harrison was the great-grandson of Robert Gordon, who was a merchant who lived south of Lake Champlain about the time of the Revolutionary War. He had owned and operated a place called...."

"...the Red Barn store," interrupted Chris.

Sean's face fell. "You mean, you knew about this before now?"

"No, I didn't," said Chris. "I know about Gordon because I've been reading a book about hidden treasure stories of New York State. But I had no clue that Harrison was related to Gordon. That's amazing news. Great work digging that up, because it establishes a link between Harrison and the legendary Gordon treasure," said Chris, patting his friend on the back.

"So is that the new focus of our search, or are you still as interested in the caves?" asked Sean.

"Don't get me wrong," said Chris. "I love caves, especially those that have never been previously explored. But you've got to admit that the stakes are now higher."

"I guess I'm not going to need my gold pan for this kind of prospecting, am I?" asked Sean."

"Not unless you think it'll be especially good in finding more of these," said Chris, holding out the two gold doubloons.

Sean's reaction was even more pronounced than Chris's mother's had been.

"Where the heck did you come up with those?" asked Sean, his mouth agape.

Chris told him the story about emptying out Louie's old chest and discovering them underneath the fake bottom panels. He then opened his cell phone and selected the menu icon for photo images.

"Check it out," he said, showing Sean the photo of the open trunk. "Somehow, the curator at the museum must not have noticed the loose bottom slats. Or maybe they just never emptied the chest all the way. Either way, no one's been in there since Louie hid those over a hundred years ago."

Sean examined the coins in much the same way as Theresa had a short while earlier.

"These things are in amazing condition," he said, noting the bright shine coming off the surface. "But you know, there is one thing still bothering me."

"What's that?" asked Chris, motioning his friend back to the car.

"The reference that I found about William Harrison said only that he was leading a group searching for silver bullion on Lake Champlain. Yet the legend in the books say it was gold; that he supposedly only dealt in gold. Where do you think the discrepancy lies?"

"I couldn't say," said Chris, sliding into the passenger seat. "But if we go by the assumption that the map at my grandfather's house was made by Harrison, then we'd have to assume that he conducted two separate searches, one in the central Adirondacks and the other on Lake Champlain. I don't know why yet, but we're moving in the right direction."

"Oh, one other thing I forgot to mention," said Sean. "I was able to track down those other names you gave me: A. Smith and T. Swain."

"Great!" said Chris, excited with the additional good news. "Where? And what did you find?"

"Between the Washington County Historical Society and the County Archives, I was able to track them back into Skenesborough in the early 1770s. Thomas Swain showed up on the register as a household of one, and Alvin Smith was apparently also a bachelor. They were also both members of a local commerce council, which indicates to me that maybe they were involved in some way with Gordon's business."

"That's as good an assumption as any," agreed Chris, deep in thought. "And it would explain what they were doing with such a large chunk of Gordon's money."

The two men talked over the possibilities as they entered the Syracuse area, following Route 690 to University Avenue. They got out of their car on Marshall Street and walked into King David's restaurant for a pile of falafel pitas. Chris had grown very fond of Middle Eastern food during his years on the Syracuse campus, and he continued to frequent the restaurant after his graduation.

On the drive north to his house, Chris voiced his thoughts about their search.

"You know, what has started out as a hunt for a single Indian cave has really turned into three separate searches," he said.

"Three? How do you come up with that?" asked Sean.

"We're still looking for the Indian caves that Dr. Meyers showed me on his maps. We're looking for a cave that was mentioned by French Louie to my great-grandfather. And we also have the search for the gold bullion that was hidden by Robert Gordon; presumably the same stuff that Harrison was looking for 130 years later."

Sean fell silent, considering the possibilities, when Chris spoke up again.

"Somehow, I can't help but feel that a couple of these are interconnected locations. Maybe we shouldn't even consider worrying about the Indian caves. Especially since we know that the real 'mother lode' is already in the form of coins and bullion, not tiny specks of dust that we've got to pull out of the ground."

By now, Sean had pulled to the end of Chris's street and rolled to a gentle stop in his dirt driveway. Together, they walked into the house just in time to see the clock strike five. They dropped the food on the kitchen table and grabbed a couple of bottles of Molson from the fridge.

"So allow me ask a question, oh Knowledgeable One. We now have more information than we know what to do with. So what comes next? When do we actually start looking for any of this stuff?" Sean asked.

"What are you doing next week?" Chris replied, staring across the table with a wide grin. "I think we can be ready by then, if your schedule will accommodate a trip into the woods."

"Sure, I can arrange that, as long as we're not gone the entire week," said Sean. "What are your plans for the rest of this week?"

"I've got a few things to handle, such as getting some wheels and letting my head heal back into a single piece. But I should be ready by the middle of next week. That'll give us a chance to plan our route, establish a search area, and take care of our own logistics."

"Is there anything that you'd like me to do in the interim?" asked Sean.

"Yes, if you have the time to do another search for me, I'd like you to try and locate records on any living descendants of William Harrison. I don't care where they're located, but I'd like to be able to contact them to find out if he left anything behind—notes, diaries, photographs, or anything that would explain why he was searching in two different places. I have a feeling that that's a critical piece of information we're missing."

"I can do that," said Sean, "but I'll tell you right now that it ain't going to be easy. I only found a couple of references to him the first time around, so locating his descendants will probably be next to impossible. But I'll see what I can find."

"As far as hitting the woods, let's shoot for Wednesday or Thursday of next week," said Chris.

"Count me in," said Sean. "I'll be ready on either day. Just let me know. We can meet in Utica and then drive one car up. Just out of curiosity, what are you going to do for transportation until you buy a car? I don't think you want to walk into a dealer and throw yourself on the mercy of a car salesman."

"No, I won't do that. I'll rent something small for the next week or two. I'll probably order something online through Jeep's fleet sales department. It's cheap, and you don't have to haggle with anyone face to face. They either accept your offer or reject it, and then you move on."

"You want another Jeep, huh?" asked Sean.

"Yes, I'm afraid I'm a creature of habit," said Chris. "I'll log on tonight and see what's out there. I don't know much about the latest lines, though, because I wasn't expecting to buy a new one for quite some time yet."

The two friends finished their meals and continued to sip on their brews for the next hour. They were both excited about the developments of the past week, and they discussed their progress as they planned their trip.

It was almost seven o'clock, and Sean was getting ready to depart for home when the doorbell rang. Chris answered the door to find a man dressed in auto mechanic's coveralls standing on the front stairs. He was making notes on a clipboard that held several papers with duplicate sheets attached.

"May I help you?" asked Chris, expecting to be asked for a donation by some non-profit organization.

"Yes sir, you can sign this line for me, please," said the man, holding the clipboard out for him to take. "Then, I can take you out for a short drive if you'd like, just to explain the features."

"A short drive? I'm sorry, I guess I don't understand," said Chris. "Who are you, and what do you need?"

The gentleman seemed a little bit surprised, as though Chris should have been expecting him.

"My name is Ed Margolis, and I work in the dealer prep and delivery office of East Syracuse Chrysler Jeep down on Manlius Center Road. I'm here to deliver your new Jeep." As he spoke, he held up a set of keys and jingled them for Chris to see.

"My...new...Jeep? But, but..." Chris stuttered. He was at a complete loss. He leaned his body out the door and looked around the delivery man. Sitting in the driveway next to Sean's Mercedes was a sparkling new Jeep Liberty. Its moss green exterior was almost identical to the color of his old vehicle, except that this one radiated that special glow that comes only from the showroom.

"I don't understand. I didn't order a Jeep. At least, not yet."

"Then it looks like someone beat you to it," said the auto representative. "It's completely paid for with a single check. I've got all the paperwork, signed and ready for you. It just needs your signature and it's yours."

Chris looked at the paperwork, including his personal information on the registration. It was all accurate, and it appeared official. As if in a daze, he took the clipboard and signed the bottom of the vehicle acceptance form. Following the instructions of the attendant, he also signed a registration form and a few documents from the dealership before handing back the clipboard.

"Here you go, sir," said Ed, handing Chris the keys. "I hope you like your new Jeep. Please remember to come and see us for service. We'll take good care of you, I promise!" He then turned and walked back toward the road, where another auto employee sat waiting in a dealership car to take them back to their showroom.

Chris stood rooted in place, his hand frozen in midair since he'd grasped the keys. His mouth was open wide, his eyes reflecting a combination of amazement and confusion.

Sean said nothing. He just walked past Chris and onto the front walkway. Letting out a low whistle, he turned back and faced his friend.

"Must be nice to have wealthy friends," he said.

Slowly, Chris' expression migrated from one of surprise, to one of understanding, and finally to amusement.

"Mom," he said simply, nodding his head.

"You think so?" asked Sean. "That would be my guess too. Come on out and let's take a look at it. I love the smell of a new car. I might even sleep in it tonight."

"Knock yourself out," said Chris, tossing him the new set of keys. "Go ahead and check it out. I'll be with you in a minute. I've got a phone call to make."

Sean caught the key ring and bounced down the walkway to investigate the new SUV. Meanwhile, Chris went into the kitchen and had a seat. He was still waiting for his heartbeat to return to normal as he dialed his mother's number.

"Hello," said the familiar voice.

"Hi, Mom. I love you, but you shouldn't have!" said Chris, without preamble. "It's gorgeous. But you know darn well I couldn't have afforded that by myself. I love it, but still, you shouldn't have."

"Whoa, easy does it," his mother said, silencing him. "What is it that's so gorgeous that I deserve all these thanks? What are you talking about?"

"The new Jeep, Mom. It's wonderful. But I should have bought that myself. There's no need for you to be helping me. I'd like to pay you back for it."

There was a lengthy pause on the line, and then his mother spoke in slow, measured words.

"Son I'm not really sure what you're looking at there, or where it came from. But I give you my word as your mother, I had nothing to do with it. If there's a new Jeep in your driveway, I promise you it didn't come from me."

"Maybe it was Dad," suggested Chris. "Yes, that must be it. I bet he set up something through the dealership here and had them rush through a same-day delivery. It's the only other possibility."

Chris could hear another silence as his mom considered the thought.

"Have you been in contact with him since your accident? Maybe you mentioned it in an e-mail?" she asked.

"No, Mom. I thought maybe you had."

"That would be tough for me to do, honey. He's somewhere between London and Brussels right now, and he won't be back in the U.S. for another three days. He couldn't have even known about the accident."

Chris closed his eyes and leaned against the refrigerator. In some ways he was happy to hear that his father was overseas. At least he had an excuse for not calling his son following the accident. But since his father hadn't even heard about the crash, he certainly was not the donor of the new Jeep.

Chris said goodbye, then walked out to join his friend in the driveway. He found Sean crawling across the front seat, practically drooling on the upholstery.

"Take a look at what this thing's got!" Sean shouted. "Power sunroof, satellite radio, about six or eight kickin' speakers, a built-in GPS navigational system... oh man, I could go on and on. Don't get me wrong, I liked your old Jeep. But this thing puts that dinosaur to shame."

"That's nice to know," said Chris, still contemplating the mystery of the anonymous gift.

"Next time you see your mom, you make sure you tell her that I like her style, OK?"

Chris directed a level stare back at him. "They didn't buy it."

"What do you mean 'they didn't buy it'? Who didn't buy it?"

"My mom or dad. It didn't come from them. My mom just told me that, and I believe her," Chris said.

Sean accepted the statement at face value. Like Chris, he wondered what benevolent party would be so interested in his welfare that they would buy him a $30,000 vehicle. Somehow, both of them thought that the answer to the riddle would soon be uncovered.

As soon as Sean departed, Chris went back into the A-frame and did some light housework. Then, to give himself time to think, he pulled his lacrosse stick off the hook in the living room and sent the hard rubber ball caroming again and again off the brick wall. Now, he not only had the mystery of the caves and the gold, but the added intrigue of a new Jeep to contemplate as well.

Finally, tired of the game of catch, Chris filled a tall glass with water and dropped in some ice. He brought the glass over to the computer and turned on the machine. If nothing else, he figured he might try to locate something else on Robert Gordon. Or maybe he could find some modern-day descendant of William J. Harrison living in either the U.S. or Canada who might know more of the story and perhaps be convinced to help him with additional information. It was worth a look.

Chris started with some basic searches, but didn't find anything new on Gordon. He was listed in a couple of reference books, but that was the extent of it. If Chris wanted to learn more, he'd probably have to drive to the town of Whitehall to visit the Skenesborough Museum. He jotted down the phone number on a pad of paper.

Next, he opened his Yahoo! account to answer any e-mails that might have arrived in the past few hours. He was anxious to hear more from his last round of interviews, and he scanned the inbox hopefully. There was nothing of interest waiting for him, so he checked his calendar for the following week, and then he fired off a quick note to Sean to confirm that he was available to start their search the following Wednesday.

Meet me at my folks' house in Utica on Wednesday morning. I'll get there by around 8:00, but if you can show up by 10:00 that would be great. I'll drive, so you can leave your car in the driveway while we're gone. See you there.

After sending the email, Chris noticed that Dr. Meyers' icon was visible on his contact list, indicating that he too was online tonight. He hadn't informed him of his progress to date, so he decided to say hello.

chriscarey1986: Hello Dr. Meyers. Thought I'd give you an update on our progress.

Cave_dweller_DrM: Thank you, Chris. Nice to hear from you. So what's new from the Salt City?

chriscarey1986: More than I can tell you about in an instant message, but I'll try. It was a GREAT day up in Blue Mountain Lake until I totaled my Jeep.

Cave_dweller_DrM: Sorry to hear that. I trust you weren't injured.

chriscarey1986: Nothing that couldn't be pulled back in place with a large roll of duct tape, thanks. But the museum did yield some great clues. I think I picked up on some details that others have missed.

Cave_dweller_DrM: Anything you have time to discuss now?

chriscarey1986: Not yet. I'd like to confirm a couple of my suspicions first. But I think I might have a lead on both some gold as well as at least one cave. It's pretty exciting.

Cave_dweller_DrM: It sounds it. But remember, you promised to let us have first crack at anything you find, right?

chriscarey1986: Of course, and I'll certainly make sure that you're my first call. I have your number programmed into my phone, you know.

Cave_dweller_DrM: Thanks, Chris.

chriscarey1986: I look forward to working with you and your colleague. By the way, I forgot to thank you for having him contact me. He's been very interested in our project.

Cave_dweller_DrM: What colleague?

chriscarey1986: Dr. Galloway, the anthropologist.

Cave_dweller_DrM: Now that's interesting. How did you get his name?

chriscarey1986: He contacted me over a week ago. He said that you gave him my name, and that he was interested in looking into the early American Indian use of caves in northern New York.

Cave_dweller_DrM: Did he say anything else?

chriscarey1986: Just that he was probably going to accompany you when you made your first exploration of the caves, assuming that we can find it. He wanted to perform the carbon dating, if possible, to confirm some of his own findings.

Cave_dweller_DrM: I find that highly unlikely.

chriscarey1986: What do you mean?

Cave_dweller_DrM: Dr. Galloway was a very good friend of mine. But I certainly never mentioned your name to him. I haven't talked to him in some time, so that would have been physically impossible.

chriscarey1986: OK. Where is Dr. Galloway today?

Cave_dweller_DrM: About five years ago, he announced that he was leaving on a two year sabbatical to Oxford, where he was supposed to be involved in some groundbreaking work on New World primates. About two months before he left, he started feeling poorly, which he chalked up to stress. He got checked out by a doctor, but they didn't find anything. So he went ahead with his plans. But his health continued to deteriorate, so he checked himself into a hospital in London where he was diagnosed with bone cancer. He came back to the States to seek more advanced treatment. But he never came back to Cornell.

chriscarey1986: Is he still officially a member of your faculty? Or can you think of any reason why he'd be interested in our activities other than on a professional level?

Cave_dweller_DrM: Chris, Dr. Galloway succumbed to his cancer almost a year ago. I was at the funeral. Whoever you've been writing to, it isn't Dr. Galloway.

The instant message from Dr. Meyers felt like a kick in the gut. Chris thanked him and immediately logged off his laptop. As he leaned back in his chair, he found that he was sweating slightly, a sure sign of nervousness. He wondered who had contacted him pretending to be a Cornell professor. It was obviously someone who wanted information about the gold. But how could they have known? He'd kept the details of their venture a closely guarded secret. It was possible that Sean had accidentally spilled the beans to someone outside their circle of contacts, but he doubted it.

Rather than sit around the house and think gloomy thoughts, Chris decided to change into his shorts and sneakers and go for a run. If nothing else, he could use the time to think over his options. He hid the two gold coins inside a pair of socks up on his loft for safekeeping. Then he set his watch timer and headed out the door.

What a difference a day could make. Just twenty-four hours earlier, he had been optimistic that they were headed in the right direction. The pieces were falling into place, and the two high school chums appeared on the edge of clearing up a two hundred-year-old mystery. But now, Chris realized that they still had clues which apparently led nowhere. On top of that, he'd wrecked his Jeep, and someone had decided to put a new one in the middle of his driveway. For free. And as if that wasn't enough, Chris just learned that he'd been discussing their newly-discovered secrets with a dead anthropologist.

It had indeed been a very strange few days.

CHAPTER 14

July 26, 2012

The sign on the door read "Syracuse Coin and Gold Exchange." Nestled in an inconspicuous corner of a shopping plaza on South Bay Road, it attracted only a small clientele of local coin enthusiasts. The neon sign on the front window declared that "WE BUY ALL GOLD AND SILVER, IMMEDIATE CASH." Inside the store, an elderly gentleman stood behind the counter, carefully examining an early American silver dollar. He augmented his failing eyesight with a large-lens jeweler's loop and a high wattage lamp.

At age seventy-seven, Wesley Hawkins had been dealing in rare coins for close to fifty years. What he lacked in eyesight, he more than made up for with an almost encyclopedic knowledge of American and foreign coinage. He was considered an expert in grading everything from copper large cent pennies right up through the valuable gold "double eagle" twenty dollar pieces. When he wasn't buying and selling, he was augmenting his income by appraising large collections for wealthy owners.

Wes was alone when the door opened and a young man walked in. He was a tall man, in his mid-twenties, dressed in faded jeans and a pale green polo shirt. Wes's attention was immediately drawn to the large bruise across the left side of his forehead. It gave him the appearance of a prizefighter who'd just emerged from the ring.

"Looks like you finished second in that fight, son," said Wes, nodding at Chris's wound.

"Ha! Yes, my knockout punch deserted me when I needed it most," replied Chris, returning the quip.

The coin expert looked at him in surprise. "I was joking. Did you really get that cut in the boxing ring? It must have been one hell of a hit."

"No, no, I was only kidding. I was in an auto accident earlier this week. I learned why airbags have been re-designed on new cars."

The dealer made a face and winced.

"Well, I hope you're OK. And now, what can I do for you?"

"I'd like to know if you are familiar with gold coins from the 1700s, especially those minted by other countries," asked Chris.

"I suppose I'm about as good as anyone," replied the dealer, modestly downplaying his well-earned reputation. "And by the way, you don't even have to say that it's minted by another country. We didn't have any American gold coins struck in that era, although there were some fine examples of territorial Colonial mint pieces, some of which can still be purchased today."

"I've got to admit, I'm hardly a numismatist myself," Chris acknowledged. "I used to collect when I was a kid, but I ended up spending my whole collection to take my girlfriend to the high school prom."

Wes laughed and threw up his arms. "Typical! And tell me, how did that turn out?"

"Lousy," said Chris, smiling as he recalled the debacle. "She dumped me the following week when she found out that I liked her best friend more."

"That's the trouble with women!" Wes chuckled. "They get mad if you don't like their friends, but you better not like their friends too much!"

"Anyway, as I said, I'm no longer a collector, but I do have a couple of coins that I'd like you to take a look at. I'm not interested in selling them because they've been in our family for a long time, but I'd like to know more about them and what they are worth."

"I'd be happy to take a look," said Wes, leaning over the counter.

Chris reached into his front pocket and extracted the same blue handkerchief that had held the coins since he'd found them inside the chest. He placed the folded cloth on top of a black felt pad that sat on the counter-top. As he unwrapped the contents, the dealer moved the lamp closer to illuminate the surface.

"Here you go," said Chris as he gently lifted the two coins out of the material and laid them on the pad. Then he sat back to listen.

"Hmmm…nice!" said the dealer, pulling the jeweler's loop into place. "Very nice. This wasn't what I expected when you said you had 'a couple of coins' to show me. I don't see examples of these in such nice condition very often."

"Rare?" asked Chris, hoping for more information.

"Not really rare, per se," said Wes, looking over the two coins in a methodical manner. "But still, these are very old, very large, and in really nice shape. I don't think they circulated for more than a year or two, if that, based on their condition. There is very little wear on either coin."

"That sounds right, based on what my grandfather told me," said Chris. Once again, he found himself in the position of having to manufacture a fake story.

"What did your grandfather tell you about them?" asked the dealer.

"He said that he'd been given them by his grandfather, who told him that they had been passed down from generation to generation since the Revolutionary War. I can't tell you any more details than that, but I know that it's been kept out of circulation for well over two hundred years. And now my grandfather has passed them down to me, which is why I'm here."

"That's a nice little present," Wes said. "You've got yourself quite a bit of cash there, should you decide to sell them."

"What would you say they're worth?" asked Chris.

"Based on their condition and the current market conditions, I'd say you could get anywhere from $2,200 up to around $3,000 for each coin, depending on how badly some collector wanted them. They're really nice."

The figure stunned Chris, who had figured that they'd each sell for around a $1,600, which was the going price for an ounce of gold.

"You said that these coins could have been used in this country even though they weren't minted here? How did that work?"

"You've got to understand that this country had no nationally-sanctioned facilities for minting coins of any kind until many years after our Declaration of Independence. Even though we officially declared ourselves independent in 1776, and the war ended in 1781, we didn't acquire a building to make coins until 1792, and the first penny was struck in 1793. Other coins followed soon after, such as the silver dollar in 1794, and the first gold "eagle" ten dollar piece in 1795."

"And before then?" prompted Chris.

"Before then, people living in this country used a hodgepodge of coins that were struck all over the world. The pieces that your grandfather gave you came from Spain. As a matter of fact, I can tell that these specific coins came from the mint in Seville."

"How could you know that?" asked Chris.

"You can see the mint mark," answered Wes. He turned over one of the coins and showed him the letter "S" stamped inside the circular chain pattern.

"There were also coins that were struck in Mexico, as well as others from Europe or South America. Each was valued based on the standards of the day. They also used gold ingots, which were crudely shaped by pouring melted gold into indentations in sand. Once the metal cooled into a solid state, it was lifted out and stamped. It was all used in trade, regardless of its source.

"So these coins we're looking at could have been circulating right here in New York State during the Revolutionary War?"

"That's correct," said Wes. "But just remember: this coin represented a lot of money back then, just as it does today. To put it into context, a copper half penny that was minted in the 1790s would buy you a full lunch. Just imagine what an ounce of gold could have purchased."

"Could I impose on you for one more question?" asked Chris, somewhat hesitantly.

"Certainly!" said the old-timer. "I'm not busy, and I always love talking coins."

"If these were worth as much as you say, do you think there is any chance that they could have belonged to a solitary woodsman who appeared to live off the land about a hundred years ago? Or would that be too much of a stretch?"

Wes looked at Chris in silence for a moment, evaluating the question.

"These didn't really come from your grandfather, did they?" asked the dealer.

Chris answered by simply looking back at the coin dealer and winking.

"I didn't think so," Wes replied. "Regarding your question, if I had to venture a guess, I'd say 'no.' Even a hundred years ago, these coins would have been long gone from circulation. Even if your woodsman could have accumulated this much wealth, which would be doubtful, it would have been in the form of coins struck in this country, such as the double eagle twenty dollar gold piece. Then again, anything is possible."

Chris lifted the two coins off the felt pad and was about to wrap them back in the handkerchief. The dealer stopped him and offered a couple of plastic-covered coin holders.

"Here: these are on the house," he said. "It would be a shame to have these get scuffed and nicked after so many years."

"Thank you, sir," said Chris. "You've been so very helpful."

"You bet," called out Wes as Chris was leaving the shop. "And you make sure to come back if you ever decide to sell those."

As Chris walked across the parking lot, his mind churned over the conversation several times, looking for information of importance. He had learned that the coins had been in use around the time of the Revolution. According to his book, this is when Robert Gordon would have left for Canada, hiding his treasure along the way.

Also, Wes said that the coins, which were minted in 1773, looked as though they hadn't circulated for more than a year or two. In other words, if Robert Gordon had dumped the coins as he headed north in 1775, that would explain their uncirculated condition. They had probably never seen the light of day until someone discovered their whereabouts.

The final clue was really more of a mystery. That was: how could Louie have come to own such a valuable piece? Did it come to him en masse, along with other pieces of the same stash? It's possible that he earned that much money from a season of trapping furs. But if that was the case, he would have been paid in American currency, which he probably would have spent on liquor during one of his sprees. Why would he own Spanish gold of such large denominations? And if there was more, where was it hidden?

Feeling pleased with his findings, Chris got back into his Jeep and called Sean. He wanted to discuss the logistics for the next week's hike. He was also interested to learn whether the search for any of Harrison's modern-day descendants had turned up any results.

Sean answered his cell on the second ring.

"Yeah, guy, what's up?"

"I've just had the two gold coins looked at by an expert," said Chris. "Nothing ground-shattering, but the guy did tell me a few things that we can use. He also said that the two are worth a combined five or six thousand dollars—not bad for an afternoon visit to a museum, eh?"

"Yes, but have you considered the fact that you now qualify as a candidate for grand theft?" asked Sean.

"You know, I guess I never thought of it that way," said Chris. "I am bringing them back very shortly, so it's really more of a loan. And since they never realized they had them in the first place, they won't be missed."

"Good luck returning them," chuckled Sean. "You're likely to have your library privileges revoked for a year."

"Thanks for the warning. Hey, were you able to find anything on the search for Harrison's descendants?" asked Chris.

"Yes, as a matter of fact, I did," said Sean. "But I refuse to tell you about it over the phone."

"Do you need to wait until you've got a secure, voice-encrypted communications line installed in your house?" asked Chris.

"Uh...no. But I just got something a lot better than that. If you're nice to me, I'll let you come over and play with it."

"What's that?"

"Only the newest set of Klipschorn freestanding loudspeakers in the state. You've got to hear them to believe them. You want to swing by later on and listen? I'll give you a data dump on Harrison while you listen to some of your dreadful blues collection."

"Sounds good. I'll stop by mom's house before I come over. Expect me at around seven, if that's OK with you."

"It should be, although Maggie might be over by then. But I don't have anything to tell you that she can't hear."

Chris smiled. Maggie often pulled her cart into Sean's yard to say hello, sometimes staying longer than her break allowed. He often wondered whether the Little Falls Golf Club noticed the disappearance of their golf steward whenever her cart passed his small cottage on the eleventh hole. Chris had never asked his friend for details, but he suspected that they had become more than mere friends.

"I'll see you then. I'll bring along a bottle of Brunello di Montalcino. The two of you can enjoy it when I leave."

"I'll hold you to that! See you then."

When Chris arrived at Sean's house later that evening, he noticed the ubiquitous golf cart in the back yard, tucked out of sight beneath the row of spruce trees. He rang the doorbell, which prompted a yelled response: "Go away!"

Chris laughed out loud as he turned the doorknob and let himself in. Maggie and Sean were on the couch watching a movie, their feet up and a bowl of popcorn on the table.

"Can't a guy get any privacy around here?" asked Sean sarcastically.

"Since when have you ever needed privacy?" asked Chris. Then, intentionally glancing at Maggie, he added quickly, "Oh…never mind."

Maggie giggled, reached out and threw a piece of popcorn at Chris. "Nice of you to drop by. Too bad you have to leave so soon." They all laughed.

Sean's friend possessed a friendly, bubbly personality that had endeared herself to the members of the club. Her short, thin frame was toned from years of exercise, and her long mane of light brown hair framed an extremely attractive and intelligent face. It was no coincidence that sales from the refreshment cart had tripled since she had taken over as course steward. They would miss her in the fall when she returned to college, where she was studying for a degree in journalism.

Chris looked across the room and let out a low whistle.

"Wow—I take it those are your new speakers?" he asked.

"The latest and greatest," said Sean, "Klipschorn Floorstanding Loud-speakers. They've got folded-horn, fifteen-inch woofers, separate midrange and tweeter compression drivers, and they're solid enough to handle 105 decibels without a bit of distortion."

"OK, what's that mean in English?" asked Chris.

"If I cranked these puppies up right now, you could hear it in the club-house. And it would sound GOOD! Want to hear?"

"No thanks. I think I'll hang on to my eardrums for another couple years," replied Chris.

Maggie stood up and looked at Sean. "I really need to take the cart back to the pro shop and punch my time card. I'll be back in a bit."

After she departed, Sean pulled a box out from under the table.

"Here's the cup and rifle stock. Sorry I couldn't find out any more for you."

"That's OK. I actually think we're doing pretty well. Tell me what you found out about relatives of Harrison."

"It wasn't easy to do, but I found an elderly surviving granddaughter living in Canada. She lives within ten miles of the place where Robert Gordon settled after fleeing the American colonies back in the 1770s."

"How were you able to locate her?" asked Chris.

"Mainly through the use of court papers," said Sean. "We knew about William J. Harrison, who was Robert Gordon's great-grandson. For a number of years, he lived in the town of Castleton, Vermont, which was only about fifteen miles away from Gordon's original store in Whitehall. When he passed away in 1941, his property was sold and his estate settled by his executor, who was also his daughter. That much I was able to track down in the real estate abstracts from Vermont."

"Nice work," said Chris. "Where did the trail go after that?"

"His daughter's name was Margaret Harrison, which changed to Margaret Surette after her first marriage. She lived in a town called Laprairie, which is across the St. Lawrence Seaway from Montreal."

"But I take it she's no longer alive?" asked Chris.

"Yes, that's correct. She died in 1970. But she did have one daughter, whose name I located through a Canadian genealogical database of Quebec residents. Her name is Annette Surette, and it appears as though she is still alive. Since she was born in 1934, she'd be either seventy-seven or seventy-eight today. If you look in the Montreal phone book, you'll find a listing for an Annette Surette in the suburb called St. Lambert, just south of the city."

"You've got her phone number already?" asked Chris.

"No, you've got her phone number...I put it in the box with your grandfather's souvenirs," said Sean, flashing a lopsided grin back at his friend."

"My, my, you get a merit badge for efficiency. I am impressed," said Chris.

"I aim to please," said Sean.

"So let's talk about next week. You're going to meet me at my folks' house at ten on Wednesday morning, fully packed and ready to go. I'll pick up enough grub to last us for five days. You have any preference what you'd like to eat? I'll stop into Eastern Mountain Sports and pick up some dehydrated packs."

"I already beat you to it," said Sean. "Give me a minute and I'll get it out of my trunk."

"Great," said Chris. "You mind if I log into my e-mail while you're doing that?"

"No, go right ahead," said Sean as he headed through the kitchen to his back door.

Chris stood in front of the keyboard and quickly brought up Yahoo! e-mail. He tapped in his username and password, and waited for his inbox to appear. However, instead, a system message appeared in a box on the screen. It read:

> Your Yahoo! mail account is still open on another computer. Do you wish to continue?

It was the second time he'd seen that message within the past two weeks. As he stood there considering the meaning, Sean returned bearing a large plastic bag.

"Here you are, sir!" he cried. "I bring you dehydrated culinary delectables from the faraway land of Dick's Sporting Goods."

"Splendid," said Chris, his attention still directed at the monitor. "Tell me what you think of this."

Sean stepped around the swivel chair and lowered his head to the display.

"Hmmm…did you remember to log yourself off your e-mail account when you left home today?" he asked.

"Yes," said Chris. "Normally, I couldn't tell you that for sure, but today I can, because we were expecting thunderstorms at home, and I wanted to unplug my laptop before I left. I am logged out, and my computer is turned off."

"Well, Yahoo! thinks you're online somewhere," said Sean.

"Sean, something funny is going on here, and I don't think it's good," said Chris.

"What's up?" asked Sean.

"I got this same message about a week ago. I thought that maybe I had left my mail account open when I stopped into the SU library, but I checked up on it and I hadn't."

"Does anyone else, like maybe your mom, use your account to send mail?"

"No, I'm the only one who uses it. And there's more that I haven't told you about. I had someone writing to me pretending to be a professor from Cornell. He said his name was Dr. Galloway. He claimed that he was an associate of Dr. Meyers, the geologist I visited a few weeks ago. We talked about quite a bit online, and he sounded very knowledgeable. He even offered to help us in our search. But then I found out that the real Dr. Galloway is deceased, and has been for over a year."

Sean slowly sank down into the chair and exhaled a long breath.

"I need to ask you a question. Were you online on Monday night, shortly before your accident?"

"No, of course not," said Chris. I was on the road from about eight that morning until the time of my accident, which was around ten-thirty. I wasn't online at any time that evening. Why do you ask?"

"Because a little earlier than that, I was online doing e-mail, and your name appeared in my list of contacts who were online. It was only for a minute or two. I tried sending you an IM, but you never responded. And then you logged out. It seemed a little odd at the time, but I didn't give it much thought."

"So what are you thinking?" asked Chris.

"I think that someone has hacked into your Yahoo! account," said Sean. "It's almost a certainty. Have you noticed anything unusual lately, such as e-mail confirmations of transactions you didn't make?" asked Sean.

"No, nothing at all, with the exception of those error messages. But I do agree that someone has accessed my account. It's pretty stupid of me to not think of that possibility given what's been happening.

"Another possibility is that someone has accessed your account to use it solely as a platform for sending out spam. It does happen. Why not check your own 'Sent Mail' folder and see whether anything has been sent from your account that you don't recognize."

Chris clicked on his Sent Mail directory and looked down the list of emails. Nothing unusual appeared in the listing; the e-mails were to friends and prospective employers.

"Nope, I recognize everything here," he said, reviewing the past thirty days' sent messages.

"OK, that's good news," said Sean. "While we're on the subject of Internet security, I think you should change the password on your account right now."

He accessed the "Settings" tab of Chris' account and stepped back out of the way.

"OK, buddy, now let's see you use some ingenuity here," Sean said. "Come up with a password with letters, numbers, and special symbols. If they're after your account for a reason, you don't want to make it easy for them."

Chris thought for a moment, then entered: chris24jr!

"Any special meaning to that?" asked Sean.

"Yup," said Chris. "Look at it…the 'chris24' could be read like 'christopher,' and the 'jr!' is just saying that I am junior. Make sense?"

"Whatever," said Sean. Although he didn't say so, Sean was a bit amazed that Chris needed to be told to change his password, given everything that had transpired over the past week.

"You know, before we go into the woods, I want to take one more good hard look at the maps and ledger, and try to put everything together," said Chris.

"What do you mean?" asked Sean.

"Well, we've got the map that we now know was drawn by Robert Gordon's great-grandson, Harrison. And we have my notes from a trip ledger that was written by someone, possibly even by Gordon himself. If we can put those two together, maybe we can find where Harrison searched, or was told to search, and find something that he overlooked.

Maybe we can even use the locations given to me by Dr. Meyers and use that as an overlay. Although we still don't know whether there is any connection between his 'legendary Indian caves' and the cave mentioned by French Louie."

"Didn't you say that your grandfather had yet another map, probably drawn by French Louie?" asked Sean.

"Yes, and that's the strangest clue of all," said Chris. "It's very primitive, although that's the way that Louie depicted things. It shows a U-shaped string of lakes, with streams and rivers all flowing out in the same direction. I've compared it to the 1903 map many times, and I just can't see where it fits in. And that's a shame, because there is an arrow that points to a specific location on the shoreline of one of the lakes. If we could figure out which one it is, we might have something."

"I'd like to have a look at that map myself," said Sean. "Maybe I could find something that you've overlooked."

"I've had all the maps digitally scanned and reproduced, so I'll bring along copies when we go into the woods on Wednesday," said Chris.

"So is that it?" asked Sean. "We have nothing left to do until we pull on our hiking boots?"

"My friend, you've helped more than you know already. As far as I'm concerned, you just need to show up, ready to go. I've still got a couple of tasks to tackle, but those should be pretty simple."

"What are they, if I may be so bold to ask?" said Sean.

"I'll probably spend a good part of the weekend matching up the earlier travel diary with the map from the Harrison expedition," said Chris. "After that, I think I'll see if I can pay a visit to Ms. Annette Surette."

"Some guys will do anything for a date," joked Sean.

"I'll have you know that most eighty-year-old women fairly swoon over my very presence," replied Chris, pretending to look indignant.

"Remind me to tell Maggie," said Sean. "Maybe she'll set you up with her grandmother."

"Speaking of Maggie," said Chris, tilting his head towards the kitchen door, "I think she's back. So I'll take my cue here and cut out." As he spoke, he gathered up the box containing the cup and rifle stock from his grandfather and slipped the paper with Surette's phone number into his wallet.

Within a moment, Maggie entered the room, now off duty. In her hand was a six-pack of Canadian ale, which she placed on the table next to the popcorn bowl.

"I hope you didn't watch the rest of the flick without me," she said, as she grabbed the DVD remote control and sat down next to Sean, close enough to confirm Chris's belief that they shared more than a basic friendship.

As Maggie settled in, she turned her light blue eyes back towards Chris. "Sean's been telling me a little bit about your hunt for caves and gold. Do you really think you're going to find anything in a place like the Adirondacks?" she asked.

"It's tough to say," said Chris. "A month ago, I would have said 'no way.' But we've made some exciting discoveries already, so maybe we will find something—assuming that someone else hasn't beat us to it over the past two hundred and thirty years."

"You gotta have faith in your dreams, right?" said Maggie.

"Yes, but even at that, it's still going to take a miracle," said Chris.

"That sounds like the title of a book: *A Miracle and a Dream*," said Maggie.

"Could be," laughed Chris. "Well, as they say, three is a crowd, so I'm outta here. I've got to get going anyway if I'm to get my beauty sleep. So I'll talk to you this weekend."

Chris spent the next two days following up on job leads. He took a telephone interview with an accounting firm in Boston and sent out résumés to a couple other east coast companies. By the time he was able to turn his attention back to the maps, it was Sunday morning.

Instead of setting an alarm, Chris always slept in on Sundays. By the time he arose and made breakfast, it was half past nine. He didn't rush himself, instead taking a long time to finish his meal while reading most of the Sunday paper. It was one of the few luxuries he allowed himself, even though he was not yet fully employed. He cleared the dishes, wiped the table, and then got out the full set of documents he'd assembled for the search.

Using his dining room table as a work surface, he unfolded the 1903 map from his grandfather, the map from Dr. Meyers, and the small, crude drawing that presumably came from French Louie. In addition to these, Chris had downloaded the pictures of the ledger pages from the Adirondack Museum from his cell phone to his computer, and then printed them out. It wasn't the complete record, but he hoped that those front pages would turn up some more clues. He also had the card with the remarks of French Louie that were recorded by his great-grandfather Calvin. Together, the maps and other documents covered the entire tabletop.

What fascinated Chris the most were the two documents with W.J. Harrison's name on top—the map and the ledger. Even though they were both owned by Harrison, they were created many years apart, perhaps over several generations. He pulled the ledger close to his face, carefully examining the stylized handwriting that was recorded in a very primitive ink. He could only guess that it was a quill-style pen that was dipped into an ink bottle, as there were many breaks in the writing.

The first entry also provided some interesting clues, although it would have been more interesting had there been a year attached to the date. As it was, it simply read "May 26," with a narrative that followed:

May 26—Aroused pre-dawn light. Portered countless measures of ingots to the bateau before bidding farewell to our fairest friends. Then, loaded our beasts with the hidden cargo, departing Skenesborough within a half an hour of Rose and Robert and company. Our guides led us west of the fort until we safely bypassed the enemy soldiers. By day's end, our party looked down upon the waters of Lake George. There we rested. 14/245 T Swain

As Chris read the paragraph, he noted the phrase "departed Skenesborough," which he knew was the original name of Whitehall prior to the Revolutionary War. He quickly looked up an online reference that listed the year of the town's name change to Whitehall as 1786. He continued on to read the following day's entries:

> May 27—Once past the fort, our guides led us south, across the bridge below the lake, then northward and west. Arrived at shore of wide river that was too deep to ford. Achak led us north to seek crossable terrain. 7/195, 7/325, 1/355. T Swain

On May 27, the journal described a fort to the south. Chris used a modern day road map of Eastern New York to trace a line south-southwest from Whitehall. Below lay Fort Ann, which was occupied by American Colonists at various times during the War for Independence.

Chris's attention was also drawn to the numerical figures at the end of each entry. They varied from day to day, and yet they all followed a pattern: a one or two digit number, then a slash, followed by a three-digit number. He had done enough orienteering to recognize the three-digit figures as bearings from a compass. He could only assume that the other numbers represented the mileage traveled on that particular leg. To test his theory, he used a ruler and the scale from the map to draw a line southwest from Whitehall at 245 degrees true for a distance of fourteen miles. He was encouraged to see that the transit line ended at the eastern shore of Lake George. He realized that the group must have approximated the distance figures, but it would still be close.

> May 28—Once across the river, which was no more than three feet to the rocky bottom, we began successive climbs into hills of progressive heights. Sufficient progress behind guides, on paths known only to them. 12/265. T Swain

Chris put down the record momentarily to consult a modern map. He could easily discern that the river they crossed at the end of the second day or early the third was the Hudson River. Fascinated, he continued to read the journal, tracking their day-by-day progress on the map.

> May 29—Hills flattened at times, but appeared larger at others. Continued west on straight transect. Compass reading may have been unreliable; wild swings in compass needle noted. No contact with other people, white or Indian, all day. 10/265. T Swain
>
> May 30—Arrived at shore of thin lake of impressive length, arranged south to north. Transit around lake to north would take several days. Passed south of lake into higher mountains. Horses finding travel difficult. 8/265. T Swain

Referring once again to the modern map, Chris followed the westward trail of the Skenesborough group through the woodlands to the southern end of Indian Lake, in Hamilton County. At this point, he picked up the 1903 topographic map and began to compare the notations recorded in the right margin with those in the journal. From May 29 through June 1, they matched exactly. It was apparent that whoever had added the lines and figures to the 1903 map had taken them directly from Thomas Swain's journal. Chris was almost certain that it was Harrison who had transcribed those notes.

He continued reading the travelogue:

> June 1—Arrived at second pristine body of water in two days. Very wild, woods very thick. Appears never to have seen people, white or Indian. Much wildlife, fish caught easily with minimal effort. Explored north end of lake, many inlets, bays and extensions. 13/265. T Swain

Rather than attempt to recreate the track on a new map, Chris simply confirmed the line drawn on Harrison's map, then followed it to Cedar

Lakes, in the middle of the West Canada Lakes Wilderness Area. Chris's own plots didn't align perfectly with Harrison's, which he couldn't understand. After applying a correction of 14° west for the magnetic variation, he kept finding himself north of the locations shown on the original plot. He checked and then rechecked his figures, each time with the same result. Based on his calculations, had the original search party marched thirty miles west on a course of 265° magnetic, they would have missed Cedar Lakes entirely, and passed almost five miles to the north. However, since it appeared that Harrison had also corrected the track for magnetic variation, he simply chalked it up to compass error.

After the entry of June 1, the handwriting changed. Another person with sloppier handwriting took over the logbook, and the entry was signed "A. Smith" instead of "T. Swain." These would be the same men that Sean had tracked down in the Washington County Archives.

> June 2—Arrived at small hellish pool of water. Upon establishing camp, experienced bear attack, Thomas broke leg under fallen steed. After much consideration, he was brought to a place out of harm's way with shelter from the elements. Although we could see the water from the cave, it was far enough removed to ease the torment of the brackish smell and the insects. We shall remain to guard and protect our injured compatriot until he is able to recommence the journey to the rendezvous. He cannot ride, as we have lost the services of both our horses. One is dead, the other is missing following skirmish with bear. Our outlook is much less positive than a week ago. 2/285, 3/005. A. Smith

Chris sat back after reading the entry from June 2 and tried to picture the events as they were described. The party had a badly injured leader, and they moved him to shelter. Also, here was the first mention of a cave. Had they known about the cave before the injury? How far was the cave from the pond? "Close enough to see the water" could have been a very long distance. Also, why had the signature changed on the daily entries? What had happened to "Thomas Swain?" Since the entry for that day noted that "Thomas" had broken his leg under a horse, Chris surmised that it referred to Thomas Swain. Perhaps he was the one they moved to the security of a cave?

Following the accident, there were no entries made in the journal for three days. Then, on June 5, the following entry was recorded:

> June 5—After careful reconsideration, Anakausuen was chosen to remain behind and provide care until Thomas regains health. Rest of party will move north, but lightened by depositing the bags with precious metals behind fake wall in back passageway. We spent today memorizing signs of lake to ensure our eventual return for gold. A. Smith

This was the last entry made before the pages became stuck to one another in the archives at Blue Mountain Lake. Anything else would have to be surmised.

Chris looked again at the map used by Harrison. He compared the tracks drawn on the faded paper with the journal notes, and he rechecked the distances two additional times. Each time he arrived at the same conclusion. If there was a cave that contained the treasure of Robert Gordon, it was probably located in the area between the Beaver Pond on Cedar Lakes and the south side of Lost Pond.

It was all fitting together well now, with the exception of the square map of Louie's. Since Louie had given his great-grandfather that map, along with the other clues, it must have meant something within the context of the mystery. And yet, try as he might, he could not fit the lakes and streams of that map into the bigger picture. He tried turning the map every which way, so that north was south and east was west, all to no avail.

It was one of only two parts of the jigsaw puzzle that did not fit.

CHAPTER 15

July 30, 2012

Monday morning couldn't have been nicer, thought Chris as he cruised along the stretch of Route 81 leading to the Canadian border. It was not too hot, and there was an unbroken ceiling of bright blue sky overhead. Although he was uncertain about how much time he'd lose crossing the border into Canada, he thought he'd be able to make the trip to Montreal in under six hours. That ought to put him in the suburb of Laprairie shortly after lunch hour.

Chris was hesitant about calling Annette Surette in the first place. He figured that she had probably received a thousand such calls from prospective treasure hunters, all looking to pick her brain about her memories from her childhood growing up with her grandfather, William J. Harrison. Chris had her pegged as a grumpy senior citizen who spoke with a French Canadian accent. However, after speaking with her, he was pleasantly surprised to find his preconceived notions to be unfounded. Throughout their brief conversation she was cheerful, alert, and if anything, spoke in a way that sounded remotely British.

Annette said that she would gladly receive a visitor, although she advised Chris that he probably didn't need to come in person. She had been only seven years old when her grandfather passed away, and she had only spoken to him a few times on the subject of his wanderings. But she would be happy to share those memories with Chris if he decided that it merited a trip to her village.

Chris followed Route 81 to the border, where he went through customs and followed the interchange onto Route 401 East. He spent the next two and a half hours covering the distance to the "Southern Ring" of Montreal's suburbs, an area some people referred to as "the 450," for the off-island area code that serves those municipalities. As Chris wound his way through the aged streets, he realized how little he knew about the province. He was expecting the hustle and bustle of Montreal, with its almost four million residents. Instead, he found a quiet semi-rural town, which was home to slightly over twenty thousand people.

Annette's dwelling was a small cape-style home on a postage stamp-sized plot of land. A white picket fence was broken by a small entrance that led to the front walkway. Chris pushed his hair to one side and tucked in his shirt before ringing the doorbell. He had replaced his worn blue jeans and t-shirt with a nicer pair of khaki slacks and a short-sleeve, button-down dress shirt for the visit.

The door was opened by a pleasant-faced woman with tightly curled locks of white hair and tortoise shell bifocals. A retired school teacher, she had worked and lived in the community for most of her life. She had never married, and lived by herself in the small home.

"Hello, Miss Surette, I'm Chris Carey. We spoke on the phone yesterday. It's so nice to meet you."

"Of course, of course, please come in," said Annette. "I'm sorry you had to drive so far to get here."

"It wasn't bad at all," said Chris. "I've always wanted to spend some time inside the old city, although this really is a lot different than downtown Montreal, isn't it?"

"Oh, my goodness, yes!" declared Annette. "I don't think I could handle all the activity of the city. This is just about perfect here; it's quiet, slow, and I know everyone on my street. I wouldn't trade it for anything."

"I hope I'm not bothering you by asking to see you. I imagine you must get calls like this all the time. It must get bothersome after a while."

"No, not at all," replied Annette. "As a matter of fact, no one has asked me about my grandfather in many, many years. He's been gone a very long time now, you know."

"Yes, I know, 1941, wasn't it?" said Chris. "My friend tracked the story of his life in order to find a living relative, which is what brought me to you. Your grandfather led a very interesting life."

"Interesting, but in many ways wasted. He spent so much of his time and resources searching for his treasures that he forgot what was important in his life," said Annette, shaking her head sadly.

"That's been the story of many men throughout time," said Chris, sympathizing with the elderly woman.

"I remember my mother when she was younger. She sometimes wondered whether her father cared for her at all. Life was always 'what we'll do after we have our money.' If only he cared how little it meant to us, maybe things would have been different."

"Do you have anything left from your grandfather?" asked Chris.

"No, nothing of any consequence," replied Annette. "We have his family bible, which has nothing written inside it. I also have his pipe rack, an old world globe, and perhaps a few other items around the house. But none of those things would lead you to anything, dear. They certainly didn't work for my grandfather."

"Miss Surette, I'd like to ask you for your opinion on a few things. There really are no correct answers to these questions. I'd just like to know what you think. Is that OK with you?"

"Yes, of course," said Annette. "But please, do call me Annette. Otherwise I'll start feeling like a senior citizen," she said, laughing at her own joke.

"Thank you, Annette," Chris said. "First of all, do you personally believe that there ever was a treasure that was lost by your family?"

"Yes, I do believe that it happened," said Annette, nodding her head. "During those early years, starting around 1775, most of the population south of Lake Champlain fled to Canada. At least, those who were loyal to the King did, which included my ancestors. I believe that a lot of people were forced to leave behind their possessions. However, according to the story, my family was forced to abandon a lot more than most."

"Do you believe that it is still there, somewhere, waiting to be found?" asked Chris.

"To be quite honest, I don't know, and I don't really care," said Annette. "Even if I knew where to find it, I wouldn't go near it for anything. There is a curse on that treasure, you know. Both of them. I couldn't understand why anyone would even dream of pursuing it."

Chris listened carefully, trying to sort out if he had heard her correctly.

"I notice you said 'both of them.' What do you mean by that?" he asked softly.

"Well, there isn't much that I can tell you except to repeat back the little bit that my grandfather told me. He said that there was enough treasure to fill several large chests. But he also said that according to his grandmother, it was lost in two different locations."

"One of the chests was dumped into the southern end of Lake Champlain, right?" said Chris.

"Yes, that was the chest that everyone used to ask about. Supposedly, it contained seventy thousand dollars in gold. Only the funny thing was, it never did."

"You mean that was a hoax?" asked Chris.

"No, it was real," said Annette. "But according to family legend, it was silver, not gold. I don't know how the story got turned around. Maybe it was because everyone knew that the Robert Gordon used to deal in gold. I don't know. But when my grandfather searched the lake shortly after the turn of the century, he wasn't looking for gold; it was silver."

"Did he ever find anything?" asked Chris.

"No. Only a continuation of the curse," said Annette. "Two men died that summer out on the boats. He gave up soon after that. He lived another thirty-six years, and yet he never resumed the search. In many ways, he died a broken man.

"What do you mean when you call it a curse?"

"Because it is a curse," said Annette, her eyes misting over. "So many men in our family have been ruined or killed because of this...this thing! It started when they first tried to move the gold out of the Colonies during the War. Robert Gordon's very dear friend perished in a mysterious accident and the gold never made it across the border. Then it was Robert Gordon himself, who was planning on retrieving the gold after the Revolution when he was killed in a hunting accident. Next, it was his son, who was returning from his job on a sailing ship to take over for his father. He disappeared suddenly and was never heard from again."

"I see what you mean," said Chris, sympathizing with the woman. However, he decided to keep his knowledge of Thomas Swain a secret, at least for the time being.

"And that's not all," continued Annette. "As I already mentioned, the summer my grandfather organized the search party on Lake Champlain, two of his best men died in strange ways. One of his foremen fell off the boat and drowned before he could be helped. It was rather bizarre, because he was supposedly an excellent swimmer. My grandfather said it was as though the water just opened up and swallowed him. I was only a child when he told me the story, but I remember as clearly as if it was yesterday."

"And the other man?" asked Chris.

"He was a young man, a kid really, who just got sick in the middle of the afternoon one day and collapsed. He never recovered consciousness, and he died that same day."

"That sounds too quick to be an illness. Did anyone else on the boat get sick?" asked Chris.

"No. They pulled off the lake to get help, and they never returned. Grandfather told me later that he thought it was heat stroke, but they never did find out. The boy's family wanted to have Grandpa brought up on charges, but nothing ever came of it."

"I had no idea that all of this happened," said Chris. "I can see why you feel snake-bit over this whole matter."

Annette only looked back at Chris and nodded. She reached for a tissue and blotted her eyes dry. Chris felt a bit awkward asking more questions, but he decided to move forward and sensitively query her about the rest of the legend.

"You've told me about the story of the silver that was dumped into Lake Champlain. And I've read about that in detail, too. But I've also found evidence that there was some gold that was carried west, into the woodlands that later became part of the Adirondack Park."

"Then it sounds as though you might know as much as me," said Annette. "According to my grandfather, most of the gold went overland to avoid capture by the American Colonists. Supposedly, two of Robert Gordon's employees were charged with moving the shipment. But as I mentioned, one of them never made it out of the woods alive. The other man, whose name I do not know, made it through to meet my ancestor in Canada. An Indian guide who had helped to steer them along the route later reported that the other employee had passed away deep in the woods. And that's about all I was told of that story."

"Your grandfather had some pretty specific information about the silver lost in Lake Champlain. Do you know if he had any similar directions to lead him to the gold that was left in the Adirondacks?"

"I only know that he had some papers handed down from his grandmother," said Annette. "I do not know what they were, or how she got them. But he seemed to think that he could use that information to follow the trail to the treasure. It never worked. He always remained furious with the men he'd brought along with him. None of those same men were with him when he explored the lake, which was two years later."

Chris reflected on Annette's answers for a moment or two, trying to figure out if her responses held additional clues. There were none that he could find, and no additional questions came to mind. He realized that he knew more about Harrison's 1903 voyage into the Adirondacks than did his granddaughter. There was little else he could learn from the last living descendant of Robert Gordon.

In an effort to be sociable, Chris changed the tone of the conversation. He told Annette about his own family and spoke of his aspirations to move into the world of business management. He sensed that she appreciated the company and enjoyed talking about subjects other than the family gold. Before he realized it, another hour had passed, and she had shared her own life story, complete with a tour of her family photo album. About the time that he felt ready to leave, he noticed a certain hesitation about her. It was as though she wanted to say something, but was having trouble doing so. He instinctively fell quiet and allowed her to speak her mind.

"Before you go, I'd like to ask you something," she said. "You asked me earlier whether I had any of my grandfather's possessions in the house, and I mentioned what little I have. But I also have a small collection of family heirlooms that go back seven generations, to Robert and Rose Gordon. They have been passed down from generation to generation, without a break, since the Revolutionary War. Would you like to see them?" asked Annette.

"Yes, very much, if you don't mind," said Chris.

Annette arose from her seat and went into the dining room, where she removed a small black box from beneath a teakwood china cabinet. She carried the box back to the living room and set it in front of Chris.

"I've never shown these to anyone," she said, lifting the lid. "I don't know if any of these items carry any significance, other than their sentimental value to me. But I have safeguarded them since my mother passed them down to me before she died in 1970. I would like to pass them down to someone before it is too late. However, because I have no children, it presents a problem to me. At least two of these items are quite valuable."

Chris reached into the bottom of the box and lifted several items out to examine. The first was an ornate gold cross, which was hand-forged and intricately carved into exquisite patterns.

"Rose Gordon received that cross as a gift from Robert's parents in London," said Annette. "The artist was Scottish, as was Robert Gordon himself. She wore that the day of their wedding."

The next item Chris retrieved was a copper coin, which was exceedingly thick and heavy. It was stored inside a small envelope for safekeeping. The coin was worn so badly that very few details remained on either side.

"According to the family legend, that currency was the first money that was ever spent in Robert Gordon's store in Skenesborough, now Whitehall, in New York. I don't know if that's a true story, but that's the way it got passed down to me," said Annette.

"He must have been very frugal to have saved his first penny," said Chris.

"Yes, especially when you consider what that penny could have bought in 1776," said Annette.

Below the penny was a small foam pad on which rested a few pieces of silver jewelry. The matching set included a bracelet and two rings, which were of hammered sterling with a darker metal overlaid in geometric patterns. Chris could not determine the identity of the second metal, although he did not believe it to be gold.

"I know very little about those pieces, although I do believe that they belonged to my grandfather's mother. Her name was Mary Harrison, and assuming that what I've told you is true, those are her only surviving possessions," said Annette.

Finally, Chris reached to the very bottom of the box and pulled out the last remaining item. Holding it flat in his hand, he brought it up to eye level for a closer look. It was a very large and heavy coin which was struck from pure gold. The now-familiar face of King Carol III stood out on the front of the coin, while the reverse was dominated by the royal shield. Chris felt his heartbeat accelerate as he looked for the date on the front. It read 1773. He flipped the coin from front to back, over and over again, just as he had in Blue Mountain Lake. It was identical to the coins he had found in Louie's trunk.

"Isn't that a beautiful piece?" asked Annette. "That, too, came from Robert Gordon's house. I know it's worth a lot of money, but I've never had it appraised."

"If I'm not mistaken, gold pieces like this would go for at least a couple thousand dollars," said Chris. "They've doubled and tripled with the price of gold. You should have this stored in a safe deposit box somewhere."

"That's probably good advice," she replied. "I'd hate to lose it, since it's been in the family so long. And it's so beautiful. Have you ever seen anything like it?"

Chris looked back at her, nodding his head.

"As a matter of fact, I have."

CHAPTER 16

July 31, 2012

The entire first floor of Chris' house was in turmoil. Sleeping bags and a tent and ground cloths and cooking gear lay in swaths that covered almost every inch of floor. It was as though an entire camping store had fallen from an unseen third floor and scattered itself evenly across his home.

Although Chris had done a lot of hiking and camping in his time, it had been quite a while since his last foray into the woods. He already owned just about everything he needed, but fitting it all into his mid-sized frame pack was a different matter. Working off a checklist that he'd drafted that morning, he slowly loaded each item, one by one, into the various compartments and pockets of the pack. As he did so, he tried to keep a mental picture of where critical supplies, such as his rain gear and flashlight, were packed. It seemed like an endless process, and he found that he wasn't enjoying himself.

To give himself a break, Chris knocked off for an early lunch, followed by a shortened three mile run. When he returned, he logged onto his laptop to quickly check e-mail. He noticed that Dr. Meyers was online, and decided to say hello via instant message:

chriscarey1986: Hello Dr. Meyers. Just thought I'd drop by to say hello and give you a status.
Cave_dweller_DrM: Hello back to you. What's new from the north country?

chriscarey1986: Not much to tell you about yet, but we leave for the woods tomorrow…FINALLY!

Cave_dweller_DrM: Last time I spoke to you, you had described a "hack attack" from an unknown entity. Did you ever find out who was talking to you while posing as Dr. Galloway?

chriscarey1986: No, Doctor, I don't have a clue. I doubt I'll ever find out, either, which is odd because so few people know about our search. But it's OK. I changed my password and the activity stopped. Thanks for the concern.

Cave_dweller_DrM: Glad to hear it.

chriscarey1986: I've got a question that maybe you could help me with. It's more topographical than geological, but I'd like to hear your opinion.

Cave_dweller_DrM: You got it. Shoot.

chriscarey1986: I've got another map, similar to the one you gave me, but it was plotted by an earlier treasure hunter back in 1903. He drew in some search lines of magnetic bearing that were recorded in either 1774 or 1775. The magnetic readings are quite clear, but yet my own plot doesn't match the one he drafted. Any thoughts? It might make me shift my search area by about five miles.

Cave_dweller_DrM: What did you use for magnetic declination?

chriscarey1986: I looked it up online to be precise. I'm using 14° west.

Cave_dweller_DrM: Hang on one minute…OK, there's your problem. Let me guess: your line passed north of the original, correct?

chriscarey1986: How did you know that?

Cave_dweller_DrM: Because the magnetic declination, or "variation," changes slightly every year, as the magnetic north pole of the Earth shifts. I just ran the geographic position figures you sent me in your last e-mail, and found that the declination in 1775 would have been a little less than 6° west, so there's an eight degree error in your calculation.

chriscarey1986: I had no idea that if could shift that much in two hundred thirty years.

Cave_dweller_DrM: Even by the time they made the search in 1903, it had migrated from 6° west to 11° west. The Earth is not a static planet!

chriscarey1986: Thanks, Doc. I appreciate you clearing that up for me. We'll be back out of the woods on Sunday night. I'll have a report on any findings to you by Monday morning.

Cave_dweller_DrM: Thanks, Chris. I wish all my students were so punctual. Please let me know if you'd ever like to come here to study. I'd welcome you into our department any time.

chriscarey1986: Thanks again! I appreciate the help.

Cave_dweller_DrM: Talk soon. Bye.

On top of the normal camping gear, Chris found himself packing numerous items that were out of the ordinary. These included some large plastic bags containing oversized maps, as well as headlamps and shovels for their explorations. Unsure of what they would find, Chris wanted to be prepared for all the contingencies they might meet. It seemed an eternity, but after four hours of sorting and packing, he finally tightened the final drawstrings and lifted the pack off the floor. It weighed in at about forty-five pounds, he figured, which would still be a comfortable-sized pack for his frame. He stood the pack up next to the door, ready to go. A long and contoured walking stick rested upright against the same wall, ready to deploy.

Meanwhile, about sixty miles to the east, Sean was going through a very similar process. However, his table and couch more closely resembled a freeze-dried version of Food and Wine magazine. He had picked up all the food for the entire five-day venture, and he had it laid out across the furniture to package in daily ration bags. It was a cumbersome process, attempting to balance out weight and space while still ensuring that they had meals that they both enjoyed. Chris had made it easy for him by saying "anything but tuna fish." Sean had wanted to pick up a vacuum-packed package of the fish, just to spite his friend. However, he thought better of it later, as he didn't want the added weight.

One unique item that would find its way into Sean's pack was a Troy Shadow X5 metal detector. This piece of equipment was unlike most other brands, which tended to be heavy and bulky. Instead, it had been engineered to be lightweight and sensitive, which made it perfect for carrying and using in remote territory such as the Adirondack back country. Weighing in at a miniscule two and a half pounds, it was one of the lightest metal detectors on the market. Sean had originally borrowed a similar machine from a friend to look for a lost ring a few years earlier. However, he was so impressed with the performance and enjoyed using it so much that he soon decided to order one for himself.

In addition to the detector, Sean also brought along a GPS receiver that would track their progress through the woods and pinpoint their precise location at any time. In general, he had little faith in the map and compass as a tool for critical navigation. He also brought along some screen-type filters of various gauge thicknesses to serve as strainers for items buried in sand and soil. Although it significantly increased the bulk of his pack, the extra equipment added less than five pounds to the overall weight of his load.

Chris walked in the door of his parents' house just a little after eight-thirty. His mother was already out in the backyard, clearing a few weeds out of the tomato and zucchini patch. She took a great amount of pride in her crop, although she gave away more than she ate. Several of her neighbors were also good friends, and she was constantly bringing them baskets of homegrown produce.

Chris stepped out the back door and onto a red slate patio, which bordered the twenty-foot-long vegetable patch. The back of the patio was ringed with assorted perennial flowers, which Theresa had grown into a beautiful palette of summer colors.

"You've got this place looking great, Mom," said Chris, announcing his presence over the flower bed.

His mother turned in his direction while wiping some dirt off her sleeve.

"Thanks, honey. It's an ongoing battle, but sometimes I think the weeds are winning."

"I stopped and picked up your favorite bagels from Wegmans. Why don't you put down your trowel and come inside to join me for breakfast?"

"I already ate, but I'll still come and sit with you," said his mother. "When's Sean getting here?"

"In another hour, maybe a little more," said Chris. "I figured we could talk a bit until then."

In the kitchen, Theresa poured two cups of coffee and set them down on the table.

"This trip sounds like a lot of fun for both of you," she said. "Is Sean as excited about it as you?"

"I think so, although I still think he'd be happier if we were sticking to the idea about panning for gold," laughed Chris. "He really seems to want to try his hand at that."

"I doubt he'd find much here in New York State, would he?" asked his mother.

"According to the geologist I met at Cornell, it's possible," said Chris. "But the chances of finding any are pretty slim, and we'd have to work for months to gather anything worth selling."

"Well, from what you've told me, you've got something a lot more exciting on your hands than a little bit of gold dust. And I've got to admit, it is kind of fun to see someone in the family looking into the story of the deathbed statement of Louis Seymour. After all, he had nothing to gain at that point, and no reason to lie."

"That's true, Mom. But you've also got to consider the possibility that he may have been delirious when he made those statements to great-grandfather. And yet, those two Spanish coins hidden in his chest prove that he did find something. So who knows?"

"Is there any chance that he might have acquired those coins through any other means? Maybe in trade for furs, or for guiding services?" asked Theresa.

"I asked that same question of the coin dealer in Syracuse," said Chris, shaking his head, "but he said it was highly improbable. He said that those coins would have been out of circulation for almost a hundred years by the time Louie hid them away in that trunk."

Chris stopped to spread some cream cheese onto a sliced bagel.

"And there's another thing," he continued. "The woman I met up in Quebec, who was a direct descendant of Robert Gordon, owned a coin that was identical to the ones that Louie had stashed away. Right down to the year and the mint mark. That's too much of a coincidence to overlook. I'd bet almost anything that Louie came into contact with at least part of Gordon's legendary treasure, and he did it through a guy named William Harrison, who was Gordon's great-grandson. I can't prove it yet, but somehow it just fits."

"Well, dear, I believe that if anyone can do it, it's you. You know, I never could keep anything hidden from you around here. You seemed to find every Christmas present as soon as I brought it home, no matter where I put it."

Then, changing the subject, she posed another question.

"So what are you planning on doing if you do find this chest of gold?" she asked. "That's a lot of money. What was it, you said $70,000?"

"Actually, Mom, it was $70,000 back in 1775, when Gordon supposedly dumped it when he fled for Canada. But the price of gold was fixed back then at $19.39 an ounce. Today, it's a little over $1,600 for the same ounce."

"So what does that come out to in modern dollars?"

"Somewhere in the neighborhood of $6.3 million, give or take a few hundred thousand."

"Good heavens! I had no idea! Chris, that's huge. You'd make national news if you found even a portion of that."

"It would be nice, but purely for historical purposes," Chris said. "You do know that we couldn't keep it for ourselves, right? New York State law says that it would belong to the state, even if we recovered it on our own property. And this is hardly private property."

"Leave it to the lawyers! But don't let your father hear me say that," laughed his mother, rolling her eyes. "So what would happen to it? Would the money just go into the state treasury, or something equally foolish?"

Chris took a moment to answer, choosing his words as he slowly sipped his coffee.

"Mom, to tell you the truth, I've been toying around with an idea for a week or two, but I don't know how to get started with it."

"What's that, dear? Maybe I could help."

"Well, one of the things that Grandpa had stashed away with his maps was a short list of things that Louie told his father. Some of those comments were meant to help him dig up the alleged chest of gold. But at least one was a request: a plea for Calvin Carey to use the gold to help take care of Louie's place. If we do find anything, I think it would be appropriate to find a way to help make Louie's wish come true."

"Hmmm... now there's an interesting thought," said Theresa. "Although I'm not sure what mechanisms are in place to help you to accomplish that goal."

"I've been looking into an idea," said Chris. "It would be a way to establish the settlement of French Louie as either a national or a New York State historic landmark. But there are a couple of issues."

"Such as?"

"The entire Adirondack Park is already a National Historic Landmark. So the powers that be might not want to designate Louie's site as anything special, above and beyond the current designation."

"But there are other sites within the Adirondack Park that have special historical significance, aren't there?" asked his mother. "I know that John Brown's Farm is one such site in Lake Placid, and I'm almost certain that there are others."

"You're right, Mom," said Chris. "It's just something I have to look into. I think that Louie's homestead represents a significant snapshot of life in the olden days of Upstate New York, and I believe it should be preserved to remind us of that heritage. What better symbol of that early pioneering spirit could you possibly select than Adirondack French Louie?"

Chris and his mom spent the next forty-five minutes or so chatting, talking over old times and discussing Chris's ongoing job search. They didn't have as much time to spend together as they would have liked these days, so they both treasured the occasions when they could sit and engage in leisurely conversation.

It was a few minutes after ten when Sean arrived in his Mercedes. Rather than pull into the circular driveway that looped in front of the house, he pulled ahead towards the old separate garage. Theresa had asked him to leave the vehicle in "long term parking" while the two of them were gone on their camping excursion.

Sean removed his fully-loaded frame pack and carried it over to the back of Chris's Jeep. He left it by the rear door, which opened into a cavernous cargo compartment when the rear seats were lowered. He then skipped up the front stairs and rang the doorbell.

Chris answered the door while still holding his coffee mug.

"Come in, stranger, and have a shot of caffeine before we hit the road."

"I just might take you up on that," said Sean. "I was up until kind of late last night trying to tune up the metal detector. Between that and a two-hour, late-night customer call, I ended up with less than four hours sleep. Again."

Chris laughed at his friend's complaint, because he knew that he never went to sleep before one in the morning, regardless of his workload. Even on nights when Sean wasn't wrapped up in his business, he was either watching a movie or chatting with any number of friends online. And late-ly, Maggie had been visiting until the late hours, which contributed to his nocturnal lifestyle.

Sean followed Chris into the kitchen and sat down at the table. Theresa hovered the coffee pot over a ceramic mug and filled it to the top. She had known Sean almost as long as Chris had, and she considered herself to be his surrogate mom after his own mother passed away three years ago. After the coffee, she offered him one of the leftover bagels from Chris's supply.

"Normally, I'd say no, but since I'm going to have to put up with your son's cooking for the next five days, maybe I'd better stuff in everything I can now."

"Hey, I read the directions on those food packs you bought: 'Just add boiling water,' right? I think even I can handle that," remarked Chris.

Sean then turned to Theresa with a conspiring grin on his face and asked, "So please tell me, how did you get him that Jeep so quickly? It's gorgeous!"

"I'm sorry, but that wasn't me or Chris's dad. My husband wasn't even in the country when it happened, and I didn't know about it until the fol-lowing day. I know it sounds crazy, but whoever got that for him knew about his accident before I did. And they have connections. It's a complete mystery to me."

"That's just plain strange," said Sean, shaking his head in amazement.

"Well, I think I'll find out soon," said Chris. "Once the final title arrives, it should say who paid the bill, even if it lists me as the owner. For now, I'm not going to think about it."

"Before you leave, could you tell me where you're going to be and when I'll hear from you again?" asked Theresa, looking at her son.

"Sure, Mom. We're parking at a place called Perkins Clearing, which is about six miles into the woods on a dirt road and roughly eight miles north of the town of Speculator, up Route 30. We're going to West Canada Lake and Cobble Hill on Cedar Lakes, where we'll spend the first couple days. Then, we'll head north through the woods to Lost Pond and look around up there with both topographic maps. If we can cover that ground in the next two days, that should leave us the full day on Sunday to come back out. We might even make it back here in time for dinner."

"I won't wait for you, but please do give me a call when you're out," asked his mom. "I know I shouldn't, but I do worry about you."

"No problem, Mom. We'll give you a shout as soon as we get back to the car."

Chris gave his mother a big hug and a peck on the cheek. Then he and Sean headed back outside and loaded Sean's pack into the back of the Jeep. It felt almost surreal; they had spent so much time planning and researching this trip, and now they were finally ready to depart. Following one more round of hugs, they were on their way.

Not much was said for the first few miles of the trip. Sean had offered to take a turn driving, which Chris had declined. As much as he missed his old Jeep CJ7, he had to admit that the new Liberty was a lot nicer. In addition to the added size and storage room, it had all the creature comforts he could ask for, along with the enhanced electronics package and surround-sound system. The fact that it still had that new car smell only added to the attraction. As they drove east on Glass Factory Road, heading toward Route 8 North, Chris realized that he was enjoying the scent.

"You like that smell, huh?" asked Sean.

"I didn't know I was that obvious," said Chris, laughing at the remark. "Yeah, I've never had a new vehicle. I think I could get used to it."

"Anyway, I've been thinking about this route we're taking ever since you proposed it. Why do you want to go to West Canada Lake first, especially via Perkins Clearing? And why bother cutting through the woods from Cedar Lakes to Lost Pond when there is a road that goes right to the place?"

"That's a lot of questions, so bear with me as I try to answer them for you one at a time. First of all, we're going to make a couple of stops en route to West Canada Lake. They won't take long, but I just want to cross off a couple of locations that were marked up on Harrison's map from 1903."

"Where, specifically, are we stopping?" asked Sean.

"Harrison annotated some spots on the hill overlooking Pillsbury Lake that look like a cave entrance. I'd like to swing by there and take a look, just to see what he found."

"If he found a cave, no matter how big or small, but then resumed his search, it must have meant that it didn't turn up anything," said Sean. "So why do we want to look in the same place?"

"Because we have technology on our side," said Chris.

Sean fell silent for a moment, then his eyes widened briefly.

"The metal detector!" he said gleefully.

"Exactly," said Chris. "We won't have to spend a lot of time in any one spot; we can go in with our light, check it out, and run the Troy machine over it."

"How about the rest of the scene around West Canada Lakes and Louie's cave? Same thing: you just want to check it out with the detector?"

"Yes, although I don't think there's much of a shot in either place," said Chris. "If Louie had somehow gained possession of the gold, he probably would have had it in his cabin, which of course was burned not long after Louie's death. If there ever was a cache of precious metals inside the structure, it would have been discovered sometime after the cabin was destroyed. Since then, several structures have stood on that exact same location. The last of those was a cabin built by the State of New York."

"What was that," asked Sean, "a ranger station?"

"Something like that," said Chris. "I think they called it an 'Interior Caretaker's Cabin.' But they burned that down intentionally sometime in the 1980s. I never did understand that move."

"We want to end up at Lost Pond for the last two days of this trip, right? Did you know we could follow a dirt road right to the pond itself?" asked Sean.

"That's what I've heard," said Chris, "although that 'road' has been in pretty poor shape for many years. As a matter of fact, when I hiked the Northville-Placid Trail, I passed the sign for the Otter Brook Trail, which is supposedly connected to a different spur of that same road. I've got news for you: it doesn't really exist, unless you've got some special tracking skills. I walked about fifty feet north trying to see some signs of it, and I couldn't find a thing. Personally, I'd rather trust our GPS for navigation that a non-existent trail."

"OK, I see your point," said Sean. "We can do that. I just wanted to know your thought process, that's all."

"Don't trust me, eh?" asked Chris, elbowing his friend.

"Hey, I'm here, aren't I?" replied Sean.

The two talked about the search for the next hour, reaching Speculator slightly before noon. Then, they turned north onto Route 30 until they reached Mason Lake, where they pulled onto the logging road that led them into the woods. As they bounced past large hardwood trees, creeks, and meadows, Chris thought, as he always did, that there is no place in the world to compare with the Adirondacks for pristine natural beauty.

In another twenty minutes, they rolled through Perkins Clearing, then turned right to follow the road to Sled Harbor. These last few miles had been off limits to the public for many years, prior to a land swap between the state and a large private paper company. Now the road was open all the way up to the trail leading to the old Pillsbury Mountain fire tower. Chris's rugged SUV easily navigated this route, despite the deep ruts and exposed rock that filled the dirt road.

Within another mile, they pulled into the small gravel parking lot that sat at the end of the road. The lot was ringed with boulders that had been strategically arranged to prevent the passage of all-terrain vehicles. As they pulled their packs out of the Jeep, Sean looked around appreciatively at the towering wooded mountains.

"That's some serious altitude for the southern Adirondacks," he said, nodding to the mountain directly in front of their vehicle.

"That's the side of Pillsbury Mountain," said Chris, pointing to the hiking trail sign. "It's got one of the original fire towers up on top, if you care to hike a couple miles straight up. On a clear day, they say you can see as far as the Green Mountains of Vermont."

"That's nice," said Sean. "Right now, all I want to find is the gold mountains."

"Ha! We'd be so lucky," said Chris as he leaned his body against a tree trunk, stretching out his calf muscles. "For the most part, we should both just look at this as a fun camping trip. Anything we find would be way above and beyond my expectations."

"Sounds like my father when he goes hunting," said Sean. "Every year he gets his license and takes his rifle and heads off into the woods. He walks for miles on end, but I don't recall that he's ever gotten a deer. For all I know, he's never even fired his weapon."

The two of them finished their stretching exercises and then shouldered their packs. The trail sign on the post pointed the way towards the "French Louie Trail" and the West Canada Lakes.

"Age before beauty," said Sean, nodding his head for Chris, who was actually just three weeks older than Sean, to take the lead. But Sean knew that his friend had planned the itinerary for the entire week and had definite ideas about which way he wanted to go.

As they headed up the path that led them up Blue Ridge, Sean commented about the solid condition of the path.

"This trail is nice and dry," he said. "It's a lot nicer than some of the eroded trails I've hiked up north. Some of those have become twenty feet wide, and you're sloshing through eight inches of mud with every step."

"That's because we're actually walking on an old roadbed," said Chris. "As recently as ten years ago, you could have driven over this with little more than a passenger car. But the passage of just a few years has allowed the vegetation to close in and take over most of it. The only reason we can walk along this half of it is that there's a steady flow of people tramping it down."

The first mile and a half was entirely uphill. They gained several hundred feet in elevation as they walked past sloping hills that were hidden beneath a mixed deciduous-conifer forest. At times, they stopped as Chris pointed out places where some of the old camps had been before they were torn out following the land swaps. But most of the time they maintained a steady pace, climbing the ridge until they reached the point where the trail split. The trail straight ahead proceeded on to Cedar Lakes, whereas the path to the left took them west toward Pillsbury Lake and the West Canadas.

"Which way?" asked Sean, taking a quick swig from his canteen.

"Go west, young man," said Chris, pointing the way to Pillsbury Lake. "Just don't get too used to the trail. We'll be leaving it within the next mile."

Chris followed Sean down a declining dirt roadbed for the next twenty minutes. At that point, they came to a place where there was a large clearing on the left, in which lay the rotting remains of a long-gone structure.

"There used to be a hunting camp here," said Chris, directing his gaze across the opening in the woods.

"Looks like it's been gone quite a while," said Sean, surveying the scene.

"It has, although I couldn't say when it was removed. It was before my time, that's for sure. It sits close to the end of Pillsbury Lake, which is where we leave the trail. We're going to head around the north side of the lake for a bit and check out some sites. You ready to get your feet dirty?"

"As ready as I'll ever be," said Sean. "You lead, I'll follow."

They marched around the wet east end of the lake, crossing over some marshy ground until finally reaching the steep hill on the other side of the water. This was the south side of what was commonly called Noisey Ridge. It was marked extensively on Harrison's map, and even the larger map from Dr. Meyers had a reference from the satellite imagery.

Once they were in the area Chris thought looked like what he was looking for, they split up and walked parallel lines, about fifty feet apart, along the topographic lines of the chart. Sean covered the lower ground, while Chris scanned the territory above. It wasn't a perfect system, and they couldn't see everything, but it allowed them to discount some of the annotations that Harrison recorded on his map signifying a point of interest.

At around four thirty, Chris stumbled upon a jumble of rock that looked at first like an opening. However, it petered out after just a few steps, affording little or no protection from the elements. To be safe, Sean removed the metal detector from the side of his pack and turned the power on. A half-dozen sweeps of the ground in front of the formation turned up nothing, so he quickly shut it off again and reattached the apparatus to the pack.

By six o'clock, they had covered all of the areas shaded on the 1903 map, although they never deciphered all of the markings written by Harrison. He had obviously found several landmarks that interested him enough to make notes, none of which were still apparent today.

Finally, Chris refolded the map from Dr. Meyers and pushed it into his side pocket. He realized that they were well into dinner hour, although they were still a full hour away from their destination.

"OK, time to kick it into overdrive and hoof it over to camp for the night. You hungry?" he asked.

"I've been hungry since we hit the trail this afternoon. I could eat a whole horse," said Sean.

"I can't help you with the horse, but how about some of that Thai chicken with rice I saw in your food bag?" asked Chris. "If we kick it into over-drive, we should be able to eat a little after seven."

With food on their minds, the two explorers made good time coming off the ridge and backtracking around the east end of Pillsbury Lake. From there it was less than a mile along the packed dirt path until they came to the Pillsbury Lake lean-to. They were relieved to find that it was empty, and they gratefully heaved their packs into the structure.

"This thing is pretty darned nice," said Sean, looking around the logs that formed the inside walls. "It looks like it's been here an awfully long time."

"Longer than you might think," answered Chris, pointing up to some inscriptions carved into the bottom of the roof shingles. Some of the dates went back over forty years. "I can't tell you when they were built, but they've been here for as long as anyone can remember. This whole part of the Adirondacks, in fact the entire park, used to be teeming with activity. Lean-tos, ranger stations, fire towers, and many more trails than exist today. It's sad, but a lot of that stuff has gone away over the years."

"Why's that?" asked Sean as he opened his backpack and removed the food bag.

"Mainly money," answered Chris. "These days, there simply isn't enough to pay for all the nice things such as recreational hiking facilities. The whole network that used to support it has fallen on hard times, and they've cut back to bare bones. You'll see several examples of that this week. It's pretty sad."

"Tell you what," said Sean as he arranged his cooking gear. "Before you start shedding any tears over the state's budget woes, why don't you go get some exercise. I need you to pump about four quarts of water."

"Will do, sir," said Chris, taking the Katadyn microfilter water purifier and jugs from Sean and heading down to the shoreline. Unfortunately, the days of drinking water straight from the lake were long gone. Those unfortunate individuals who committed that blunder often found themselves anchored in the outhouse for extended periods of time. The parasite Giardia lamblia, known affectionately as "beaver fever" because it is carried by the resident beaver population, could wreak havoc unless properly filtered out of the drinking water.

It took Chris a surprisingly short amount of time to filter the large quantity of water into the folding plastic storage jugs. They wasted little time in getting the stove lit and the cooking water boiling. Within fifteen minutes, they were sitting over a nice hot meal.

"This stuff is pretty darn good, if I must say so myself," said Sean, digging into his Thai dish.

"The lasagna is pretty tasty too," agreed Chris. "But then again, almost anything tastes good in the woods. You take the same thing home and try making it in your kitchen, it just doesn't taste the same."

"So tomorrow, you want to head over to West Canada Lake?" asked Sean.

"Yeah, that's the plan," said Chris. "I'd like to get a really early start, so that we can make it over there by about nine o'clock. That's so we can check out old Louie's homestead and still have time to make it over to

Cobble Hill in the afternoon."

"You think anyone's ever been over that area with a metal detector?" asked Sean.

"I'd say it's a pretty safe bet," replied Chris, taking a dinner roll from the food bag. "Even if it takes a couple days to carry it in there, you've gotta figure that someone has tried searching it with one, given all the years it's been there. Still, even if we don't get a hit on anything valuable, it should be interesting to see what the detector finds. I'm glad you bought that thing; it'll save us a lot of wasted time."

"How about all the other areas that Harrison recorded on his map?" asked Sean. "Do you plan on making any other stops to check those out as we head over to West Canada Lake?"

"No, I don't," said Chris. "First, I don't think we have time, if we want to leave ourselves two full days to search around Lost Pond. We've got to do our thing at Louie's and then move on quickly. Also, nothing else matches the sketch that Louie gave to my great-grandfather."

"You mean the small drawing with the collection of ponds or lakes?"

"That's the one," said Chris.

"Did you bring that map?" asked Sean.

"No, that's the only one I didn't bring," said Chris. "It didn't provide any information that would help us, because it was drawn in such crude detail and proportion-less scale. And it didn't make a lot of sense, because all the streams ran to the north, or what appeared to be north. If you look at a real map of this region, there's no single location that matches that description. Also, I've looked at that paper so much that I could probably recreate it right here on the spot for you."

"And yet there was that arrow pointing to someplace," said Sean. "I'd love to have about five minutes with Louie, just to find out what he meant."

"That would answer a lot of questions, wouldn't it?" said Chris.

Since the sun was going down, the two men set about their evening chores, including clean-up and preparing the lean-to for the night. They rolled out their sleeping bags, and then gathered enough wood to keep a small fire burning until about an hour after dark. They didn't need the blaze for cooking, or for warmth. But both of them had always enjoyed the primeval urge to gaze into the bright orange flames of the fireplace as they listened to the sounds of the approaching Adirondack nighttime. The dancing flames sent darts of color into the shadows of the lean-to, while the calls of the loons echoed from over the lake. It was purely magical, and the two sat rooted in place until the fire was reduced to a pile of glowing embers. Then, they slept.

It was five thirty when the shrill beeping of Sean's alarm watch pierced the morning silence. Chris's watch followed suit about a minute later, rousing both men from slumber. It took them a matter of minutes to crawl from their sleeping backs and pull on their hiking clothes.

"Nothing like getting an early jump on the rest of the world," said Sean, hopping from one leg to the other to get the circulation going.

"Uh, huh. Although in our case, I doubt we'll see anyone else for the remainder of the day. Not many people use these woods during the week, even in the middle of summer. Once we hit the Northville-Placid trail at West Canada Creek, we may run into a couple other hikers doing the whole 134 mile trail, but probably no one else."

They ate a quick meal of hot chocolate and pre-packaged breakfast bars, then packed up and hit the trail. The morning mist had condensed thickly onto the undergrowth, which grew across the middle of the trail. They soon found themselves soaked to the skin as they pushed their way through the vegetation.

"Are you sure that this is the trail?" asked Sean. "It seems as though someone would have been assigned to clear at least a little bit of this stuff away."

"It all goes back to what I was telling you yesterday. They used to have trail crews back here to keep the undergrowth cut back. But they couldn't afford the people anymore, so nature has moved in and taken over."

They moved ahead at a brisk pace, passing a lot of flooded ground where beavers had moved in and constructed dams. In another half hour, the dirt road narrowed to a slim path, which wound its way past Whitney and Sampson Lakes. From there, the trail followed the contours of the terrain, up and down many steep hills through a magnificent canopy of hardwood trees. Whitney Creek eventually appeared to their right, and the trail followed along on a parallel course until the creek emptied into Mud Lake, just east of the headwaters of West Canada Creek.

They reached the junction of the Northville-Lake Placid Trail at eight thirty. Although the morning sun had dried the dew from their clothes, they were both damp from perspiration from the hike. They had covered six to seven miles in about two and a half hours, which was a lot of ground considering the fact that they were traveling with full packs.

Sean looked up at the sign that was nailed up on a white birch tree. "Right turn, correct?" he asked.

"Yup, we're almost there," replied Chris. "A little over a mile and we'll be walking across Louie's clearing."

Chris had a clear recollection of the site on the eastern end of West Canada Lake, as he had spent a day there when he passed through years earlier. However, as he and Sean covered the final yards south of the clearing and emerged from the hemlock trees, he gasped at the changes brought on by just a few years.

Very slowly, he stepped across the ruins of the old caretaker's cabin as he moved toward the lakeshore. What most caught his attention was the view of the lake, which was now completely obscured by a thicket of grown trees. It was as though the woods had grown up overnight, completely reclaiming the land that humans had borrowed for a hundred years.

"You look lost," Sean said, noting his friend's bewilderment.

"I think I am lost," said Chris, looking from side to side. "I can't believe how this place has changed over the past fifteen years. I was here with the Boys Scouts when I was a kid, and the clearing was filled with grass. It was overgrown, but I could still walk across it. Just look at it now. You'd never know that this was once a manicured lawn!"

Together, they walked around the front of the foundation, which was filled with crushed stone that had once been brick. They followed a path down to the water, where there was a small tent site next to a large rock.

"Believe it or not, we just walked across what used to be a front lawn," said Chris. "And this tent site used to be a small dock, where the caretaker kept his boats tied up. Things sure do change quickly."

They looked around the lake for a few minutes before retracing their steps and stopping in front of Louie's fireplace. It was an impressive pile of large stones, mortared together and supporting a massive, long stone that was laid across the top as a mantelpiece. According to legend, Louie had found that rock on the other side of the lake and had floated it across in his boat just for that purpose.

"Well, we've got a lot of work to do here," said Chris, looking at his partner. "We might as well get started so that we can finish up here and move on by early afternoon."

Both men took off their packs, and Sean began assembling the metal detector. Meanwhile, Chris retrieved a packet of old photographs he'd brought along that showed the arrangement of buildings at Louie's camp.

"Where do you want to start?" asked Sean, adjusting the settings on his detector. "It looks as though this entire place was part of a building. My guess is that I'll get signals no matter where we look."

"You're probably right," said Chris, surveying the scene. "But let's start by covering this central area, which was once Louie's main camp. Then, we can work out from there."

"What are we looking for?" asked Sean. "Should I set the sensitivity for a single coin, or for a larger target?"

"Let's look for a larger target for now," said Chris, scanning the remains in front of them. "I doubt that Louie would have kept anything valuable in his house, but yet there's something that bothers me."

"What's that?" asked Sean as he donned the headset and commenced sweeping with the detector.

"Louie was known to keep his stash of maps and other secrets stored away in metal tins, which he hid up in the rafters of his camp. The last time he left the camp was in February of 1915, and he never returned. He died in town, without ever having a chance to move any of his possessions. So anything he didn't give away prior to his death would have either been discovered earlier, or it's still here. And no one has ever reported finding gold at this site, or anyplace else where Louie built a camp."

As he spoke, Sean removed the headset and put down the detector. He began digging beneath a pile of cinders, investigating a strong signal.

"Whatever it is, there's a lot of it," said Sean, quickly removing close to a foot of rock and debris before arriving at the target.

"Oh, wow. It's the screen from an old door, and part of a hinge. Lovely!" said Sean, tossing the junk to the side and remounting the apparatus.

"Anyway, as I was saying," continued Chris, "if Louie hid anything too well in his camp, it may have burned to the ground at the same time as the rest of his settlement. In which case, it might still be here, buried beneath all the materials from the later cabins."

"You know, there's always the possibility that someone might have discovered the gold, if it was ever here in the first place, and plundered it without announcing their find," suggested Sean.

"You mean, so that they wouldn't have to turn it over to the state, as the law dictates?" said Chris, building on Sean's thought process.

"Yes, that's the idea," said Sean. "Even if the discovery was made many years ago, the value of gold bullion would still have made it an incredibly profitable venture. Why give it up for nothing if you don't have to?"

Chris didn't answer that question, instead deciding to watch Sean and help select logical search patterns within the ruins of the old encampment.

Sean stopped sweeping four more times over the next ten minutes, each time using the trowel to dig up bits and pieces of various household items. One interesting find was the front cover off an old wood-burning stove, which was probably from the caretaker's cabin rather than Louie's shack. Another promising signal turned out to be a pile of spent brass shell casings from a high-powered rifle.

For the next three hours, the pair swept a series of parallel lines, each about three feet apart from the last, until they had covered the entire area occupied by the old caretaker's cabin.

"Is it possible that Louie's camp was offset from the ranger station at all?" asked Sean, looking for more possible search sectors.

"It's always possible," said Chris, looking back at his old photos. "But the one picture I've got that shows Louie's camp and the fireplace put both buildings roughly in the same spot. Let's try working the ground just south and east of the foundation. According to the book, that's where his outbuilding and chicken coop were set up, along with his garden. You never know where he might have buried a container around here."

Once again, they commenced sweeping, this time around the back side of the brick remains. After a few minutes of work, Sean stopped and looked down at his equipment.

"I've got something promising here," he said, taking out his trowel and dropping down to his knees.

After a few minutes of searching, Sean came up with a relatively large coin, which was worn and caked in dirt. He removed his canteen and dampened a bandana, which he used to rub the coin until a silvery gleam shined through.

"Oh man, look at this!" cried Chris, triumphantly holding up a Walking Liberty half dollar, dated 1939. "Ain't she purdy!"

Chris took the coin from Sean and turned it over in his hand.

"It sure is," he said, admiring the attractive design of the silver piece. "It was probably dropped by some hunter or fisherman passing through in the 1940s. But it's not what we're looking for."

"Picky, picky! I think you're just jealous," said Sean with mock indignation.

They continued sweeping the area until they had covered most of the clearing, stopping every few minutes to investigate yet another signal. Chris volunteered to do some of the digging, which often involved cutting through a tough layer of overgrown weeds and roots. Each time they stopped, their hopes grew, only to be dashed by the find of another metal nail, screw, fire grate, or coffee can. It was tedious, frustrating work that left them hot and tired.

Shortly before one o'clock, Chris straightened his back and stretched, looking up at the sky. It was as though he had failed to notice that it had grown quite hot, with the few wisps of cirrus clouds failing to block the penetrating rays of the mid-summer sun. For the third time that day, he felt his shirt sticking uncomfortably to his back.

"What do you say we relax by the shoreline with some lunch, then pack up and move out?" he asked.

"Sounds like a winner to me," said Sean, ripping off his headset. "This place is driving me crazy. Remind me to come back here if I ever decide to go into the scrap metal recycling business. There's enough here to make a guy rich."

They picked up their packs and carried them down to the lake without bothering to hoist them onto their backs. Sean found a comfortable spot in the grass, where he plopped himself down and loosened the drawstring on his backpack. He removed the food bag and went to work identifying the components of their noon meal. As he spoke, he opened the refillable tubes that held peanut butter and jelly and spread liberal quantities across slices of whole wheat bread.

"Have you ever been to Louie's cave on Cobble Hill?" he asked.

"No, never been there," said Chris. "But I've got it pointed out on Dr. Meyers' map in exquisite detail. I don't think we'll have any trouble find-ing it," Chris said.

"Regardless, it shouldn't take long to search once we get over there," Sean said.

As they ate, Chris removed his boots and dangled his feet into the cold lake water. Sean finished his sandwich and lay back in the grass, feeling the sun beat down on his face. It wasn't long before his eyelids began to feel heavy, and he quickly dozed off into a fitful nap. Chris looked back at his friend and chuckled. Ever since he had known Sean, he'd observed this behavior. The man who could stay awake working on a computer firewall problem until three in the morning could also fall asleep at the drop of a hat when given the opportunity. Sean liked to call it his "screensaver mode," which he employed whenever possible.

Rather than awaken his friend immediately, Chris decided to have one last look around the site before resuming their trek. He pushed himself to a sitting position, then pulled on his socks and hiking boots. Quietly, he tiptoed past Sean's inert form and walked back into the remains of the building site. There, he noticed some flat boards that had become shelters for the garter snakes that lived in the clearing. He nudged one of these boards with his boot and gazed in amusement as two thin, striped snakes slithered away over the weeds in search of deeper concealment. As he watched, he couldn't help but wonder: were these two related to the many "friends" (snakes) that Louie had carried into the woods to keep in his garden?

After a final lap around the clearing, including a lengthy inspection of Louie's famous fireplace, Chris headed back to the lake to collect his belongings.

"Wake up!" he shouted, banging his metal cup against the frame of his pack. "All aboard for Cobble Hill and Cedar Lakes."

"Alright, I hear you," groaned Sean, who had commenced a slow and rhythmic snoring. "Give me a minute and I'll run you into the ground."

Within ten minutes, they had repacked their sacks and started down the trail once again.

"So now what?" asked Sean, feeling more energy with every step.

"Now, we head about four miles to the east, then give Cobble Hill the once-over treatment. I figure we should be able to wrap that up by about five thirty and make it to the Third Lake lean-to by supper time."

Sean looked up at the sky, which had gotten noticeably more cloudy over the past few hours.

"Looks a bit darker than it did this morning," he said.

"Yeah, the long-range forecast called for some rain, possibly even thunderstorms this evening and through the night. We'll have to keep an eye out for that and make sure we get into the lean-to before it starts."

"Or we could stay in Louie's cave tonight," suggested Sean. "Either way, we can still search the site, because the X5 is completely waterproof."

"We'll see when we get there," said Chris. "Given my 'druthers, I'd opt for the lean-to. There's fresh water right there, the scenery is better, and there's an outhouse just next door."

"Ah yes, all the conveniences of home," said Sean. "How silly of me to forget!"

With Sean in the lead, the two hiked east, leaving behind Louie's hermitage and the picturesque West Canada Lake. They rounded the corner of Mud Lake, marveling at the primitive wildness that encompassed its marshlike setting. Overhead, a great blue heron soared, flapping its expansive wings as it gained altitude. Then, it was into the woods, their steps carrying them past Cat Lake and Kings Pond.

They stopped only once along the way, and that was to watch a doe with a pair of young fawns cross the trail far ahead. With that one exception, they moved rapidly along, reaching the jumbled rock of Cobble Hill by about four thirty. Once there, they used Dr. Meyers' map to locate the cave-like space that Louie had adopted as a temporary stopover. Sean was amazed at the geometrical shape of the shelter.

"Just look at this place," he murmured, gazing up at the perpendicular walls and squared corners of the enclosure. "I know it's just a coincidence, but this place looks like it was built by an engineer."

"Nature can do strange things," said Chris, nodding in agreement. "Of course, it's just the way the rocks tumbled off the formation and came to rest, but it does look like someone used a blueprint to build it, doesn't it?"

Sean once again detached the metal detector from the outer strapping of his pack and prepared it for operation.

"Did you bring along extra batteries for that thing, or should we be conserving our search hours for Lost Pond?" asked Chris.

Sean's face registered a smug look as he held the machine aloft.

"My friend, may I remind you that this is a Troy Shadow X5. It uses a single nine-volt battery, which I replaced on Monday. Since I put in a lithium cell, we should get about fifty hours of use before it dies. Even if we do burn through that much time, I brought along a replacement."

"Remind me never to doubt you again," said Chris.

"Hey—I was a Boy Scout. Remember: 'Be prepared!'"

After a quick drink and five-minute rest, Sean was ready to begin scanning the area around the camp. This time, the activity would be a little more productive, with a lot less garbage than at Louie's West Canada Lake camp. The fact that there had never been a structure occupying the site would be a factor that worked in their favor. Also, the cave was off the trail a bit; not far, but enough to escape the notice of most hikers.

"How long do you figure it'll take us to do a complete scan of the interior, plus maybe the surrounding thirty feet?" asked Chris.

Sean quickly surveyed the scene, mentally measuring the area.

"Not more than a half hour, depending on how deep we want to go and how far from the entrance we want to search. But it's all pretty concentrated, so it should go quickly."

Sean once again donned the headset and commenced a slow, methodical line search, starting from the back of the cave and working forward. For many years, a metal cot and bedspring had occupied the site. It had literally fallen apart on the spot, so the detector beeped almost continuously as it picked up remnants of the steel frame.

Chris once again manned the trowel and performed the excavation services whenever the machine indicated a find. Almost all of the signals were generated by scrap metal of one form or another. However, at one point near the north wall of the cave, Sean received a signal that was both strong and concentrated. As Chris dug down through the packed soil, the machine loudly buzzed. Finally, he reached into the bottom of the hole and pulled out an impressive-sized knife blade. It looked as though it had once held a bone or antler handle, although that part had long since vanished.

"I wonder who that belonged to." said Sean.

"I'd love to say it was Louie's, but I believe his hunting knife is on display up in Blue Mountain Lake. Then again, this natural shelter is hardly a secret. It's in all the hiking guides of the area, and even in the old days it was used often by hunters as an overnight rest stop. My guess is that knife's probably been here a long time, maybe forty or fifty years. But I doubt it was ever Louie's."

"Leave it on top of my pack," said Sean. "I'm curious; I think I'm going to take it to a knife maker I know back home and see if he can tell me anything about its age."

"Knock yourself out," said Chris, tossing the blade on top of Sean's pack. "You can carry all the steel out of here you want."

The next twenty minutes of scanning took them outside the cave, where they continued their search lines for another thirty feet in both directions from the cave entrance, covering ground that others might have missed in the same pursuit. At one point, the detector announced a very strong target of large mass. However, a quick excavation uncovered only a few feet of rusting chain, probably left over from the old logging days.

"OK, buddy, I don't know about you, but I could use a visit to the nearest diner," Sean said, regrouping his gear.

"We don't have far to go," said Chris, helping replace the headset into its storage bag. "Another half hour, tops, and we'll be sitting in the Third Cedar Lake lean-to."

"Race you, chump!" said Sean, throwing on his pack and starting quickly for the trail.

"No thanks," replied Chris. "First one there has to start cooking dinner."

"You take the fun out of everything," grumbled Sean.

Chris' estimate was almost exact to the minute. They needed only a little over twenty five minutes to reach the secluded lean-to. It was empty, and a nice supply of dry kindling and firewood was piled against the side wall.

"Now there's a nice surprise," said Sean, dropping his pack on the worn floorboards. "There wasn't a single stick of good wood left in the Pillsbury lean-to. Someone was pretty considerate here."

"It's not as surprising as you'd think," said Chris, also removing his pack for the day. "This lean-to is over a quarter mile from the Northville-Placid trail, and it's a bit harder to find than most the others. Most of the time only the local fishermen make it back here. They tend to leave wood behind more than the rest of the hikers, because they know that it'll probably be a friend of theirs who uses the lean-to next. Regardless, I always try to leave at least a small pile for the next party. It's just good etiquette back here. And in the winter, it could mean the difference between life and death."

The two fell silent as Sean lit the stove and Chris pumped water through the filter for supper. They both felt fatigued, and little was said until they had finished preparing the meal and were sitting down to eat. Famished, they both dug in simultaneously.

"Do you remember last night, when I said it all tastes good in the woods?" asked Chris.

Sean nodded "yes" as he gulped a mouthful of the dehydrated chili-mac dish.

"Well, I lied. I've had better chow back here than this stuff."

"Yeah, I've got to admit, it's not the best," agreed Sean. "I don't think it's fully rehydrated, either. But to tell you the truth, I don't really care. I'm so hungry I think I could eat my shoes."

"I'd pay good money to see that," laughed Chris, leaning back against the lean-to wall.

"So what's on tap for tomorrow? Anyplace else you want to look around here before we head up to Lost Pond?"

"No, not really," replied Chris, studying the dirt under his fingernails. "I don't know whether Louie had a camp at the east end of this lake. And even if he did, I've never seen anything saying where it was, so we'd have no idea where to look. I think we should head up to Lost Pond as early as we can tomorrow, which would leave the afternoon and all day on Saturday to poke around up there."

"I take it that we'll be relying on the GPS to get us up there," said Sean.

"For the most part, that's correct," replied Chris. "I spoke to the forest ranger from Indian Lake last week, and he claimed that there still is the remnant of a trail that goes from the back of the Beaver Pond on Cedar Lakes to Lost Pond. But he also said that he derives a good part of his overtime pay searching for hikers who get lost on that trail. So to answer your question, we'll be using the good old-fashioned map and compass, with the GPS as backup."

"Sounds like a plan," said Sean. "I'll save some time tomorrow morning to program in the coordinates, but it shouldn't be too hard. It's only about three miles, a straight shot to the north. It doesn't look like tough terrain, either."

"Great. We should be able to make good time getting there. That's a good thing, because once we arrive, I foresee a couple of problems," said Chris.

"Such as?" asked Sean.

"Well, for one thing, we have to trust the written record of Thomas Swain, who supposedly perished somewhere close by the pond. Everything after him was recorded by Alvin Smith, who wasn't as neat about keeping records. But one of the first things he wrote, which was in his log entry of June 2, was that they could 'see the water from the cave.' That could mean several things, especially given the changes in the land over the years."

"You mean the density of the woods surrounding the pond?" asked Sean.

"No, it's even more complicated than that," said Chris. As he spoke, he unfolded copies of two different topographic maps showing Lost Pond, which were produced fifty years apart. "If you look at the original topographic map of 1903, then you look at the next U.S. Geographic Survey map from 1954, what do you notice?"

"Wow, that's quite a difference," acknowledged Sean. "The map from 1903 barely shows the pond as being anything more than a puddle, but in the 1954 version, it looks like a decent volume of water."

"Exactly. That means that either one of the maps is wrong, or the lake has changed in size over time. Either one could be correct."

"How could the pond grow that much over the course of fifty years, especially since the topography hasn't changed at all?" asked Sean.

"Easy. Castor canadensis."

"Huh?"

"The American beaver," translated Chris. "When they migrate into an area, they build dams to stop up slow-moving creeks. Sometimes, raising the water level just a little bit can flood a pretty good amount of acreage. My guess is that's what happened at Lost Pond."

"If what you're saying is true, then this cave might be a lot closer to the water today than it was in the 1700s."

"That's exactly what I'm saying," said Chris. "Or even than it was back when Harrison searched this place a hundred years ago. But who knows? Maybe they had beavers in the 1700s. I just don't know, which troubles me. And if there is a cave there, how come no one has found it in all the time that a trail has been available to the public? It seems as though someone would have stumbled on it. We have a written record that it exists."

"Well, that's one advantage that we have over everyone else," said Sean. "No one else would have looked for it because they didn't have the same historical journal that you found at the museum. It's true that Dr. Meyers had an idea from his studies, but that's never been confirmed either."

As Sean spoke, Chris went about setting up a fire, arranging the tinder beneath some dry twigs and larger sticks. After a short time, he applied a single match, and soon had a crackling fire inside the rock fire pit.

"Wow, you really were a Boy Scout, weren't you?" said Sean.

As the two settled back to relax in the lean-to, Chris went on to explain his thinking on French Louie's homestead.

"One of his last statements to my great-grandfather in the winter of 1914 was 'You use the gold to take care of this place.' I hope this doesn't sound too corny, but I'd love to find a way to make Louie's wish come true, even if it is over a hundred years later."

"That's assuming that we find an appreciable amount of gold, and we're allowed to use it to preserve the site. That's highly doubtful, since we can't keep the stuff even if we find it," countered Sean.

"Maybe we can't lay claim to ownership of the gold itself. But if we can find a way to get some positive public relations going for us, we might be able to do some good things here," said Chris.

"What do you mean by that?" asked Sean.

Chris repeated the information he'd shared with his mother the day before, about how to have a location designated as a historic site.

"So you think that's possible at the site of Louie's original camp? To have it designated as a national historic site?"

"Either a national or a New York State historic site, one or the other. I think it would be a fitting tribute to one of the most famous characters of the region to preserve the site, including the fireplace, as an example of the Adirondack woodsman and his lifestyle. And just imagine, if we could prove that Louie was tied into the fable of the Gordons' gold, that would make our case that much stronger."

"I wonder whether they'd try to construct a replica building," Sean wondered out loud.

"I doubt it. I'd be happy if they put up a plaque and paid to maintain the site. But let's not worry about that just yet. Either we make a big find, or none of this is worth discussing."

While they were speaking, Sean prepared two mugs of hot chocolate. Handing one to Chris, he held the other aloft and proposed a toast.

"Here's to Louie. May we fulfill his last wish and help to preserve the legend."

"Here, here," said Chris, raising his mug in support. "Let's do him proud."

CHAPTER 17

August 2, 2012

The next morning seemed to come late, as neither of the two friends bothered setting an alarm. Even though it was after seven, the sky was still relatively dark due to the heavy cloud cover. A light rain was falling across the lake, and heavy mists were rolling in from the west.

Chris sat up, lazily surveying the weather conditions. Sean, who was barely awake, had decided to hunker down further into his sleeping bag. Chris looked back at the lump in the middle of the goose down bag and shook his head in wonder. Then, he reached out with a long leg and gave it a gentle kick.

"Hey, watch it!" came a muffled shout. "Can't a man get a decent night's sleep in this hotel?"

"Nope, sorry," Chris answered. "Checkout time is eight thirty. If we stay any later, we have to pay for an extra night."

"That's OK. Put it on my credit card," joked Sean, still concealed inside the bag.

"Looks kind of messy out there," observed Chris, pulling on a windbreaker. "We might even have to get our feet wet today."

Sean popped his head out the top baffles of his sleeping bag just in time to see Chris pull the Svea stove from his backpack. After priming it with a little white gas fuel, he applied a match and soon had a pot of water coming to a rolling boil.

"I say we live it up a little today," said Chris. "How does a ham and cheese omelet with hash brown potatoes sound?"

"Let me guess, just add water, right?" asked Sean.

"You betcha, just add water!" replied Chris.

"You're going to kill me before we're through with all this freeze-dried stuff," said Sean.

"I aim to please," said Chris, already opening the foil-lined pouches.

Despite Sean's protests, the breakfasts were actually quite tasty, and both men ate heartily until their plates were empty. Then, they packed up their backpacks and prepared to hit the trail. Chris looked at his watch as they stretched their sore calf and thigh muscles.

"It's only eight twenty. Looks like we won't owe the hotel manager for the extra night after all," he said.

"That's OK, I'm not ready to leave quite yet," said Sean. "I want to program our way points into the portable GPS before we go. This might take a little while, so bear with me for about fifteen minutes, OK?"

"It shouldn't take that long at all," said Chris. "I've already done the hard part for you. Here you go." As he spoke, he handed Sean a slip of paper with all of their planned way points listed in column format.

"Wow! I'm impressed," said Sean, taking the paper. "I ought to bring you along more often."

Sean turned on the GPS and waited until it was fully operational. It was a small device, weighing only a few ounces, yet Sean claimed it was "worth its weight in gold" in the event that they became lost amidst the mountains and valleys of the deep woods. Even when he stayed on the trails, he enjoyed playing with the device as he continued to familiarize himself with the available features and functions.

When he finally completed the programming, Sean looked up at Chris and gave a thumbs up.

"OK, sir, you've got the lead today. I'll just follow along and let the funny little box beep if we go off course."

"We'll be fine for the first two or three miles," said Chris. "I'll only start worrying once we leave the back of Beaver Pond and start heading north. Then, I'll be relying on my wingman to keep me straight."

Chris and Sean mounted their packs and retraced their steps back to the Northville-Placid Trail, then followed the main path north and east, over a very pleasant stretch of trail, until they reached the Beaver Pond lean-to after about two miles. It was relatively dry, in spite of the light drizzle that still fell from the sky. They had both decided against wearing rain gear, as the layer of waterproof clothing often generated more moisture in the form of perspiration than the rain itself.

Beaver Pond is simply an oblong extension of Cedar Lakes. The Northville-Placid Trail crosses the narrow strip of water that connects it to the rest of Cedar Lakes. Although several camps used to exist along the north shore of Beaver Pond, they have been gone for at least fifty years, and hikers rarely venture into that area today.

The pair took a short break at the spring hole to quench their thirst and then started the trek around the east side of Beaver Pond. The wet vegetation once again soaked their clothes as they pushed doggedly ahead. The thick undergrowth of young spruce and hemlock made the going extremely difficult, and they both picked up scratches from the sharp branches that blocked their way.

"Oh, sure, this part of the trip around the Beaver Pond is going to be a piece of cake," said Sean, sarcastically mimicking Chris.

"I hadn't counted on this type of ground cover," grunted Chris, heaving more branches out of his way. "I think that once we gain a little elevation and move away from the lake it should get better."

"I certainly hope so," concurred Sean. "I think we're creating our own trail as we go. We ought to get paid for this by the state!"

"It would only count if we put up trail signs as we went along," said Chris.

"Are you kidding me? I think I've already marked several trees with blood. What more could they want?"

The two decided to alter their course to the east a bit, allowing them to escape into an area where the woods were less dense. They could still see

Beaver Pond through the trees, which had shifted to a mix of birch and maple. They followed the contour of the pond as it bent east, then north. Finally, they arrived at the coordinates Sean had programmed into the GPS for the trail to Lost Pond. Looking around, Sean was puzzled.

"Your forest ranger friend was right. I know we're at the right place, but I don't see anything that resembles a trail."

"My guess is that is hasn't been used for decades," said Chris. "Even that Otter Brook Trail I was telling you about, if it goes unused for even a few years, becomes pretty hard to follow."

As he spoke, Chris pulled out his compass and took a quick bearing. He lined up his map and faced northeast, pointing into the woods beyond.

"I say we go that way," he recommended.

"According to the GPS, you're pretty close," said Sean, who directed them a few degrees farther east. "We've got a few small bends in our route; otherwise I think you'd have it perfect."

Their route was selected to take advantage of the topography. It followed along the contour lines of the landscape and avoided climbing over the three thousand-foot-tall mountain that lay directly north of Beaver Pond. It was relatively flat, with just a slight downhill trend through mostly open forest. They made good time for going cross-country, and within about forty-five minutes of leaving Beaver Pond, Sean recommended a course change.

"I have us at this junction right here," he said, pointing to a low point on the map. "If we turn about eight degrees to the west and cross that little saddle of a hill, we should be within less than a mile of Lost Pond."

"I agree," said Chris, looking at his compass. "I'd recommend about 320 degrees magnetic, which is pretty close to the GPS. Let's go for it."

Shortly after their turn, Sean pointed at a spot off to their right.

"If I didn't know any better, I'd say that that looks like the bed of an old trail, heading northeast up that hill."

"It could be," said Chris. "Remember, the trail from Beaver Pond didn't actually go to Lost Pond. It diverted to the right and ended up at Little

Moose Lake. You may be seeing remnants of that trail."

With Sean in the lead, the duo continued walking, up over another rise, then down a long, gentle descent onto lower ground. Before long, they emerged into a lightly wooded plain where the ground began to feel squelchy beneath their feet.

"My friend, I think we've arrived," said Chris, nodding at the open water ahead.

"So it would appear," said Sean. "Where do you want to set up camp, since we forgot to call ahead for a reservation?" His attempt at humor alluded to the fact that there are no lean-tos around Lost Pond, and very little in the way of choice tent sites.

"How about over there," Chris said, pointing to a low patch of flat, dry ground south of the pond. "It looks about as good as any place around, and we could use that large fallen log as a bench. And you gotta admit: the price is right."

"Looks good to me," said Sean, following Chris across the clearing.

"We'll just set up the tent quickly and drop our stuff inside. I can't see the point of wasting much time setting up any more than that. We need to use our time searching for a cave," said Chris.

"Should we even bother with the metal detector?" asked Sean.

"I don't see what it would give us," said Chris. "From reading the journal of Thomas Swain, it sounds as though we've got to find the cave in order to get anywhere. But just for the heck of it, we can try a few lines around the lake sometime before we leave on Sunday."

"I can't see any harm in it, but I doubt that it would turn up anything," said Sean.

Working in tandem, they quickly set up the tent and stashed their gear inside. The rain had stopped entirely, although the air had a hot and humid feel.

"I could go for a swim," said Sean, noting the sweat pouring off his forehead.

"I wouldn't dive in head first," advised Chris, nodding at the brown water. "I doubt that's more than shoulder high in most places."

They proceeded to remove the maps and guides from Chris's pack, arranging them on top of a large ground cloth.

"Let's see the map that Dr. Meyers sketched out for you," said Sean, reaching for the document. He unfolded the segments and located the pond on the upper half.

"Not much there to help us," observed Chris. "He circled the areas north and south of the pond. Those are the only places that would support a cave around here. It's basically an old creek bed running east and west."

"Where do you recommend starting?" asked Sean.

"I think we should start on the north side, just because it's smaller and less area to search. We've only got about five or six hours of sunlight left today, but we have the entire day tomorrow. Let's leave the larger slope to the south for then."

"Sounds like a great idea to me," said Sean. "We've got a lot of hillside to cover. I think I'll bring along the survey tape and make sure we know where we are after each pass."

"Good idea," said Chris. "No point covering the same ground twice."

Sean went into a side pocket of his pack and retrieved a roll of bright pink stretch tape. It was made specifically for tying around trees as a preliminary marker.

"You ready to get started" asked Chris, "or do you need to spend another half hour shopping around in your bag of tricks?"

"I'm ready to go now. But I've got an idea. Before we dive in blind, let's run up the hill behind our tent site and look over the north slope carefully for a few minutes. Maybe we can localize our search for a cave entrance if we can pick out the prime rock formations from over the pond. It won't take more than ten minutes, and it could save us a whole lot of time."

"That's a good idea," said Chris. "You do OK for yourself when you use that brain of yours for something besides talking to computers, you know that?"

"Thanks. I try," said Sean, already leading the way into the tall grass.

The two scrambled their way through thick brush until they reached the incline that led them uphill. From there, they pulled themselves up through a steeply sloped hillside with mixed conifers and deciduous trees overhanging a thin layer of undergrowth. All the while, the clouds were dissipating, allowing the warm sun to heat up the afternoon air.

On top of the incline, Chris and Sean surveyed the opposite shoreline, sweeping east to west and up the north hill. Part of the ground was obviously compacted dirt and soil, whereas other areas were filled with jumbled rock and vertical slabs. They noted as much detail as possible while focusing on those areas with concentrations of solid rock.

Before returning to their tent, Sean reached into his fanny pack and produced four granola bars.

"We never did stop for lunch today. How about a sample from the buffet table? Your choices are chocolate chip or peanut butter."

"I'll try one of each, thanks."

The two stood in place while munching their snacks. Chris stared absentmindedly at his boots as he ate, watching the ground water as it seeped into his muddy footsteps. Already he felt the heat sapping the energy from his body, and Sean look similarly worn. The temperature was climbing, and the humidity was higher than normal. After another swig from their canteens, they backtracked down the hill and headed over to start their search.

"Just think: the cave we're looking for was used by someone almost 240 years ago," said Chris. "Doesn't that make the hair on your neck stand up?"

"I guess so," replied Sean. "But I'll be a lot happier when we actually find it, assuming that it is here somewhere."

Chris's eyes narrowed to a squint as he looked westward across the pond.

"I'm not sure, but I think I see where the Otter Brook Trail comes into the clearing over there."

"I think I see what you mean," agreed Sean. "I wonder if we'll see any people hiking through before Sunday."

"I doubt it," said Chris. "The ranger I spoke with said that most of that trail is in pretty bad shape. I guess they had to improve parts of it for some operation or search a number of years ago, but we're in a pretty obscure part of the woods. There's little reason for anyone to come this far in for the sole reason of visiting a shallow little waterhole."

The two walked around to the north side of the pond, laden with the materials needed for the search. Chris carried all the maps and records, which were attached by a rubber band to a pad of writing paper. Sean carried the surveying tape and the rest of their supplies. They separated on the hillside by about thirty feet, with Sean higher up the slope than Chris. Then, they began their first search line.

Progress was tedious at times, and they didn't move ahead with much speed. Before long, they decided to increase the distance between them to fifty feet, with the objective of covering more area with each pass. Starting on the eastern side of the hill, they worked their way west until they were beyond the pond itself. They continued a bit further before climbing up another fifty feet in elevation and starting the next line, this time from west to east. By working this pattern, they were able to cover a one mile long strip of ground once every hour. That line was about one hundred feet wide, covering elevation gains of up to thirty feet.

By four o'clock that afternoon, they had covered the first three hundred feet of hillside without detecting a trace of a cave. The heat felt even more oppressive than earlier.

"I don't know about you, but I'm about beat," said Sean. "I could go for some down time."

"Some forty-niner you'd make!" said Chris, referring to the eternally backbreaking job of the old-time gold prospectors. "I tell you what: we've already covered most of the places that I'd deem as promising. Let's just climb up another hundred feet and make one more pass down the hillside before we call it quits for the day, OK?"

"Deal," said Sean, eager to get back to the campsite.

Together, they started their last transit for the day, weaving back and forth as they moved across the slope. At one point, Chris stopped to examine some craggy outcroppings with projecting slabs of rock that might have concealed an opening.

"Hey, come check this out," he called, his voice attenuated by the solid surroundings.

Sean followed the voice up and over sharp a ledge, where he found Chris sitting in a small square rock enclosure. A natural chair had been formed against a vertical face, complete with a flat seat and an arm rest. A two foot-long overhang even resembled a canopy.

"Well, will you look at that!" said Sean. "It's none other than His Royal Highness, King Carey on his royal throne! How may I be of service, your majesty?" As he spoke, he bowed forward in a mock show of servitude.

"OK, cut the crap. I thought you might like to see it," said Chris, rising from the seat. "You've got to admit, it is pretty neat."

"Sure is," said Sean, staring in wonder. "Mother Nature pulls some pretty good tricks from up her sleeve when she wants."

Sean descended back to his search line, and the two resumed their transit across the mountainside. By the time they reached the eastern end of the ridge, it was slightly past five o'clock.

"Time to head down, but first let's check out our search area for tomorrow," said Chris, nodding at the mountain directly across the pond.

"It looks both longer and higher than the hill we're on right now," said Sean. "We'll have to cover a lot more ground than we managed today."

Chris consulted the map, pointing out the topographic lines of the terrain.

"You're right. That mountain makes this one look like a molehill," said Chris. "Check it out: it's five hundred feet taller, and the ridge runs for miles, all the way down Otter Brook. But don't despair. Remember, it's got to be somewhere closer to the pond, because the journal written by Thomas Swain said that 'they could see the water from the cave.' My guess is it's somewhere within the first half mile along that ridge, and no more than three hundred feet up. Let's scan the landscape for a few minutes and see if anything looks like an opening."

Sean and Chris slowly panned back and forth across the face of the mountain, starting near the pond and then expanding their search. They concentrated once again on the locations with exposed rock, trying to pick out areas with the highest probability of an entrance. After several minutes of observation without an obvious candidate, they called it quits. Any discovery would have to come from another day of laborious sector-by-sector searching.

They meandered back down to the clearing and headed around the lake toward their tent site. They said little as they walked, but deep inside both men were contemplating the same facts. They had been on the trail for three days now, and they had nothing to show for it except for an old half dollar. Tomorrow would be their last day of searching before they hit the trail for the trip home on Sunday.

"You look like you could go for a nap about now," said Chris, addressing his friend.

"I'm OK," said Sean. "I'm sure I'll sleep well tonight, but I've still got a bit left in the tank."

"How about I'll run out and gather the firewood, while you just hang close to camp and get supper going?" Chris asked as he unzipped the front flaps on the tent.

"You don't fool me," said Sean. "You just don't want to eat your own cooking again."

"Why should I have to—I'm in the woods with 'Master Chef Sean.'"

"Flattery will get you everything," said Sean, flopping onto his sleeping bag. "Just let me rest for a couple minutes, and I'll soon start preparing a masterpiece."

Chris laughed, knowing that he'd probably have to awaken Sean when he finished collecting the wood.

"OK, buddy, I'll see you in a while. Don't snore too loud; you'll scare off the wildlife."

Chris then headed up the hill just south of the tent, where they had climbed earlier in the day to scout out the north ridge. He followed their footsteps up the hill to a spot where several dead hardwood trees had dropped limbs on the ground. As was his way, he formed three or four smaller piles of branches, and then combined them into a single large stack to carry down the hill. However, just before he bent to hoist the final load onto his shoulder, he stopped to examine something on the ground. He looked even closer, his face set in a contemplative scowl.

"Hmm," he said, lost in his thoughts. "Now that's interesting."

With that, he lifted the firewood off the ground and started back down the hill.

Contrary to Chris's expectations, Sean was not asleep at the campsite. He had retrieved and filtered water from a nearby creek and had started boiling it for the evening meal. He had also retrieved several large rocks and formed them into a fire ring for their nightly blaze. He looked up from the cook pot as Chris dropped the weighty pile of limbs next to the fire pit.

"It looks as though someone has had a fire here before," said Sean. "We might as well use the same spot."

"OK," said Chris.

"You know, for all the heat and humidity and bugs around this place, it's actually got a quiet solitude that is kind of appealing," said Sean.

"Yup," said Chris.

"Hopefully the weather will hold out for us tomorrow," continued Sean. "It would be pretty miserable trying to repeat today's search in a downpour."

"Uh huh," came the muttered response.

Sean wasn't used to receiving one-word answers from his friend. Figuring that he was either tired or not feeling talkative, he remained quiet until the dinner was ready.

"Here we are," said Sean as he placed a bowl of turkey tetrazzini and rice on the log they were using as a table. "It's not exactly worthy of a Michelin star, but it smells edible."

"Thanks," said Chris, looking down.

"What's the matter there? Cat got your tongue?" asked Sean.

"Would you do me a favor?" asked Chris, looking serious.

"Sure, whatcha need?"

"Could I see the bottom of your boot?"

"Huh?" asked Sean, a bit shocked. "Sure. Why?"

As he spoke, he lifted his leg backward from the knee, exposing the bottom of his hiking boot for Chris' inspection.

"That's what I thought," said Chris, looking back at Sean with concern.

"What's wrong?" asked Sean. "You look like you're expecting trouble."

"Have you seen anyone else around here today?" asked Chris. "Or heard any noises, or seen any signs of anyone?"

"No, of course not," answered Sean. "We're the only two people here, although I suppose someone could have come down the trail and checked out the lake while we were up on the mountain searching. But I sure haven't seen anyone. Why?"

"Well, you've got Vibram soles on your hiking boots, and so do I. While I was up on the hill behind us gathering wood, I came across the footprints that you and I made earlier when we climbed the hill to scout out the other side of the pond. There's a muddy patch up there where we both left our tracks, side by side. But at one point, another footprint crossed out track, on top of mine. It was a chain-link bottom, like the kind you find on one of those waterproof rubber-bottomed models. It didn't belong to either of us."

"Jeez, I wonder where that could have come from," said Sean. "It could have been another hiker passing through?"

"It's possible," said Chris. "But whoever it was, they didn't go up the side of the hill like us. Their footprints came from the west, on a course that was perpendicular to ours. It wouldn't be bothering me, except that I can't think of a single reason why someone would be up there other than for hunting or trapping—and neither of those activities is in season right now."

"Was there anything else you could make of it, such as where they were heading?"

"No, I could only pick up one good print and part of another before the person headed onto dry rock and vanished pretty quickly. But I could tell that the print was made from a smaller boot than yours or mine. If I had to venture a guess, I'd say that it was either a smaller man, or else a woman."

"Well, I'm glad that it's not Sasquatch up there," remarked Sean. "I'd feel a bit uncomfortable if you came across a print made from a size 23 boot."

"OK, let's forget about the mystery tracks for the time being and stuff our faces," said Chris. "What was that you said about turkey tetrazzini?"

"Piping hot and served over dinner rolls," said Sean, lifting the dish once more. "Come and get it before it's all gone."

The two men both cleaned their plates in relatively short order. Then, Sean pulled out the food bag and brought out a surprise.

"And now, for your dessert pleasure…Oreo cookies!" he said, brandishing a small sealable bag. "Step right up and get your sugar buzz right here!"

"Oh, man, it's a good thing I didn't know you had them in your pack yesterday," said Chris. "I would have raided your pack in the middle of the night."

"It wouldn't have worked," said Sean. "I've got a motion-detector burglar alarm installed on the food bag. Try to get in without the secret code and it zaps you with a stun gun."

Once dishes were washed, Sean pulled his foam ground pad out of the tent and lay it across the middle of their camp site. He lay down on his side, content to watch the sun set in the valley to the west. Meanwhile, Chris retrieved the map that Harrison had used during the search in 1903 and reviewed the notes that went along with it.

"This is interesting," he said, showing the map to Sean. "Look how much different the map from 1954 is from the 1903 version. Some of the altitudes are off by more than a hundred feet. Even the contour lines of the hills are shaped somewhat differently."

"You've got to figure that Harrison's map was made in a day when large-scale surveying techniques still carried some inaccuracies," said Sean. "I'm sure that they're much better today than in the 1950s. With satellite mapping, details can be measured to the precise fraction of an inch."

Together, they pored over the details of Harrison's search while plotting out their own for the following day. There was a certain thrill in the air that came from knowing that they were so close to finding something that had remained hidden for so many years, even though they knew that their chances were small, with so much ground to cover and only two of them to search.

Chris pointed out the features on the map that they had observed from the smaller hill on the north side. He drew a tight box around a small area just south of the pond. It concentrated on the ground that was closest to the water and between 2,400 to 2,600 feet in elevation.

"I think there's at least a fifty percent chance that this is where we'll find it, somewhere in here," he said. "If we don't, we'll move a quarter mile east, then west, and expand the search horizontally rather than vertically."

"What makes you think it's not further up the hill?" asked Sean.

"Because if it was much further than that, we'd have a tough time seeing the pond," Chris replied. "Also, think about it: assuming that Swain and his group were traveling through the low lands, avoiding the higher hills, he would have been injured on flat ground, meaning the area around the pond. Why would they want to carry him way up into the hills? My guess is that they never would have found the cave had it been way up on the mountain. I think it's below 2,600 feet."

"Sounds like a logical assumption to me," said Sean. "Let's go with it and see what happens."

Sean looked around, noticing the light disappearing from the sky overhead. In the west, the setting sun was rapidly disappearing over the horizon, bathing them in long spears of magnificent light and shadow. He suddenly regretted not bringing his digital camera to preserve the memory.

"Looks like it'll be dark soon," said Sean. "I'd better get the firewood broken up. Why don't you use your pyromaniac skills to get a foundation of kindling set up in the fire ring so all we'll have to do is light the match?"

"Sounds like a deal to me," said Chris. "I never could resist setting up a good blaze."

Sean went to work, taking the branches that Chris had collected earlier and breaking them up into foot-long sticks. Chris had brought down an impressive pile of wood, so they'd have enough to keep a fire going for several hours. As Sean worked, using his knee for leverage, the pile grew in height until it was almost three feet tall and four feet wide. "Enough to toast a couple bags of marshmallows," he thought to himself.

As Sean worked the woodpile, Chris rummaged around the nearby woods, pulling out small dead twigs and birch bark to use as kindling. It was getting darker, and he had trouble seeing well without a flashlight. However, he was able to collect enough to serve the purpose. He carried the heap of fire starter material back to the campsite and arranged it in layers inside the fire ring. Sean tossed him a few larger sticks to weave into the pile, and soon they were ready to burn.

"Hang on before you light that thing," said Chris. "I want to go into the tent and grab my flashlight. I'll get yours too."

Once the flashlights were out, Sean applied a lighter to the base of the timber and gently breathed air into the base of the fire. It was a matter of seconds before the flames flickered through the pile of twigs, sending a series of cracks and pops through the night air. Chris added some larger sticks onto the base until they soon had an impressive bonfire blazing away.

"Nice job," said Chris. "What say we throw on some water for a little hot cocoa?"

"I could go for some myself," said Sean, setting up the pot.

Because the site had no genuine fireplace, there was no grate onto which they could settle the cook pot. Instead, they had to settle for pushing it up against the growing pile of embers. However, the fire was hot, and it wasn't long before they heard the water bubbling. Sean poured the liquid directly into the mugs, and they were soon enjoying their hot beverages. They both leaned back, using the log as a support, and gazed up into the night sky.

"You know, I haven't said this before, but just think about all the things that would happen if we found the cave, much less the gold that might be inside," said Chris.

"We'd certainly have our pictures in the local paper," said Sean, looking back into the fire.

"Yeah, we'd get our names in print, that's for sure," said Chris. "But I wasn't even thinking about that. I meant that we'd be the first people in modern times to explore this cave; heck, maybe even get to name the thing. Also, we'd be able to write the final chapter of a treasure story that has been circulating for over two hundred years."

"So which excites you more? The thought of finding the cave or the treasure?" asked Sean.

"I'm not exactly sure myself," said Chris. "We couldn't keep the treasure even if we found it, so maybe the cave is a more interesting prospect. But I'd still love to try to influence someone, perhaps the Governor, to use the money to designate and preserve Louie's place on West Canada Lake as a State Historic Site. So there are lots of factors involved here."

They both sat back to enjoy a little silence while sipping on their drinks. In the background, they could hear the sounds of small animals scurrying around in the brush, and an owl hooted from across the lake.

"Pretty magical out here, isn't it?" asked Chris.

"It sure is," replied Sean, his voice trailing off to again enjoy the sounds of the Adirondack night.

"Sounds like we've got half a zoo surrounding us," said Chris, listening as the bullfrogs commenced their concert of throaty calls. Another owl chimed in from their own side of the pond, and more noises emerged from the woods.

Then, from quite nearby, a loud "crack" interrupted the other sounds as a large stick snapped in two. Sean and Chris both froze momentarily, listening for additional clues as to the source.

"That sounded like something a bit bigger than a rabbit, didn't it?" said Sean, his head turned around.

"Yeah, but noises always seem louder at night, especially when you're in the middle of the woods and you can't see the critters in the dark. It's a funny phenomenon, but I think everyone tends to imagine a moose when it's really a mouse. It happens all the time."

Sean grabbed his flashlight and shined it in the direction of the sound. At the end of the beam were two large boulders, each about five feet tall and standing about six feet apart. All he could see in the circle of light was some tall grass between the rocks and a few moths that were attracted by the light. He shut the off the flashlight and returned to his drink.

"Hey, you never said how the interview went with the accounting firm over in Boston. How did that work out, anyway?"

"It went OK, I guess," said Chris. "All we did was talk on the phone, and I'm not sure whether they'll hire anything more than an entry-level bean counter via a phone interview. I'll have to see what they say when they call back. That is, if they call back."

Sean was about to offer some words of encouragement when yet another branch snapped in the direction of the two boulders. Immediately following the staccato of the snap was a dull thud, as though a body had fallen and hit the ground. Then, more silence.

This time, the volume and proximity of the sounds caused both Sean and Chris to sit up in alarm. There was no denying the presence of a large animal within thirty feet of their fire. Only its identity remained unknown.

Sean once again illuminated the large rocks with the beam of his light. Meanwhile, Chris hunched over, whispering in his ear: "You go back around the outside of that boulder on the left. Have your light on, and make a pretty good amount of noise. I'm going to tip-toe around the right side and see if I can catch a glimpse of whatever the heck is back there."

"What happens if it's a bear?" Sean asked, his voice barely audible above the crackle of the flames.

"I'll tickle his belly and run like hell!" said Chris, his teeth visible through his wide grin.

"Last one back is a rotten egg for a year," quipped Sean, already scuffling towards his assigned station.

Chris felt rather strange, stalking silently through the rough grass as he approached the right side of the tall rock. He wasn't sure what he would do if he came face to face with a bear, or even a large buck, or perhaps a doe with a fawn. It was bad enough that he'd lost his Jeep to a deer within the past few weeks. But he wasn't comfortable listening to the sound of something that big so close to their backs. If nothing else, he would flush it from its hiding, then return to enjoy the campfire with his friend.

The closer he got to the boulder, the more adrenalin he could feel surging into his veins. He was able to creep ahead without making a sound until he could almost reach out and touch the surface of the rock. Then, leaning on its gritty vertical surface, he eased himself along until he was almost to the back corner. His heart was thumping so loudly in his chest that he thought it must be audible to the deer, or bear, or whatever it was.

From around the other side of the rock he saw the silhouette of Sean's light. It was growing in intensity as Sean approached the corner of the boulder.

And then he saw it.

There was something there. It was large, and black, and moving in his direction. Chris froze only long enough to get a second glimpse of the form. It walked in an upright position. The form was human, dressed in black pants, black sweater, and a black knit hat that pulled down over the face, leaving only the eyes and mouth exposed. The person was backing away from the light, as if he or she was about to turn and run. Chris, however, made a split decision: he was not going to let that happen.

Using every bit of his rugged six-foot-two frame, he lunged at the shadowy figure, taking advantage of the element of surprise. As Sean rounded the rock with the light, Chris wrapped his arms around the person and used a twisting motion to spin them both to the ground. He landed on top and quickly pinned the intruder face down to the earth. As he did, an unearthly, high-pitched scream pierced the night.

"Stop it! Stop it! You're hurting me," came the voice from beneath him. "Let me go!"

Sean shined the beam at the torso of the individual trapped in Chris's iron arm lock, while Chris reached up and ripped the hat from the intruder's head. As he did, a flood of long, shiny black hair cascaded out of the cap and onto the ground. Chris looked down into the face of an attractive, twenty-something woman.

"Don't hurt me, don't hurt me," she pleaded, looking up into the glare of the light. "I can explain this."

Chris was at a loss for words.

"What the...wait a minute. I know you!" he stammered.

"Yes," she replied quickly in a strained voice. "We met at Cornell, in Dr. Meyers' laboratory. Remember?"

"Oh my God, it's Cathy, right?"

"Actually, it's Kristi. Kristi Kincaid. From the Geology Department."

"Don't tell me you've been following us for three days," Chris said, slowly releasing his grasp on the frightened woman. "And who else is with you?"

"No one else is with me," said the graduate student, accepting a hand up from Chris. "And no, I haven't been following you all week; it's just been for the past day."

"Do you realize you're lucky you weren't just almost beaten to a pulp?" Chris asked, his voice on the edge of rage. "What's the deal, sneaking around, following us up here? What the hell are you doing?"

"I'm looking for the same thing you are," said Kristi, glaring back somewhat defiantly. "Only I feel like I have a right to be here."

"You have a right to be here? What the heck is that supposed to mean?" Chris shot back.

"I've been working with Dr. Meyers for three years now, busting my butt in that lab day in, day out, trying to wrap up my degree," said Kristi, her voice rising. "I've been helping him do just about everything that he's got his name on, and for what? So that he can keep me in the background while he gives information that could potentially lead to a new cave discovery to someone he's never met? I don't think so!"

"Uh, look, Kristi, why don't you come and sit down with us and we can talk this thing out," offered Chris. "We've got some awfully good hot chocolate mix over by our campfire; we'd love to share a cup with you."

"It's even got mini-marshmallows," added Sean.

Kristi looked up and briefly laughed. "Well, as long as it's got mini-marshmallows, how can I refuse? Sure, I'll join you for a cup."

"By the way, my name's Sean," he said, gesturing for Kristi to follow them back to the fire.

"Yes, I know," said Kristi.

Sean didn't ask how she happened to know his name, but the question stuck in his mind for a later conversation.

"Please make yourself comfortable," said Chris, pointing out their log seating. "Sorry we don't have any padding, but it wouldn't fit in the station wagon."

"That's OK. I'm a geologist, remember? I'm used to hard seats."

"We've still got some hot water on the fire, but I'm afraid you'll have to drink out of the metal cup that comes with the stove. I didn't think to carry along a third cup," said Sean, mixing up the cocoa in the lid of their cooking stove.

"That's fine," said Kristi, settling herself down in front of the fire. "I guess it's better than getting tackled and driven into the ground by a couple of football players."

"Actually, neither of us plays football," said Chris, "although I played lacrosse in college, and my friend here used to take judo lessons a few years back. But as long as we're explaining this to you, perhaps you could explain what you're doing tracking us through the woods like this? If you wanted to help us look for the cave, we would have welcomed the assistance. Why did you have to sneak around like a cat burglar spying on our activities?"

"Quite simply, I didn't think you would welcome my presence back here, or anywhere, for that matter, if you were looking for a new cave. I thought that you'd want that recognition for yourself. The little bits of conversation I caught that first day in the laboratory made it sound as though you were close to discovering some of the lost Indian mine caves of the Adirondacks. I couldn't believe when Dr. Meyers offered you information that he had never shared with me. To tell you the truth, I was furious."

Chris looked saddened by the statement, and he shook his head slowly while looking at their guest.

"I wish I'd known that was an issue," he said. "It was never my intention to get in the way of your research. But there are so many things that you could have done, such as ask Dr. Meyers for the information yourself. You could have even asked me to come along with the two of us. We would have welcomed the company."

"To tell you the truth, I never knew that Dr. Meyers had anything down on paper regarding the Indian mine legends. He never mentioned a thing to me. He's my degree advisor, and he knows that I'm concentrating on underground formations. So why wouldn't he have told me?"

"I'm sure it wasn't done intentionally," said Chris. "It must have been an oversight on his part, because Dr. Meyers knew that we're also trying to find traces of gold minerals, as well as a potential lead mine. I might also add that although his map was interesting, it provided very little in the way of usable information. Mostly, it tracked the old folklore tales based on Indian stories and correlated them to satellite imagery photographs of the same territory. Some of that land is surrounding us as we speak."

"Yes, I know," said Kristi. "I also know that you're looking for more than some 'trace minerals.'"

Chris looked at Sean, who stared back at him in disbelief. Somehow, the newcomer had not only learned their schedule, but the main purpose of their search.

"Kristi, I want you to tell me how you know as much as you do," demanded Chris. "I've met you once, in Dr. Meyers' lab, and we spoke for all of two minutes. Yet you knew exactly where to find us and when. Who has been giving you the lowdown on us?"

"You have," said Kristi, returning Chris' stare.

"Explain," said Chris, continuing the interrogation.

"You've told me almost everything you're doing," said Kristi. "Or perhaps I should say, you told Dr. Galloway, who told me."

This time, the silence lasted a full ten seconds. Chris hung his head, looking at the ground in amazement. Meanwhile, Sean simply let out a long sigh.

"So let me guess... you're Dr. Galloway," Chris ventured, finally looking back at Kristi.

"One and the same," said Kristi.

"But when you first sent me those IMs introducing yourself to me, how did you get my screen name? From Dr. Meyers?"

There was a long pause while Kristi looked down at her hands, flushing noticeably in embarrassment.

"No, actually, uh... I borrowed your user name and password when you weren't looking," she said uncomfortably.

"You WHAT? When?" came Chris' reply.

"In the first-floor lounge of Snee Hall, back on campus," said Kristi. "You went in there after your meeting with Dr. Meyers. I followed you and watched you log in."

This time, the silence lasted even longer. It was Sean who finally broke the air.

"Chris, now I can guess why you kept getting that message that someone else was logged onto your account on a different computer," he said quietly, his eyes avoiding Kristi's.

"Is that true, Kristi?" Chris asked calmly, looking directly into her eyes. "Did you log into my e-mail account as well, and read my mail?"

Kristi's eyes instantly filled with tears, and she momentarily turned away.

"Yes," she responded in a choked voice. "Yes, I did, but only to find out where you were going with the cave exploration. You must believe me. I had no desire to read your personal business. But I just had to find out where you were looking."

"You realize that's a federal offense, don't you?" asked Chris, although truthfully he didn't know whether hacking into an e-mail account was illegal or not. "And my guess is that Dr. Meyers wouldn't be too pleased to hear of your clandestine activities either."

"I know," sighed Kristi. "I don't even want to think of what he'd say if he knew that I borrowed Dr. Galloway's name. The two of them were quite close at Cornell."

"Yes, I know. Dr. Meyers told me about that last week."

"You knew?" said Kristi, her eyes opening wide. "Then you knew that the instant messages from Dr. Galloway were fake."

"Not at first," admitted Chris. "I didn't learn about that until after I'd answered several of your questions. I was talking to Dr. Meyers online and I thanked him for forwarding my name to his colleague. That's when the whole story fell apart."

"I noticed that you changed your Yahoo! password too," said Kristi. "I really feel badly about this. I didn't want to end up looking like this. Really, I didn't."

"I bet," said Chris, still looking quite perturbed.

"Well, now that I'm here, at least I could help you search," said Kristi. "I've been studying cave formations in New York and the Northeast for six years now, so I should know something that could help you out."

Chris looked silently at Sean, who returned an almost imperceptible nod in return.

"OK. You can help us. But what do you hope to get out of this whole thing?" asked Chris.

"If I can help you find the cave, I'd at least like to be mentioned in the credits, and maybe have the opportunity to report it to the geological register," said Kristi. "For a geologist who will soon be looking for a job, that would look good on my résumé."

"I know all about résumés," laughed Chris. "I've been looking for a job since I got out of graduate school this spring. But then again, you've had access to my e-mail, so you probably know about that too."

"No, I don't," said Kristi, looking slightly hurt. "I didn't go into a thing that didn't look related to your search for a cave. I told you: I felt bad enough already."

"Regardless, I'm afraid that I've already promised Dr. Meyers that I'll call him first if we find anything. So you may not have much time by yourself to do caving before a cast of your contemporaries arrives."

Kristi looked sideways at Chris, a trace of a smile crossing her face.

"You promised Dr. Meyers that you'd call him first. But it doesn't have to be immediatly, does it?"

"My God, you really do think like a criminal, don't you?" Chris asked.

"Only when it comes to furthering my budding professional career," Kristi said, her brown eyes gleaming in the firelight.

"Well, tomorrow we're going to search as much of the hillside on the south side of the pond as we can, given the amount of daylight we'll have. We've drawn it out on our map and divided it into search sectors."

"I watched you for some time yesterday," said Kristi. "I saw you roving back and forth across the other hill. I take it you didn't find anything worthwhile."

"Nothing more than Chris's throne," said Sean, recalling the interesting formation on the north side of the pond.

"Excuse me?" said Kristi, looking puzzled.

"Never mind," said Sean, choosing not to explain the matter.

"No, we found nothing that looked like a cave entrance," said Chris.

"I wouldn't have thought so," said Kristi. "The mountain in back of us is much better suited to the formation of a cave. It's bigger, with more rock and also a fair amount of water. Remember, most caves are formed by ground water trickling down through existing cracks and eroding the rock over many millennia."

"I'm aware of the basic theory," said Chris, "although I hadn't thought of looking for an uphill source of water before starting our search."

"It isn't always easy to find," said Kristi. "It doesn't have to be a visible water source, such as a river or stream. All it requires is a steady supply that will provide a small amount of seepage into porous rock such as limestone. I've already spent some time up on top of the ridge to the south of us looking for good possibilities."

"We'd certainly welcome your expertise in the search process," acknowledged Chris.

"Yeah, anything that could help us narrow down 'the box,'" said Sean, referring to the area they'd selected on their map.

"I'll do everything I can," Kristi promised, putting down her empty mug and rising off the log bench. "For now, I think I'm going to head up to my tent and turn in for the night."

"Where are you camped?" asked Chris, looking around for signs of a tent.

"I'm completely out of sight, up the same hill where you collected your wood," replied Kristi. "As a matter of fact, if you walked another two hundred feet farther across that little plateau up there, you would have seen my tent."

"When did you get here?" asked Sean.

"Just a day before you," replied Kristi. "I've been scouting the mountain out since then, but I wanted to see specifically where you looked. I needed to see where Dr. Meyers sent you on his map." As she spoke, she shrugged her shoulders apologetically.

"Do you want one of us to walk you back up to your tent?" asked Sean.

"No, it's OK, but thanks," said Kristi. "I've got a good light; I'll be fine."

"We're setting an alarm for six, and we should be on the mountain searching by seven," said Chris.

"I'll be there," replied Kristi as she turned to walk away. "See you in the morning."

Once she was out of earshot, Chris turned back towards Sean and made a sarcastic face.

"Do you need a big strong man to walk you back to your tent?" he mimicked while rolling his eyes at Sean.

"Well, you never know. Maybe she's afraid of the dark," said Sean.

"The only thing she needs to fear are guys who can't seem to leave a pretty girl alone," joked Chris. "I'm surprised you didn't ask for her phone number."

"Don't let Maggie hear you say that," said Sean. "She'd never come to visit anymore."

"Well, Mr. Don Juan, I don't know about you, but I've had enough excitement for one day. I'm turning in now," said Chris, preparing to head into the tent.

"Sounds like a plan," agreed Sean. "I'll set my alarm."

Within a matter of minutes, they were both sound asleep.

Chris' eyes opened at least twenty minutes before the alarm sounded its shrill report. Unable to drift back to sleep, he began to think about the events that had led up to today. Everything had happened so quickly, and in such rapid succession. He felt a nervous energy coursing through his system, urging him on to the day's search. And now they had a third person to consider, one who had stalked them over the past few weeks and was now asking to join their ranks. Chris felt a certain uneasiness with Kristi, as she had already displayed a healthy dose of duplicity in her actions. However, she was here now, inextricably linked to the search for the cave.

Sean's alarm soon sounded, and the two men arose in unison. They were quiet as they dressed and went about their chores. The morning was chilly, and Chris found that he needed his fleece jacket while preparing breakfast.

True to her word, Kristi came stumping down the trail at about five minutes of seven. Her long black hair was pulled back into a pony tail. She wore a fleece vest over a safari-inspired, short-sleeve shirt, along with a pair of nylon cargo pants. Chris hadn't been able to see her face clearly the previous night, and he was surprised at how attractive she looked in the morning sunlight. Her dark brown eyes radiated an intelligent beauty that he found very becoming.

"I'd offer you some coffee, but Chris made this batch," said Sean. "That means you could stand the spoon in the cup without it touching the sides."

Kristi laughed. "A little bit on the strong side, huh?"

"The last time I had a cup of his java, I was awake for three and a half days," said Sean.

"Is that true, Chris?" Kristi asked, turning her eyes in his direction.

"Absolutely!" replied Chris. "I like my coffee to be a bit on the chewy side. Lots of grinds left in the bottom for extra effect."

"Not me," said Kristi, shaking her head. "I like about six shots of my amaretto-flavored sweetener stirred in before I touch the stuff."

Chris shuddered at the thought of the syrupy goo diluting his caffeine.

"Anyway, we're ready whenever you are. Take a look at the area we want to search first, and then we'll work our way outward from there." Chris showed the map to Kristi as he spoke. "Do you see anything wrong with our search pattern?"

"Why did you choose to focus on the terrain closest to the water?" asked Kristi, unaware of the other clues at Chris and Sean's disposal.

"It's largely guesswork," explained Chris. "However, we have records from more than one source that state the caves are within visible distance of the pond. If we go much further west, I think we'll lose that visibility." Chris decided to stop there, without providing additional details. He felt gun-shy about providing Kristi with a full accounting of their knowledge.

"OK, we could do that," said Kristi. "But there are some really nice ledges and fractured formations about a mile west of here that might be good candidates. How long do you have to look?"

"We're leaving here on Sunday morning, whether we find anything or not," said Chris. "How about you?"

"I've got to be out of here by Monday afternoon," replied Kristi. "You didn't come in through the Otter Brook Trail, did you?"

"No, we came in by bushwhacking up from Cedar Lakes. And we've got to go out the same way," said Chris.

"OK. Then let's use your map to search the hillside closer to the pond today," said Kristi. "I can go back over the area west of here after you leave."

Chris pulled a notepad from his shirt pocket and jotted down a number.

"Here: it's my cell number," he explained. "PLEASE call me if you find anything after we've left. I can be back here in a matter of hours."

"Is this because you want to come along as a fellow spelunker, or are you only interested in finding yourself a treasure?" asked Kristi, with a hint of a smile on her face.

"I'm every bit the cave-lover that you are," said Chris. "I may not have the degree to back it up, but I've been spelunking for twelve years now, and I'm sure I don't have to remind you that you shouldn't be going in any cave by yourself."

"Aw, how sweet of you to be concerned over me," said Kristi, her voice tinged with sarcasm. "I didn't know you cared."

Sean snorted and tossed his head in mock disgust.

"This is getting out of hand already. Let's get moving before I throw up."

"Yes sir!" said Chris, snapping a crisp salute Sean's way. "Please, sir, lead the way."

With Sean in front, the three searchers headed a quarter mile east, then climbed the steep hillside together. When they were about a hundred feet up the incline, they split up to search their parallel lines across the face of the hill. With Sean on top, Kristi in the middle, and Chris down below, they were able to carve out large chunks of real estate with each pass. Sean tied surveyor's tape to the end of each sector so that they wouldn't search the same area twice. Meanwhile, Kristi identified several geological points of interest for the others to view, including places where underground development may have begun.

Moving in unison, they spent the first three hours of the morning covering the ground southeast of the pond. They stuck to their plan and stopped after searching the first three hundred feet of elevation gain. By that point, the pond was largely obscured by the trees, and there was little chance of finding anything higher.

Sean surveyed the search map again, pointing out their next target.

"We'll pick up our next pattern box right at the western line of this first area. We'll start at the same altitude, which will be about fifty feet up from the lake, and work it east to west. We should be able to get at least two passes done by lunch hour. We'll work the rest of the hill after we eat."

Chris placed the map in front of Kristi for her inspection.

"Based on the features you observed from the top of the ridge, are there any places that you think deserve more focused attention?"

"Not especially," said Kristi, taking the map from Chris. "But I did see some nice drainage channels leading to some clefts here, and here," indicating two points on the map. "There are also a number of places along the 2,500 to 2,600 foot shelf, right in the middle of this range, where I'd slow down and look a little deeper."

Chris took the map and folded it back into Sean's daypack.

"OK then, are we all set to start the next search box?" he asked.

"I don't know about you, but I could go for a drink and a quick bathroom break," said Sean.

"How about you?" asked Chris, looking at Kristi.

"I'm good," she replied quickly, eager to start again.

"OK then, slacker," Chris said to Sean. "Since you're the only one who needs to visit the powder room, we'll wait up here while you refresh your makeup."

"I'll try to be quick," said Sean as he departed. "Don't find the gold without me!"

Sean headed down the mountain toward the tent, leaving Chris and Kristi alone on the slope. Realizing he knew very little about his new prospecting partner, Chris decided to pass the time with some light conversation.

"Well, since you know all about me, how about telling me a little bit about yourself," he said with a smile. "It's only fair, don't you think?"

Kristi looked back with a warm smile of her own.

"Gee, there isn't a heck of a lot to say," Kristi replied quietly. "I was born and raised in a small town that you've never heard of, not far from Denver, Colorado. I thought that I wanted to be zoology major until I got to college. I took a geology course as a freshman, and I've been hooked ever since. I love being outside, and I love hiking and horseback riding. Besides that, I'm just looking to finish up my masters degree and go to work for a major company back in Colorado. Well, how did I do?"

"How did you do?" asked Chris, looking puzzled.

"Yes: you just heard my life story in twenty seconds or less. I warned you it would be boring."

As Kristi spoke, Chris couldn't help but notice her shining hair and bright smile. She looked radiant, even though she'd been in the woods for three days. He also liked watching the corners of her mouth curve up into a pair of dimples when she smiled.

"Oh, come on," said Chris. "I'm sure that your life has been anything but boring. From what I've seen so far, you're definitely not a shrinking violet. I'd bet you had half the college boys on campus chasing you around."

"No, hardly that," said Kristi, laughing at the thought. "Those of us who were serious about school didn't get out and about as much as some of the others. And once you become a graduate student, you can forget about it. I'm only twenty-four, but yet I think the undergrads consider me to be over the hill. Nope, no fiancée or boyfriend, if that's what you mean. Maybe it's better that way. Maybe it allows me to have more freedom to do what I want, when I want."

"So, you never feel lonely at all?" asked Chris, hoping he wasn't being too personal with his questions.

"Oh, maybe sometimes," said Kristi, kicking some pebbles with her boot. "But I guess I'd rather be by myself than be with someone just to have a date for the weekend. I never could understand that."

"Yeah, I know what you mean there," said Chris. "I dated a lot through my four years of college, but I always ended up with girls who wanted me to make the bar scene every Saturday night and then get married as soon as they graduated. Somehow it never really worked out, and I never ended up with anyone for more than six months. But it's OK. I've always had good friends, and I made it to all four of our class formals. It's been a lot of fun."

Kristi asked him about his grad school years in Syracuse, when he was living in his house off campus. Chris told her about his attempts to balance his full course load with his obligation to provide company to his mother back in Utica. He liked the way she listened to him while he talked. It was as though he hadn't had a chance to talk with a girl his age for quite a while, and he enjoyed her company.

"You did better than me," Kristi admitted. "I made it to a couple of sorority dances my freshman and sophomore years, but not much after that. I don't know why, either. I guess I never thought about it much."

"See, if you had tried eavesdropping behind our tent just a couple of years earlier, you could have had a date too!" Chris said, smiling back at her.

Kristi blushed, looking down at the ground.

"That wouldn't have been such a bad thing," she said, her cheeks turning a shade more flushed. "You know, I am really sorry about invading your privacy the way that I did. I know you must be upset with me, and I deserve everything you're thinking.

"Nah, please don't worry about it," said Chris, patting her on the shoulder. "I understand your motives, although I wouldn't like to see you make a habit of that."

"No more, I promise," said Kristi. "Although I might end up sending you e-mail instead of stealing it."

"I'd welcome that. And now, I see my trusty compatriot coming our way, so I believe we're ready to roll."

Within a minute, Sean finished climbing back up the hill to where Kristi and Chris were seated. In his hand, he carried granola bars for the three of them.

"Here you go," he said, passing them around. "I stopped at the candy machine at the bottom of the hill."

"I hope you also picked up a six pack of beer for dinner," joked Chris. Kristi just rolled her eyes.

"I see you've managed to impress our new friend already," Sean said sarcastically, nodding in Kristi's direction.

"My mom told me to always make a good first impression," replied Chris, leading the way toward the next section of mountain.

The next mile of mountainside heading west was more rugged than their previous search box. The trio often had to stop to either climb or drop below impassable outcroppings. They tried to remain within visual range of one another to ensure complete coverage of each search line. Only by preserving the steady, almost-parallel line pattern could they be sure that they had not missed a critical fissure or opening in the rock that might lead to a cave. It was slow, hot work that had them sweating profusely within the first mile of the new leg.

In order to increase the speed of their search, they again decided to widen the distance between them to fifty feet. This meant that each pass at the mountain would take them another one hundred fifty feet up the slope. They would have to remain vigilant for any clues in the geological strata that might yield evidence of an opening. Using Kristi's experienced eyes to anchor their movement, they felt that they could cover more territory while also catching the fine details. They only had time to do this once, so every minute and every yard of ground was important.

By the time noon arrived, they had completed one pass across the mile-long sector, and had moved up another hundred and fifty feet and started to work their second pass. They toiled, yard by yard and slab by slab, to stay in formation, while observing every possible crag and cranny.

Although they had not yet completed the next full transit line, Kristi was ready for a break. "How about we call a time out for lunch," she said. "I could go for some food and a ten minute nap."

"Hey, now that sounds like my idea of a break," said Sean, always ready for a quick snooze.

"Oh no, you don't," said Chris. "If I let you doze off now, I won't be able to get you up again until dinner. Remember our fishing trip last year? You slept the entire Saturday afternoon away."

"I was just leaving a couple of fish for you, old buddy," Sean scoffed.

"I'll tell you what," said Chris. "I'll go to the tent and grab our lunch stuff, while you see if you can get us that table over by the window." As he spoke, he pointed to a comfortable-looking ledge about forty feet to their left.

"Shouldn't be a problem, as long as we don't need a reservation," said Sean.

"I'll be back in ten minutes with lunch for three," said Chris.

"Wait a minute," said Kristi. "Don't get anything for me. I'd rather get rid of stuff from my own food pack so I won't have to carry it back out on Monday. I'll go back to my tent and get my own lunch, if that's OK with you."

"See, she's already afraid of your cooking," said Chris, poking Sean in the side.

Kristi slapped Chris playfully on the arm. "I am not. And you're a goof."

"OK, on that note, I'm out of here. See you in ten minutes," said Chris. He bounced to his feet and quickly picked his way down the hillside toward the tent.

Kristi also departed quickly, en route to her own tent at the top of the plateau. Sean was left by himself, suddenly wondering: "Did I miss something here?" He climbed over to the ledge suggested by Chris and settled himself down to wait, using his day pack as a head rest. It was a cool spot, nestled underneath some small maple trees, and he soon felt the familiar hand of sleep pulling him in.

"See, I knew it," said Chris, whose voice seemed to come from afar.

"Knew what," replied Sean, cocking a half-closed eye in his direction.

"Knew that you'd fall asleep by the time I got back," said Chris.

Sean pulled himself back into a sitting position and shook the drowsiness out of his head.

"Kristi's not back yet?" he asked.

"Nope. She had to go farther and uphill. She should be back any minute now," said Chris.

"It sure does seem like you've fully forgiven each other," said Sean, hinting at his perceived notion.

"For what?" asked Chris.

"Her for hacking your e-mail account, and you for your flying tackle and take-down last night in back of the tent. You've got to admit, for all that's gone on, she does look at you kind of a lot."

Chris shrugged his shoulders. "I hadn't noticed," he said absently. "She's a nice girl, and she's interesting to talk to. Not much I can say besides that. I've just met her, same as you."

As he spoke, Kristi's footsteps sounded from across the ridge, approaching diagonally down the hillside. She appeared carrying a small purple stuff sack, along with an additional canteen.

"I'm back. Did you guys miss me?" she said, laughing as she sat down on the flat rock.

"Everything OK in your trailer?" Sean quipped.

"Yes, although I think a mouse nibbled its way into a bag of cashews," she replied. "The corner of the plastic was chewed away, and there are nut crumbs on the floor of the tent. Besides that, everything looks fine."

They sat down and laid out their lunches, using bandanas as tablecloths and re-filled water bottles as cups. Sean opened a can of spreadable chicken meat and began to distribute it over some very crushed wheat rolls.

"Yum, doesn't that look delicious," said Chris, smacking his lips sarcastically.

"It's about the only thing left on the menu," said Sean. "You can always try the next restaurant."

"Of course not," replied Chris. "I'd never miss one of your creations. Do I get extra credit if I can correctly identify the main ingredient?"

Sean rolled his eyes, and Kristi giggled.

"Don't encourage him," Sean said to Kristi, nodding Chris's way. "He only gets worse."

Chris stretched and wrapped his arms around his knees.

"You know, this is a very nice spot to take a break," he said. "When I walked down to the tent, it felt about twenty degrees warmer down there. It's nice and cool up here under the trees."

"I think we've got the cool air rolling off the mountain," suggested Kristi. "Where I come from in Colorado, the air coming over the mountains can give us some massive storms. But then again, we've got over fifty mountains taller than fourteen thousand feet. The Adirondacks are quite small by comparison."

"But they are still unique, despite their relatively small stature," said Sean. "The high peaks of the Adirondacks get some of the most severe weather in the country, and much of the flora and fauna is representative of ecosystems found in true tundras. It's really a pretty amazing place."

As Sean spoke, he finished assembling the lunch.

"Here you are, sir," said Sean, handing a sandwich and snack bar to Chris. "Get them while they're still fresh."

Chris rolled over to accept the offering, and then re-situated himself further back on the ledge. Meanwhile, Kristi opened a foil packet of tuna and squeezed it onto a slice of thick rye bread. She complemented the meal with some chocolate-covered raisins, which was a departure from her normally healthy diet.

They ate in relative silence, listening to the sounds of the birds twittering in the trees. The rustling of the leaves and the dripping of water sprinkling down the rocks completed the natural symphony surrounding them.

"I do agree with you," said Sean. "It is nice and cool here."

"Almost too cool," said Kristi, who now was feeling a bit chilled. "Where I'm sitting, it almost feels like I've got an air conditioner blowing on my back."

Chris stopped chewing and set down his sandwich. His face was a mask of fascination. He stood up and walked away from the other two, stopping about twenty feet away and then turning and slowly retracing his steps, hands spread to his sides as he walked. As he moved in front of Sean and Kristi, he stopped, looking at the hillside and vegetation directly in front of them. Then, he resumed his course, continuing another twenty feet beyond their resting place.

"Hmm…odd," he said, turning around and starting back to his original position. When he arrived back at his place on the ledge, he sat down once again, but only momentarily.

"Very odd," he said, standing up once again.

"What's so odd?" asked Sean, looking at his friend, bewildered.

"You're right, Kristi" said Chris. "It is cool here. It's too damn cool here. That's not cool air coming off the mountain. That's air that's been chilled to about forty degrees. And it's coming from somewhere that we can't see!"

Sean and Kristi both stood up and looked straight ahead at the side of the mountain. Directly in front of them, not more than fifteen feet away, was a vertical jumble of rock that was almost completely covered by a thick growth of trees, brush, and vines. The roots from a tree growing above the tangle seemed to intertwine with the thicket, resulting in a densely-woven tapestry of seemingly impenetrable organic materials.

Chris approached the overgrown curtain of biomass, feeling the flow of cool air intensify as he moved closer to the wall. He pulled aside some of the obstructing limbs, using both his arms and legs to tease his way through the growth. Underneath was a wall of gray rock that was split by a dark and empty crack, approximately five feet high and four feet wide at its base.

Chris turned around with a broad grin on his face.

"My friends, I believe it's time we went back for our headlamps."

CHAPTER 18

After breathlessly racing back to their tents to retrieve their headlamps and spelunking gear, Chris and Kristi met again outside the entrance, waiting for Sean to make their initial entry into the darkness. Sean took a few minutes longer to climb back up to the ledge, since he was carrying the metal detector and all its accessories.

"Wow, you really did come prepared," said Kristi, looking at the electronics.

"I'm not sure that we're going to need it in there," said Sean, arranging his gear for the search. "But it's always better to be ready just in case."

"Well, I'm only interested in the cave itself," said Kristi. "Anything man-made is beyond the scope of my studies, although I love looking at early Indian cave art."

Chris spoke as he strapped on his headlamp and flipped on the battery power.

"We have no idea whether anyone has ever been inside this particular cave before, so it's all still academic."

"That's right," said Sean, looking somewhat dismayed. "Could you imagine if there is more than one cave system out here? We could spend our entire time checking out the wrong place," he groaned.

"Never mind," said Kristi, her eyes gleaming with anticipation. "This is all I ever dreamed of: the opportunity for a first exploration." She turned to Chris and Sean and regarded them with a pleading expression. "I have one favor that I need to ask of you."

"Name it," said Chris. "What do you want?"

"If it's OK with you two, I'd love to be the first one in. It's been a dream of mine for my entire adult life."

Chris looked at Sean, who shrugged his shoulders back at Kristi.

"Sure, knock yourself out," said Sean. "It doesn't matter to me."

"I'd never want to step in the way of a woman's lifelong fantasy," added Chris.

Under most circumstances, Kristi would have made some response to Chris's colorful remark. However, all she could manage was a nervous nod of her head and a quick set of shallow breaths, as though she was hyperventilating. Then, she turned on the manual flash on her digital camera and moved toward the crack in the rock.

The cave opening was roughly triangular in shape. It was slanted to the left, with a crooked point on top. None of the three would be able to enter without stooping.

"Here goes," Kristi said quietly as she ducked her head and stepped through the fissure.

Outside the entrance, Sean looked at Chris, who nodded back at him, then pointed to the opening.

"Age before beauty," he said jokingly.

"Hey, that's supposed to be my line," replied Sean as he turned on his headlamp. He promptly ducked his head and guided the metal detector through the entrance.

Chris brought up the rear, following the others into the darkness. Ahead of him he could see his two fellow explorers as they followed the contour of the cave down a flight of naturally-formed steps. The entrance bent to the right slightly before emerging into a decent-sized room that was about thirty feet long. It was roughly rectangular, although it was wider near the front than it was in the rear. The back of the room slanted downward, and an exit shaft appeared in the beam of their lamps that quickly divided into two smaller tunnels.

"Someone's been here before," said Sean, shining his light into the middle of the main floor. There, arranged on the gravel and dirt base, stood a nicely-formed stack of small and medium-sized rocks. They had been piled into the shape of a long, truncated pyramid, almost as though someone was trying to cover up a log. It had clearly been crafted by other-than-natural forces.

"Let's see what the Shadow X5 picks up," said Sean, turning on the metal detector and adjusting the controls.

Almost immediately, the machine let out a loud screech that didn't require a headset to hear. Sean waved the detection coil back and forth over the length of the rock pile, noting where the tone was most prominent.

"There's definitely something major under there," said Sean, looking back at Chris. "Sounds like it's long and thin, but with pretty good density. I can't wait to see this."

Sean immediately dropped to his knees and began moving rocks from the pile. Chris, who was more than curious, joined him instantly. Even Kristi, who was more interested in the formation of the cave itself than she was in anything they might find in it, could not resist watching the two as they uncovered the source of the signal.

Within a minute of removing the first rock, Sean uncovered an orbital-shaped object with a hole in one side. Because his beam was focused more on the wall ahead of him than on the floor, he didn't immediately recognize the find until another few stones had been removed.

"Well, hello there," Sean declared, looking down at the vacant stare of a skeletal skull. "I hope you don't mind having company."

Sean and Chris both sat up on their knees, looking at the remnants of the long-ago deceased traveler. Behind Sean, Kristi stood with her hand over her open mouth, staring in disbelief.

"Oh my god," she said slowly, bending over and peering into the open eye sockets.

"I wonder who he was, and who buried him," she mused out loud.

"Unless I miss my guess," said Chris, "you are looking at the final resting ground of Mr. Thomas Swain. May he rest in peace."

"How long has this body been in here?" asked Kristi. "And is this part of what you expected to find?"

"Assuming that we're correct in our story, Mr. Swain died in either 1774 or 1775," said Chris. "Personally, I'd bet on the latter of the two years. And yes, in a perfect case scenario, we were expecting to find this body here, although we have no idea who buried him."

"Maybe if we removed more of this rock, we'd come across some clues," suggested Sean. "And we still want to take a look at what's been setting off the detector."

"I suppose Mr. Swain won't object to our incursion," agreed Chris, resuming the digging position.

"Well, while you two gentlemen are doing your thing, I'm going to do mine," said Kristi, removing a tape measure and writing pad from her pack. She commenced measuring and photographing every square inch of the outer room, including the floor, ceiling, and side walls. She used the pad to sketch out the dimensions, noting the measurements she'd taken.

Meanwhile, Sean and Chris continued their excavation, moving more of the rocks away from the skeleton. Working from the head down, they moved past the shoulders and rib cage. It was when they approached the area of the hip that they saw the first glimpse of metal.

"Looks like an old rifle barrel," said Sean, fingering the outer casting of the cylinder. "It's pretty corroded, but there's the front sight. Not much else it could be. I'm sure we'll uncover the rest of it as we move farther down the guy's leg."

Chris didn't say anything. He just stared thoughtfully at the barrel, which was aligned with the remains of the skeleton's leg.

"You know what I think?" he said, rubbing his chin with his hand.

"What?" asked Sean.

"I think that if we brought this thing home with us, and we tried fitting it up with that old muzzleloader stock you took to the museum, they'd match up perfectly."

Sean shot a quick glance at Chris as he caught his breath.

"You think, you think that the stock of the Brown Bessie came from this cave?" he asked.

"I think it came from this gun," Chris replied.

"OK," said Sean. "If we follow that logic, and if we know that Louie ended up with the stock, that means that Louie must have been here at least once after this guy was buried."

"Or, it could mean that someone else carried the stock out of the cave and either gave it to Louie, or Louie found it somewhere in his travels."

"What's your guess?" asked Sean.

"I think that Louie found this cave sometime after the Harrison map was drawn. After all, since Louie ended up with Harrison's maps, we know that he must have been with him, probably hired on as a guide. And we know…at least we think that Harrison's group never located the gold, or he wouldn't have continued searching."

Their conversation was suddenly cut short by a scream.

Kristi, who was only ten feet away from the two men, was kneeling on the ground near the entrance. Chris and Sean were by her side in an instant.

"What is it, Kristi?" shouted Chris, bending over her. "What's wrong!"

At first, Kristi stayed frozen in place, her hand gripped against her stomach, seemingly unable to reply. Suddenly she looked up at the two, her face silhouetted by the lamp on her forehead.

"Oh my god. Oh my god," she repeated, over and over again. "Come with me."

Kristi bounded up the rocky steps and through the cave entrance, followed by Chris and Sean. Once they were all outside, the two men looked at her, squinting against the light of the sun's rays, waiting for her to explain. Instead, she simply extended her arm and opened her fist.

"Look," she said, her voice trembling. "It was buried in the dirt on the floor, near that big boulder." In her hand she held an irregularly-shaped ingot of shining gold. It was about the size of a man's thumb, and it had a stamped marking on the side.

Sean took the piece from Kristi's hand and held it close to his face, examining the details. His face could not hide the exhilaration he felt from the discovery.

"Feel how heavy this thing is," he said as he passed the ingot to Chris.

"What a strange shape," remarked Kristi, her voice finally returning to normal. "It was obviously cast somewhere, but the mold must have been very crude."

"Ingots like these were produced in North and Central America before they had proper coinage machinery here," explained Chris. "They used packed sand, into which they made an indentation with a finger or thumb, and then poured the refined melted gold. Once the gold had hardened and cooled, they removed the sand and stamped it with the appropriate weight."

"How do you know all this?" asked Kristi, looking at Chris in wonder.

"I heard it from a coin dealer back in Syracuse," said Chris, examining the stamped markings. "Either coins or ingots were used in larger transactions, although the ingots soon gave way to the standardized coinage once the country was established and opened its first mint in the 1790s."

"Why didn't your metal detector find this piece as you entered the cave?" asked Kristi. "Isn't it big enough to give off a signal?"

"Oh my goodness, yes," said Sean. "I could find something that size if it was buried under two feet of dirt. But I didn't turn the detector on until we saw that pile of rocks in the middle of the front room, and even then I only scanned that one small area. I can't wait to see what else we come across in there."

"Well, come on then, partner," said Chris. "We're burning daylight out here. Let's get going."

"Before we go back inside, who's going to hold onto the ingot?" asked Sean.

"Well, since Kristi found it, I think it's only fair that she gets to hang on to it," said Chris. "But given the laws of the State, it really doesn't matter. Even if the gold carried no historical significance, it's not like any of us could keep it anyway."

"What do you mean?" asked Kristi, her face clouded with disappointment. "What 'laws of the State?'"

Chris looked at Kristi sadly, realizing her unfamiliarity with the statutes.

"I'm sorry to tell you this, but no matter how much gold or silver we find, we aren't entitled to keep any of it. Any appreciable amount of gold or silver found or mined in New York State becomes the property of the State."

Kristi looked like a kid who's just been told that they couldn't have a puppy.

"That's not fair," she said. "If we hadn't found it, it would have sat here forever and never done anyone any good. That thing's got to be worth…"

"About seven to ten thousand dollars," continued Chris, estimating the weight of the piece.

"You're kidding," said Kristi.

"Why would I kid you?" asked Chris, looking into her eyes with a smile.

"I think I'm going to scream," said Kristi.

"Not again!" said Sean. "You almost broke my eardrums with that first outburst."

"OK," said Sean, leading the way, "Kristi, you hold the ingot. Everyone: back in the cave!"

Once back inside the darkness, Kristi continued her measurements and photography while Sean and Chris resumed their exhumation of Swain's remains, uncovering the hip and then the bones of the legs. When they were finished uncovering the lower extremities, Chris bent over and gave a low whistle.

"Look at the lower right leg," he said, pointing out the badly fractured bone ends. "Even two hundred years later, there's little doubt what caused this fellow to go down. Something smashed the hell out of his tibia and fibula bones. He couldn't have walked out of here for a couple of months."

"Doesn't it look like the barrel of the gun is aligned with the broken leg?" asked Sean. "I bet someone removed the barrel to use as a splint."

Chris looked at Sean with astonishment.

"My friend, I think you've solved a mystery that's lasted for over two centuries. I'm almost certain you're right."

Working in tandem, they moved the last rocks off the bones, laying bare the entire skeleton. Sean pulled the heavy gun barrel away from the grave, and then passed the metal detector over the remains again. He was surprised to receive a beeping signal indicating more metal, even though none was readily visible. By waving the loop over the remains a few more times, he was able to localize two small focal points, each returning a signal that indicated that perhaps a single coin was buried beneath the soil.

"Could you give me a little extra light right here?" he said to Chris, pointing down to an area no more than three inches in diameter. "I'd rather not move any of this fellow's parts if I don't have to. Maybe if we could see better, we could avoid digging for whatever's setting off this signal."

Chris focused his head lamp on the bull's-eye indicated by Sean, while Sean used a stainless steel probe to gently prod beneath the skeleton's right hand. He quickly retrieved a round object that was too thick to be a coin, but yet appeared to carry significant ornamentation on at least one side. After wiping off the dirt, Sean was able to make a positive identification.

"Brass button," he stated definitively.

He passed the button to Chris, and then started probing for the other hot spot. With Chris again providing illumination, Sean was able to locate the other object beneath the bones of the lower pelvis.

"Looks like we might have a matching set," he said, pulling out a second circular metal object with patterns identical the first. "I'd bet that Dr. Rehnquist at the museum could identify the year and place that these were made."

"That's a thought," said Chris. "We should bring one along with us to have it checked out."

"How about Mr. Swain here?" asked Sean, looking at the skeleton now exposed on the gravel floor. "Do we cover him up again, or leave him as is?"

"Let's leave him out for the time being," said Chris. "He's been cooped up for over two hundred years. He deserves a little fresh air, doesn't he?"

In the back of the chamber, Kristi was laughing at the conversation.

"Listen to the two of you talking. You sound as though he's still alive!" she said.

"Well, isn't he?" joked Sean. "Look at that! He just winked at you!"

"Stop it," said Kristi. "Whenever you two are ready, I'd like to look at the first fifty feet or so of tunnel."

"We could do that," said Chris. "But I would like to do a sweep over the floor of this outer room, just to see that we're not missing anything."

"How long do you think that will take?" asked Kristi.

Chris looked back at Sean, who quickly estimated the area of the floor.

"Not more than twenty minutes, unless we get any signals. But I can't imagine finding much, because the floor is rock, so nothing could be buried."

"OK, I'll wait for you," Kristi offered.

Sean picked up the detector and started sweeping the rock surface, working from the back of the room to the front. He was methodical in his approach, working in arcing patterns that overlapped across the left, then right sides of the chamber. Chris kept pace, side-by-side with Sean, using his headlamp to provide extra lighting.

They had covered about half the space when Chris suddenly spoke out.

"Hey! Wait a minute. Let's take a look at this."

Sean was surprised, because he had seen nothing and heard nothing from the detector. Chris knelt on the floor and picked up a small black piece of stone.

"This doesn't look like it belongs here," he said. "Check this out."

In his hand was a triangular-shaped rock that looked as though it had been sharpened to a point.

"Let me see that," said Kristi, stepping up with her own light.

Chris handed her the stone, which she briefly examined before looking back at him.

"Nice find," she said, holding it up between her thumb and index finger. "This is an arrowhead, probably Iroquois, which has been chiseled out of chert."

"Chert? What's chert?" asked Sean.

"It's a coarse type of siliceous rock, which is a form of flint. I'm not an expert on Native American tools, but I do know that it was used by the Indians in this part of the continent to make things like spears and arrowheads, as well as scraping tools. It could be chipped into a razor-sharp edge, which was lethal in the hands of a skilled hunter."

"I've never seen rock like this in the Adirondacks," said Chris. "Is this something that you'd expect to find locally, or was this carried here from some distant location?"

"You could find it in Upstate New York, but it's more prevalent on the Niagara Peninsula and throughout southern Ontario," Kristi explained. "It's a pretty common by-product of glacial activity. The bigger mystery appears to be how and when this piece was carried in here, since it's a safe bet that your Mr. Swain never created one of these himself."

"We can answer that question," said Chris, pointing to his pack. "We have the journal left behind by this gentleman. He was guided into the woods by at least two Iroquois guides, so it's entirely possible that this belonged to one of those Indians and was even used to hunt for the food that they ate."

"Look at that," said Sean, pointing to a darkened area of the rock floor. "It looks as though there could have been a fire there a long time ago."

Kristi knelt on the floor and ran her fingers across part of the surface. She examined the black stain on her hand, noting the way it smudged her fingertips.

"It's tough to say because it's so old," she said. "But I'm fairly certain that this is organic material, not mineral. So it's quite possible that this could have been where they set a fire. We'll be able to tell when the university team arrives with the equipment."

"Oh, you mean, Dr. Galloway, with his carbon-dating gear?" asked

Chris, rolling his eyes.

"You'll never let me live that down, will you?" she said.

"Maybe someday," Chris replied, winking back at her. "Actually, you're pretty handy to have around."

Sean continued the sweeps with the detector, slowly and methodically working his way toward the front entrance. When he was about two-thirds of the way up to the natural steps, the detector started singing once again, indicating a metallic presence. It was concentrated within a twelve-inch radius, and it seemed to contain several fragments of metal. Sean also noticed a small amount of hardened black material, which had decomposed into very small granules.

"Give me some more light," he said, looking back at the other two.

Chris and Kristi combined their beams to flood the spot with light, as Sean began sifting through a small heap of organic material containing bits and pieces of hardware. Also present in the mix were a few small chips that shined a bright yellow gold. Sean picked up one of the shavings and handed it to Kristi.

"What do you make of this?" he asked.

"It looks like a bit of refined gold that has flaked off a larger piece, such as an ingot or large coin," she replied. "But wherever it came from, I can tell you that this isn't a piece of raw ore. And it came from someplace else besides here."

Chris scooped up some of the dark material, noting its light weight and dry, crusted feel.

"At first blush, I was going to say that this was the remains of charred wood. But under the light, it looks like this could have been some form of leather which has fallen apart through the ages. It's kind of tough to tell, though, because there just isn't enough of it left."

Chris had no way of knowing just how close he was to the truth. The early saddles that were used in this country were comprised largely of cloth and wood, with leather added for support. Even though the cloth material had long since disintegrated, traces of the leather and metallic fasteners were still evident.

Sean held up some iron bits that looked like primitive connector pieces.

"Whatever it was, I think these were used to hold it together," he said, inspecting them closely.

"Should we screen out this pile, just to grab the few bits of gold we can find?" Chris asked.

"Sure, hand me my bag, will you," Sean said to Kristi, who passed him his small satchel of accessory parts. He reached into the bag and pulled out the trowel and a lightweight medium-gauge soil filter.

"Let's just get rid of the big stuff first. Why don't you do the honors," he said, handing the trowel to Chris as he held the filter device with both hands.

"Sure. I never could resist playing in a sandbox," said Chris, shoveling the first scoops of material into the filter.

As he scooped, Sean maintained a vigorous shaking motion. Most of the smaller stuff passed through the sieve, but the bigger pieces stuck, and Sean discarded them by hand. He repeated this process, scoop after scoop, until they were nearly through with the pile.

Then, it was Chris' turn to get excited. "Hello!" he said, giving great emphasis to the first syllable. As he spoke, a large gold coin slid off the trowel and onto the material on the screen.

Chris reached in and picked out the gold piece, instantly noting its similarity to those from the museum in Blue Mountain Lake. He looked at the date on the front, which read 1773.

"This one's a year earlier than the other two, but it could have still come from the same batch," he said.

"You found more of these?" asked Kristi, her eyes wide open.

"Yes, but in a much more civilized location. It's a long story; why don't we save it for the campfire tonight?"

As they spoke, Sean retrieved a smaller filter and began sifting the debris through a second pass.

"Once we get through this, let's just pick out what we can find, and then move on," said Chris. "There's probably not enough here to merit much of our time, unless they are bigger chunks."

They worked their way through the remaining heap, handful by handful, until they were near the bottom.

"Here's another keeper," said Sean, pulling out a pea-sized bit of solid gold.

"It looks like it was broken off of another ingot, like the one I found earlier," said Kristi.

"Wow. Forget how valuable this stuff is; it's just plain beautiful to look at," said Sean, marveling at the way the nugget reflected the light of their headlamps.

"And pretty darn rare, too," added Kristi. "If you took all the gold that's ever been mined and put it all in one place, it would only make a cube about eighty-two feet on each side. No wonder it's so prized."

Sean continued sifting until he had exhausted the pile of organic matter, not finding much else worth saving. He slipped the doubloon and the larger nugget into a small cloth bag inside the metal detector coil holder. Then, he and Chris completed searching the remainder of the floor until they had reached the cave entrance.

"What time do you have?" asked Kristi, looking at Chris and Sean.

Chris looked at the illuminated dial on his Juregensen watch.

"I've got about three thirty, a little after," he said.

"Could we move back into the exit tunnels now?" she asked. "I'd like to look around at least an hour or two before we call it quits for the day."

"Of course," said Chris, understanding her desire to start her exploration.

"Me first?" she asked, looking imploringly at the other two.

"Women always go first," said Chris. Sean nodded his agreement.

They entered the small opening at the rear of the chamber, walking in single file. Even Kristi, who stood at five feet seven inches, had to stoop to avoid hitting her head on the overhead rock. Sean left the metal detector up front in the main room due to the space constraints.

They spent their next two hours exploring the first hundred yards of tunnels, including several that interconnected with one another. A large room, about forty feet by thirty feet, was of particular interest to Kristi because of the flowstone formation on one end. It resembled a rock waterfall, with multiple shades of yellow and off-white calcite.

They could have covered more ground, but Kristi was photographing and mapping each formation as they progressed.

"I'd love to see where this thing comes out," she said, looking into the inky-dark depths ahead of them. "You can just feel the air current moving through here. There must be at least one other entrance, even though we probably won't find it today."

"No, we probably won't," replied Chris, glancing once again at his watch. "It's almost five thirty now. I think it's time we headed back to the surface."

Together, they turned and retraced their steps to the outer routes they'd taken from the entry chamber. Seeing light coming from another intersection, Kristi decided to follow it back to their destination. She was within thirty feet of the front room when she stopped to examine a pile of rubble.

"This didn't happen by accident. Someone moved these stones here," she said.

"I'd agree with you," said Sean, noticing the same collection of uniform-sized rocks stacked loosely in a pile.

"It's worth checking out," said Chris. "We could probably move this stuff by hand in a couple of minutes."

The two men returned to their knees and began to haul the rock away from the original pile. Sean couldn't resist adding a bit of off-tune music to the occasion.

"Yo ho ho, yo ho ho, I'm a miner, don't you know!" he sang, his notes echoing along the stone passageway.

Within five minutes, they had moved all the rock, and they had discovered nothing.

"If you ask my opinion, it looked as if something was hidden there at one time," said Kristi.

"Well, my oh my… weren't you the one who was 'only interested in the cave, not the gold?'" asked Chris.

"Well, yes. But that first ingot I found sort of enhanced my interest somewhat," she said, giggling out loud.

"Women," said Chris, rolling his eyes again.

The adrenaline rush of the day's activities finally began to wear thin as the three walked back down the mountainside. Kristi accepted an invitation to join Chris and Sean for supper and a brief campfire. However, they all agreed that they were too tired for a lengthier communal event.

As Kristi hiked back up the hillside to fetch her food and utensils, Chris went in search of wood and Sean left to filter more water. Within fifteen minutes, they had reassembled at the tent near the pond. It was Chris's turn to do the cooking, so the other two stood nearby as they chatted about the events of the day.

"All in all, a pretty darn successful day, don't you think?" said Chris as he set up the camp stove. "We found the cave, we found Thomas Swain, and we even got a few ounces of gold to show for it."

"Sure beats panning all summer to find a few stray flakes," agreed Sean.

"How much is in the grand prize, if you do manage to find it?" asked Kristi.

"A lot," said Chris, intentionally vague in his answer.

"Oh, come on, you can tell me," said Kristi. "After all, I did help you find the cave, didn't I?"

"We think it might be as much as seventy thousand, although some of it might be in silver instead of gold."

It was a little white lie, but Chris felt no guilt. The actual value in current dollars had grown to over six million, but that was more information than she needed to have. At least for now.

"Oh wow," said Kristi. "That's a lot of loot. But, if you don't get to keep any of it, why bother? It'll only end up going to the State anyway."

"I never could resist a good mystery," said Chris, smiling up at her.

"He read every one of the Hardy Boys books when he was a kid," added Sean.

"I'll tell you what's a good mystery," said Kristi. "Did you notice that we didn't see a single bat on the inside of that cave? Not even in the front chamber. I've never been in a cave that didn't have at least some bats."

"That's not really a mystery," said Chris. "Did you see what we had to chop through in order to gain entry to that place? I doubt there's any way that a bat could have detected an opening in the rock; it was a solid wall of trees, roots, and other debris. It would have been impossible for anything to fly through that thatch."

"That's right," said Sean. "We wouldn't have found it ourselves if not for a big stroke of luck. Had we waited another five minutes to eat lunch, we wouldn't have been sitting on that ledge, which means that we never would have noticed the difference in temperature."

"Well, we did sit there, and we did find the cave," said Kristi. "Now, my next question is, who is going to call Dr. Meyers and report it?"

"Something tells me that I know the answer to this question," said Chris, looking back at the geologist. "Does she have long black hair and pretty brown eyes?"

"Oh, thank you, thank you," said Kristi, hugging both the men in turn.

"Wait a minute; we haven't said 'yes' yet," said Chris, feigning reluctance.

"Yes, you have. I can see right through you," said Kristi. "You have no idea what this will mean to my new career, especially if I can find some really extraordinary formations inside. I'd like to get something published as soon as I can."

"I did promise to call Dr. Meyers personally if we found anything," said Chris. "But we'll wait the extra day for you to talk to him on Monday. Just make sure you mention that we were here, OK?"

"Of course," said Kristi, laughing at the remark. "After all, I've got to tell him that it was your trip. You just invited me to join you after we met at Cornell and I told you how much I wanted to come along."

"Oh, good grief!" exclaimed Chris. "So that's going to be the story? I must have the word 'SUCKER' tattooed across my forehead."

Following a tasty meal of chicken and rice over biscuits, the trio sat comfortably by the unlit fire that Sean had set up. He'd piled a few sticks and kindling in a lackluster manner, not really feeling up to participating in the nightly blaze.

"You know, I think I've about had it," he said, stretching out his legs in front of him. "If you folks don't mind, I'm going to turn in right after cleanup," he said.

"That's OK," said Chris, sipping the last of his Kool-Aid. "We've got a long day tomorrow. I think I'll turn in fairly early tonight as well. But I did want to give Kristi a tour of King Chris's Throne."

"What?" asked Kristi, a baffled expression creasing her face.

"Just a really neat geological formation Sean and I found yesterday, up on the other hillside. It's not really that spectacular, if you don't want to see it."

"I'd love to see it," said Kristi. "I love anything geological. Please, lead the way!"

Sean agreed to do the remainder of the dishes, leaving Chris free to escort Kristi back up the hill north of Lost Pond. Together, they scrambled up the rock outcroppings, climbing around and over many of the same slabs that Chris had climbed with Sean a day earlier. They reached the stone chair after about fifteen minutes of frenetic movement, without stopping to catch their breath. By the time they arrived at the site of the throne, they were both winded from the exertion of the ascent.

"Oh, nice. Very nice!" said Kristi, examining the natural cut in the rock that formed the seat. "You're right, it really does resemble a throne."

"Eh, like I said, it's nothing really that amazing. I just thought maybe you might like going for a walk after dinner," said Chris.

"I'm honored," said Kristi, seating herself in the alcove. "Hey, this thing really is pretty cozy, isn't it," she laughed.

"I'd prefer something with a little more cushion," said Chris, smiling back at her.

"Ooh, let's run up to the top of the hill and catch the sunset," said Kristi, looking off at the western sky. "It looks like it'll be a good one tonight."

Chris followed her up another couple hundred feet to the top of the hill, where they found a comfortable level patch to flop down and watch the colors unfold. It was a gorgeous evening, with the skies turning a vibrant orange and red, graduating into darker shades of purple in the east. They spent the next hour talking about simple things like family and friends, their dreams and aspirations. The longer the conversation lasted, the more Chris yearned to stay. Only the onset of darkness prompted him to suggest returning to camp.

"Come on, Future Dr. Kincaid," said Chris. "I'll escort you down the hill and back up to your tent. Let's grab some lights along the way. It's going to be getting pretty dark within the next twenty minutes."

"I'll stick right behind you," said Kristi, following in his footsteps.

They proceeded to descend, exercising caution when necessary. When they came to a vertical drop of about six feet, Chris took it in a single leap. As Kristi sat and prepared to slide off, Chris put his hand up to give her a stable hold.

"Thanks," she said, landing on both feet with a thud.

Chris held her hand long enough to ensure that she did not tumble to the ground. However, as they turned to walk back around the pond, she still had a grip on his hand, and had entwined her fingers into his.

"I hope you don't mind me using you for balance," she said, keeping her eyes focused straight ahead.

"Are you kidding me?" replied Chris. "It would be my pleasure. Heck, I haven't had a date all week."

"Oh, so that's what you think this is," said Kristi, intentionally bumping Chris with her hip, "a devious attempt to get a date on a Saturday night?"

"Hey, sorry for the slim pickings, but I'm the only show in town," said Chris, enjoying the exchange.

"A girl could do worse," replied Kristi.

Considering that a brief thunderstorm rolled through the area on Saturday night, the next dawn revealed a bright blue sky. It was somewhat chilly, but the weather looked promising for the walk out of the woods.

Chris and Sean had already eaten breakfast and were in the process of rolling up their tent when Kristi appeared at the bottom of the hill. Braced for the cool air, she wore a bright-orange fleece pullover and a pair of red wind pants over her khaki shorts. Her hair was pulled back in a pony tail, revealing her tanned and radiant face.

"Good thing I came down when I did," she said, looking at the nearly assembled backpacks leaning against the log bench. "Would you really have taken off without saying goodbye?" she asked.

"Of course not," said Chris. "We just didn't have time to conduct room service for breakfast this morning."

"I've actually been up for over two hours," said Kristi with an indignant snort. "I've already downloaded the photos and my measurements into my laptop, and recorded most of my Day 1 observations. So there."

"Well, excuse me for assuming that you were still cocooned in your beauty rest," said Chris. "But I would have stopped up no matter what. We still need to trade e-mail addresses and phone numbers... unless you want me to keep using that Galloway address. You don't, do you?"

"No, of course not," giggled Kristi. "Here: I already wrote it all down for you—my e-mail, phone, and everything." She handed him a piece of paper that had been ripped out of a spiral-ring notebook.

"That's efficiency," said Chris.

"I try," replied Kristi.

"Are you sure you don't want me to call Dr. Meyers, just to let him know that you're wandering about in the cave by yourself tomorrow? That does have me a little nervous, you know."

"You don't have to worry," said Kristi. "I'm a big girl, and I've got extra lights and supplies, and I'll stay away from any pits. I promise."

Sean finished putting the tent into its bag and wrapped up the last of his packing.

"OK, I'm set to go if you are," he said to Chris. "I just need a few minutes in the little boy's room, and I'll be ready to hit the trail."

Sean headed up the hill to find some privacy, leaving Chris and Kristi alone in the clearing.

"I'm glad we've had a little time to talk these past couple days," said Chris. "I've enjoyed getting to know you."

"I have too," said Kristi. "It was even worth being tackled by a Division I varsity lacrosse player!"

"Sorry about that," said Chris. "But given the circumstances, I don't feel too bad about it. I hope I didn't leave any bumps or bruises."

"Only to my ego," replied Kristi.

"Hey, listen," said Chris, his eyes showing genuine concern. "Promise me you won't do anything foolish inside the cave until your team catches up with you, OK? Otherwise I'd be worried sick until I knew you made it out safely."

"Aw, that's really sweet, thank you," she said. She leaned forward and gave Chris a kiss on the side of his cheek.

"Now it's my turn to blush," said Chris, smiling back at her.

"I didn't know I ever blushed in the first place."

"Anyway, just be careful, OK?" Chris reminded her.

"I've got a good idea," said Kristi. "I'll be out of here by tomorrow night. And then I'll want to brief Dr. Meyers on Tuesday or Wednesday. How about I come up to Syracuse at the end of next week and bring along photos of anything I find that's worthwhile inside the deeper regions of the cave? Maybe I could even help you brainstorm where to look next."

"Sure, you're welcome any time," said Chris. "We really could use help at this stage. We've got to go back to the drawing board and try to see where the gold was taken after it was removed from the cave. It obviously stayed there for a period of time. Now, we need to zone in on its final destination."

"Any ideas?" asked Kristi.

"A few," said Chris. "I want to go back again and look at the circumstances surrounding Harrison's search, and also check out French Louie's maps one more time. We may be coming back in here again soon." He winked at Kristi as he spoke.

"Would you count me in?" asked Kristi. "I'd love to come, but this time with an invitation."

"Consider yourself invited," said Chris.

As he spoke, Sean returned from the hillside and made some final adjustments on his pack straps.

"Ready, amigo?" Chris asked him as he readied his own gear.

"Ready as I'll ever be," said Sean, lifting his pack onto his shoulders.

Both of them turned and faced Kristi, who hugged each of them in turn.

"Thanks for everything, both of you. I hope you can make it back here sometime this month. This means so much to me," she gushed.

"It's been a pleasure meeting you," said Sean. "We'll probably be back soon, especially if we can clear up any more of the mystery."

"And I really wish I could stay longer now," said Chris. "But I still have my interviews coming up this week, and some other things to take care of as well. Maybe we'll see you, though, before you come back in with your team."

"It's a deal!" said Kristi.

Sean and Chris said their farewells and turned to start their walk back through the woods to the Beaver Pond off of Cedar Lakes. Once they reached the junction with the Northville-Placid Trail, they figured it would take another three hours to get back to the Jeep. They had covered about six feet of their journey when Kristi called after them.

"Oh, uh, guys… aren't you forgetting something?" she asked, a sly expression crossing her face.

Both men turned back to see what she had in mind.

"Forgetting something? What do you mean?" asked Chris, looking a bit puzzled.

"The ingot!" Kristi exclaimed, holding out the large chunk of gold in her hand. "You forgot to take the ingot that I found."

Chris remained rooted in place, a puzzled expression still on his face.

"Remember you said that I could hold it for the rest of the day, but any gold and silver found becomes the property of New York State? Remember? And by the way, I've determined that it weighs somewhere between two to three ounces."

"Ingot? What ingot?" said Chris, looking at Sean.

"Beats me. I didn't see any ingot," Sean replied.

"I think she's become delusional. We'd better get going."

Before Kristi could say another word, Chris and Sean turned around and walked off into the woods.

CHAPTER 19

Sean and Chris were out of the woods by two in the afternoon and rolling into the Careys' driveway in Utica by four. Excited by the discoveries of the week, their thrill was tempered only slightly by their inability to find the actual treasure. With growing certainty that the legend of Gordon's gold hoard was true, they knew that they would continue chasing their leads until they laid their hands on the prize.

Theresa Carey was just walking back up the driveway from her mailbox when the Jeep pulled between the stone gateposts. She smiled at her son as he drove past and parked in back of Sean's Mercedes.

"Welcome home! I was just thinking about starting some dinner; will you join me?" she called out through the open driver's window.

Chris opened the door and bounded out of the vehicle in a single movement.

"Hey, Mom! Sure, how could we resist. But maybe we'd better eat outside on the patio; we haven't had a shower in four days."

"That's more information than I needed," said his mother, giving him a hug. "You boys relax. Dinner should be ready in about half an hour."

Chris took advantage of the interlude to take a shower and remove the four days of sweat and bug dope from his skin. Meanwhile, Sean transferred his gear from the Jeep into his trunk. They met in the kitchen in time to help Theresa move some rotisserie chicken from the oven to the table. Not much was discussed until they were all seated for the meal.

"So, are you boys going to keep me in suspense, or are you going to fill me in on your trip?" Theresa asked as she passed around a plate of potatoes.

Sean and Chris looked at one another, then simultaneously blurted out the same reply.

"We're going to keep you in suspense," they said, bursting into laughter.

"Thank you," she replied, responding to the sarcasm.

"Mom, it's been a great week. We couldn't have asked for anything better. I've got so much to tell you about that I feel like a balloon about ready to burst."

"Well, don't keep it a secret, Son. Let's have it. I know you didn't find the great treasure you told me about, or I would have heard about it already. But you must have found something of interest while you were in there?"

Sean felt the sudden need to interrupt and field this question.

"As a matter of fact, Mrs. Carey, Chris did find something while he was in the woods. I think he found his next girlfriend."

"What?" said Theresa, shooting a glance at her son. "You didn't mention anything about a girl to me. Is she coming over?"

"Mom, stop," pleaded Chris. "Sean's just playing games with you. We did meet a woman in there who is a graduate geology student at Cornell, but she's not my girlfriend. Please."

"Well, you make sure to bring her over here to meet me when she's in town. I always like to meet the girls you're dating, Honey."

Chris rolled his eyes and shot a level stare at Sean for mentioning the subject.

"Anyway, Mom, it looks as though Grandpa's been sitting on a lot of good information for at least seventy years. The things that I saw on his papers and maps do exist, and we did find them. As a matter of fact, I think we found everything but the gold."

"Well, if the cave exists, and the gold exists, then you should have found one when you found the other, right?"

"Not exactly," Chris explained. "We did find traces of gold that was stored there once. And we found another one of the doubloons, which was almost identical to the coins I found in Louie's trunk at the Adirondack Museum. Also, the graduate student we met found a gold ingot that weighed several ounces, which was also probably from the same cache. But it looks like rest of it's been removed from the cave, probably many years ago."

"Your grandfather will be pleased to know that he was able to help you get as far as you have. He'd probably love to have a shot at finding the rest himself, if he could still get around."

"Did he ever show you that old gun stock that French Louie supposedly gave to Great-Grandpa?"

"Yes, a long time ago. Why?"

"We found the barrel of that same gun, sitting in the cave next to a skeleton," Chris said. "It was in pretty bad shape, but it matched up."

"A skeleton? Oh my!" Teresa exclaimed. "Do you think it's possible that the gold is still buried along with the skeleton somewhere inside the cave? Did you have a chance to explore the entire place from end to end?"

"No, we only searched the first several hundred feet of the cave's passageways, Mom. But that was much farther than anyone could have made it without lighting. It got pretty black once we transited through the first large chamber. Also, there were lots of signs of human activity in the outer room, but none at all beyond about thirty feet into the first tunnel. I don't think it's possible they went any farther."

"So what happens next?" asked Theresa. "Have you run out of ideas on where to search, or is there anything else up your sleeve?"

"I'm going to take a break for about a week," replied Chris. "I have an interview in Boston on Wednesday, which is a good sign because I interviewed with them by phone last week. I've also got a pile of letters to get out by next weekend. After that, I want to do some more investigative work and check out a couple more sites for us to search. I'm not ready to give up yet."

"I could use some time myself," said Sean. "But we don't want to wait too long; once we get into September, it starts getting a bit frosty back in those mountains. Maybe we could look at going back in another two weeks?"

"I'm OK with that," said Chris. "Maybe we could take a day or two and do some deeper exploration inside Carey Caverns."

"Too late. I bet your new friend from Cornell has it named already," laughed Sean. "Why don't you call her up tonight and ask her. While you're at it, see if she still remembers your name!"

The next several days passed by in a blur. Chris received a phone call from an ecstatic Dr. Meyers on Tuesday afternoon, thanking him for his part in finding the cave.

"Was the map I gave you much help?" the professor asked.

"It was," said Chris. "To tell you the truth, several bits of information led us to the right part of the right hill. And then, we just got lucky. But I'm sure that Kristi has told you about that."

"Yes, she hasn't stopped talking about it since she returned," said Dr. Meyers. "And I might add, she hasn't stopped talking about you since she's been back, either. You made quite an impression on her."

"Did she tell you how we met?" Chris asked.

"No, but I remember that I introduced you when you were down here, didn't I?"

"Oh, uh… yes. Yes, you did," said Chris, deciding not to pursue the topic.

"Kristi said she's done a masterful job of hiding the entrance. We're going to hold off on announcing this until we can get all the way through the cave and map out as much as we can reach. Once we announce a new cave to the public, we'll have hundreds of people back there checking it out."

"When are you planning on going in yourself?" asked Chris.

"I want to start that process next week. I'm going in there a week from today, along with about a half dozen folks from the department here. It should be quite a party. You're welcome to join us if you'd like," said the doctor.

"We might take you up on that, Dr. Meyers. Thank you for your offer."

"OK then, Chris, thanks again for taking such an interest in this. I'm sure you and Sean will both be mentioned when we go public with the discovery."

Dr. Meyers was about to hang up the phone when Chris chimed in with another question.

"Dr, Meyers, I wonder if I might be able to ask you one more question?"

"Go ahead."

"I don't know if Kristi told you this in her report, but there is a body in the cave."

"Yes, the skeleton that you found near the entrance," Dr. Meyers replied.

"One and the same," said Chris. "Just out of curiosity, what's going to happen to that?"

There was a pause at the other end of the phone as the professor considered the possibilities.

"Well, I understand that it's been there for a very long time; possibly since the Revolutionary War. Is that correct?"

"I believe so, yes," answered Chris.

"Since they are human remains, the authorities are going to have to be involved. I also imagine that there might be some historical interest in this person as well. They may try to locate any living survivors of the family, which is highly unlikely, assuming that they can even identify the deceased. But if they can, the family will decide how the remains will be handled. If they can't, the bones will probably be buried in a simple plot in a local cemetery."

"Could you please keep me in the loop on that?" asked Chris. "I have an idea for the deceased, who, by the way, I believe to be one Thomas Swain."

"Ah, so you've given some thought to this already," said Dr. Meyers.

"You might say that Mr. Swain and I have become fairly well acquainted these past several weeks."

"I'll do whatever I can," said the professor. "And thanks again for your help. I hope we get to see each other again soon."

The following day, Wednesday, was a long one for Chris. He was up at four in the morning and on the road within an hour in order to arrive in Boston's business district for a one o'clock interview. Dressed in black pinstripes with a white shirt and dark silk tie, he amused himself comparing his ensemble to the hiking garb he wore the previous week. However, this was "business dress" in the financial industry, especially inside the big city corporations.

Chris's interview went well. It lasted until the end of the day, because he was asked to meet with three different department heads after his initial interview with the hiring manager. By the time he walked out the front door, rush hour was in full swing.

Rather than stop for dinner, he grabbed a hot dog from a street vendor and carried it into his Jeep. The drive home would take him at least six hours and probably more, given the congestion on the highway. He had been on the road for about an hour when his cell phone rang. He didn't recognize the number that appeared on the display.

"Hello," he called out, setting his phone to hands-free operation.

"Well, hey there, stranger," said a familiar voice. "You've been out of the woods for three whole days now, so I thought I'd call to make sure you didn't forget me entirely."

"Kristi! Hi! Thanks for calling me. I've been thinking about calling you."

"Oh, of course you have," Kristi replied sarcastically. "You were about to call me this very moment, but I beat you to it, right?"

"Oh stop, please," Chris said, rolling his eyes. "I've been busy: very busy. As a matter of fact, I'm in Boston right now."

"Well, OK then, you're excused, I guess."

"So tell me about your day on Monday. How far in did you get, and what else did you find?

"I explored two smaller passageways, each leading in different directions from a centralized chamber that was not far from the big room that we found on Saturday, the one with the flowstone formation. There were several more really impressive accumulations of calcite back there as well. And there's something else I noticed when I made another pass at the tunnels leading away from the front room."

"What's that?" asked Chris.

"Do you remember that dark organic material that you sifted through with Sean in the outer room on Saturday? Remember, that's where you found that coin?"

"Of course," replied Chris.

"I found a little more of that stuff down the channel where you two found that small rock pile. That's the one that you moved, thinking that there was something buried underneath."

"I remember that."

"I brought some of that stuff home with me and put it under the microscope. It's leather! It's darn near petrified, and there isn't much of the original structure left, but there's no doubt in my mind."

"So what are you thinking?" asked Chris.

"I'm thinking that it was probably a leather satchel of some kind, and that it was originally used to carry a portion of the gold. I went back to the rock pile back there, and I found a few flakes of gold mixed in with the gravel on the cave floor. Wherever I've found the decomposed leather, I've found traces of gold. That's not a coincidence."

"I would agree," said Chris. "Nice work, Kristi."

"I took a ton of photos, too, including one of an interesting underground stream that you'd love to see. Are you accepting visitors up there?"

"Sure. I'd love to have company," said Chris. "How about Friday?"

"I can do that," replied Kristi. "I can make it up there by about six."

"Sounds great. I'll get some Chinese takeout and we can eat while you give me the photo tour."

"I'd like that a lot," said Kristi.

"I'm looking forward to it too, Kristi. I'll email you directions to the house. It's a little out of the way but I imagine you'll get here OK."

"I've got GPS in the car. I'll find you. See you around six."

It was mid-morning on Thursday when the shiny new green Jeep pulled up in front of the Syracuse Coin and Gold Exchange. Wes Hawkins was showing some Indian Head pennies to a young boy when the door opened. Chris nodded as he entered the store and was acknowledged by the numismatist.

"Give me a few minutes and I'll be with you," Wes said, winking over the counter.

Chris looked around the place with mild interest as he waited his turn. He flipped through a notebook holding pages of old foreign currency and then looked at some silver coins through the countertop. Meanwhile, the novice collector finished his purchase and walked out, watched by the storekeeper.

"I wish I had their kind of money back when I was a lad," said Wes. "That young kid just bought two Indian Head pennies for seventy five bucks. Jeez, I would have had to work all summer to make that kind of money," he said, shaking his head.

Chris decided not to beat around the bush. He withdrew a small leather key holder from his side pocket and opened it on the shiny glass counter. He opened the snap and picked out the 1793 doubloon, along with the broken end of the ingot that they had found inside the cave.

"Last time I was here, you said you could find a market for some gold. I think I'd like to take you up on your kind offer," said Chris.

"Last time you were here, you seemed pretty reluctant to part with either of those two doubloons. What made you change your mind?" asked Wes.

"Those weren't mine to sell," said Chris. "If you'd take a look, you'll notice that this one is from a year earlier. I'd also like you to weigh the bit of gold bullion there and make me a combined offer."

The dealer donned his eye loop and examined the coin closely. He scowled as he worked: a practice perfected from years of experience in the business. He never liked to show his thoughts or emotions as he worked, for fear of raising the customers' expectations.

After he finished inspecting the doubloon, he viewed the piece of ingot under the same loop, prodding it and verifying that it was indeed solid gold. He then moved it to a balance scale, where he weighed the bit to a hundredth of a gram.

"Nice coin," he said simply as he returned to Chris' place at the counter. "I'd love to know your source. I'd buy more than one, if you had them."

"For now, that's the only one," said Chris. "And I won't have any more to sell after this one piece. It's for a special reason."

"It always is," said Wes, shaking his head with a wistful smile. "Anyway, the nugget is a little more than seven grams. Based on today's spot price of gold, I can offer you about $400 for it. For the doubloon, I'll add in another $2,400. So you're looking at about $2,800, if you want to do this."

Normally, Chris would have balked at accepting an immediate offer. It was his nature to do some comparison shopping, especially for such a commodity as rare coins, because he knew that there were unscrupulous dealers who would rob you blind given the opportunity. However, from his observations and his previous meeting with Wes, he instinctively trusted the elderly business owner.

"I'll take it," he said, extending his hand.

"Good," said the shopkeeper, reaching for his records. "I could give you cash, or if you'd rather, I can write you a check."

"Cash is fine," said Chris. "I have plans for this money, and I'd like to keep it hush for the time being."

"You got it," said Wes. "I'll be right back."

He stepped into the back room and opened the safe. When he returned, he counted out twenty-eight hundred-dollar bills into Chris's waiting hands.

"There you go," said Wes, writing out a receipt for the transaction. "Signed, sealed and delivered."

Chris was about to leave, but he turned back to face the dealer again.

"Just out of curiosity, what usually happens to a coin like this after you buy it?"

"I've got a buyer lined up for almost any Colonial Era coin that comes in. He's got a large collection and deep pockets."

"How much do you think he'll pay for this one?" asked Chris.

"I know for a fact I'll get at least $2,900 for it, just because of the date and the condition."

Chris smiled and shook his head at the dealer, thinking of his quick five hundred dollar profit. "Nice work, if you can get it," he said ruefully, departing the store.

The next afternoon, Chris found himself busy cleaning up his house and stowing the remainder of his gear from the camping trip. As he worked, he scoffed at himself, reminding himself that Kristi was no different than any other visitor he'd had over to visit. However, he found himself worrying more and more about wanting to make a good impression on his new friend. He'd never been that way before with any of his female friends, and yet he felt something different with her. He found himself wondering whether she was having any of the same thoughts.

About an hour before she was due to arrive, he drove out to a small local Chinese restaurant and bought several dishes to satisfy a wide range of tastes. He couldn't remember what Kristi had brought with her to eat at Lost Pond, so he had to trust his instincts and order some of his own favorites. He stood in the front of the eatery as the chef prepared large containers of shrimp with Chinese vegetables, sesame chicken, Chinese barbeque pork, and chicken fried rice. He added a few egg rolls for good measure, and finished off by asking for some extra fortune cookies. He was surprised by the weight of the bag as he hoisted it off the counter for the quick trip home.

Once back at the house, Chris put the food into the oven to keep it warm. He then turned on some light jazz and sat down to watch a few minutes of baseball with the volume turned off. Still nervous, he considered opening a bottle of wine, rejecting the idea as being too presumptuous.

The doorbell rang at about six fifteen. Chris answered the door to find a very different looking Kristi standing on the steps. She was dressed in a light pink blouse with faded blue jeans. She had abandoned her ponytail of the woods, instead allowing her shining black hair to flow freely down her shoulders and back. It had a natural wave that Chris hadn't noticed before, and it curved around her face and neck in a most becoming style.

Chris stood motionless, transfixed for a second or two, before welcoming her into the house.

"Wow, you look a little different than the last time I saw you," he said, giving her a big hug.

"Oh, so I looked bad out there in the wilderness last week?" she teased him, returning the embrace.

"There you go again. You're not going to give me any break, are you?" asked Chris, looking back at her affectionately.

"Not as long as you can remind me about Dr. Galloway," returned Kristi.

"Speaking of which, I noticed when I spoke with Dr. Meyers that he didn't seem to know about your little ruse."

"No reason he has to know," said Kristi, shrugging her shoulders. "I wanted to find the cave; I found the cave. Now how about we call a final truce over that topic?"

Chris could tell that she was ready to drop the subject permanently.

"You got it. I'll never mention it again," he replied. "Now, how about some Chinese delicacies right out of the wok? It sure beats the heck out of the freeze-dried cardboard we had last week."

"Sure. I'm famished, since I had to miss lunch today. We can look at my pictures later."

Chris opened the oven and moved the food cartons to the small kitchen table, where Kristi had seated herself awaiting the meal. Chris smiled to himself watching her, as she sat with her legs folded completely underneath her body. He never could understand how anyone could feel comfortable in that position, but it was a testament to the flexibility of her long, lean body.

They spent the next hour talking about unimportant things and laughing at each other's stories. To Chris, it felt as though they were merely continuing the conversation they had initiated outside the cave. He noticed the same ease he'd experienced at Lost Pond: the shared laughter, the comfort level at exposing his own fears and weaknesses. He liked Kristi, and he was very glad that she had come to visit, even if it was only for the "official" reason she'd given for the trip. Inwardly, he hoped that she was experiencing the same emotions, yet he could not read her well enough to make that determination.

After the meal, Kristi helped to clear the dishes, and then she pulled her laptop computer out of a black leather carrying bag. She was in the process of setting up the photo presentation when Chris's phone rang. He read Sean's number on the display, and answered accordingly: "Hey, bud, long time no hear."

"What do you expect? I've been working fourteen hour days this week trying to catch up from our little goose chase to Lost Pond," answered Sean.

"So what's up?" asked Chris.

"I was about to ask you the same thing," said Sean. "I'm in Syracuse, about three minutes from your house. I thought I'd drop by and chat about our next steps, if you've got time."

Chris exhaled a deep breath and allowed his head to drop down. It wasn't that he didn't want to see his friend, because he always enjoyed his company. But he didn't want the additional company tonight. However, he was too polite to decline the offer, and he doubted that Sean would ask to stop by unless he had a good reason.

"By all means, guy, feel free to stop by. We can make it a party. Kristi just came over about an hour ago. We don't have much food left, but you're welcome to join us for coffee."

Sean hesitated momentarily, not sure how to interpret Chris's offer.

"You sure you want me to stop by? I didn't know she was coming up. If I'd be getting in the way…"

"No, no, please come on over. We'd love to have you. See you in a few, OK?"

Kristi watched him hang up the phone, and she correctly read his body language.

"Was that Sean?" she asked.

"Yupper," replied Chris.

"You don't seem particularly happy to hear from him," she guessed.

"Oh, no, he's my best friend, and I always like having him over here. Especially with his crazy schedule, we don't get to visit very often any more. But you want to know something funny?"

"What?" she said, looking directly into his eyes.

"Ever since you told me that you wanted to visit tonight, I've been looking forward to you coming up here. I mean, I've really been looking forward to seeing you again. I don't know why, but I...I...I just had a wonderful time talking with you and being with you back in the woods. I hope you don't think that I'm being too forward. I'm just telling you what I felt."

Kristi smiled and reached out, putting her hand on Chris' arm.

"Thank you, Chris," she said warmly. "I'm glad you said that, because I feel the same way. You're a really easy person to talk to, and I've been looking forward all week to seeing you again."

Chris wasn't sure where to go from there, but he was glad that he had opened the door to seeing her again. He felt an inner satisfaction that he could look into her eyes without camouflaging the feelings that he had for her.

"OK, now let me show you all the good stuff I found after you guys left me on my own," Kristi said, firing up the slide presentation. She started advancing through the digital photos, showing some truly impressive formations from several chambers deep inside the cave. As she spoke, she provided in-depth geological commentaries on the pictures, as well as speculations on how the features were formed. Her knowledge was very extensive, which backed up her initial claim that her interest was really in the discovery of the cave rather than the treasure.

She was about twenty photos into her presentation when the doorbell rang. Chris never bothered rising from the couch. Instead, he swiveled his body about and called toward the door: "It's open."

Sean walked in carrying a brown paper bag.

"Delivery! A special dessert, if you two still have room. It's tiramisu from The Italian Eatery."

"Ooh, yeah, I love it," said Kristi, her eyes gleaming. "How did you know?"

"I'm clairvoyant. Didn't Chris tell you?"

Kristi giggled, elbowing Chris in the side. "No, I guess he forgot."

Chris simply looked at her again, obviously enjoying herself, her wide smile set across her attractive face. He couldn't understand how someone of her personality and looks hadn't been chased by half the male students at Cornell.

"How about we have some of this while we talk about our next trip?" asked Sean. "That is, unless you got a job offer out of your interview this week?"

"No, not yet, anyway," said Chris. "They're hiring a business unit manager, but it's for a group in their Manhattan office. I don't want to live down there, thank you. They also have a couple of audit jobs in Boston, but those didn't thrill me either. Of course, I told them that I was interested in all of them, so we're still talking, but I'm going to continue with other interviews as well."

"Cool," said Sean. "Because I want to get back into the woods at least one more time before the season's over, maybe in another week or two?"

"I might end up beating you back in there," said Chris, glancing back at Kristi. "I've been invited to go on the exploration trip that Dr. Meyers is planning. As a matter of fact, you're free to come too."

"No thanks. Not if it's only spelunking. I'd like to focus on finding the rest of the gold, assuming that it was relocated somewhere in the vicinity of the Lost Pond cave."

"But how do you know that it was?" asked Kristi. "How do you know that there's anything more back there?"

"We don't," replied Chris. "But we do have a number of clues that suggest that it was the subject of a search in the first decade of the last century. We also know that it was found, probably by Louis Seymour, otherwise known as Adirondack French Louie. But that's when the trail goes cold. He left a few maps that depict possible hiding spots where he may have reburied the stash, although we've been unable to crack the code so far."

"Would you mind if I took a look at your maps?" asked Kristi. "Maybe I'll see something that you overlooked."

"Sure, you're welcome to it," said Chris, standing to retrieve the box where he'd stored the documents. "You OK with that?" Chris asked Sean, who quickly nodded his concurrence.

"Sure. More power to you if you can make sense of Louie's drawings."

Chris used a towel to clean and dry the kitchen table before laying out the large topographic map with Harrison's original annotations from the 1903 trip. He also held the map given to him by Dr. Meyers.

"I don't think we need this one anymore," he said, holding up the latter.

"No, I agree," said Kristi, glancing over the shaded areas that her professor-advisor had sketched in using a colored marker. "I'm still a bit torqued that he never offered to give me the same information, but there's not much I can do about that."

Chris ignored her remark and introduced the reprinted copy of the daily journal that had been recorded by Thomas Swain over two hundred years earlier.

"I found these in the archives at the Adirondack Museum. They were written sometime in 1774 or 1775 by a man named Thomas Swain, and his grandson somehow obtained them and transferred his notes onto this other map. French Louie somehow got a hold of them, and presumably used them to track down the gold. There are some parts of this story that we don't know, but that appears to be the main chapter in the book."

Kristi spoke while concentrating on the maps. "And how do you know that Louie didn't take the gold and use it for his own personal expenses?"

"Because shortly before he died, he gave some maps and drawings to my great-grandfather. Those maps have been passed down through my family, along with another piece of paper containing some of the things Louie said...verbal clues. One of his last statements to my great-grandfather was, 'you use the gold to take care of this place.' That's it. Now, he wouldn't have said that if he'd already spent the gold, would he?"

"No, I see what you mean," said Kristi. "It sounds like he had some very definite ideas as to how he wanted it used."

Sean chimed in next from his position behind the table.

"Louie also left behind a hand-drawn map showing a bunch of lakes and streams, with an arrow pointing to a specific spot at the corner of one lake."

"Yeah, but good luck deciphering that one," laughed Chris. "Louie was well-known for creating maps that only Louie could read. For the most part, all of the lakes are the same size, and the streams run out of the lakes in the same direction. As much as I've tried, I can't seem to match it up to anything in the West Canada territory. I've tried rescaling it, expanding the distances between the bodies of water and even eliminating the streams entirely, but nothing seems to work."

"Did Louie ever travel outside of the area, or did he station himself in that one part of the woods only?" asked Kristi.

"He was well known for traveling long distances on foot," said Chris. "But for the most part, his later years were spent entirely within the West Canada Lakes region, with the occasional visit to Speculator or west to Jocks Lake. There's no way he would have lugged that much weight over such a long distance."

"Where is the map that Louie drew showing the lakes?" asked Kristi, looking back at Chris.

"Hang on, I'll get that for you," said Chris, rummaging deeper into the same box.

He placed the hand-drawn page on the table on top of the 1903 topographic map.

"Here it is, although I can't say for certain that it even represents this area. Like I said, nothing seems to match."

Kristi placed both hands on the table and leaned over, pursing her lips as she concentrated on the rough sketching. Chris and Sean stood in back of her, interested in her observations.

"I've aligned it with the arrow pointing down, at that lake on the top left side. But I really couldn't tell you whether Louie meant that to represent north or not. If you think that it's aligned incorrectly, just turn the paper and have at it."

After staring at the small square sheet of paper for a minute, Kristi giggled, and then continued her inspection.

"What's so funny?" asked Sean.

"Oh, nothing," replied Kristi. "Maybe I should have been a psychiatrist."

"Whatcha mean?" asked Chris. "Are you seeing something that we didn't?"

"No, it's just that this reminds me more of an ink-blot test than a map. I keep seeing an image in here rather than a location. It's rather disconcerting."

"What do you mean?" asked Chris.

"If you were giving me a psychological profile test, and you showed me this paper and asked me to say the first thing that came to my mind, I'd say 'fireplace.' It looks like a fireplace to me. See, all the rocks, and these squiggly lines are the flames coming up out of the fire." She giggled again. "I know, I know... I'm probably crazy. I'll keep looking to see if anything matches the map."

Chris felt as though a lightning bolt had struck the top of his head and traveled the entire length of his body. He spun sideways to look at Sean, whose face registered a startled expression. His mouth was agape, his eyes open in an exaggerated glare. He was about to speak when Chris quickly placed his finger over his pursed lips, motioning for silence. Since they were standing in back of Kristi, their movements were outside of her field of view.

The fireplace. French Louie's fireplace.

How could he have failed to see the fireplace? Now that Kristi had suggested the intent of the drawing, it all became crystal clear to both men. Louie had been trying to show Calvin Carey where to find the gold by drawing a picture rather than a map. But no one had been able to see that, until now.

Sean couldn't tell what Chris had in mind, but he instantly put on his poker face and went along with him. Kristi continued to examine the two documents closely, her eyes roving over the features. As she perused the papers, Chris opened his cell phone and quickly tapped a text message to Sean. Even though his friend was standing right next to him, he couldn't state his intent out loud. His message was brief and to the point:

chriscarey1986: Leave in ten minutes, wait somewhere for about 30 minutes before coming back. Let's talk after Kristi leaves.

Sean felt his phone vibrate silently on his belt holder. He released it from the clasp and looked at the message from Chris, nodding his understanding. It all transpired in cathedral silence, as Kristi completed her review.

"If there's anything there, I can't find it," she said, leaning back. "I'm sorry, but now I see what you mean. Even the shape of the lakes and how they're distributed doesn't match a thing on the map. That's a tough one."

"That's OK," said Chris, his face a mask of indifference. "I don't know what to make of it either. Hopefully we can find a way to work around it, or we may never find the final resting place of the Gordons' treasure."

While Chris and Kristi were talking, Sean moved into the kitchen to get himself a glass of water. He was filling the glass at the sink when his eyes wandered onto a scrap of yellow paper sitting beside the soap dish. It was a customer receipt from the Syracuse Coin and Gold Exchange that had been written the previous day. It listed a cash payment of $2,800 for a gold doubloon and a small amount of gold bullion. His eyes lingered on the paper for a few seconds as he tried to digest its meaning. Chris had not mentioned selling the gold they'd found in the cave, nor had they discussed their intent to do so. And yet he trusted Chris with his life, and knew that he'd never do anything behind his back. He decided to ask his friend about it later.

"So, did I hear someone say the word 'tiramisu?'" asked Kristi, looking at the bag on the table.

"You bet. Best stuff in town, too," said Sean, opening the package.

"I'll get the plates," said Chris. "It'll be a nice nightcap. I've got an early start tomorrow, so I'd better crash kind of early tonight."

"Seems to me you'd want to avoid using the word 'crash' to describe any of your activities," suggested Sean.

While Kristi cut and served the tiramisu, Chris retrieved a bottle of amaretto which he had stored in a cabinet. He poured three small measures into some tiny cordial glasses he kept for special occasions.

"Here's to good friends," said Chris, raising his glass in toast towards the other two.

"And here's to finding enough gold to sink a damn battleship," said Sean, already tasting the first piece of the dessert.

Shortly after finishing the tiramisu, Sean took his cue and started heading toward the door.

"Well, I've been up since four this morning. It's getting dark out, and I don't want to fall asleep on the road," he said. "I'll catch up with you again soon."

Sean shook hands with Chris, and then gave Kristi a hug.

"I hope we'll be seeing you again soon?" he asked her.

"I hope so too," said Kristi, shooting a quick glance back at Chris. "That is, if you don't mind the intrusion."

"Not at all. But you better watch out for this guy," replied Sean, nodding towards Chris. "He's got a funny way of talking people into things without them knowing it."

"Stop it," cried Chris, faking a horrified expression. "You're giving away my trade secrets."

Sean simply winked back at Kristi and then let himself out the front door.

Chris watched him go, and then turned back toward Kristi.

"So you're planning on going back into the cave next Wednesday, is that correct?"

"Yes, that's the plan for now. Dr. Meyers wants to get as much of the background work done as possible before we go out with the announcement. Once we do, I'm sure that the State Department of Environmental Conservation will want to go in, not to mention the Adirondack Park Agency, plus a horde of amateur spelunkers from every corner of the Northeast. How about you? Are you planning on coming in with us?"

"Probably not the first day," replied Chris, his eyes avoiding hers. "I'd like to, but the time just isn't there right now."

Kristi's eyes registered instant disappointment.

"That's too bad. I was hoping that we'd be able to spend a little time together while doing some exploring," she said.

"I'd like that quite a bit," said Chris, stretching his lanky frame while yawning. "It's just that time is kind of a precious commodity right now. As a matter of fact, I think I'd better be getting to sleep pretty shortly. I've got another early start tomorrow."

Kristi directed a steady gaze at Chris.

"Is everything OK?" she asked. "When I got here, you seemed so happy to see me. Now, all of a sudden, I feel like unwelcome company. What's wrong?"

Chris turned and walked up close to her, taking her hand in his. He addressed her softly.

"Kristi, I do want to see you. Very, very much. But right now, there are things going on that I just cannot discuss. Within a week, I think it will all be over. But right now, it's really kind of strange. But there's one thing you must promise to believe, OK?"

"What is that?" she asked.

"As soon as I'm done with this, you and I will have plenty of time together, OK?" He bowed his head and kissed her lightly on the forehead. "As a matter of fact, you'll probably get sick of me in a hurry."

"That will never happen," she said, looking up into his eyes. Tilting her head upward, she returned his kiss before turning toward the door.

"I'll call you before I leave for Lost Pond, OK?" she asked.

"You'd better," Chris replied. "Otherwise I'll think that you don't want to see me anymore."

Kristi had been gone for about twenty minutes when Chris heard Sean's car pull back into his driveway. Chris had left the front door open and was sitting on the couch with his feet up when Sean walked into the front room. He was wearing an ear-to-ear grin, which was met by Chris's own gleeful expression. They traded high fives before a single word was spoken.

"YES!" yelped Sean, dancing around in celebration. "I think we've just been handed the last clue on a silver platter."

"It would appear so, although I don't want to get our hopes up too high," said Chris.

"So, I take it that you don't trust Kristi enough to let her in on this?" asked Sean.

"Don't get me wrong," said Chris. "I like Kristi. I like her a lot. But I'm not really sure how far to trust her yet, considering our rather dubious introduction of last week. After all, we've already seen what she's capable of when it benefits her own purposes. I think I'd rather hold off on telling her everything until we're ready to act."

"And just when do you think that should be?" asked Sean.

"As soon as we can get our packs and gear ready to go," said Chris. "I don't think I could bear the suspense of waiting another week."

"I'm glad to hear you say that, buddy. I'm in the same boat," said Sean.

"You realize, I hope, that if we do end up making 'the find' this trip we'll probably be in the woods for the better part of a week, right?"

Sean winced, thinking of his workload piling up back home.

"Guess I'll have to call a couple clients and push things back a bit," he said. "I should be able to squeeze in the extra time, as long as there aren't any emergencies over the weekend."

"I'd like to do a little advance planning before we head in," said Chris. "There are some people who should know about this, although not quite yet."

"What do you mean?" asked Sean.

"At the very least, I'd like to notify the Forest Ranger who is responsible for the area inside the West Canada Lakes. Then there's the State Historic Preservation Officer, who probably has an office in Albany, who would want to be in on this. I also think we should contact either the State Police or the State Treasury Department. If the entire pile of Robert Gordon's gold is really parked next to Louie's fireplace, we'll need help getting it out. Having an armed guard will be a pretty good idea, considering that we're talking about over six million dollars."

Sean just shook his head, overwhelmed with the extent of the loot. It was almost beyond his comprehension.

"By the way, I've already unloaded the bit of gold we found in the Lost Pond cave last week," Chris said.

"Oh really?" asked Sean, pretending not to have already seen the receipt.

"I hope you don't mind. I wanted some cash to take care of a little detail that's been bugging me since we discovered the cave. No one will ever know that we found anything there. You OK with that?"

"Sure. Are you going to fill me on the details, or do you plan on keeping me in suspense?"

"Would you mind if I kept it a secret until I determine whether we can make it happen?"

"Sure," replied Sean. "Just let me know if you're going to use it to buy a ticket to Maui. I want to tag along."

"Nothing so dramatic," said Chris. "I just want to correct a wrong that's been left untended for too many years."

After a bit more discussion, the two decided to prepare to leave for their dig at Louie's camp the following Monday. Chris volunteered to make the appropriate calls to the various State officials, in case they did strike pay dirt. However, he had an additional favor to ask of Sean.

"I'd like you to run one more genealogical search over the weekend, if possible. I'd like you to search for surviving descendants of Thomas Swain of Skenesborough, now Whitehall."

"Sure, I can do that," said Sean. "I've become rather good at scouring all the databases. If he's got any living relatives, I should be able to find them."

"Good. You'll see what I have in mind very soon," said Chris.

"I hate when you go into cryptic mode on me," said Sean, throwing up his hands.

"I like to keep you guessing," said Chris with a grin. "See you Monday morning, six sharp, at my mom's house?"

"You got it," replied Sean. "I'll bring the food."

"Don't forget the metal detector and your screening sieves. Also, a camp shovel would come in handy too. I'll bring a duffel bag."

"I've got a small shovel I can bring along," said Sean. "But a duffel bag? What's that for?"

"Just in case we do find the entire pile of gold in one place," replied Chris. "We won't be able to move it by ourselves. So the best we'll be able to manage is to hide it inside an innocent-looking duffel bag while one of us runs out to fetch the cavalry."

"You're optimistic. I like that," said Sean.

"My glass is always half full. See you on Monday."

CHAPTER 20

It didn't take Chris long to realize that their timeline was overly zealous. His hiking clothes were barely cleaned from the last excursion when he had to start packing on Saturday morning. At ten o'clock, he started making phone calls to the slate of officials in Albany, only to learn that nobody was reachable over the weekend. He had some success contacting the Department Of Environmental Conservation office, which had a duty officer assigned to the phones. However, when Chris explained that he was on the verge of discovering a huge sum of gold from a hidden location in the Adirondacks, the representative muttered something derogatory into the phone and then hung up on him. Even the State Police department wasn't interested in hearing about it, assuming that he was a crackpot calling to gain attention.

After spending a couple of discouraging hours on the phone, Chris returned to his packing, sorting through his gear and clothing until the backpack was once again ready to go. Then, he settled down to a quick lunch while reading his e-mail. As he perused the contents of his inbox, a new message arrived from Kristi. It contained only six words:

"Please call me whenever you want."

Chris smiled as he read the e-mail. He reached over and grabbed his cell phone without stopping to think about a reason to call. No time like the present, he thought, as he pressed the "dial" button next to her name in the directory. She answered on the first ring.

"Well, hey, that was quick," Kristi said while answering her phone.

"Ah, the disadvantages of Caller ID," said Chris. "A guy never gets to announce his identity anymore. Everyone knows who's calling before they answer the phone."

"Well, at least I answered it, didn't I?" chided Kristi. "I could have just let it ring."

"You wouldn't do that to me now that I've asked you out to dinner after your cave exploration."

"You never asked me out to dinner," said Kristi.

"OK, so I did now. What do you say? Maybe dinner and a movie?"

"You're on. But this time, how about you come down to Ithaca and we'll go out down here. I'd love to show you around the town."

"Sounds great," said Chris. "But you're going back into the woods next week, and I may be as well. Maybe we could do it the following weekend, if we're both already out and cleaned up. If not, let's shoot for the week-end after."

"Promise?" asked Kristi.

"Cross my heart and hope to die," said Chris.

"You sure are dramatic for an accountant," giggled Kristi. "I love it."

"You've got my cell number. We'll talk as soon as we're out."

Chris hung up the phone, feeling happy that Kristi had seemed so eager to see him again. Setting that aside, he resumed his packing until he was completely ready to hit the trail. All the while, he felt a growing sense of suspense, as though a knot was slowly tightening in his stomach. They had made so much progress, and yet they were running out of clues. Either they found their quarry this weekend, or they ran the risk of coming up empty.

Chris was greatly relieved when the alarm went off on Monday morning. He had set both his digital clock as well as his cell phone alarm to ring at four, giving him time to eat and pack the car before starting the drive to Utica. He couldn't rid himself of the feeling in his gut as he drove the quiet streets to his mother's house. To alleviate some of the nervousness, he tossed an Aerosmith CD into his Jeep's stereo and cranked the volume.

It had rained hard during the night, and some of that precipitation was still falling when Chris pulled into his mother's driveway. Because of the early hour, he decided to wait in the car rather than go inside the dark house. He listened to some distant rumbles of thunder as he waited for Sean to arrive.

Within a few minutes, the familiar white Mercedes rolled up alongside the Jeep. Sean hopped out and leaned into Chris's passenger side window.

"You ready to get the show on the road?" he asked, feigning impatience.

"I've been sitting here waiting for you, good buddy. You let me know when you're ready to roll."

Together, they moved Sean's pack, metal detector, and other gear into the back of the Jeep. They then made a quick stop for coffee and donuts before pulling back onto the road. Within five minutes they were rolling along Route 8 North, which would lead them up into the heart of the southern Adirondacks.

"I don't know about you, but I feel like I've been walking on eggshells ever since Friday," said Chris.

"I know what you mean," agreed Sean. "I hardly ate a thing yesterday; I was so keyed up about this trip. I was half tempted to hike in there yesterday with just the detector to see if anything was buried where the map indicates."

"This is probably a dumb question, but how could we have missed looking there last time?" wondered Chris. "It's right there, sitting just off to the side of Louie's house. It must be about the only spot we didn't check with the detector."

"Well, for one thing, it isn't exactly right next to the site of the old camp. It's actually off to the side and out in front a bit, by at least forty feet. Keep in mind that our time was limited there, and we had no reason to suspect that Louie would have hidden anything beyond the boundaries of his own camp. We also had to scan the garden, as well as the spots where the outer buildings had stood. I don't think there's any way we could have covered all the contingencies."

"Yeah, you're probably right," said Chris. "Anyway, if it's there, we'll find it this time."

"You should be glad we didn't find the jackpot at Louie's camp on the last trip, assuming it is there now."

"Why is that?" asked Chris.

"Because you never would have met your new flame if we hadn't gone on to Lost Pond," said Sean. "Speaking of that, what's up with you two? She sure seems to like you."

"It's kind of mutual," said Chris, smiling inside and out. "We haven't had much time together, though, so I might still find a way to screw it up."

"Nah, have faith in yourself, man," laughed Sean. "Everything happens for a reason. I really believe that."

"Hey, by the way, did you have a chance to do that search on Thomas Swain?" asked Chris.

"I did, but you're not going to like my report," said Sean. "Unlike the search for Gordon's descendants, I couldn't find a thing for Swain. Apparently, he had no children and no wife. Unless I go overseas to England and try to follow his family tree back the other way, I'm afraid I'm at a dead end. I'm sorry."

"That's OK. And there's no need to bother looking overseas, either," said Chris, shaking his head, "as long as he's got no family looking for him."

"You mean, for his remains?" asked Sean, looking across at Chris.

"Mm hmm," muttered Chris, as he stared vacantly out at the road.

Sean decided to let the topic drop, and the two of them rode most of the way up to Speculator in relative silence. Meanwhile, the rain resumed, slowly at first, but then harder as they moved north. By the time the Jeep bounced up the rocky dirt road through Sled Harbor, it was coming down at a moderate pace.

"You think this is going to let up anytime soon?" asked Sean, looking at the sky as he climbed out of the vehicle.

"I hope not," replied Chris. "More rain means fewer people. And if there's one thing we don't want around us this week, it's people."

"I've got a great idea for keeping people away from the dig once we're done digging, but how do we keep people from watching us excavate?"

"Chances are pretty good we won't see more than one or two groups back there anyway. So what we'll do is camp in the clearing, near the lake, and then wait until the sun goes down. If we need to dig, we should be safe once it gets dark out," said Chris.

"Sounds good," said Sean. "I've got a whole package of extra batteries, so we should have all the light we need."

"What's your plan for keeping people away from the pit once we've got it dug up?" asked Chris.

"Ah, now it's my turn to be cryptic. Watch and learn, young man," replied Sean.

As Chris had predicted, the trail was devoid of people as the two men made their way down the trail past Pillsbury Lake, bending westward into the heart of the West Canada Lakes. They had both donned ponchos and positioned pack covers due to the continuous downpour, which ricocheted off the trees around them, forming large pools on the ground. At times, they found themselves up to their ankles in mud, which sucked at their boots and slowed their progress considerably.

Because of the conditions and their heavy packs, it took them almost four hours to reach the lean-to at Sampson Lake. It was almost one o'clock, and they'd eaten very little along the way.

"I could use a break about now," said Chris, slinging his pack to the wooden plank floor of the lean-to.

"I'll second that motion," said Sean, following suit. "You want some lunch?"

Chris responded only by nodding his head "yes."

"Hang on, I'll find something quick to eat," said Sean.

As he released the top flap on his backpack, Chris poked at the wet ground with the toe of his boot.

"You know, this rain could work to our advantage in more ways than one," he said thoughtfully. "Not only will it keep people out of our way, it should also make the ground a lot easier to dig."

"Hopefully it'll back off a little though, or we'll have the pit filling in with water as fast as we dig it."

"How about the X5 detector?" asked Chris. "Will a little water in the hole bother its sensitivity?"

"Maybe a little," replied Sean. "Its optimal operating range is 0-75% relative humidity, so anything above that will degrade the detection process a bit. But remember, this machine is designed to work in the rain without sustaining any water damage, so it can handle a little abuse if need be. Besides, it's not like we're searching for a single coin at any great depth. Our target should be pretty large, so we should get a fairly strong signal. I'm not expecting any problems from the equipment."

As Sean spoke, he pulled out a couple of power bars and a large bag of trail mix. Together, they sat and absentmindedly munched on their snacks.

"How long before we make it to West Canada Lake?" asked Sean.

"If we get moving, we could probably be there in a little over two hours," said Chris. "It depends on the trails. If they're really bad, it may take a bit longer. But we'll be there by four no matter what."

"That'll work just fine," said Sean. "That should give me time to set up the detector and run a few rings around the fireplace to localize our target. We'll want to do that when no one else is around. Then, once I mark it out, we can use your plan and start digging as soon as it gets dark."

"You brought your sieve with you, right?" asked Chris.

"Yes, I did. You wanted that so we could clean any dirt away from the bullion, right?"

"Yeah, I figure we could use the lake as a cleaning station," said Chris. "As long as no one is around to watch us, we should be able to drag any coins or ingots down to the waterfront and get them cleaned off before storing them inside the duffel bag. We don't know how much we'll find, but at least we'll have a place to hide everything. The duffel itself will go right inside our tent."

"I've never slept with six million dollars before," laughed Sean.

"We're not sure we'll find anything," said Chris. "That's why I'm anxious to get going; are you ready?"

"Ready as I'm going to be," replied Sean, pulling himself to a stand. "Last one back on the trail is a rotten egg."

Reenergized by the break, they motored up the hill from the lean-to and commenced the final five-mile segment of trail leading to West Canada Lake. Sean was in the lead, bulling his way through the wet bushes that overhung the path. Chris stayed right with him as they maintained a healthy pace of almost three miles per hour. Even with another short break at West Canada Creek, they still managed to arrive at Louie's clearing by three forty-five. Before setting up their tent, they checked the two lean-tos in the vicinity, finding that both were unoccupied.

"I'd much rather stay in one of those tonight," said Sean, looking off in the direction of the lean-to south of the lake.

"Me too," said Chris. "But each of those shelters is several hundred yards away and out of visual range. We wouldn't be able to keep an eye on the fireplace from either one. So I don't see any alternative but to park ourselves right here and get going."

By the time they began unpacking their things, the rain had slowed to a gentle mist. Chris unfolded the tent and began to insert the internal poles, while Sean removed the metal detector from its protective sheath.

"I'm sorry," said Sean apologetically. "I know I should be helping you set up. But I've been waiting for this moment all summer. I can't wait to do a quick test and see if we've got anything. OK?"

"I wouldn't expect anything different," replied Chris, smiling back at his friend. "Have at it. No matter what happens, we'll wait a few hours to dig, but I can't see any harm in doing a few sweeps now."

Sean moved further back into the clearing, away from the fireplace, and turned on the machine. He tuned it up, setting the sensitivity on a medium level to get started.

"There's metal all over the place," he said, looking across the ruins of the old ranger station. "Just like last time we were here. But most of it is probably junk left over from the station."

"You can tune that stuff right out, can't you?" asked Chris.

"Yup, I'm doing that right now," said Sean. "I'm increasing the discrimination setting so that it only picks up a metal that it deems of interest, such as copper or silver."

"Or gold?" questioned Chris.

"Or gold," nodded Sean.

When the setting finally met Sean's approval, he commenced sweeping, moving the detector back and forth in a series of slow arcs across the ground. The many bits of old steel and iron generated nothing more than barely perceptible background noise, which Sean ignored. He worked his way across the overgrown earth until he reached the right side of the fireplace, where he followed the contour of the stones around the base. He detected almost no signal through his headset as he moved the coils along the side and then around the back corner of the massive structure. If they had interpreted the drawing correctly, he would soon be on top of the exact spot where Louie had buried the gold.

Sean stepped around the back of the fireplace and began sweeping to his right, toward the lake. Chris had ceased his activity and was watching intently. Sean's sweeps were slow and deliberate, overlapping one another as they moved methodically westward, six inches at a time. He was about halfway across the back of the fireplace when he stopped and froze in place for a moment, listening to the buzzing in his headphones. He reached out with his left hand and turned a knob on the control panel.

"Getting anything?" asked Chris quietly.

"Oh yeah, just now," said Sean. "Sounds good."

Continuing his path, he moved to his right, bit by bit, until he was sweeping over the rear left corner of the fireplace. His next sweep extended about a foot behind the same back corner, at which point he froze in place like a statue.

"Oh my God," he muttered, his eyes the size of silver dollars. "Oh my God."

"What is it?" asked Chris. "What are you hearing?"

"Give me a minute. Please!" said Sean, his voice wavering slightly.

He reached down and turned the knob again, then one more time, as he scanned the ground in back of the fireplace. Finally, after about three minutes of sweeps, he stopped. He raised his head and stared at Chris with an expression that he did not recognize.

"It's here," he said, whispered in a hushed tone, "right beneath the coil."

"Are you sure?" asked Chris, looking at the spot indicated by Sean's gesture.

"I've got the discrimination set all the way up, and the sensitivity set all the way down, and the signal is blasting my damn ear drums off. I've never heard a tone like this, and I saw this machine tested on a one-pound block of silver. Something's down there, and it's very big, and very good."

"Great work. Now shut that thing down and put it away," said Chris. "In case anyone comes by, we don't want them to even see us looking here."

Sean simply nodded back, quickly removing the headset and breaking down the detector. Chris finished setting up the tent, which was not more than twenty feet from the fireplace. They then placed the metal detector and the shovel inside to keep them hidden from straying eyes.

For the next hour, the two went about their normal camp routine as though little was different. They set up camp, filtered their water, and gathered wet firewood as though they were going to start a blaze. All the while, they were too excited to do much talking, instead being preoccupied with the upcoming dig.

"I guess there isn't much point in guarding the spot, is there?" asked

Sean. "After all, whatever is buried there has been down there for at least a full century. No reason to worry about it now."

"Not until we uncover the first bit of gold," agreed Chris. "That's when we might have issues."

"Not unless the local bears have an appreciation for precious metals," countered Sean, "because I don't think there's anyone else around for several miles."

"I know. I've never been so happy to see rain in my entire life," smiled Chris.

Neither Chris nor Sean was hungry, both being too excited to eat. However, just to kill some time until dark, they decided to prepare a regular dinner, served on Chris's tin camp dishes. It was sweet and sour chicken and rice, served over a package of dry fried noodles that Sean had carried into the woods as a special treat.

Shortly before dinner, the rain ceased entirely, and the sun poked its rays out from beneath the clouds in the west. They washed their dishes and prepared their camp for the night. But once they were inside the tent, it was a different scene entirely. Sean set out the sieves, which they would use to wash the dirt from any larger coins or ingots that came out of the pit. Meanwhile, Chris unpacked the duffel bag and opened it to receive the final cleaned bullion. He also unfolded an extra ground cloth that he had brought into the woods to cover the hole in case they needed to take a rest from the digging.

As the sky deepened from orange to red, Sean gazed around the site, assessing their readiness to get started.

"Think we should do one final check of the area, just to make sure we're alone?" he asked.

"It couldn't hurt," agreed Chris. "Why don't you go ahead and get everything ready to start while I run off to look at each of the lean-tos. It shouldn't take me more than a couple of minutes."

Sean watched his friend jog down the trail, heading northwest to the upper lean-to, as he retrieved the shovel and sieves. Chris reappeared five minutes later, crossing their site en route to the shelter on the southern side of the clearing. He was back within moments to give the all-clear.

"All's quiet on the Western Front," he assured Sean, who was rigging up their headlights.

"That's great," said Sean. "I've got new batteries in both our lamps, and I have enough replacements to keep these things going until tomorrow. That's a good thing, because if that signal I heard earlier was any indication, we just might be pulling stuff out all night."

"That wouldn't be such a bad thing," replied Chris.

"You want to dig first, or should I?" asked Sean.

"Whatever is your pleasure," replied Chris.

"I'm so keyed up, I think I'd like first crack at it," said Sean. "If I don't get rid of some of this energy somehow, I think I'll explode. You can relieve me when I get tired."

"What's your plan for getting down to the metal?" asked Chris. "Are you going straight down from the top?"

"No, I've made marks around the apparent edges of the target zone," said Sean. "I'd like to come in from the sides, just to see what this stuff is packed in. Not that I'd expect any case or container to have survived, because I'm sure any trace of wood would have long since disintegrated. But I'd like to try to avoid scattering or damaging the contents as much as possible."

"Sounds like a plan," nodded Chris. "Go whenever you're ready. I'll try to keep my light trained on your shovel."

Sean looked down and placed his shovel to the ground. Placing his foot on top of the spade, he forced the blade into the ground and started the excavation.

"Here's to our success," he said, lifting a shovelful of wet dirt from the ground.

"Let's keep all the soil we dig in one pile," suggested Chris. "That's so we can cover our tracks in a hurry, if we need to."

"We can do that, but it's really not necessary," said Sean, chuckling.

"Oh, that's right. You have a plan. How silly of me to forget," said Chris sarcastically.

"Don't worry about it," laughed Sean. "No one will want to go near this hole once it's dug."

Chris continued digging along a line that was roughly six inches south of the center of their target signal. He had excavated down about twelve inches in depth and was moving forward when the shovel hit a rock.

"That didn't sound good," said Chris.

"No, I didn't expect that," agreed Sean.

Moving to his left, he tried again, but ran into the same obstruction.

"Why don't you just dig along the edge of the rock until you come to a place where you can work your way around it?" Chris suggested. "Then maybe the two of us can pry it out of the ground."

Sean gave it a shot, moving in both directions, east and west. After considerable testing, he determined that it was a single rock that extended about eighteen inches from one side of the trough to the other. Rather than battle the weighty stone, he decided to move down to the other side of the square where the detector indicated the metal. It was about three feet away from the spot where he had made his initial probe with the shovel.

Digging deliberately, Sean quickly reached a depth of about ten inches before once again striking rock.

"OK, Einstein, now what?" said Sean, looking up at Chris.

"First, hand me the shovel. It's my turn to toil for a while," said Chris.

"Then what?" asked Sean, handing him the tool. "What do you have in mind for Plan B?"

"I'm going to start removing dirt from the top, a bit at a time, until I come down on the top of this rock. Then, I'll expand the hole until we can see exactly what we've got," said Chris.

"Not very scientific, but it might work," said Sean.

Chris began digging at a steady, controlled pace, lifting even amounts of soil from the hole with each stroke. As he worked, the mound of dirt next to the hole grew until it was several feet tall. Because of the clouds, they had to rely almost entirely on their headlamps for illumination. After about five minutes of digging, Chris' shovel finally scraped against the same rock that had greeted Sean earlier.

"This thing appears to be pretty level," said Chris, turning to look at Sean's silhouette. I think I'm just going to keep expanding this hole outward until I get to the edge that you hit earlier. Then, at some point, we should be able to tell what shape it is and maybe how to move it out of the way."

Chris resumed his work, digging, lifting, dumping, then starting the process over again and again. The minutes ticked by slowly as each thrust of the shovel was met by the screech of metal on stone. When he finally reached a point where the shovel no longer hit rock, he turned the shovel over to Sean for the next shift.

Working in sequence, they labored for about ninety minutes, excavating a hole that was about two feet by three feet. The stone itself was smaller than that, but they needed to add some working space around the edges in order to get their hands around the outside of the bulky mass. While Sean moved large shovels full of dirt, Chris was busy with the trowel, strategically working to free the corners from the confines of the soil.

Suddenly, Chris spoke up. "Hey, hold on a minute," he said, still kneeling over the north end of the pit.

"What's up?" asked Sean, wiping the sweat from his brow.

"I think I have a little movement here."

"You're kidding," said Sean. "How is that possible? This thing is huge."

"If I'm not mistaken, it's not one big stone, but two smaller ones. And unless I miss my guess, they're not as big as you think, or at least, not as heavy as you think. Check this out."

Sean stood back as Chris used his fingers to find a small crack that ran from one side of the pit to the other. Once located, he inserted the small trowel into the fracture and pulled back, using a lever motion to slide the rock forward.

"See. I think we've got two rectangular flat rocks that are sitting on top of a series of vertical slabs, forming a compartment. Based on how easily this one slid, my guess is that they aren't that thick, either. I think we should try to get our hands around this one rock and lift it right out of the hole. If nothing else, at least we'll be able to see where we need to go after that."

"What time is it?" asked Sean.

Chris looked at his wristwatch.

"Quarter to eleven," he said, holding up his arm. "Time to get moving."

"I'll keep taking more dirt off the top, while you try to dig around the outside," suggested Sean. "I think we're almost there."

"Let's do it," replied Chris, using the trowel to work under more of the corner surfaces.

Finally, after another ten minutes of scooping, Chris motioned for Sean to stop again.

"I think we've got enough of the edge exposed to get a grip on it," he said, pointing to the overhanging shelf of rock. "It's really only about an inch thick. We should be able to get the shovel under it and then pry it upright."

This time, Chris and Sean moved around to the same side of the hole. Sean worked the pointed tip of the spade underneath the middle of the flat-edged stone and then began to push down, using the side of the hole for leverage. The rock sheaf lifted up ever so slightly, allowing Chris to shove his trowel underneath another portion of the stone. With supreme exertion, they were able to move the great weight upward, an inch at a time, until it finally reached its tipping point and lifted easily into a standing position. With a push of his boot, Chris sent the tablet tumbling backward away from the hole, striking the ground with a resounding thud.

For what seemed like an eternity, Chris and Sean stood rooted in place, unable to fully comprehend what they saw. Where the hefty plate sat just a minute ago, there now rested a dark layer of soil that was laced throughout with the gleam of gold.

Resisting the urge to scream out in celebration, they instead traded a vigorous set of high fives, followed by a short embrace. They both then fell to their knees next to the pit and began clearing the dirt from the precious metal.

"Go grab the sieves from the tent," said Chris, barely able to control his excitement. "Let's see what we've got here, get it cleaned off, and then start moving it into the duffel bag."

Sean retrieved the strainer devices, and they both began loading handfuls of gold-laden soil onto the wire mesh boxes. They decided to work in tandem on this stage, with each of them shaking out the soil and small rocks from their own sieve until they were left with only gold coins and the occasional ingot. The deeper into the pile they moved, the less dirt and fewer stones intruded into the mass of gold. They began shuttling a series of loads from the sieves into the duffel bag inside the tent, dumping their payload and then returning for more. Chris was stunned by the sheer weight of a single load of the shining coins, which had been the source of the legend for over two hundred years.

"Do you have any idea how much this is worth?" asked Sean. "How much each and every load we're taking into the tent is worth?"

Chris held up the box he had in his hands at that moment, assessing the contents.

"About a hundred and fifty thousand dollars for the numismatic value coins, but probably only about ninety or a hundred thousand if we sold it for the bullion alone," he replied.

"Kind of sad that this will all end up going into the governor's coffers, isn't it?" asked Sean.

"Maybe not all of it," countered Chris. "I think we can make a strong case to use some of the proceeds to sponsor the historic site proposal."

"Nice idea," grunted Sean, lifting another heavy load from the pit. "But won't that involve cutting through a lot of red tape and securing State sponsorship?"

"Probably," said Chris, following closely behind Sean with yet more coins. "But I could dedicate a bit of time to it this fall, unless I start working sooner than I expect. I can be pretty persuasive, you know."

"I know, I know," laughed Sean. "I've paid the price for that on many occasions."

Returning to the pit, Chris directed his beam underneath the remaining flat stone, which still sat perched on top of the other half of the pit. He examined the sides of the enclosure containing the coins, mentally sizing up its dimensions and construction. After a short inspection, he rocked back onto his heels and glanced up smiling.

"You know what I think he did?" he asked, looking back at Sean.

"Who?"

"French Louie," said Chris. "I think he dug a large rectangular hole, and then lined the bottom and all four sides with the flattest, thinnest stones he could find. It's almost like slate, but he didn't have access to slate. Anyway, if you look at how this is constructed, it's almost like he built an in-ground chest of stone and then filled it in with the gold. The two flat plates over the top would have kept out most of the dirt. Then, he simply covered the top with a foot of soil and let nature do the rest."

"It's strange that he didn't use any of it," said Sean, peering into the hole with Chris. "With all that gold, he could have had anything in the world he wanted."

"Oh, I think he already had what he wanted most in life," said Chris, looking around him appreciatively. Even in the small amount of visible light, he could make out the wondrous forms of the towering spruce around the clearing and hear the melodious sounds of the clear, fresh water rippling against the shore. "You couldn't buy a nicer piece of land for any amount of money."

"At least he was able to provide clues to the location of the cache so that it would be found at some time."

"Speaking of time," said Chris, "I think we'd better get back to work. I doubt we're halfway through yet, and it's closing in on midnight. We need to get this done within the next couple hours."

"I'm on it," said Sean. "Let's go."

Using the two sieves as carrying cases, they were able to move the next eighty pounds of coins and ingots to the tent in less than an hour. However, as they began to reach deeper into the underground vault, another problem became apparent.

Water.

As Sean extended his hands down to scoop more of the bullion, he reached into a layer of ice cold water that had risen and filled the bottom of the hole. Chris also experienced the freezing sensation as he positioned himself for his next load. Even though the air temperature was in the seventies, the water felt as though it was in direct contact with a layer of permafrost.

Neither Chris nor Sean would have believed that it was possible to chill water to that temperature without the benefit of ice, and they soon noticed that their fingertips were becoming numb.

"I'm going to take a minute or two and thaw out here," said Sean, rubbing his hands together while blowing on them.

"I think I'll join you," said Chris. He removed his fleece vest from a pocket in his backpack and used it to wrap around both hands.

"I'm not sure about this, but I think I felt something hard at the bottom of the hole," said Sean.

"So did I," added Chris. "I'm pretty sure it was another rock, which Louie probably laid across the bottom of the pit as a floor. Let's take a look and see if we can catch a glimpse of it."

Both Chris and Sean pointed their headlamps straight down into the hole from directly above.

"It's tough to see through the muddy water, but I'm fairly certain that I'm right," said Chris. "And that's good news, because that means we're close to the bottom. I'm sure we've left a fair amount of 'strays' in there, but I'd like to bet that we've got about ninety percent of it out already."

"I've got a good idea," said Sean as he walked back to the tent. He returned with a pair of two-quart cook pots.

"Did you ever participate in a bucket brigade contest?"

"No, but I once knew a guy who was a volunteer fireman," quipped Chris.

"Close enough. Let's give it a try."

Sean knelt down next to the hole and lowered his pot to the bottom. He tipped it sideways, allowing it to fill with the silt-laden water before lifting it back out again.

"Here you go," he said, handing it to Chris to dispose of before lowering the next pot into the pit.

Chris accepted the filled vessel and dumped it out several yards away before passing it back to Sean. By then, Sean had already filled the second pot with more water. Working in rapid succession, they were able to drain almost all of the water out of the pit within about ten minutes.

"OK, it looks like we're almost down to rock," said Sean, sweeping his beam across the bottom of the hole. "I don't want to scoop out any more or we'll run the risk of throwing away some bits of gold with the water."

"It looks like we've cleaned most of it out anyway," said Chris, looking over his friend's shoulder. "We should be able to cherry pick now and grab whatever's left."

Despite the dirt and wet grass, both men lay flat on their stomachs and picked out leftover pieces of gold. They retrieved a few dozen doubloons and smaller ingots from the cracks and corners of the bottom before finally declaring that the site was picked clean.

"Why not get the detector and do one more final sweep over the pit, just to ensure that we're not missing something major?" said Chris.

"Good idea," said Sean, returning to the tent for the device.

He was back in a minute with the case and the headset, which he quickly set up and tuned for the hunt. He lowered the coil into the pit and moved it from one side to the other, scanning the area thoroughly. He then moved outside the pit and inspected the ground around the opening in all directions, in case Louie had buried the gold in more than one spot. When he was finally satisfied, he turned the volume on the headset down to low and addressed Chris.

"I think we've just about drained Fort Knox, my friend," he said. "I'm still getting a light signal from the bottom of the pit, which might come from a single coin or nugget that we may have overlooked. Or maybe there's room between the bottom and side rocks where something may have slid down out of sight. Either way, it's small, and not easily accessible."

Chris looked at his watch and saw that it was almost one. "I'm glad that most of the gold we took out of there was pretty clean. Otherwise we'd be washing coins until almost dawn," he said.

"I know what you mean. I've about had it," agreed Sean. "I've been going non-stop since four o'clock yesterday morning. I can barely keep my eyes open."

"Let's get this hole at least partially filled in before we call it a day," said Chris. "And then we'll roll the sleeping bags out with the duffel bag between the two of us. I want to be able to reach out and touch that thing anytime I wake up."

"You go ahead and start getting ready," said Sean. "I'll cover the hole. Besides, there are a couple things I still want to do."

Chris looked at his friend, who was removing a placard from his back-pack. He smiled coyly at Chris as he slid out of the tent without allowing him to see its inscription.

Chris walked the few paces down to the lake to retrieve some wash water. As he prepared himself for sleep, he recognized the sounds made by Sean as he shoveled dirt into the hole and then pounded a few sticks into the ground. He laughed as he worked, obviously up to some form of devious humor. However, Chris was too tired to investigate, instead deciding to ignore his friend's action until the following morning. Sean returned to the tent ten minutes after Chris, still chuckling.

Exhausted by their activities, both men slept until eight thirty the following morning. Chris was the first one awake. He smiled as his hand felt the familiar bulk of the bullion through the canvas duffel bag.

Thinking that he'd let Sean sleep for a bit longer, he wriggled out of his bag and pulled on his jeans and shirt. He then unzipped the flap on the tent door and backed out of the domed tent. It was a glorious morning, with puffy white clouds moving across a mostly blue sky. Looking around the site, he saw something that quickly caught his attention. He walked over to investigate, a wide grin splitting his face.

There, next to the filled-in hole from the previous night, Sean had erected a makeshift seat consisting of a thick limb resting in the crotches of two heavy Y-shaped branches. Two other sticks had been hammered into place next to the seat. One simply held a roll of toilet paper. The other supported the sign, which read:

"Sean's Outhouse. Seats by reservation only."

PART IV

THE REST OF ETERNITY

CHAPTER 21

By prior agreement, they had selected Chris as the one who would hike out of the woods to notify the authorities and arrange for assistance with the recovery. They both realized that this would leave Sean alone to mind the multi-million dollar treasure. However, as long as it resembled the tent of any other hiker, he should be fine. Chris's plan was to hike out of the woods at dawn, stop in Utica, call on the State Police, and then return with additional food and supplies to last until the authorities arrived on the scene.

After wolfing down a couple of granola bars, Chris hoofed it out of the woods and back to his Jeep. He stopped at his mother's home only long enough to inform her of their discovery, and he solemnly demanded that she remain silent on the matter until it had been announced by the State.

"To do otherwise might put Sean in grave danger," he said, considering what some unscrupulous criminals might do in order to put their hands on six million dollars in gold.

His next stop was to the State Police in Utica, where he spoke with a special investigator, Detective Marty Hampton, and explained his situation. The seasoned representative arranged a security detail, and then contacted the local Forest Rangers as well as his counterpart in the Department of Interior. Agreeing with Chris regarding the importance of secrecy, he placed an immediate gag order on each of the departments that would be involved in the recovery of the gold.

After spending only a matter of hours outside of the woods, Chris turned around and immediately headed back toward Speculator. Despite being on the verge of exhaustion, he was determined to make it back to West Canada Lake by the early morning hours on Wednesday. It worried him that his friend was alone, unarmed, with the massive treasure literally sitting inside his tent. As long as the secret was maintained, no one was in danger. However, if anything leaked out from the State Police Department office, there was no telling what might happen. Chris even considered bringing along a weapon before quickly dismissing the idea.

By the time Chris arrived at the trailhead and parked, it was already past six o'clock. He had eaten a sandwich in the car so that he wouldn't have to stop for a meal. He was able to make it beyond the Pillsbury Lake lean-to before darkness set in. By the time he arrived at Sampson Lake, it was pitch black. As he paused for a brief rest to eat some chocolate and quench his thirst, he considered stopping for a few hours of sleep. The lean-to at Sampson Lake was within the next mile, and he could have easily given in to his desire for rest. However, he forced his mind back to the tent at West Canada Lake and the welfare of his friend. He replaced the batteries in his headlamp and pushed ahead on the trail.

By the time he emerged from the trees at the south end of Louie's clearing, it was eleven thirty. He directed his flashlight at the tent, which was barely visible between the tall weeds and the dense spruce trees. There was no sign of movement. As he approached, he heard only the sound of his own footsteps. There was nothing outside the tent to indicate that anyone was home.

He turned off his lamp and bent to unzip the front doorway flap. Only then did he hear a grumbling voice come from inside:

"Jeez…all you had to do was to hike eleven miles out, drive for two hours, visit a bunch of officials and cut through a mass of red tape, arrange for an armed guard, go shopping, drive two more hours, and then hike another eleven miles to get back in here. You've been gone for almost eighteen hours. What the hell took you?"

Considering the incredible worth of the bullion itself, the welcoming committee was relatively subdued. Eight New York State Police officers, accompanied by a U.S. Treasury Department marshal and a member of the State Historical Division, followed two Forest Rangers into the clearing at West Canada Lake at noon on Thursday. The State Police officers all wore their side arms in plain view, in an obvious display of protective force.

One by one, the members of the recovery group were allowed into the tent to view the huge pile of coins and ingots. To a person, they were left speechless at the golden mass that filled the overloaded duffel bag. No one could ever recall seeing such a vast amount of wealth amassed at any one place.

Rather than wait another day to hike out, the State Police officers decided to take a one hour rest, then turn around and carry the gold out of the woods that same afternoon. They divided the bullion into eight equal piles, which they loaded into specially reinforced bags supplied by the Treasury official. They had intentionally carried light loads to accommodate the additional cargo. Meanwhile, the Forest Rangers had arranged special permission with the New York State Department of Environmental Conservation to bring a succession of multi-passenger all terrain vehicles into the woods as far as Pillsbury Lake. This would reduce the return hike by three miles.

The officer in charge of the State Police detachment was a friendly, outgoing veteran of the force with extensive experience in special operations. Lieutenant Ken Folsom had been on the force for close to thirty years, yet still maintained the physique of a boot camp graduate. He remained close to Chris and Sean for several hours of the return hike, questioning them on the detection and excavation of the treasure. He was most interested in the detective work that went into locating the final place where they had uncovered the cache.

"Let me know if either of you gentlemen are ever interested in joining the force," he said, looking at Chris and Sean with admiration. "We could use your kind of street smarts on our team."

After another three hours of hiking, they arrived at the location where the ATVs were parked, awaiting the journey out of the woods. The gold was loaded into specially-secured, locked containers, which were attached to the back of each vehicle.

As they were climbing onto their respective rides, Sean noticed Chris looking at his watch repeatedly.

"A penny for your thoughts," he asked Chris, replacing his canteen onto his belt holster.

"It's almost six o'clock on Thursday. I was just wondering where Kristi might be right now. She's been in the woods with her team for two days. I bet they're having a good time roaming through the rest of that cave."

"Don't tell me you'd rather be at Lost Pond right now," Sean said, rolling his eyes skyward.

"No. This has been pretty special. But I am looking forward to seeing her again soon."

As Chris was speaking, Lieutenant Folsom stepped up to address the two men.

"We'll take you back to your vehicle now, and you can go back to your homes tonight. But I imagine there's going to be some folks looking for you as soon as the news stations get hold of this story," he said.

Sean and Chris both looked at the officer for a moment, digesting his words. Then, Chris looked at Sean with an expression displaying mixed emotions.

"I'll tell you the truth; I hadn't even considered that. This will probably generate a newspaper story or two, won't it?" Chris said.

"A newspaper story or two?" laughed Lieutenant Folsom incredulously. "Obviously you two don't know how things work in the media business. This kind of thing will go way beyond the local news broadcasts. It'll probably get some national coverage, and I'm sure you'll have a lineup of reporters from newspapers, magazines, and television stations clamoring for interviews. Life might be a bit interesting these next few weeks."

Chris closed his eyes as he wiped the sweat off his brow. He already had his hands full with the job search and interview process. He had hoped to divide any remaining spare time between exploring the new cave and visiting Kristi. This was a fly in the ointment he hadn't expected.

On their drive back to the Careys' house in Utica, Chris and Sean discussed the issues that would be affecting their lives in the coming weeks. Chris was worried that some of Lieutenant Folsom's questions may have forced him to divulge details of the cave at Lost Pond that might compromise the Cornell expedition. He indicated to the officer that he had promised to keep the location of the caves a secret until after the university had made the initial exploration. However, once the story broke, there was no telling how much would be released as the news-hungry media pressed to learn more of the details.

"Maybe we should call Dr. Meyers now, just to give him a heads-up," suggested Sean.

"That's a great idea, if only we had a satellite-capable phones," said Chris. "Even that wouldn't reach him if he's down inside the cave. I guess I could leave him a voice message, but I'd still hate to think of a swarm of people arriving to check out the place while their group is still inside."

"What about the remains of Thomas Swain that are still in the outer chamber?" asked Sean.

"I spoke to the Forest Ranger about that. He said that the County Medical Examiner would go in and remove them, just to look them over and confirm that there isn't anything suspicious. I think they'll be able to determine that pretty quickly."

"And then...?" said Sean, leaving his statement open.

"Then, they will either release them to the surviving family, or they'll dispose of them 'in an appropriate manner.'"

"We both know there is no surviving family," countered Sean.

"Now that's just not true," said Chris, acting indignant. "We are his surviving family!"

Monday, August 18, was a typical late summer day in the state capital. It had been over a week since Chris and Sean had returned from their final venture in the West Canada Lakes with the haul of a lifetime. To their credit, the various officials involved in their story had done a magnificent job of keeping the lid on it. Chris and Sean had been in contact with Dr. Meyers, who had successfully mapped out the entire Lost Pond cave, which included a second entrance almost a half mile away. Kristi had made many of the first-entry explorations herself, and she received accolades from the college as well as the caving community at large. She asked Dr. Meyers to relay to Chris that she would be listing both of them as co-finders in her publication on the system.

Chris and Sean had been asked to arrive at the State Capitol Building early, in order to meet the governor and receive a briefing on the status of the treasure. Members of the governor's staff were present, as well as the director of the New York State Historical Society, who was introduced to those assembled as Mr. Peter Wembley. Chris was especially interested in being introduced to the Historic Preservation Officer, a middle-aged woman named Lillian Burnett, who was also present at the gathering. He and Sean managed to pull her aside for a private conversation about thirty minutes before the press conference began.

"I can't tell you how much we appreciate your contribution to the story of the Gordon Treasure," she said, looking at them with admiration. "For over two hundred years, people have wondered whether that was fact or fiction. You finally solved the mystery."

"Thanks, but you're giving us entirely too much credit," said Chris. "We didn't know anything about Robert Gordon when we started out on this hunt. As a matter of fact, our initial goal was to try to do some recreational panning for gold as part of a hiking trip. Later, we added in the fun of seeking out an old Indian cave. But neither of us knew anything about a treasure that was buried in Lake Champlain; none of that came out until we were actively planning our trip.

"Well, I guess everything turned out better then you expected, didn't it?" said Lillian, a wide grin crossing her face.

"Actually, not quite," said Chris, hesitating as he tried to find the right words.

"Not quite? I don't understand. How could things have turned out any better? In ten minutes, the whole country will know about your magnificent discovery, and every museum in the region will be able to add an exhibit showing this newly discovered chapter in our colonial history."

"Actually, that's what I wanted to talk to you about," said Chris, lowering his voice. "I think we should try to have the homestead site of Louis Seymour, otherwise known as Adirondack French Louie, dedicated as a New York State Historical Site."

"It really is deserving of this honor," added Sean. "Louie epitomized the spirit and lifestyle of the frontier woodsman in the Adirondacks, and we'll never see someone of his ilk again. And in addition to that, you won't even need funding to maintain the place. There's over six million dollars in gold that no one counted on recovering. One of Louie's dying wishes was that the gold would be used to 'take care of the place.' I think we owe it to him."

Lillian stood there listening to them with a confused expression on her face, alternating her attention from one to the other.

"Yes, yes, I highly agree with you, although you won't have to worry about using the gold to fund the maintenance on the place. The state government will do that using dollars already allocated to preserving historic sites. But I thought I told you all about this when you submitted the paperwork for the designation last week."

"Paperwork? What paperwork?" asked Chris, stumbling over his words.

"The State Register of Historic Places Application that you filed in our office," Lillian replied, looking back at Chris curiously. "The description, the history, the significance and sources... you did a wonderful job of it all. And those maps you submitted were so professional; they were the nicest I've ever seen. I see no reason why that application won't just fly through the approval process. You really did your homework on that one."

"But... I... I...," Chris stuttered.

"Oh," said Lillian, taking him by his arm, "it looks as though the conference is set to start. You should be taking your seats now." She pointed Chris and Sean to a pair of seats, side by side, to the left of the podium.

Chris's head was spinning as he allowed himself to be ushered to a chair on the raised stand, where he was seated in front of no less than two hundred reporters and news station cameras. He and Sean had been so busy with the events surrounding the discovery of the gold that he hadn't had time to even think about filing the Historic Site papers. They were extensive documents that required significant background work and preparation. They would have taken him at least a month to research and develop. How could this have happened without his knowledge?

The stand on which they were seated had a podium in the center and several seats on either side. Sean took the seat directly to the left of the podium, where the Governor would introduce the news. Chris sat next to Sean. To the right of the podium were chairs for the head of the Department of Environmental Conservation, along with the Directors of the Historical Preservation Site Office and the Historical Society.

Still in a state of shock, Chris barely took notice of the other people who joined him on stage, until he heard a familiar voice next to him.

"Hello, stranger. Long time no see."

Looking up to his left, he was surprised to see the distinguished face of Dr. Meyers smiling back at him.

"I hope this seat isn't already taken," the professor said as he pulled out the chair.

"No, no, by all means, please," said Chris, reaching out to shake his hand. "I can't wait to hear what else you found in your exploration."

"Certainly: I'd be glad to tell you about it," said Dr. Meyers. "That is, whatever Kristi hasn't already told you. Do you realize that she hasn't stopped talking about you since she came back from that first trip into Lost Pond? I think you've got an admirer," he said, digging Chris in the ribs.

"I'm hoping to do some caving with her as soon as we both find some spare time," said Chris. "To tell you the truth, we've both been so busy I haven't had time to ask her."

"Why not talk to her as soon as we're done here," said Dr. Meyers, nodding to the back of the crowded audience.

Chris looked out at the rows of packed seats and noticed Kristi, standing in the back of the room. She was dressed in a red pantsuit, with her shining hair flowing over her shoulders and a big smile on her face. Her eyes met Chris's, and she waved vigorously.

"I didn't know she was going to be here," said Chris.

"I couldn't keep her away," said Dr. Meyers. "Once she found out that they wanted to announce the cave and the discovery of the treasure at the same time, she demanded to come along. Naturally, since she had a hand in finding the cave, I couldn't refuse." As Chris looked out into the crowd, he also picked out his mother, who had driven to the capital from Utica for the occasion. Standing next to her was Maggie, who had taken the day off from her duties at the golf course to attend.

The conference started with an introduction by the Governor, who spoke for fifteen minutes about the history of New York and the glorious legends that abound from the Revolutionary War. He pontificated on the contributions made by the common citizens of the state in discovering and preserving that history, and then introduced the other members of the panel.

Next, Dr. Meyers was called forward to announce the discovery of the new cave system, accessible through public lands, describing its characteristics and how it had been found. He limited his remarks to about five minutes, and kept the language simple enough for all to understand.

Finally, the Director of the Historical Society gave a few background remarks regarding the origins of the story, and Chris and Sean were brought to the podium to discuss their find of the legendary cache of gold. Chris summarized the treasure-hunting venture, and he and Sean took turns relaying different aspects of the adventure, after which the eager press corps took over and launched into a marathon session of questions.

It was close to noon by the time Chris and Sean were able to extricate themselves from the last knot of reporters. It seemed as though they had told the same story over and over again, from multiple angles, until they just couldn't talk about it any longer. As the final few reporters departed, Sean and Chris were left standing with a small gathering of their friends and family—Chris's mother, Kristi, Maggie, and the Director of the Historical Society. Before Chris could say anything, Peter Wembley motioned to attract his attention.

"I got your e-mail last week," he said directly to Chris. "I was able to contact the Hamilton County Medical Examiner, and they gave you the go ahead. They took custody of the remains from the cave and will transport them as you requested."

"That's great," said Chris, ignoring the questioning looks from Sean and the others. "Will you be able to join us? It will be Wednesday morning at ten o'clock. We'd love to have you there."

"Yes, I saw that in your e-mail too. I'll be there… wouldn't miss it for anything," Wembley replied.

With that, he turned and strode off, leaving Chris smiling and the others noticeably puzzled.

"What was that all about?" asked Sean, holding hands with Maggie. "Are you cutting deals behind my back for the made-for-television movie rights?"

"No, nothing so dramatic," laughed Chris. "It's just that our friend, Mr. Swain, has been sitting in a cave by himself for over 230 years. I thought it would be a fitting tribute to let him spend the rest of eternity with his friends."

CHAPTER 22

The Wood Creek-Kinner Cemetery stands on a grassy hillside just past the town line of Fort Ann. It is visible from the lanes of historic Route 4, although most people drive by without giving it a second glance. The headstones in the graveyard are old and weathered; many have been worn smooth by the stresses of climate and time. The inscriptions on some are barely legible, while still others are broken in half and lying on the ground.

At the back of the cemetery lay a freshly covered mound of dark brown soil. In back of the newly dug grave was a black granite memorial stone, standing upright and incongruous with its neighbors. Engraved in sharp relief letters were the words:

Thomas P. Swain
Merchant—Friend—Loyal Compatriot
1741–1775
Returned home August 20, 2012

In attendance were Chris, Sean, Kristi, and Maggie, along with Peter Wembley and several members of his Historical Society office. Four rows of seats were arranged in front of the grave, which sloped downhill toward the creek. The back rows were filled by members of the Whitehall Historical Society, as well as the mayor of the small town. Only Chris's mother had found it impossible to attend, due to a prior obligation to an ill friend.

Much to Chris's surprise, Annette Surette had accepted the invitation, and she had been driven down to the graveyard by her granddaughter.

"How could I miss this?" Annette said, taking hold of Chris' hands. "Mr. Swain gave his life trying to protect my great-great-great-great-grandfather. The least I could do was to come and pay my respects."

The ceremony was brief, a memorial tribute given by a Lutheran minister who presided over a local congregation. Yet it was conducted with the dignity and decorum that Chris and Sean felt was due to this man who had died a lonely death in a solitary cave, so long ago and so far from his home and loved ones.

After the service was over, Chris and Sean engaged Peter Wembley in a brief conversation about the cemetery, which held the remains of many local residents from as far back as the early 1800s.

"How were you able to get funding approved for the monument on such short notice?" asked Wembley. "Was it state funded?"

"Uh… yes. Unofficially," said Chris.

When the two men looked at Chris for additional comment, he simply winked at them, indicating that it was best left undisclosed. Only when Peter departed did Sean inquire about the cost of the gravestone.

"Let me see, if I had to guess, I'd say that the stone cost around $2,800, based on your transaction for the gold we found at Lost Pond."

"Actually, it was about $3,000, but who's counting," said Chris, admitting that he'd had to use some of his own money, in addition to the proceeds from the sale of the coin and ingot.

As the group moved away from the cemetery and back toward the parking lot, Kristi caught up with Chris and took his hand.

"So when will I see you again?" she asked. "I've got some time before the students arrive back on campus, and most of my dissertation is ready to go. I'm about set for a bit of time off."

Chris looked down into her appealing brown eyes and smiled.

"If that's an offer, you can count me in," he said quickly. "How about dinner Friday night, and then whatever on Saturday and Sunday?"

"If I might ask, what is 'whatever'?"

"Exactly!" said Chris, throwing his arm around her shoulders. "It's whatever I can do, as long as you're there, too."

Chris felt overjoyed at the way events had turned out over the course of the past few weeks. He couldn't explain, even to himself, the elation he felt anticipating the time he'd spend with Kristi. He felt so comfortable and at ease whenever she was around, and he just wanted to be with her whenever his crowded schedule allowed.

As the pair descended the grassy slope to the parking lot, Kristi noticed a sudden change in Chris. His face became abruptly serious, his body upright and taut. He dropped his arm that had been wrapped around her shoulders, and craned his neck to gain a better view of his vehicle. Without speaking, she followed his stare down the hill and into the lot, where a stranger stood by himself. His back was towards Chris, so he could not see the man's face, and only the back of a dark gray suit and a matching Fedora hat were visible over the top of the other parked cars.

As Chris approached the lot, he noticed there was something familiar about the figure: his build and stature. But it couldn't be...not what he was thinking. It was only when the man turned around and faced Chris that he realized his intuition was correct.

"Dad!" Chris said, bounding the few final steps to greet his father. "How long have you been here?"

"Hello, Son," his father said, smiling warmly. He threw his arms around Chris and embraced him tightly. "I got here just after the service started. I would have joined you, but I didn't want to interrupt the minister's invocation. It looked like a wonderful ceremony, though."

"How did you even know about it?" asked Chris. "Did Mom tell you where we were?"

"Well, yes and no," said his father. "She told me about the ceremony and how to find you. But the rest of the story, with the cave and the gold, that's all over the country. I've been hearing it from everyone, ever since Wednesday, when it hit the news wires. You seem to be the man of the hour, Chris."

"It wasn't just me, Dad," said Chris, motioning to his friends. "Sean was the one who got the whole thing going when he suggested that we go panning for gold. And he also hooked us up with the geology professor who suggested the area where we should start our hunt."

"Of course," said Chris Sr., who had known Sean since he was in high school. "It's great to see you again, Sean."

"Dad, I'd also like you to meet Kristi. She's a geology graduate student at Cornell who helped us find the cave at Lost Pond."

Kristi's hand had been hooked inside Chris's arm. She let it drop slowly.

"It's very nice to meet you," she said, reaching out to take his hand.

"Theresa told me about you," said Chris' father, returning the handshake. "You made quite an impression on her on Wednesday. And she's not someone who is easily impressed."

"Aw, she's such a nice lady," said Kristi shyly. "We had a lot to talk about. While these two guys were talking to all the reporters, she told me all about Chris's weaknesses."

"Yeah, and I bet you memorized them all," said Chris, looking at her in amusement.

Meanwhile, Chris's father changed the topic, stepping back to admire the new Jeep.

"I take it you're pleased with it?" he asked in a solicitous manner.

"Yes, but…" Chris left his sentence dangling in midair.

"Anything you want added to it? I didn't have much choice given such short notice," said his father, still looking through the driver side window.

"Then, it was you," Chris said haltingly, looking back and forth between the Jeep and his father. "You're the one who had it delivered to my house."

"Of course, Son. I'm surprised it took you this long to figure that out. Guess I can still slip one past you if I have to, huh?"

"But how? How did you know? I asked Mom about it the day after my accident, and she said that you were in Europe. You couldn't have possibly known I'd been in a wreck the day before."

"It was easy; I have a lot of friends who are well-connected. Do you remember the name Anthony Morelli?"

Chris wracked his brain trying to match a face with the name his father had mentioned.

"No, can't say as I do. I don't believe I've ever met anyone by that name."

"Oh, yes you have. But I really can't blame you for forgetting. It was about two o'clock in the morning, and you'd just had your cranium bell rung by a large beech tree."

The light suddenly went on in Chris's head.

"Dr. Morelli, at the hospital in Utica!"

"One and the same," said his father, smiling back at him. "We served together in the Rotary Club before I moved down to D.C. to run the practice. We still keep in touch via e-mail, and he gave me a shout as soon as you checked out of the hospital that morning. It was already close to nine o'clock in Brussels, so I was able to jump right on it. I contacted our main office and had one of the office managers place an immediate rush order that would be delivered the same day. I hope you like the color, by the way."

"Yes, Dad, it's great. It's actually pretty close to my old Jeep, just a shade lighter with the metallic finish. I love it. So anyway, how did that work, with you being overseas?"

"Son, we've got a staff of over sixty lawyers working out of our headquarters office. If we can't coordinate the details needed to buy a car in a day, we've got a problem. All I did was have the information from your last registration transferred to the new one, and then wire a payment from my bank directly to their finance office. The registration was easy, since we both have the same name. Oh, in case they didn't tell you, you've already got the extended version of the warranty, so make sure you don't pay for any of your own repairs until you go over one hundred thousand miles."

Chris just laughed and shook his head.

"I've got to admit, Dad, you had me stumped. Once I ruled out Mom, and she said you were out of the country and that she hadn't talked to you,

I couldn't tell who my secret benefactor was."

Chris's father shifted his feet and cleared his throat nervously. He appeared uneasy as he looked at his son with an apologetic expression.

"Chris, I hope you know that these past few years haven't been easy for me. I feel bad as anything about missing your graduation this year, and the last one, too. And while I wanted to give you this Jeep as a graduation present, regardless of your accident, I know that it still doesn't make up for me not always being there when you needed me. I'm sorry for that, Son."

"Oh my God, I think I'm going to cry," said Kristi, standing off to the side.

"It's OK, Dad," said Chris. "Everyone knows how busy you are running one of Washington's most successful law practices. It's amazing that you're able to make it back as often as you do."

"Well, some of that's going to change. Maybe not this year, but within the next two or three, I'm going to be scaling back my involvement and spending more time up here with your mother and you. Even if you wind up working in another city, we'll see more of each other than we have these past four years. Who knows? I may end up retiring soon."

"I could never picture you retiring completely," said Chris. "You love your work too much to spend your entire day watching television and playing bridge."

"You know, I think you're right, at least partially," said the elder Carey, a smile crossing his face. "Anyway, if I gave up the practice of law completely, I'd lose all of my influence in government. That means I wouldn't be able to get my little pet projects pushed through the bureaucracy, such as historic site designations for hermits living in the middle of the Adirondacks."

Chris' jaw dropped open in amazement, and he was momentarily left speechless.

"I guess you weren't expecting that either, were you?" his father laughed.

"Oh my God, no!" shrieked Chris. "We've wanted to apply to have the site of French Louie's cabin designated as a state historic site ever since we got involved in this chase. But it would have taken us months to get underway with the application process. There was so much information they wanted, and it all had to be in perfect order."

"Yes, state governments do tend to be pretty demanding. It's as though they have their own little fiefdoms, and no one is permitted to step around their due processes. But once again, having a large staff of junior attorneys has its advantages. We had their application done and out the door within three days of downloading the forms."

"But how did you know that we even wanted to go that route?" asked Chris. "I certainly never had that discussion with you."

"You can thank your mother for that one," said his father. "She told me that you'd brought the topic up several times. I even bought another copy of the book *Adirondack French Louie*, to keep on my night table in Washington. He was quite a man, that Louie. It'll be an honor to say that I...or we, had a hand in obtaining that special designation for his homestead."

"Well, you certainly expedited the process," said Sean. "We weren't expecting to get an application in front of the board this month, which would have meant waiting until the next quarterly review board in November."

"That's right, Dad," agreed Chris. "Thanks to your intervention, we might be able to see the site at West Canada Lake designated sometime this month. You might even be able to participate in the dedication ceremony, if they do such a thing."

"Uh, no thanks," said Chris Senior. "Remember, I reviewed the application before it was submitted to the committee, and I saw how far back into the woods this place is. I'm a little too old to be strapping on a fifty-pound pack for a three-day hike."

"I understand," said Chris. "Don't worry; you're excused. But as long as you're feeling in such a helpful mood, I wonder if you might be able to help me out with a potential legal issue."

"What's that?" asked his father. "I'm sure you haven't gotten yourself into any trouble with the law."

"Well...probably not," replied Chris. His face was an odd mixture of concern and devious glee. "But you might say that I 'borrowed' something that didn't belong to me, even though the folks who owned it never knew that it existed."

Chris's father, Kristi, and Maggie all looked at him with question marks in their eyes, waiting for him to explain his cryptic riddle. Only Sean seemed to understand the statement, nodding slowly as he remembered the original clue that Chris had uncovered at the Adirondack Museum.

"The coins," he said simply.

"Yup," Chris replied, shifting his eyes from Sean back to his father.

"I'm afraid I don't understand," he said. "What coins?"

"Let me explain. When we first started investigating the possibility that French Louie was involved in a search for the lost gold, I paid a visit to the Adirondack Museum and found two gold doubloons hidden in a secret compartment of Louie's old trunk. That's what first proved the authenticity of your grandfather's artifacts. Remember the muzzleloader stock and the old tin cup?"

"Of course I do. Go on."

"Anyway, I knew as soon as I found those that they'd been hidden by Louie sometime before he died, and that the museum had never known they were stashed away under the fake floorboard of the trunk. So I borrowed them, just to have them identified and make certain that they indeed could have been part of the Robert Gordon treasure. It all checked out, and they provided a key link with some more clues we found at the Lost Pond Cave. But you see, I never wanted to actually take the coins. I only wanted to borrow them. And therein lies the problem."

Chris' father threw his head back with a great roar of laughter.

"So now you're feeling honest, but you're afraid that you'll be arrested if you try and smuggle several thousand dollars worth of gold back to its owner. Is that it?" he said.

"In a nutshell, yes," Chris replied, a twinkle in his eye.

"This is not a problem," said his father, still chuckling at the irony of the situation. "Just leave them with your mother, and I'll have someone pick them up and take them to the Governor's office. He owes me a favor or two. I think he'll smooth the way for the safe and easy return of those heirlooms to their rightful owners. I'm sure they'll be very understanding, if not grateful, for your role in their discovery."

"Speaking of honesty," said Kristi, "you never did explain why you didn't say anything when I happened to give you the 'missing link' clue about the meaning of French Louie's fireplace drawing. Were you afraid that I was going to go in ahead of you and claim your precious gold?" She looked at Chris with a semi-serious pout on her face, feigning sadness.

"No, of course not," said Chris. "But we also couldn't risk having word of the location leak out, no matter how innocent it might have been. Do you have any idea how many people would have been racing to get their shovel in the ground ahead of ours had a single word of this gotten out?"

"Oh, so you think that women can't keep secrets?"

"I'm sorry. Could I make it up to you with an all-expense paid trip to Boston to take in a game at Fenway, then dinner at the Union Oyster House?"

"Ooh, really?" cried Kristi, her eyes lighting up in surprise.

"You'd better watch him," said the senior Carey, gesturing toward his son. "He's always been pretty good with the bribes."

Following their reunion of sorts, Chris and his father exchanged another round of handshakes and hugs. Then, it was time for the renowned lawyer to resume his journey back to Albany and then on to the nation's capital.

"We'll talk soon, Son, OK?" said Chris' father, putting his hand on Chris's shoulder as he turned for his car.

"Sure, Dad. And thanks again for everything—the help completing the historic site application, as well as the little 'graduation present,'" said Chris, nodding at the new vehicle. "But most of all, thanks for coming up here for this. You don't know how much it means to me."

Chris Senior simply nodded and tipped his hat, then climbed into his BMW Z4 roadster and pulled slowly out of the parking lot.

"Don't forget your mother's birthday," he called out through the open roof as he punched the accelerator. And then he was gone.

CHAPTER 23

The dedication ceremony for the Adirondack French Louie Hermitage historic site was conducted on a cloudless Wednesday afternoon in September. As Lillian Burnett had predicted, the flawless application package impressed the historic site approval committee with its well-grounded justification for attaining the designation. The vote was unanimous, and the site was added to the State Register within a week of its passage.

Special permission was granted to allow a helicopter to fly into the clearing at West Canada Lake to deliver the site markers, which included a plaque, a metal marker, and a signboard. The plaque was placed into a special cement base, which was situated near the stone fireplace erected by Louie in 1913. Nearby was the signboard, which was supported on two legs and held an annotated map of the clearing, with laminated photographs of Louie's camp and outbuildings. Yet a third marker, which was flat and made of bronze, was sunk into the ground at the spot where Chris and Sean discovered the Gordon treasure. The story of the gold was spelled out on one side.

Because of the remote location of the encampment, only a select handful of government representatives chose to make the trek. Chris was pleased to see that both Peter Wembley and Lillian Burnett were in attendance, both carrying packs and tents for an extended stay. A number of local hunters and fishermen, some of whom had grandfathers who knew

Louie, also showed up to pay their respects. Presiding over the ceremony was a young staff member from the Governor's inner circle, who used the occasion as a paid vacation from his Albany desk job.

"They did a nice job of this," said Sean, looking over the various displays and plaques. "Does this mean that the State will actually come in and take care of the place?"

"It looks like they've already made a good start," said Kristi, who had walked in from the Moose River Plains that morning. "Someone cut out a lot of the high weeds and grass within the last few days."

The three of them strolled over to the back of the fireplace to gaze at the location where Chris and Sean had toiled to lift the stones off the underground vault. The rest of the stones had been removed, and the bare earth was quickly sprouting a layer of new growth.

"You'd hardly know that anything was ever down there," said Chris, shaking his head with wonder.

"I like to think of all the thousands of people who stood in this very spot, from the time Louie lived here until the day we dug up the gold, completely unaware of what lay just beneath their feet. Just think of it. If they'd only known," said Chris.

"Do you think he'd mind?" mused Kristi, looking around the clearing.

"Do you think he'd mind what?" asked Chris.

"Do you think French Louie would mind if he saw all these people, and these signs scattered all over the place? I heard that he rather enjoyed his solitude," Kristi replied.

"He did. But he also enjoyed people, as long as they were the right type," said Chris. "Anyway, you'd know it if he minded. He would have done something by now."

"Huh?" grunted Kristi. "How's that?"

"Because Louie always said that he was 'coming back' after his death. So he must be here now, amongst us. I'm sure he would have let us know if he was angry."

"Oh, like, maybe he would have thrown a special lightning bolt our way?" asked Kristi, giggling at Chris.

"Sure, why not," replied Chris. As he spoke, he gave Kristi an affectionate kiss on the top of her head.

Within a few minutes, the brief ceremony began, in which the site of Adirondack French Louie's homestead was officially declared a New York State Historic Site. Whether Louie was there to witness the event is still a matter of debate. The chances are pretty good that he was, because the sun reigned supreme throughout the afternoon, the bugs stayed down, and it was one of the nicest days that anyone could remember in the history of West Canada Lake. By da holy feesh, it was.

ABOUT THE AUTHOR

Larry Weill has led a career that is as diverse and interesting as the subjects in his books. An avid outdoorsman, he has hiked and climbed extensively throughout the Adirondacks and the Northeast since his days as a Wilderness Park Ranger. He has also worked as a financial planner, a technical writer, a trainer, and a career Naval officer.

A self-avowed "people watcher," Larry has an interesting knack for observing and describing people and their many amusing habits and traits. He is the author of the popular books *Excuse Me, Sir...Your Socks Are On Fire*, *Pardon Me, Sir...There's A Moose In Your Tent*, and *Forgive Me, Ma'am...Bears Don't Wear Blue*. The trilogy describes his time as a Wilderness Park Ranger and the interesting people and experiences he encountered while on the job.

Larry makes his home near Rochester, New York, from which he makes frequent ventures into his beloved Adirondack woods. *Adirondack Trail of Gold* is Larry's first foray into fiction, but not his last. Stay tuned for future additions to this exciting new series.